SIGNIFICANT

Dear Gary,
May this adventure inspire many more
future conversations with those you meet,
that each one might know their unfathomable
significance.
Love, Bill

SIGNIFICANT

W. J. BROWN

AMBASSADOR INTERNATIONAL
GREENVILLE, SOUTH CAROLINA & BELFAST, NORTHERN IRELAND

www.ambassador-international.com

Significant

ISBN: 978-1-62020-713-0
eISBN: 978-1-64960-003-5

Cover Design and Interior Typesetting by Hannah Nichols

AMBASSADOR INTERNATIONAL
Emerald House
411 University Ridge, Suite B14
Greenville, SC 29601, USA
www.ambassador-international.com

AMBASSADOR BOOKS
The Mount
2 Woodstock Link
Belfast, BT6 8DD, Northern Ireland, UK
www.ambassadormedia.co.uk

The colophon is a trademark of Ambassador, a Christian publishing company.

DEDICATION

To one of the most significant men I will ever know,
James H. Campbell, my wife's amazing father,
whose mother gave him the opportunity to do great things.

And

To one of the least recognized significant women in my family,
Kristin Tobin, my niece who passed far too young,
whose mother Christine gave life to her in tragic circumstances
and whose son Trevor is accomplishing much as a U.S. Marine.

And

To all surprised moms who sacrifice so much to make their children
significant in this life.

"Your ordinary acts of love and hope point to the extraordinary promise that every human life is of inestimable value."[1]

—Desmond Tutu

Archbishop Emeritus of Cape Town

"We're all human, aren't we? Every human life is worth the same, and worth saving."[2]

—J.K. Rowling

Harry Potter and the Deathly Hallows

ACKNOWLEDGMENTS

The creative spark for this story came from the early life story of my father-in-law, who was found on a doorstep in Detroit on November of 1928, wrapped in a blanket with a note, 'take care of my baby Theodore.' Some ninety-one years later and still counting, my father-in-law continues his extraordinary life as an accomplished professional pen-and-ink artist and published writer. More importantly, he has left a tremendous legacy as a husband of one wife for more than seventy years, father of three gifted daughters, and highly engaged grandfather and great grandfather. He has changed the destiny of my life and of thousands of lives. Thus, I begin my acknowledgements thanking him.

In addition to my father-in-law, my immediate family have been constant fans, especially my wife Nancy and my two daughters, Natalie and Heidi, gifted writers, communicators, and actors that constantly amaze me. My uncle on our Italian side of my family, Dr. Vincent Arone, also garners my gratitude for his enthusiasm for my first novel, *Into the Winds of Fear,* and encouragement to continue to write fiction. The unconditional love and support of my family and of my wife's family has been such a great gift to me.

I also have the pleasure of living my life with so many amazing friends, too many to note all of them here. To all those in the Fellowship of the Smoke, I thank you for dreaming together. I thank my fellow professors and writers, Ben Fraser, Terry Lindvall, Gil Elvgren, and Dennis Bounds for dousing me with considerable encouragement in between doses of delightful mockery, never believing (or at least not telling me) that there weren't any valid reasons why a social scientist like me couldn't write good fiction.

Likewise, my students' many hundreds of affirmations of liking and even loving my first novel has been a constant source of motivation.

I thank my dear friends in YWAM, especially Gary Stephens, Mike King, and Kenny Jackson, whose contemplations and conversations created space for me to apprehend God's inspiration to write about adopted children who become heroes.

Writing a story is easy; crafting it into an engaging and enjoyable read is much more challenging. I would not have achieved the latter without the assistance of Timothy Beals, President and CEO of Credo Communications, Dr. Quentin Schultze, Professor Emeritus at Calvin College who helped me to connect with Tim, Karen Ball, literary critic and consultant, and Heidi Livingston and Ruthie Walker, for their important editorial contributions.

Finally, I acknowledge you, the reader, for whom this story is written. You were constantly in mind as I did my utmost to give a powerful voice to one very special child prodigy.

PREFACE

IN RESPONSE TO THE GROWING international threat of hostile countries placing weapons in space, on June 18, 2018, President Donald Trump announced that the Pentagon would begin developing a sixth independent military branch of government. The president's directive birthed the United States Space Force, the first new military service since 1947, the year when the U.S. Air Force was established. On August 29, 2019, Air Force General John "Jay" Raymond was tasked to lead the U.S. Space Command, which will function as a forerunner to the U.S. Space Force. Congress authorized the U.S. Space Force in December 2019 while military space threats from China and Russia continue to escalate. Negotiations and competition for dominance in space will be the critical testing grounds for maintaining international peace or catapulting the planet toward a devastating catastrophe.

Now the time has come to write the next great chapter in the history of our armed forces, to prepare for the next battlefield where America's best and bravest will be called to deter and defeat a new generation of threats to our people and to our nation. The time has come to establish the United States Space Force.

—U.S. Vice President Mike Pence

August 9, 2018

Washington, D.C.

I know in my heart of hearts this will be the generation that restores life in America.

—U.S. Vice President Mike Pence

February 22, 2018

National Harbor, Maryland

CHAPTER 1

I COULD NOT RESIST THE temptation. I knew I shouldn't have gone back into my parents' bedroom, but I did. It was a rare opportunity. I sat on my mom's side of the bed, facing the bathroom, and looked at her journal sitting next to the small reading lamp. She had once read Dad a poem she had written in her journal, a very meaningful poem with beautiful words that made my dad cry. I think I was about five years old when this happened. It was then that I knew very special words were written in that book. Now, I was older and a much better reader; my desire to read precious words from my mom's journal overpowered my desire to not intrude into my mom's privacy. It was hard for me at age seven to understand the boundaries of privacy. After staring at the book, I picked it up and started at the beginning.

As I thumbed through the pages, my feelings of guilt rose. As much as I wanted to put it down and leave the room, I could not. It was Columbus Day, a school holiday, and I was home alone. Mom had just left for work but I knew my dad would be returning home soon from his morning exercise routine at the Y. I knew I had a short window of time to read my mom's deepest, most private thoughts.

I suppressed the guilt and after about four or five minutes of leafing through the journal, reading bits and pieces, I stumbled upon some riveting words that captivated me. The entry date was August 20, 2005. Mom wrote this account:

> It is three years to the date that Elana told me about the most frightening and horrific experience in her life, and yet, through her pain and grief, I have received unimaginable joy. This fact is so difficult to reconcile, but I know that I must one day do so. Elana revealed what had happened to her while we were in the hospital together so I could understand why she had decided to give up her baby. I feared that I had made wrong assumptions about her choice, and her nightmare confirmed that I had. Her story was very difficult to hear but it was important that I understood.

Elana told me how she had staggered out of the dark shadows of New York's Central Park nearly naked, running as fast as she could with large tears streaming down her face. One minute she was enjoying a casual run at dusk during a warm November day without any concern, and the next she found herself being dragged off the running path by a powerful man who clasped his large hand across her mouth so she could not scream. Sensing the strength of his powerful arms, she knew she would not be able to escape. The act of violence upon her defenseless body was so fast and shocking that she couldn't remember many details of the rape, other than the large knife the rapist used to cut her running shorts and rip them off her body. She also remembered hitting the man in the larynx with her fist while kicking him in the groin as he stood. She said her counterattack stunned him long enough to get to her feet and run for her life.

I cannot fathom what Elana had experienced. What if that had happened to me? Would I have been able to escape? Elana shared with me that in a state of complete confusion, she spotted a homeless man on the path close to where she had been attacked. She came upon him so fast that he froze in fear as she reached down and grabbed one of his blankets to cover herself. She did turn her head toward the direction from which she had come and saw the perpetrator step out of the shadows and onto the walking path, turning in the opposite direction from where she had run. Elana caught a glimpse of his dark features. The attacker ran, heading deeper into the park.

Elana said she knew she should find a police officer, but she was far too ashamed in her semi-nude state. Instead, she flagged down a taxi and begged the shocked driver to take her to her apartment, promising him she had cash at home and would pay him. She seldom carried cash on her to prevent losing much money in case she was robbed. She told me through her tears she wished to God she had met a robber that night, not a rapist. She said she tried to stop sobbing during the taxi ride home but without much success. The cab driver refused to accept payment. He said, "you have suffered enough; you owe me nothing. But you should go to the police." Elana described to me how she grabbed the man's arm and squeezed, still unable to talk and utter the words thank you.

I asked her if she called the police. "No," she said, "once safely inside my apartment, I could not get into the shower quick enough." After twenty minutes she came to the realization that a hundred long showers would never wash away the shame she felt. She told me how she blamed herself by asking over and over, "How could I let myself get raped? How could I be so careless?" She told me she knew there would be no justice. She had read there were more than 17,000 rape kits in New York City that sat in a police storage facility untested.

She told me she had to leave the city. She packed her bags the next morning, left a note for her landlord, and caught a train to Detroit where her cousin lived. Listening to her nightmare, I realized Elana's love of New York had been robbed from her. She told me how she had wept as she left the city of her greatest dreams and greatest nightmare. This was why she was giving up her baby, although she had first decided to terminate the pregnancy. I understood, but it was too painful to write about and contemplate until now. What would I have done if I had been Elana? I had already made that choice once. Would I have terminated my pregnancy or changed my mind like she did? She had made a courageous choice since she was too emotionally broken to raise her child. I think it was a good choice. I am glad she made that choice. Would I have considered my unborn to be significant, even as a consequence of rape? How could I ever explain this to Johann?

I closed my mom's journal in confusion and shock; I thought I knew what rape was, but I was not sure. I had to Google it later. The last question was like a bullet rattling around in my head. What was Mom afraid of telling me? Who was Elana and why was she in Mom's journal?

As more questions seemed to swirl around in my brain, I heard the garage door opening. Shoot, Dad was home. I had lost track of time. I closed the journal and put it back on the nightstand just as I had found it and exited my parent's room just as dad was coming into the house through the garage. I tried my best to remove the guilty look on my face as I met dad in the kitchen while I made my way to the toaster, popping in a slice of bread that I didn't want. Dad took no notice of my guilt. I was lucky.

"Want some toast, Dad?" I asked.

"No thanks, Johann."

My secret remained undiscovered and over time, my guilt subsided, but my determination to learn what mom had not been able to tell me intensified. As much as I wanted to go back into my mom's journal to find the answers to my questions, I decided that I would never read her personal journal again behind her back. And I never did.

─────────────

I awoke shaking in a cold sweat. I looked at my clock—3:35 a.m. I wondered if I had been screaming out loud, but no one came into my room. My parents were sound asleep. Then I remembered in this recurring nightmare no one ever seemed to hear my screams, because no one ever came to me to see what was wrong. The dream was always the same and yet always different. Someone was trying to kill me, but in different ways. In each dream, no one could hear my anguish. I always awoke just before death.

I turned on the light of my nightstand and looked over at my computer. The college application for the University of Chicago I was filling out was still open on the computer screen. I needed to finish it soon, as it was late October and the deadline was November 1. I hated filling out applications and this one was no exception. I had gotten stuck on the section that asked me to "write a 1500 to 2000-word narrative about your life from the time you were born and include your family history."

The problem was there were many unknowns in my family history. I didn't know much about my birth or true family heritage. My dad was born in Iron Mountain, Michigan, and his parents were

German immigrants. I knew my mom's family was fourth generation Irish-Italian-Cuban heritage and she grew up just outside of Boston. They met as students at Boston University in the early 1990s and were married right after they both graduated from college. My dad completed a Ph.D. in English Literature and my mom completed medical school to become an OB-GYN. They found jobs in New York and lived and worked in Manhattan for many years. They were visiting my dad's parents in Michigan on the day of the 9/11 terrorist attacks. The attack changed their world, as they both had close friends killed in the World Trade Center. They wanted to get away from the bad memories and moved to Detroit in January of 2002, where I was born. Just before my fourth birthday, my mom received a great job offer to work in a hospital in Chicago. My dad then applied for a teaching position at Wheaton College and received an offer. My parents found a spacious three-bedroom apartment in the city near Addams-Medill Park. Although they loved being in the city, they could not find a suitable school for me, so they moved to Downers Grove, Illinois, so I could attend a school for gifted children there.

The circumstances surrounding my arrival into this world always seemed to be shrouded in mystery, as I never heard my parents talk about that time period in their lives. Their years in Detroit following the 9/11 attacks were a difficult time for them, so we didn't talk about it. Not understanding my family history in Detroit was something that gnawed at me. Every time I broached the topic of our family history, my parents quickly changed the subject. I had no siblings to talk to about it either. I knew from my mom's diary something was hidden about my past. Then one day that all changed; it was sudden and dramatic.

I remembered it well. I leaned back in my chair with my blank document staring at me and I let my mind wander. It was a crisp winter day, the Saturday just before Christmas in 2013. After breakfast, my father said, "Johann, please go up into our attic and find your grandfathers' strong box. You know the one?"

I nodded yes, as my father had shown me the box the previous summer.

"There is the deed to our house on the top of all the papers in there. Please bring it down to me."

I found and opened the old German strong box and after pulling out the deed, my curiosity overtook me. I started to dig through and scan the many layers of documents until I made my way to the bottom of the box. I found a long form birth certificate with my birthday, August 20, with my name on it and with an "unknown" listed on the line for my father's name and "Elana Abelman" listed on the line for my mother's name. After staring at the name Elana, I felt like I'd been struck by a spell and transported into a fairy tale—I was sure that Elana was the name I read in my mom's journal all those years ago!

I wanted to run but my legs wouldn't move. After several minutes in a stupor, I clenched the birth certificate in my right hand and stood up to go back downstairs. When I did not come back, my dad decided to check on me and came up into the attic. He found me standing near the box, not moving, with tears in my eyes, clutching my birth certificate. He just stood there with me in silence and wrapped his arms around me.

When I regained some composure, all I could utter was, "Is Elana my real mom?"

"It's a long story, son." My dad was gentle, whispering. "Let's go get your mom and we will tell you about Elana."

My dad held me close as we walked downstairs together. He had to hold me up because I could not walk well. As soon as my mom saw the tears streaking down my face and the birth certificate clutched in my hand, tears began rolling down her checks. We all walked into our sunroom and sat down.

My dad was apologetic.

"We were waiting to tell you the whole story about Elana and your birth, Johann, when you were older, but now that you know, we must tell you."

"But I don't know," I said in anger and confusion. "I don't know anything!"

My mom tried to soothe my anger and hurt. She grabbed both of my hands.

"I'm sure, Johann, you have noticed that your skin color is brown, your eyes are dark brown, and your hair is dark brown and curly, unlike me or your dad."

"But you're part Cuban, Mom, and your skin is a darker complexion like mine."

"You're already beyond six feet tall," my dad said, "taller than most everyone your age, and you will be much taller than me."

I looked intensely into the faces of my parents. "Is Elana my real mom?"

"Elana is your biological mother, but I am very much your real mom."

My dad looked deeply into my eyes.

"No one knows the identity of your biological father, but I am very much your real dad."

I could not speak and just sat there, emotionally numb.

My mom then began to share Elana's story.

"I met her in the Hutzel Women's Hospital in the Detroit Medical Center where you were born. After giving birth to you prematurely, your mother Elana gave you up for adoption. You stayed in the hospital for several weeks until you became healthy. Your birth mother left the hospital after your birth, and she did not leave any contact information. She put her sister's address in Detroit as her home address, but when we checked it later, we found out that her sister had lived there but had passed away in a car accident. Elana had disappeared."

I then stood up. "Why did she leave, Mom?"

"She left because she had no way to take care of you. Elana came into the hospital so that she could give you to a family that would love and care for you and give you the best life possible."

As I heard these words, I felt anguish for a mother I had never known. I leaned into my mom and tried to control the hot twitching I felt in my eyes. After a while, I looked up into the eyes of the only mother I had ever known and said, "Thank you, Mom."

I then looked at my father and recognized that fierce gaze of unconditional love, a love that I had always known. I said, "Dad, you are my dad."

"I'm so sorry, Johann," my dad said through controlled breathing, "that you had to learn the truth about your birth this way. Something happened to Elana. She was raped. Do you know what that means?

"I know." I didn't dare reveal how I knew after first reading my mom's journal.

"You understand now why we wanted to wait to tell you. We could not explain sexual assault to you when you were a child. Even now, you are still a bit too young to understand sexual passion and why there are sexual assaults like rape. We had planned on telling you this whole story at an older age. I should not have let you loose in that strong box. I don't fault you. I myself would be curious about the other papers in the strong box if my father had given me the same task."

My mother drew me close to her and squeezed tight.

"You are the love of our lives, Johann. You know we are close friends with Dr. John Bishops. He knew we had been trying for years to have children, but we were not able to conceive. I was on duty in the hospital when Dr. Bishops contacted me about a woman coming off the street in early labor who wanted her child to be adopted. I met Elana in the ER and stayed with her during her emergency delivery. Dr. Bishops thought of me and your dad's desire to adopt a child and called the hospital legal team. They said they could make it work—an immediate custody and adoption. I was shocked when I was called to Dr. Bishop's office after your delivery to find your dad there with several lawyers and administrators. We didn't have a lot of time to make a decision about adopting you. That's when I asked to speak to Elana after surgery, so I could hear her heart and know what she wanted. I wrote it all down; let me tell you what Elana said in her own words."

My mom went into her bedroom and came back with her personal journal, the same one I had read from when I was younger. As she read the entire entry, the story of Elana's rape, the words were all familiar. It was the second time I became fixated on my mom's account of Elana, this time as told in her own voice. When my mom got to the part of the story where I had stopped because of my dad returning home from the gym, I held my breath in anticipation. These next words were the ones waiting for me that I had never read before:

> When I met Elana in the ER, I was filled with compassion. I spent as much time with her as I could during her labor and continued to stay by her side until it was time for the delivery of her twenty-six-week old baby. I will never forget Elana's parting words before she went into the delivery room. She squeezed my hand tight and said, "Katarina, the doctor said it's a boy, and if he survives, I want you to have him. I'm giving him up for adoption not because I don't want him, but because I love him and want him to have a good life, the life he deserves. I tried to terminate this pregnancy earlier today but knew God had a different plan, so I prayed that God would lead me to the right person. It's no accident you are here tonight. I know you will love him as your own. I can see love in your eyes and I can hear it in your voice. I cannot give my son the life he deserves and I could not take his life. It's not his fault I was raped. It's not my fault either. If you will adopt him, I will be so grateful. I give my son to you and your husband, Katarina. I ask that you keep the name Johann as his first name, and that you love him as your own son."

I broke again when my mom finished reading. I realized that I had two moms who loved me. I could understand that my biological mother knew the best chance I had to survive and have a decent life was to be adopted. My father then grabbed my shoulders and looked into my eyes. His words were tender yet powerful.

"Johann, I know this is hard. Even though it might seem we are not the same blood, we are. We all go back to Adam. We are all of one human family. But even stronger than blood are the soul and the spirit. You know we are body, soul and spirit. My soul and spirit and your mother's soul and spirit are one with yours. We are bound together in one family."

After going through the memories of that day, I sat there transfixed, staring at the essay question on the computer as I had recalled the most traumatic event in my life. Should any of this go into the essay? Was it appropriate? Would the admissions' reviewers even know that I was adopted? I decided they would not have that information about me, so I left it out of my essay. I wrote about the happy childhood that I had with my parents and about how I had grown to love astronomy and baseball, in that order. I felt good about the essay when I finished—1836 words. I was, however, emotionally spent. Once again, I wondered about Elana. She was my first mother who protected me and who brought me into this world. I wondered if she was still alive.

CHAPTER 2

WHILE I WAS WAITING TO hear from the University of Chicago's admission's office, the coach of the University of Chicago's baseball team showed up at my home. My dad invited him in and called me down from my room where I was engrossed in a new George Washington biography. I hated to break away and was a bit perturbed when my father introduced me to Coach Kevin Knightley. I knew that the university had a Division III baseball team and that the admissions representatives I talked to had told me the team had a great interest in me, but I never expected a personal visit from the coach. I changed my expression and my attitude and even apologized to the coach for my delayed response in coming down from my room.

"It's great to meet you, Johann."

Coach Knightley offered a big smile and firm handshake.

"I have heard much about you."

His voice was warm and personable. I didn't know what to say.

"If you heard about my summer league batting average, I must be honest and let you know I'm not that great of a hitter. I had a hot streak last July."

That was stupid. Why did I say that?

"I wasn't thinking about your .312 summer league average or your .278 average last season. I was thinking instead of your 1600 total score on the SATs. We need smart players, not just good athletes."

He did know my batting average. Impressive.

"I am one of those players, Coach, who is more dependent on knowledge than on athleticism."

"I also heard about your modesty, like downplaying your summer batting average as you just did. You have a very good overall batting average for a shortstop, even without that hot streak."

"I get doses of humility from my parents. They don't let anything go to my head, not even my SAT scores. My mom reminded me that 682 other students also scored a 1600 composite score on their SATs this year."

"It's still impressive." *This coach knew how to encourage.*

After about thirty minutes of friendly conversation with the coach and my parents, I decided that I liked him. He was friendly, easy-going, full of humor, principled, and respectful. Before he left, he told me, "Johann, I know you have a love for astronomy and you have a bright academic future. I know also that you love baseball. We have one baseball scholarship left and I am offering it to you. I know you already have an academic scholarship so the baseball scholarship would cover the shortfall in tuition and living expenses that the other scholarship doesn't cover. I would not be here if I thought baseball might jeopardize your academic career. I believe that you can do both, that you don't have to decide one or the other—not now. You're going to be sixteen in August and have lots of time to make career decisions. There is an open door from me to be a part of our team and still put academics first. I can't promise you can even make it as a starter this year, as we have a very good player who can play shortstop. I think you should be given the chance to be a part of our team if you want to keep playing baseball. Just take some time and think about it and talk it over with your parents. You have my complete respect for whatever decision you make."

He then thanked my parents and my dad walked him out to his car. They talked for about five minutes before the coach left.

"Dad, I like him. But I'm not convinced I can do both. Baseball would be from February through June, five months of my life. It's intense."

"I know son, but just think about it. Talk with the other players who also are at the university, first for academics, and second for athletics. Then decide."

My dad returned to the house to help my mom just as another visitor pulled up into our driveway. I recognized Police Chief Ryan as he stepped out of the car.

"You must be 6'2"," he said as he stretched out his hand toward me. Chief Ryan was always a larger than life hero to me, a tall imposing figure, but now I could nearly look him in the eye.

"Almost," I said as I shook his hand. His grip was as rock hard as I had remembered it.

"I'm still looking up to you, Chief."

"Not for long," he replied.

"It's good to see you, Chief. You want to come in?"

"No thanks, I'm on my way to a meeting. Just give this package to your dad," he said as he handed me a large envelope filled with several papers. "Tell him it's for our City Council meeting next week."

That night I had difficulty falling asleep. I thought about all my accomplishments as an athlete that I had worked hard to achieve. I had always wondered why sports seemed to come easy to me. Perhaps my biological father was athletically gifted. I would never know. Even my ethnicity was at best, a guess: part Mediterranean, part Hispanic, and then Elana is a Jewish name common in Eastern Europe, which made for many possibilities. I knew my biological father had a dark complexion, but Elana was unsure about his ethnicity. Then there was some mystery about why I also could roll the letter *r*. I figured I must be part Italian or Hispanic. I just didn't know. The ironic thing is I doubt that I had much German blood despite my full name—Johann Smedley Oberhausen. I could conclude that being a pretty good athlete must have come through both my biological parents.

Am I irresponsible if I drop athletics? I wondered. *I don't know. How can a sixteen-year-old know what to do and I'm not even sixteen yet? I know my dad would love me to play baseball. How will I ever get to sleep thinking about this?*

The more I tried to sleep and forget about the decision I had to make, the more I went back in time, reflecting on my childhood. My earliest memories were at age three, or at least those were my earliest dreams that I could recall. That was when I remembered my parents' amazement that I had counted all the Honey Nut Cheerios that my cousin had thrown into my crib. Carla, age eight at the time, had counted aloud to twenty-seven as she tossed twenty-seven Cheerios at me. I had returned the favor by tossing them back at her, counting aloud to twenty myself. Then I told her I had eaten seven of them. My parents knew I was precocious; they just didn't know my proclivity for math and were shocked that I could subtract.

I remembered my favorite Christmas gift at age six—my first Rubik's cube. I loved solving it along with every Sudoku puzzle that my parents could find, books and books of them. I also loved

500-piece and 1000-piece jigsaw puzzles. My mind could remember shapes and sizes of almost any puzzle piece I set my eyes upon.

My favorite pastime was playing chess online with my friend Nikki from Ukraine and my friend Thomas from Italy. It was so much fun being young and unknown except by a few people. None of my opponents except Nikki and Thomas knew that I was a young kid growing up. Cyberspace was the place that I used my middle name, Smedley. It was a name from long ago. Not many people had ever heard of the name except those who knew the famous Major General Smedley Butler, the highly decorated United States Marine who won the Medal of Honor twice.

I thought about how Elana had chosen my name Johann; why, we don't know, and how my parents came to choose Smedley as my second name. They had known about Major General Smedley Butler, having grown up in Philadelphia and having attended the Haverford School where the famous Marine and writer had also attended and starred as captain of the baseball team and quarterback of the football team. His school was shocked when thirty-eight days before his seventeenth birthday, Smedley left school to enlist in the Marine Corp by lying about his age so he could fight in the Spanish-American War in 1898.

Lying awake in bed, I thought about how I knew nothing about my biological parents but understood I had acquired amazing math skills from them. My adoptive parents, Markus and Katarina, although both intelligent, were not plagued with the intellectual curiosity that I had from a young age. My constant dinner table questions often perplexed them. I remember becoming obsessed with rainbows at age ten, wanting to better understand the double refraction of light in double rainbows. I wanted to know what conditions caused such outcomes.

Others my age didn't ask the questions I did. I wanted to know how a hawk could see such long distances while in flight on a loft of air and yet stay focused on the prey. I saw one swoop down and snatch a sandwich from a child's hand. I wanted to know how it did that.

My mind often interrupted my sleep. On this particular fitful night, I thought about my nearly sixteen years on Earth and my place in the universe. What did it all mean? I knew the miracle of my own eyes by which I could see the Milky Way. How could the human eye discern so many millions of variations of color, size, weight, motion, velocity, depth, and volume, and somehow see into the solar system? I knew that the extraordinary complexity of the human being and of the universe were two sets of facts that pointed to a Creator. *Why did God design me? What was my purpose and my destiny? Was I supposed to be a great baseball player, or astronomer? Or something else?* I wanted to know.

———————

I looked at my alarm clock again one very early morning the week before the end of the school year. I was so glad there was no school requiring me to rise early. School was sometimes fun and other times disappointing. I attended classes in the gifted program of a reputable private school in Downers Grove called the Avery Coonley School. It was one of the best in the nation, but most classes seemed to be more about acquiring information, learning it, and then reproducing it in the form of tests, quizzes, and exams. That bored me because I found that easy to do. My parents called it a photographic memory. It was my greatest gift, I suppose, but was annoying at times. I could remember most everything that I had seen, including almost everything I had read. I needed more than knowledge; that was easy for me to get. I wanted more attention on wisdom and beauty, on understanding the best ways to use knowledge. I could see the world's knowledge production was multiplying but wisdom was declining. I was fortunate; my parents taught me wisdom.

While my friends were playing MMORPGs, I was reading my parents' books by ancient writers like Plato, Aristotle, and Homer. While my friends consumed hours of television, I was reading mid-twentieth century writers like G.K. Chesterton, C.S. Lewis, and J.R.R. Tolkien. While my friends were transported into world wars with zombies in online games, I was being transported into the Peloponnesian War, the land of Narnia, and the great battles of Middle Earth. I would have found myself alone, except for one attribute that made all my friends envious and made me a good athlete—I was fast on my feet—real fast. To me, running was like breathing; it was a part of living. I didn't think about it much—I ran whenever I could. Maybe I was part Maasai. My parents said that by the time I could walk I could also run.

I remember when Mom first realized how fast I was. I was twelve years old when we first traveled to the University of Chicago for some testing. On the way by car to the train station to catch the early morning train, we ran out of gas. My mom did not panic.

"Don't worry, Johann, your dad keeps a couple gallons of spare gas in the trunk."

We checked the trunk and the gas container was empty. Dad was at a conference in Denver, so he could not help us. Who could we call at 5:30 a.m. to bring gas? These were the days before Uber. We did not have AAA and there were no police nearby on the country road where we were. The nearest gas station was a couple of miles away.

"I'll run to the station, Mom, and get some gas."

"It's too far, Johann, we'll miss our train."

"I can make it, Mom; I'm fast," I assured her as I took off running. The whole trip took me less than thirty minutes and we did not miss the train.

Running fast enabled me to steal bases in baseball and to break away from defensive players in soccer. In football, I could run kickoffs and punts back with such elusive speed it was difficult to catch me. Despite these athletic gifts, I did not think much about it because my speed felt so natural. Although I was fast, I did not like track. I felt too isolated. Instead, I preferred team sports and my baseball and soccer coaches loved me for that, for wanting to promote the team and not myself.

The irony was that although I did not like attention focused on me, when I ran, all eyes were fixed on me. My coaches said it was not my speed alone, but the combination of being fast and graceful. I could take no credit for appearing to glide across a football field or soccer field. I could take no credit for taking second base before the catcher managed to get the ball out of his glove. I could take no credit for emerging from a pack of players with the ball coming straight for the goalie before the goalie recognized I had broken through the defense. The goalies did not fear me though. I was not very accurate in kicking a soccer ball. Neither was I a great hitter in baseball. I had a good average, but often bunted my way onto first base. I loved the challenge of beating out a throw to first base. I would miss that the most if I gave up playing baseball.

Exhausted from thought, I fell asleep, thinking about how much I liked Coach Knightley, despite the fact that his offer was keeping me awake half the night. Then it came to me, just before I fell asleep, and I knew what I needed to do regarding the baseball scholarship.

CHAPTER 3

I ROSE EARLY BEFORE MY parents were up, grabbed a banana, slipped out of the house, and walked to Avery Coonley. It was a mild December Saturday morning and the six inches of snow we had the week before had all melted. I first spotted Julianna as I walked across the beautifully landscaped campus, admiring the architecture. Even from across the field I could see she was becoming more beautiful each time I saw her. She saw me, smiled and waved as we approached each other.

Julianna Giamatti, a business student at Northwestern University and Avery Coonley alum, worked for TD Ameritrade in downtown Chicago. Her father was our town's fire chief and we had been friends since third grade.

We both saw Alan arriving from another direction.

Julianna gave me a warm embrace and Alan extended his arm and fist toward mine and as I met his with my own. Julianna then embraced Alan.

"Yo, Johann."

"Thanks for coming, Alan. And you, too, Julianna. You always show up when I need you. I have to decide whether or not to accept the baseball scholarship."

"I've got twenty minutes, Johann, before I need to go coach our men's volleyball team."

"I'm coaching the women's team, Johann, and I have the same amount of time. Let's go over to my office and talk."

Gentle flashbacks filtered through my thoughts as I remembered how Julianna was the first girl I had a crush on. As we walked to the office, I was grateful that we were still good friends. She had become the older sister I had always wanted. I also thought about all the hours I had spent at the school during the past nine years and how Alan was one of my first advocates. When the bullies came after me walking home from school before I became a recognizable athlete, Alan had a knack for showing up to keep me from getting pummeled. I could share any problem or fear with Alan, knowing he would hold it in confidence. Alan was now like a big brother to me.

I loved this place. This was where I had made dozens of life-long friends, most of them gifted in remarkable ways. The Avery Coonley School offered special programs for gifted young people who wanted to excel and yet not be bullied because of their peculiar proclivities. I loved the school: it was a second home.

It didn't hit me until we sat down in Juliana's office that something wasn't right. Alan and Julianna both had worry etched across their faces.

"I'm glad you called us," Alan said. "If you had not called, we would have called you."

"What's going on?"

"First, Johann, how can we help you?" Julianna always had that unselfish concern for everyone else first.

"You remember the baseball scholarship I told you both about?"

They both nodded.

"I think I know what to do, but I need to run my thoughts by you. I have to let them know by the end of this month. My dad would like me to accept it, but I just don't see myself as a professional baseball player. I see myself being a great astronomer. I know I can do both but I want to put all my energy into pursuing astronomy. But it's hard because I love playing baseball and I'm good at it."

Julianna got right to the point the way she often did. "You have to go where your heart takes you, Johann."

"I agree," Alan piped in. "Your dad will support you no matter what you choose."

"I know, I just hate to disappoint him. He has done so much for me."

"Your parents are both proud of you, Johann. You will not disappoint them."

Julianna gave me a big hug as only an older sister could. "You'll make the right choice, Johann."

I felt good and gained confidence about the upcoming decision now that I had Alan and Julianna's affirmation. But while I had become more comfortable, they both continued to shift in their seats. Alan wasted no time telling me why.

"Susan hacked into a live telephone conversation last night at an *Eleutheria Club* meeting. One of our intelligence agencies was recording it. If it's real, there's a serious biological warfare threat against the U.S. being formulated overseas. We need to meet again tonight. Can you come?"

"Yeah, what time?"

"Let's meet at five in case anyone has evening engagements," Alan said. "I'll let everyone know."

Susan Livingston was an extraordinary hacker and fellow alum who worked for Microsoft. I knew she must have intercepted some alarming information.

———————————

That evening, I took my bike to the Metra rail station in Downers Grove and caught a train for downtown Chicago, getting off within walking distance of Dursen Shoes on North Milwaukee Street. I loved the city, despite the violent gangs, crime, shootings, drug problems, and other horrible realities of many urban areas that keep people away. I always saw the good side of Chicago and I had so many friends who lived in the city. I loved Chicago culture, sports, restaurants, museums, clothing stores, shoe stores, and most of all, bookshops.

In 2001, after the 9/11 terrorist attacks, many of my friends, all alums of the Avery Coonley School, formed a private club called the *Eleutheria Club,* taking the name from the Greek word ἐλευθερία, an ancient Greek term for the personification of liberty. Most of these friends who founded the club were computer and technology geniuses who had hacking skills that rivaled those of Julian Assange, Kevin Mitnick, Gary McKinnon, and Adrian Lamo and the LulzSec group. The difference between these hackers and the *Eleutheria Club* was that our group sought to help U.S. counterterrorism experts by feeding them information on terrorist threats they might uncover with our IT skills. Our club had no formal membership or formal organization—there was nothing to sign and no dues to pay. It was secretive and all relational, with minimal structure; although we did elect a club president every three years.

Just after my fourteenth birthday, Alan invited me to my first *Eleutheria Club* meeting. He wanted me to join them.

"You know I'm not an experienced hacker, Alan. Why would you all want me?"

"First of all, you're my friend Johann. Second, you have much to offer. Many of the new security threats involve space warfare that none of us know much about."

"I'm not a space warfare expert . . . "

"But you will be," Alan said. "We have plenty of IT wizards, Johann. We need people who know astronomy and physics and who are learning about space warfare. Warfare is moving into space."

"I'm new at this stuff."

"But you're a faster learner," Alan said.

"I guess. If you guys really want me, I'll join your club."

Becoming part of the *Eleutheria Club* was that simple. Now, those in the club had become my closest friends.

I entered Dursen Shoes a couple of minutes before five, just as the store was closing, and made my way downstairs into the large and fully furnished 1200 square feet of underground surveillance equipment, meeting rooms, and a lounge area, including a functional kitchen. The sophisticated communication technology with advanced online surveillance capabilities was purchased by the owners, John and Joy Dexter, who purchased the equipment for their son. The Dexters were wealthy board members of Avery Coonley and John was an avid ham radio operator with an extensive international network of ham radio friends that he had nurtured during the past thirty years. Their son, David, was one of the original founders of the *Eleutheria Club*.

Alan and Julianna greeted me with subdued smiles as I entered the communication center. We sat on some sofas drinking coffee until Susan, Christina, and Darrell joined us. Susan, an accomplished software engineer and cyber-security expert, was recruited by Microsoft early in her senior year at Avery Coonley. Her hacking skills were well known. Christina, also an IT expert and bright star, graduated two years before me and had become one of the leaders of the *Eleutheria Club*. Her parents immigrated to Chicago from

Singapore two years before she was born. After Julianna, she became one of my closest female friends.

I didn't know Darrell very well as he had not attended Avery Coonley, but he had forged a strong friendship with both Alan and Christina. He was a military veteran and language expert with family roots in Hong Kong. Darrell, who worked for the U.S. Citizenship and Immigration Services, was known to be calm under pressure. It was a gift I wanted.

Susan put her secure iPad on the table in front of the sofa and with very little introduction, said, "Listen to this audio recording I hacked into last night in real time. I recorded it as it was also being recorded by a U.S. intelligence agency."

"How was your flight from Johannesburg to Istanbul, Mr. Churgrill?"

"No problems, General Sarkovsky."

"So, your fear of being on a no-fly list was unfounded?"

"No, it was the case, but I was able to take care of it prior to my flight, and I'm no longer on the list."

"We have a short window here. Let's discuss the business at hand."

"Vodka?"

"No thank you, just some water. I never mix business with alcohol."

"Can you deliver what I asked, General, at the price that I offered?"

"Yes I can, but with a small price adjustment."

"What adjustment?"

"The price will be 260 million."

"You call sixty million a small adjustment? That's insane! I said last week that we will pay 200 million."

"It's costing more than anticipated to purchase the biological agents and transport them to the Iranians and then on to their destinations. You have access to great capital, you can find 260 million."

"The government and the bankers will already be asking many questions with such large amounts of money crossing borders. My backers told me no more than 225 million."

"Then contact your backers and tell them I am authorized to accept no less than 250 million euros. You could pay 225 million now and another twenty-five million a month after the event. That's my best offer."

"I can pay 230 million euros total in unmarked euros, Swiss francs, and South African rand. 200 million one week from today and thirty million the day after the attack. I cannot pay more than that. Remember, you will have ten million shares of stock, which will make you a fortune."

"Agreed. You pushed me beyond the limit and I hope there is no pushback."

"Then we have an agreement for 230 million euros."

"Yes," the general said. "Have your people draw up a formal business contract."

"Now, when will the payload be ready to launch?"

"It will take eight to twelve months to get it in place."

"That is too long, I want it launched within six months."

"That's nuts. No one can build and launch a WMD in six months."

"The Chinese can," Churgrill said. "They will be ready. Their rocket site is nearly ready and they have built their weapon in four months."

"Putting a weapon on a Russian satellite will take more time; it takes a minimum of 180 days just to get a ride into space!"

"You have six months max. I am paying you 230 million euros. Be resourceful."

"Well, there is one possibility."

"Indeed, I found out last week a new weather satellite is already being built by your country and will be launched next February. You should be able create your weapon in time to place it on that satellite."

"We can if the agents get to the Iranians quickly."

"Then you agree to my time frame, General?"

"Yes, we will plan to set the WMD on the Russian weather satellite being launched in February."

Susan paused the recording. "Most of the remaining conversation is not important, except for one short discussion that I will play after we talk about this."

"Who are these people?" Darrell asked.

Alan leaned forward and took hold of the conversation.

"Our follow-up research indicates the man with the South African accent, Atlas Churgrill, is a businessman and billionaire who once ran for president of South Africa and who is a former ambassador to the United Nations. He has long been suspected of illegal activities, including money laundering, narcotics distribution, diamond smuggling, and human trafficking. Julianna's done the research on Sarkovsky."

"General Nicoli Sarkovsky is a high-ranking retired general, and he's an associate of the president of Russia," Julianna explained. "He has many high-level contacts in Russia and has access to the president and to all the engineers who have worked in the Russian space program."

"What is the agent in the WMD?" Christina asked.

"We don't know yet," replied Alan. "But I have a question for you, Johann. Is this credible? Can a WMD be added to the payload of a weather satellite?"

"I believe so. A biological WMD can be very small and very light-weight. This would not be a difficult task for a team of experienced aeronautical engineers."

"Then we have to take this seriously. Now let's listen to the end of their conversation."

Susan reached across the table and turned on the recording again.

"I'm skeptical of the simulation report you sent, General."

"I understand, I also was skeptical when I saw the results of the last test indicating zero deviation. But I checked the procedures and numbers multiple times—it is what it is. There was no mistake."

"Isn't that unusual?"

"The person who conducted these simulations is a brilliant scientist. The results are unusual because there almost al-ways is a small degree of deviation, but on the last set of simulations, it just happened to be perfect. One hundred percent of the targets were hit."

"How do you explain that?"

"You can't explain it. My scientist said this might occur once in ten thousand simulations. The calculations, instrumentation, and results were doubled-checked. They were recorded accurately. There was no deviation. The satellite weapon being developed performed perfectly in the simulations. Remember, the other tests did have deviations that require design adjustments. The average deviation over the five tests was less than one percent, with a hit rate of over ninety-nine percent each time."

"And are you still confident, General, that China will blame the U.S. for this attack?"

"Yes. And the U.S. will blame China. They are both preparing for space wars. Before they can control the situation, things—"

[Churgrill interrupts]. "Before they can control the situation, things will spin out of control."

"Exactly, and the military leaders will overreact."

"How certain are you of this scenario, General?"

"One hundred percent."

"Nothing is one hundred percent assured, General, not even your next breath. But am I certain that you can instigate a war between China and the U.S.? Yes, I am. And that war will make you wealthy and will secure your political future."

"Not as wealthy as you," Sarkovsky said.

"This isn't about the money. I have plenty of that already. Only an act of God can stop this now, General."

"I think God will stay out of this," Sarkovsky said. "The U.S. is overdue this catastrophic reckoning for all its greed and China will pay for all its sins, too."

Susan stopped the recording. "That's the heart of this conversation. The end goal is igniting a space war between the U.S. and China with WMDs, all to the benefit of Russia."

We all sat there in silence, trying to absorb the gravity of what we just heard.

I spoke up. "So, what are we going to do, if anything? The U.S. intelligence agencies must know about this."

"Someone in an intelligence agency did record it. But we don't know who. We're trying to find out our through our contacts."

Alan took charge of the meeting again.

"Susan, let me play devil's advocate. How authentic was this recording? Couldn't two well-trained actors have created such a conversation? Was it a true encounter or were two people spreading purposeful disinformation, knowing that they were being recorded by one or more foreign agents?"

After much debate, our consensus was that the conversation did not sound scripted. It sounded unrehearsed and genuine.

Alan posed another question. "Do U.S. government agents who have heard this recording believe this is a genuine conversation? And if they do believe it's true, who do they believe the agents are that are being sent to Iran to create the WMDs?"

These last questions remained unanswered.

I returned home on the train, waiting with great anxiety to get some clarity about this threat.

CHAPTER 4

I AWOKE IN THE NIGHT with the same cold sweat that had become commonplace. I had thrashed my sheets, as if I had been in a life and death wrestling match. The killer in my recurring nightmare had come for me again. It was always a man with weapons that differed from dream to dream. In this dream, he wielded a long sharp knife and was seeking to dismember me alive—a horrid thought like some demon-possessed person in the worst horror movie I could imagine. Most people are dismembered after they are dead; this killer wanted to dismember me while living.

Sometimes I awoke thrashing my arms wildly like a cat trying to protect itself from a predator. Other times I realized I would be kicking my killer while lying on my back, as in a bicycle motion. My most poignant memory of these nightmares was the grotesque sinister face of the killer and the white gown he wore splattered with blood. I felt an evil presence in my room for what seemed like hours after these nightmares ended. I hated them.

I shuddered as I turned on the lamp on the bureau next to my bed and looked at the clock—4:24 a.m. I had been in a daze. It was the early morning of May 31. Today I had to communicate my final decision whether or not to play baseball for the University of Chicago. When the fear left me and I fell back asleep, I awoke hours later with my thoughts not on my reoccurring nightmare and not on whether to play baseball at the University of Chicago, but instead, on our upcoming camping trip to Yosemite National Park.

When I came downstairs for breakfast, my parents were like little children on Christmas morning waiting to hear of my decision regarding baseball, although they tried to hide it.

My dad picked up the morning newspaper on the kitchen island where my mom had placed it.

"Wow, I can't believe it's already the end of May," he said aloud to no one in particular but loud enough for us to hear.

"I know," my mom said, "where did the month go?"

For a moment they both pretended to forget about this being the day I needed to tell the university my final decision.

Then Mom started reviewing all the tasks she had intended to complete in May, playing dumb, as if I did not know what was going on.

She then asked my father, "How about you honey, did you get all your May goals completed?"

When I could stand it no longer, I thought it was time to call my parents on the carpet for their elaborate charade.

"And now, Mom, are you going to ask me if I completed all my May tasks, just to make sure I didn't forget today is the last day to make a decision regarding Coach Knightley's offer?"

"Oh yes, you did have a big May goal." She was still playing dumb.

"And you just thought of it now, Mom?"

She just looked over toward me with a slight smirk, and then focused back on the pan of bacon she was frying for breakfast. I noticed Dad was smirking, too, as he tried to hide behind the paper.

"Okay, okay," I said. "Yes, I have made a final decision. But I want to tell you during our special time camping in Yosemite."

"But you have to tell Coach Knightley today, and Yosemite's next week!"

"Exactly, Mom. I will talk with Coach Knightley today, but I will save the news for you and dad for during our Yosemite trip."

My mom protested. "You will keep us in suspense for another week?"

My dad kept his cool. "It's okay, Katarina. As long as Coach Knightley knows today, we can wait for Yosemite."

"I want to tell you on Half Dome."

"And you trust me not to get the information from Coach Knightley?"

"Yes, Dad, as mischievous as you are, you must promise to wait."

"Fine, I promise I will not ask Coach Knightly about your decision."

After a pleasant breakfast, despite my parents' occasional quip about waiting for Yosemite, I knew I wanted some time alone with my dad.

"Dad, do you have time to talk this morning?"

He had anticipated this question and had taken the morning off, recognizing that today was decision day. We went into the sunroom and sat down while Mom went to take a shower.

I began the conversation.

"I know what I want, Dad, but I want to make sure I do what's best. You know the university would like me to become a student athlete. I've done that most of my life. I want to focus on academics now, but I also love baseball. I admit, I'm infatuated with the possibility of one day trying to make the Chicago White Sox farm team, but I wouldn't want to be taking time away from the astronomy lab. I know enough to realize a contract in major league baseball is a dream unobtainable. So why play college if I'm not going pro?"

"I agree that thinking of a possible pro contract this early is a bridge too far, though you remind scouts of Ellsbury. Not that you one day might have the potential of a player like Jacoby Ellsbury, but the hours of practice require a whole-hearted commitment to the sport. Also, Ellsbury is one of the best with an enormous amount of talent. I know you are a gifted player, but to even approach his level would require a total commitment to an unimaginable amount of hard work."

"My passion is astronomy, Dad. I want to pursue the stars, not stardom. I want to understand the unknown, but I don't know if I'm ready to give up baseball."

"You know, Johann, that not many astronomers are financially successful or well known. Even Galileo was ridiculed and imprisoned because men did not like to change their paradigms about the nature of the universe. History is full of men who ran blindly with new theories, applying them beyond their original intentions, as both Galileo and Darwin discovered."

"I know, Dad. I have read enough of their work to know that neither scientist had any intention of replacing God's central role as the Creator of the universe. They didn't want fame or glory, but it came."

I looked at the *National Geographic* and astronomy magazines stacked on the table. Sunlight danced on the cover image of the Amazon River, making a beautiful distraction. "As much as I love science," I said, "I also value the philosophy of science. Remember how I devoured Kuhn's book, *The Structure of Scientific Revolutions*, during the last winter break?"

"Yes, I remember our discussions."

"Well, I read up on Kuhn and learned how he abandoned his scientific career in order to explore the nature of scientific discovery. I learned much from him. I know that great discoverers are seldom held in honor during their lifetimes. I'd be fortunate to discover anything new!"

"It's part art and part science. Timing and history have to align in unusual ways in order to realize that one has even made a consequential scientific discovery."

"But the idea of hunting for something new and consequential is just as tantalizing to me as the chance to play professional baseball. But both baseball and astronomy are fun, just in different ways."

"I think you will know what is best for you, Johann. Take your time thinking about it and don't try to please me or your mother. I won't ask you again until we reach the summit of Half Dome."

Those words from my father released all the pressure I was feeling. I knew whatever I decided to do, my parents would support me one hundred percent.

———————

Nicole Jacobson came into my life the week before our Yosemite trip and became my first romantic interest. It was more infatuation on my part, since she was a recent college graduate and several years older than me. I was a teenager with no romantic experiences. None, zero. I never messed around. I had no girlfriends in high school. I was too busy with sports and academics and family trips, and too intimidated to try and pursue a girlfriend.

It's not that I didn't notice beautiful women like Julianna. I did notice. I just always felt too incompetent and too young to act on my instincts. My closest female friends like Julianna and Christina, both part of the *Eleutheria Club*, treated me like a younger brother. They never showed romantic interest in me, and I didn't dare make passes at them for fear of being ridiculed as well as being inappropriate. I was like the little brother in the group.

Then Nicole came along, or I should say, her personal journal came along. I had arrived at Dursen Shoes for an *Eleutheria Club* meeting just a few minutes after the last customer left before the store closed. That customer was a young woman from Silver Springs, Maryland, who was in Chicago attending a weekend conference. She had a broken heel and needed a new pair of shoes so she found Dursen Shoes. While she'd been trying on a pair of shoes, her personal journal fell out of her bag and landed under the bench she was sitting on. She didn't notice it had fallen out in her hurry to get back to the evening session.

I saw the journal under the bench and opened it, looking for the name of its owner. I found Nicole's name on the inside cover, along with her address and phone number.

I felt conflicted once I realized it was someone's personal journal, and then had a flashback to reading my mom's journal. But I could not resist perusing some of the entries. I was captivated by the last one she wrote. She said she was on the airplane on her way to Chicago for a conference and she wrote about the horrendous day just before she left. After reading it I felt close to her. She had recorded a recurring nightmare that had many similarities to my own nightmares.

> I awoke, screaming silently again as I put my hands up to my throat to stop the choking sensation I had imagined in my recurring nightmare. I was drenched in perspiration and was tense with a palpable fear in my spirit. The dream

always had the same theme—someone was trying to suffocate me, with one hand holding me down and the other covering my face. I felt my life slipping away as I struggled to breathe. Then it ended before I died and like many times before. I awoke shaking.

That part I understood. The rest of the journal entry for that day was technical, but it was not good news:

Slept another hour and awoke to emergency phone call. My boss called me to rally my team to prepare for a biological threat. We have to produce twenty-eight million doses of camelid antitoxin heavy-chain-Ab V_H (VHH) to neutralize intoxicating BoNT proteases, the lethal Botulinum toxin. Was grateful Shelley brought me Dunkin Donuts coffee and donut, and a sandwich for lunch. Just what I needed. Forget the trim body goal. Who cares if we are fighting an agent that will kill us all?

Director of national intelligence will provide more details. Nationwide, we need 270 million doses of heptavalent Botulinum antitoxin to cover all the urban population, about eighty-one percent of the total U.S. pop. We already have twenty-two million doses in storage. Need to produce another twenty-eight million doses in our U.S. lab. Need eighty percent twenty milliliter glass vials and twenty percent fifty mL glass vials. CDC has about twenty-five million doses distributed to twenty CDC Quarantine Stations throughout the U.S., including one in San Juan, Puerto Rico, one in Anchorage, and one in Honolulu. About sixty percent of those doses are the fifty milliliter vials. The CDC lab outside of Atlanta is in the process of producing another twenty-five million dozes for distribution. The Zurich, Switzerland, lab and the Singapore lab are producing thirty million doses each. The remaining 107 million doses will need to come from the Emergent BioSolutions Corporation lab in Canada, which we will need to replace since they also are preparing for a potential attack on Canada.

We may not have enough sodium sulfide. Have plenty of sulfur but iodine shipments have been slow and we don't have enough on hand right now to make 50,000 vials of HBAT. Got production going well before leaving for Chicago.

I closed the journal and knew that I needed to talk to this woman. I found out through the store sales manager that evening that Nicole Jacobson, his last customer, was attending a conference nearby on biological threats. I left a note for her with the store manager. It said, "I found your journal and would like to talk with you. My name is Johann Oberhausen. Please call me." I then provided my cell number.

I received a call just before I left my dorm room that morning.

"This is Johann."

"This is Nicole Jacobson. Johann, I want to thank you for finding my journal in Dursen Shoes. It had some very important information and I was sick with worry when I lost it."

I liked the sound of her voice. She was very personable.

"You are welcome, Nicole. I would have brought it over to the conference but I didn't know how to find you. I knew you would come back for it."

"That is kind of you, Johann, to think about finding me right away. I had to be at a 5:30 panel so I rushed out of the store."

"Do you have any free time tonight?" I asked. "There is something important I would like to talk with you about face-to-face regarding a national security issue."

"The conference ends tonight at five and I have no plans for dinner."

"Are you staying near the conference site?"

"Yes, I'm at the Hilton where the conference is."

"Great, I know an excellent Italian restaurant not far from there. Can you meet me at Vivere on West Monroe at seven?"

"That is perfect."

"I'll make reservations, I look forward to meeting you."

I arrived early after trying to find something nice to wear. As I waited for her at the reception area where guests are seated, I scrutinized everyone who came through the door. I had not asked Nicole for any physical description and I had not given one to her.

Finally, a woman walked up to the desk and asked to be seated with Johann Oberhausen. She had long brunette hair that reached well below her shoulders. She had a warm smile and energetic disposition. I came over to the reception desk and introduced myself to her. It was helpful that I was nearly six feet two inches tall, but I knew she could see that I was young. I was relieved when she did not show any reaction to my youth.

"Thank you so much, Nicole, for taking time to meet with me."

After we sat down and small talked about our homes in Maryland and Illinois and about our families, I turned the conversation serious.

"I need to apologize to you, Nicole. I read from your journal."

"You must be the curious type. Of course, I forgive you, Johann. I might have done the same thing."

"I was looking for your name and address, but after I found it, I could not resist the temptation to peruse your entries. Your last entry hit me hard."

"Yeah, the day before I came here was crazy."

"Do you mind if we turn off our cell phones off and put them away?" I asked.

"That's fine," she said. "Why the extra security?"

"You'll understand in a minute. But first, what I want you to know is that you are the first person I've met who understands my recurring nightmare, because you have the same one."

"You have dreams of someone trying to kill you?" She leaned toward me.

"Yes," I said. "Sometimes a man is strangling me with his bare hands, sometimes cutting me up with sharp knives, and other times suffocating me with a pillow. And always leaving me shaken."

"I've had mostly suffocation nightmares. No knives, thank God," she said.

"If you believe in the spiritual realm, would describe all these dreams as demonic?"

"Yes. That's a good description," she said.

"The second part of your last day's journal entry also was frightening."

"Do you understand antitoxins?" Nicole asked.

"No, but I understand the real threat of a biological attack."

I then explained a little bit about our surveillance club and bits and pieces of the conversation Susan had intercepted between Churgrill and Sarkovsky, trying to not ever mention their names.

"The threat is real," she replied once I finished. "This is just another confirmation. But this information could be helpful if we know the biological agent is made by Russia but coming from Iran. We will have a briefing soon by the national director of intelligence."

"Do you have cameras in your building?" I asked.

"You mean surveillance cameras?"

"Yes," I said.

"I think so. Why do you ask?"

"My friends are security experts and I was just curious how safe your work environment is, given the sensitive nature of your operations," I said.

After the serious conversation, we both enjoyed dinner and each other's company.

"I hope you will not be offended, Johann, if I asked how old you are? You will be a freshman this fall at the University of Chicago, so I'm guessing you're eighteen or nineteen?"

"I'll be entering college as a sixteen-year-old freshman. I graduated from high school two years ahead of my age group."

"We have that in common, too. I just graduated from Johns Hopkins University at age nineteen, two to three years ahead of my age group. So, we are about three years apart."

I was surprised but glad she was not uncomfortable by our age difference.

After the evening ended, she said, "Call me, Johann, when you get back home from Yosemite."

CHAPTER 5

OUR DRIVE TO YOSEMITE VALLEY on Highway 41, following the Merced River, was as beautiful as I had ever remembered it. We first flew to San Jose for the night, rented a car, and then drove to the valley, entering from the west early in the morning. As we approached Inspiration Point, my mom shouted, "Please stop, honey!"

Dad pulled over and we saw what Mom had seen: a majestic view of the valley. We could see Half Dome, along with El Capitan and Bridalveil Falls. The falls beckoned to us to come for a closer view, so after driving back down to the valley floor and parking the car, dad said, "Let's hike up to the base." The late spring snow melt provided plenty of water to cascade down the 620-foot drop.

The rocks were quite slippery on the way down, and Mom took a bad fall on her arm. As Dad and I helped her up, she cried out in much pain.

"This arm is hurting bad, but it's not broken," she said.

My mom was a doctor so I suppose she was right, but I could see her still grimace.

My dad made a sling for her and we hiked back down to the parking lot. We continued on the road a short distance to get a better view of El Capitan, the largest sheer face of granite in the world which rises to 7,573 feet.

Our last stop for the evening before we camped was a brief visit to historic Yosemite Chapel, built in 1879 as part of the original Yosemite Village. Not far away, we found our tent site at the Upper Pines Campground in Yosemite Valley. After we pitched our tent, my dad said, "Let's get a fire going to cook dinner."

It was already late afternoon when Mom covered our picnic table with a red tablecloth and set out a couple bottles of red wine, a container of pine nut hummus dip, sliced celery, red and green peppers, and carrot sticks. We watched the coals whiten as we snacked. Dad then placed the steaks Mom had been marinating in her special sauce on the grill. As the sun set behind the trees, I thought, *can life be any better than this?*

"I didn't think you could do it," my mom said to me as she crunched on some celery dipped in blue cheese.

"Do what?"

"Keep a secret for one week."

"Your father and I have a bet. I say yes, he thinks no."

"I can confirm one of you is right. How's your arm?" I asked, strategically changing the subject.

"I'm going up Half Dome no matter what," she replied. "I am pretty sure that it's a deep bruise or slight fracture, but not broken."

My dad then chimed in. "I sure hope your diagnosis is right."

After dinner, I asked my dad some simple questions as we scanned the constellations in the night sky.

"Do you believe in destiny?" I asked.

"If you mean do I believe God destined us to accomplish specific things, then yes."

"Me, too."

"But there's always the effects of free will, Johann."

"What do you mean?"

"The free will of man can interfere with the destiny of God."

"But God has all power to make His will happen."

Mom then joined our conversation, pouring some more chips into the bowl on the picnic table.

"But He seldom uses that power when it means taking away the free will of man. He lets us choose."

It wasn't easy to accept, but I knew she was right. The world was full of people who made bad choices. I needed to make good choices.

———————————

Early the next morning, we began our sixteen-mile round trip hike up to Half Dome. Mom took off her sling and said that her arm pain was bearable.

"How is it?" Dad asked after we passed the one-mile marker.

"Not throbbing; it feels okay, just sore."

My mom's excellent physical condition and experience as a former college athlete in soccer and softball had prepared her to hike up the mountain despite some pain. So did her love of hiking.

"You know, Mom, all my friends assume that I inherited my athletic skills from you."

"Hey, what about me?"

"Sorry, Dad; they all think of you as a crazy professor and give you the credit for my photographic memory since you remember every poem you've ever read."

"Hey, I worked hard for that reputation. So, they think you got your craziness from me?"

"It's not from me," Mom said.

About halfway up the mountain, I began to think about my adoption, a subject I had avoided thinking or talking about after that emotional day many years ago. My parents were the only parents I had ever known, and I had long ago made peace with the idea that Elana could not care for me. It did not stop me from thinking about her now, though.

"Did you and Dad try to have children before you adopted me?" I asked my mom.

She looked at me with some sadness in her face.

"We tried, but after a dangerous tubal pregnancy, the doctors had to remove my ovaries."

"I'm so sorry, Mom. I didn't know."

"Your mom and I explored many options, Johann, but then you fell into our laps and we decided you were the one for us."

"How so?" I already knew the story but wanted to hear it again.

"We'll tell you more secrets on top of Half Dome," my mom said with a sly smile on her face.

Nailed by my mom. I made her wait, so now she was making me wait.

When we nearly reached the summit, we had to finish the last 400 feet by cable. My dad worried about my mom's arm, but by taking her time, she had just enough of her arm strength to pull herself up the cables. I noticed her wince a couple of times, but she toughed it out.

When we reached the summit, it was very windy and difficult to communicate. After taking a couple of pictures and recording the view on our phones, I turned to my parents and said, "Dad wins the bet."

My mom smiled and then told me, "I knew it. I just didn't want you to know I knew."

"How?"

"I'm your mom; I know you. And Dad knew, too, without Coach telling him."

"So much for my dramatic announcement."

"We'll tell you our secrets on the way down; it's too windy to hear each other."

But I wasn't about to let my mom off the hook. After about a half mile back down the mountain, we were all ready to talk.

"So, tell me how I fell into your laps. I know you told me the whole story when I was younger, but I want to hear it again."

"After the ectopic pregnancy and eventual loss of my ovaries, we were devastated," my mom explained. "We considered in vitro fertilization but that was costly. We settled on adoption."

"But we had no idea of how long adoption took and we didn't realize that it also was expensive, especially for international adoptions," my dad said. "Everything was on hold when you came along."

"You mean when Elana came into the ER?"

"Yes, exactly."

"Can you tell me any more about her?" I prompted.

"When Elana came in, she triggered a memory of my first pregnancy at age twenty. After a night of heavy drinking together, my boyfriend ignored my pleas and took advantage of me. I could have brought charges against him for rape but refrained because we were both drunk. After I found out I was pregnant, my boyfriend abandoned me and had no interest in becoming a parent. I felt I had no choice but to end the pregnancy, so I did."

Stunned, I was silent, not knowing what to say. I looked down.

"I don't think I ever overcame the guilt of that decision until we adopted you."

When I looked up, tears were beading in her eyes.

I uttered softly, "I'm so sorry." It sounded hollow.

Mom then stopped walking, turned to me, and looked into my eyes.

"On the day we adopted you, I felt closure from the day I had always regretted, that day when I ended the life of my first child."

She gave me a strong embrace as she looked at the swaying trees beyond me.

We began walking again in silence. Dad was now fifty yards ahead of us and we needed catch up. During the rest of the journey hiking down from Half Dome, we did not talk too much. The three of us were deep in contemplation. I could not help but think of how my life would have been enriched by an older brother or sister.

We returned to our campsite exhausted. I wolfed down some Italian sausage, gouda cheese, and gourmet crackers with my mom while Dad made a campfire. After the flames transitioned to glowing embers, Dad went into our tent and returned with a box of Graham Crackers, a bag of large marshmallows, and two chocolate bars. My dad found the metal marshmallow roasting sticks he brought and before long we were all washing down our s'mores with hot chocolate. As I took in the evening, the reality of being part of a loving family made me grateful. What would have happened to me if I had not been adopted? I thought.

I realized that my parents seemed to be among the happiest people on Earth, and I was part of their happiness. I knew adopted kids were not easy to parent, and it could have gone all wrong with me. I knew that knowing that I wasn't abandoned by my mother was a big reason I was able to make it through my teen years without anger, confusion, and isolation.

As we sat around the campfire looking at the stars on that crisp cool night, the three of us experienced a moment of transcendence—the pure joy of being a family that loved each other and who belonged to one another. I felt peace about turning down the baseball scholarship.

Just as we were all getting sleepy, my father perked us up by proposing a toast with a bottle of port wine he had retrieved from his backpack.

"What's that?" I asked.

"This bottle was given to me by my father as a going away gift when I came to the United States from Germany at age twenty-one. This bottle of port is thirty-eight years old. My father told me, 'Save this for a special occasion in America; it cost more than your air ticket to Boston.' My father had always delighted in my decision to immigrate to America. He was seven years old when he had first met the friendly American soldiers from the 101st Airborne Division who had come to his small Bavarian town in April of 1945. They had been pursuing Hitler but were kind to the German children, sharing their chocolate, cookies, and unusual items like baseball cards. An American soldier introduced my father to baseball and gave him a Lou Gehrig baseball card. He kept the card until his death and refused to sell it, even after its value had sky-rocketed after Gehrig's premature death to ALS.

"At that time," my father explained as he poured three glasses of port, "baseball was little known in Germany. My father promoted the sport in Bavaria, helping to start Munich's first adult baseball league."

This was all new information to me. It was making sense.

"Is that why you wanted me to pursue baseball?"

"I must confess, I had mixed emotions when you shared your desire to pursue astronomy alone without baseball," my dad replied. "But your decision resonated as the right one, so I'm uncorking this thirty-eight-year old bottle of fine port wine."

My parents lifted up their glasses in a toast to my pursuit of astronomy. I didn't know what to expect, but I liked the taste of the thirty-eight-year-old port. I fell asleep sitting by the campfire and my dad put a heavy blanket over me. It was a very good trip to Yosemite.

CHAPTER 6

"HAPPY BIRTHDAY, JOHANN!" MY PARENTS and friends shouted after I blew out the sixteen candles on my cake.

"Do I get a car?" I asked my parents in jest. "How am I going to get around as a college student?"

My dad laughed.

"Better than a car," he said, "I'll spray paint your bike a new color and add new reflectors for night riding."

I arrived at the Alper House residence hall at the University of Chicago four days later, wondering which one of the 109 other students assigned with me I would meet first. It was an ideal location for me, a couple of minutes' walk from the Laboratory for Astrophysics and Space where I wanted to spend a lot of time. The Alper House had a coffeehouse and provided neighborhood services, including making special meals for the elderly and arranging for students to help out in local schools. The House also organized camping trips to the Indiana Dunes, which I planned to take advantage of, and were involved in intramural sports, featuring competitive teams in soccer, flag football, and volleyball.

After I arrived on that first day, I walked up the stairs and found my room. The door was closed so I knocked to see if anyone was there. The door opened and I was greeted by a lanky, well-dressed teenager with curly brown hair, a large head with a receding hairline, a wide mouth, thin nose, very white complexion, and a broad smile.

"Hi," he said with his hand extended. "I'm Mark."

"Hi Mark, I'm Johann. I'm your roommate."

Within two minutes of light conversation about ourselves, I could surmise that Mark had a quirky personality and that we were going to get along fine.

"I hope I didn't interrupt anything," I said, noticing that Mark seemed to have been going through a stack of important papers.

"No, just shifting through this package of orientation materials to help me get settled. I just arrived here from New Jersey."

"Coolness—a great state with great people."

"That's a kind thing to say, Johann. Most just think of *Jersey Shore*, gangsta culture, and pharmaceutical plants. And then COVID-19. I'm from a small town called Whitehouse Station. It's very different from the urban sprawl. We have a couple thousand residents."

"I grew up in Downers Grove just west of Chicago. It's much bigger but still a cool community. But I would love living in a much smaller place where you get to know people."

"That's what we'll have here. This place rocks."

"Excellent, I'm so glad I'm here."

I felt so jazzed about getting such a stellar roommate. Mark was a computer science major with a risky hobby of currency trading. I was quite impressed when he set up three medium-sized computer screens on wall mounts above his desk so he could follow three currency pairs at the same time. Currency trading was a silent sport so I was glad to see he brought no sound system and no television, and neither did I. We were both content to play music off our phones and to watch TV programs on our computers using headphones so we did not disturb one another.

My first class, chemistry, began the Tuesday before Labor Day. As I rode my bike across campus, I thought about what it was going to be like as perhaps the youngest student that year in the freshman class at the University of Chicago. Then I met Mizzi Zagred in my chemistry class.

During the second week of class, I noticed her phone went off the charts one morning with text messages. I sat close enough to her to see the birthday emojis.

"Happy birthday, Mizzi," I whispered from behind, trying to not be overheard by the professor.

She turned and smiled and shocked me by saying, "Sweet sixteen—it's going to be an awesome year."

Mizzi had officially enrolled at age fifteen into the university as the youngest student. I was the second youngest.

In addition to chemistry, my class schedule included math, biology, philosophy, and an advanced physics course. I later learned, as did Mizzi, that Yo Timothy Shano had entered the Pritzker School of Medicine at the university at age twelve in 2002. After finding out about Yo, we didn't feel so young.

I stepped into my second class, PHSC 12600 Matter, Energy, Space, and Time, to find Dr. John E. Keppler standing at the front of the class with our course professor. Keppler introduced himself as the head of the Kavli Institute for Cosmological Physics and the Enrico Fermi Institute. He left out his introduction that he was the S. Chandrasekhar Distinguished Service Professor in the Department of Astronomy and Astrophysics, which is housed in the Kavli Institute.

"I know you are all going to have a great time here, and it will be even better when you come visit us at the Kavli Institute. We have some amazing people here, including my good friend who is your professor for this class, Dr. Hans Schroeder."

He introduced Dr. Schroeder, who then asked all of us to introduce ourselves and share where we were from and what our primary study interests were. At the end of class, Dr. Keppler returned and asked me and Mizzi to stay longer after class and talk with him. I was a bit intimidated but also excited.

"You two are the youngest students in the university this year, and you both chose this advanced class. I am glad you did."

Mizzi and I both smiled.

"It was unusual for both of you to get into an advanced class in your first year, but after I saw your strong admissions test scores, I encouraged Dr. Schroeder to give his approval. I don't want either of you to feel intimidated because you are younger. Share your ideas. Be bold and don't be afraid."

We both floated out of the classroom on a cloud.

"Was that not everything?"

"It was, Mizzi. He's legendary."

I shared with Mizzi my dream to one day work in the lab at the Kavli Institute.

"That's totally rad, Johann. I hope it happens soon."

Although Dr. Keppler was not teaching our physics course, he contacted me and Mizzi later that week and invited us to visit the Astronomy and Astrophysics Lab at the institute. He also told us about the lab positions available for students. I was surprised that we could even apply as freshmen.

"Selection of lab assistants is not based on age," he assured us. "It's based on aptitude and passion for the work. Think about applying."

We were in the clouds again.

"Am I in a dream? Is this real?"

"I'm not sure I can apply, Johann." Mizzi had sadness in her voice.

"Why not? You are so good."

"My mom is going through breast cancer treatment, and she needs me. I've been commuting almost every weekend to Milwaukee."

"Oh man, I'm so sorry. You are doing the right thing though. Our parents are irreplaceable."

———————

Near the end of our third physics class, Dr. Schroeder shocked us with his next statements.

"This semester we are going to simulate a crisis. Earth is in a collision course with a comet and we have to determine what we need to do to survive."

During the next several weeks Dr. Schroeder laid out for our class the challenges with forecasting the trajectory of comets and their proximity to Earth. He was an electrifying speaker that would stop and call on any student at any time, sometimes using our first names and sometimes using our last names.

Our fourth class of the semester was engaging. "The comet that recently collided with the path of our sun provided new data," he bellowed. "What are we going to do, Oberhausen?"

"Pore over that data and analyze it."

"And what are we looking for?" he asked, looking squarely at Mizzi.

"Its size and trajectory."

"Excellent, Mizzi. And what else, Angela?"

"The sun's influence on the size and trajectory."

"Correct, Farrentino, you've been doing your homework. Now, there are some theories about comets colliding with Earth in the past, but the evidence of such events is still an open debate. Who knows about the mysterious blast in Siberia that leveled hundreds of square miles of forest?"

Several students raised their hands.

"Was it a comet, Susan?"

"It could have been caused by the fragment of a comet, but also might have been a meteor or asteroid."

"Good answer."

He walked toward the back of the room and then turned abruptly toward Kevin Smith, who was right beside him.

"How big was the explosion, Kevin?"

"A 100-megaton hydrogen bomb?" he guessed.

"Good guess, but bigger."

That was my opening.

"A 1000-megaton hydrogen bomb," I said.

"Correct, Johann, but fortunately it impacted a rural area where no people lived."

"What if it had hit St. Petersburg?"

Angela spoke up. "It would be catastrophic with mass casualties."

"Precisely! That's why our work here is important. And that's your task this semester. To determine where a comet might collide with us and determine how to stop it."

I loved the challenge of figuring out how to stop an impending disaster. Dr. Schroeder divided our class of eighteen students into three teams of six students. I was placed on Team Alpha and was happy to see that Angela was on my team. The other four members of our team were from Barcelona, Singapore, New Delhi, and Haifa. Angela was from Sorrento, Italy, and I was the only American.

This is going to be a great team, I thought to myself as I looked around to see the many different types of expressions on the faces of my classmates. I was intrigued by Angela and wanted to befriend her. I asked her out for a bite to eat after class and she obliged. She was graced with long, auburn silky hair, green eyes, and a beautiful olive skin complexion. She was sculpted somewhat like a beach volleyball player with her dark tan and muscular figure, and she carried a strong presence when she entered a room. She wore a minimum amount of make-up and a modest amount of jewelry, and sported two small tattoos visible in summer clothing, one on her lower back just above her waistline and one high on her right shoulder. The shoulder tattoo looked like a sort of medal and the tattoo on the small of her back was only visible when she leaned over and was wearing a short blouse. It appeared to be an airplane on the water. When I saw it, I had to find out more. I wanted to hear that story.

We found a cafe on campus to grab a bite to eat. After some ordinary chitchat about our families, about her life in Italy, and my life in a Chicago suburb, I asked, "Angela, did you win a medal for flying a plane?"

She just laughed. "Curious about my tattoos?"

"Yes. A medal and a plane?"

"The medal tattoo is the medal of honor that my father received for his courageous conduct as an advisor in the Vietnam War."

"That's so cool."

"The plane tattoo is U.S. Airways Flight 1549 sitting on the Hudson River with the passengers standing on both wings, just after Captain Chesley Sullenberger had set the plane down on the river in an emergency landing."

"You were there?"

"I was on a sightseeing trip, strolling along the Hudson River in the perfect position to take a magnificent photo that crossed the globe. After I won an award for it, I asked an artist to memorialize it on my back."

"What a great story Angela. I'd love to hear more. Are you free for dinner tomorrow?"

She paused for a few seconds. "I am."

"I know some great places within walking distance from here. Let's meet here at six tomorrow."

The serious demands of our advanced physics class filled most of our conversation. We talked a lot about our expectations of being new students and what we would be learning, and Angela shared one personal decision that gave me some insight into her character.

"I wouldn't have said yes for dinner, Johann, if I had thought you were not a serious student. I'm not interested in relationships right now. I've had more than my share and I want to focus now on my studies. How old are you by the way?" Angela asked.

"I'll be seventeen on my next birthday. And you?"

"I'm nineteen," she said with a smile on her face.

After four weeks of class, each team was given an envelope with the specifics of the problem they needed to solve. The path of the comet on an impending collision with Earth was provided, as well as the point where it was expected to survive the entry into Earth's atmosphere. The impact on Earth was estimated to be in the Middle East, somewhere between Cairo and Amman, with a high probability of impacting Egypt, Israel, Lebanon, Jordan, and the Mediterranean Sea. My teammate from Haifa, Moshi Cohen, was stirred up by the prospect of an eighty percent strike probability somewhere in Israel. Although he knew we were responding to a simulation, Israelis had lived for many years with the real fear of total destruction from an enemy with nuclear weapons. Moshi thus took the game seriously, since it was a real possibility that his country needed future scientists who understood how to protect their country against such threats.

In addition to Moshi, Mizzi was an Egyptian immigrant to Toronto who was born in Cairo. The simulation ignited her emotion. Like Moshi, it was intense considering the devastation that such a comet would inflict on the city of Cairo and its twenty-two million people. A direct hit would incinerate the city and its inhabitants, an unfathomable horror.

As strong as their dedication was to solve the crisis, neither our team nor Mizzi's team conceived of the intervention that would prevent the comet from impacting Earth. That honor would go to Melinda Parkinson from team Gamma. She discovered that the consistency of the meteor made it vulnerable to magnetic fluctuations. By creating a magnetic field during one of the episodic fluctuations, the trajectory of the meteor could be altered by nearly one degree, resulting in its slight resistance to the gravitational pull of the Earth.

Of course, Dr. Schroeder had provided enough information in the envelopes of each team to decipher the solution as Melinda had, but there also was a lot of distracting information that Dr. Schroeder provided that was not useful. Melinda worked her way through the distractions quickly, separating the relevant information from the irrelevant information. She was the first to find the nugget of information that pointed toward the solution, which then had to be enacted.

Once Melinda's proposed solution was verified by Dr. Schroeder, all three teams worked on ways to create the magnetic interference. This gave my team the chance to shine. We worked through many long nights in October and November. I spearheaded the development of a magnetic plate constructed from one hundred solar panels big enough to generate enough current to create the magnetic field but light enough to launch into space and be put onto the international space station.

Angela developed the manufacturing process to create the plate and Moshi created a plan to obtain all the materials for less than $10,000, meeting the budget criteria for the solution. Our team then determined how to attach the plate to the next commercial satellite that Russia was launching in sixty days.

Mizzi played a key role on team Beta, creating an effective strategy for negotiating with the Russians to carry their plate into space. Russia may have entertained some thoughts regarding their strategic advantage in protecting the Middle East from a catastrophe acting independently, but Mizzi's Russian contacts decided to play the game with Schroeder's university team. Mizzi's grandfather had been a diplomat in Egypt during Sadat's presidency and had direct interaction with Russian diplomats for two decades. She understood how the Russians thought and how they negotiated. Her strategy would ensure that the Russians would be given credit for rescuing the Middle East from cosmic catastrophe, gaining political capital to spend there in the future. Our class felt good about our chances of solving Schroeder's problem before the end of the semester.

In early October, just as I felt I was getting into my studies, I received an urgent call from Julianna.

"Hey, what's up?" I was happy and in the mood for a cheerful conversation.

"Susan has found more disturbing surveillance information. Can you come to Dursen Shoes at seven?'

"I'll be there," I said.

When I arrived, the store was closed and Christina let me in and led me down the stairs in the back of the store. Seated around a table drinking fresh cappuccinos were Susan, Julianna, and Alan. Christina and I joined them. Everyone had somber faces. Alan opened the meeting.

"Before we begin to discuss new information, we must understand that the information we have has put us all in danger, and it will put you in danger, Johann, since it is new to you."

I nodded.

"No one but us in this room can know, with the exception of Darrell."

"But shouldn't our government contacts in the surveillance know?"

"They know," Susan replied. "What we have is their surveillance information. But right now, we don't know who we can trust in the U.S. government, and we don't know who has this information and who doesn't."

"What about our regular trustworthy contacts?"

"One or more of them have been compromised," Alan replied.

Julianna explained further.

"Johann, if we let anyone in the U.S. government intelligence community know that we have this information, then we would be a threat to them. Even our own government might not protect us."

"So, think about this carefully, Johann." Christina looked directly into my eyes.

"Is knowing more worth risking your life and possibly the lives of your family?"

"My family? What does my family have to do with this?"

"There are ruthless people planning great harm. Whoever they are, they might not hesitate to target our family members and close friends. They might kill anyone they think could possibly know anything about their plot."

I sat there stunned for several minutes in silence, thinking to myself. *What right do have I to risk the lives of my parents, my relatives, and my close friends? How could I ethically do such a thing?* Even my close friends at the University of Chicago who know nothing could become targets by professional assassins.

"I can't risk the lives of others. It wouldn't be right."

"We completely understand," Alan said, "But what if you knew that the lives of your family, your relatives, and your close friends are already at risk?"

Again, I could not answer right away. Alan waited for my reply.

"If that was true, then I should find out what was going on, but only if I could help stop whatever plot was risking their lives."

I looked up at Alan. "If I can help stop whatever is planned and help protect my family and the innocent lives of others, then count me in."

Susan look relieved, and quickly introduced the surveillance she had received from Maryland with the help of Nicole Jacobson.

"As I shared before, Johann's friend, Nicole, provided information about their security cameras. But once we were into the system, I found out someone else was already tapping into their system. It was compromised. I notified Nicole, and they've just shut the system down. But here is what we have from a recent meeting."

As we looked at Susan's computer monitor, we could see Nicole, as she worked her way through two security doors and grumbled to herself, "I hate being late," loud enough to be picked up.

She sat down at a conference room table with several others, and two additional experts were videoed into the meeting with other researchers in Switzerland and Singapore. The first to speak was the director of national intelligence, Honorable Daniel Ties, who led the briefing.

"Thank you all for coming on such short notice. I want you to feel free to interrupt me at any time and ask questions. You remember four weeks ago we asked you all to accelerate your production of HBAT? At that time our intelligence agents in the field had picked up chatter about plans for a biological attack against the United States. It took us some time, but we have now confirmed that the threat of a biological attack is credible."

One of the senior scientists asked, "What kind of attack?"

"We believe the threat is for a national attack in multiple cities in multiple regions of the country. We are not sure about the agent—our best guess is Botulinum toxin, which is why the president directed us to increase HBAT production."

"What terrorist group could execute such an attack?" asked another scientist.

"Not a terrorist group," responded the director. "We are talking a nation-state attack."

"A major war?"

"I'm afraid so," Director Ties confirmed. "A war that we have to win!"

"Oh no," Nicole blurted out loud enough for everyone to hear clearly. "No one wins a war like that."

Awkward silence followed.

"You all remember the Botulinum attacks in Chicago that we thwarted in 2005?" the director continued. "The one at the Sears building?"

Several nodded.

"That would've been a great disaster had not some very brave people fought against the terrorists. At that time, we did not have enough HBAT to treat all those affected by a major attack in a city like Chicago. Today, we do have enough. In addition to our own production capacity in North America under the CDC, Emergent BioSolutions in Canada has a large production capability to produce the antitoxin. The greatest challenge is timely distribution.

"If the agent Botulinum is confirmed, we must acquire and distribute 330 million doses of heptavalent Botulinum antitoxin, one for every man, woman, and child in the nation, to prepare for an imminent Botulinum attack. Such a task normally takes six to eight months to accomplish, but we may not have six to eight months once the agent is confirmed. We might not even have six to eight weeks," the director concluded.

"How is it possible for us to produce that much antitoxin in such a short period?" Nicole asked.

"The production is possible with an international effort but the distribution is a logistical nightmare," the director replied. "A total of 465 U.S. government distribution centers has been established to date that could disseminate HBAT, corresponding to the number of congressional representatives in each state. Alabama has seven locations, for example, while Alaska and American Samoa have one location each. California and Texas, in contrast, have fifty-three and thirty-six distributions sites respectively. Senator Rand Paul's national plan for building the distribution centers based on the population distribution laid out in the congressional map has helped us to be much better prepared, but the challenge is 427 distribution centers must receive shipments of HBAT from five HBAT manufacturing labs in Silver Springs, Atlanta, Winnipeg, Lausanne, and Singapore."

One of Nicole's team members then asked the director, "Where do people go to get their antitoxin?"

"Residents would need to go to their voting locations where they cast their election ballots to pick up their HBAT supplied for all the family members in their household. And that is the great challenge at hand—motivating complete compliance to the government's antitoxin distribution plan. Nationwide voter turnout to voting locations during presidential elections has consistently been less than sixty percent since the 1970s. If compliance mirrored voting behavior, the potential loss of forty percent of the population in certain cities and regions of the country to a biological attack would be staggering. Hopefully people will come to protect themselves."

We watched the facial expressions of those in the conference, and Nicole and her colleagues looked stunned. Not a word was uttered in response to what the director had just shared. He continued.

"Despite twenty-five years of get out the vote campaigns, the highest voting participation in recent history was only about forty-one percent of the total population. It would be nearly impossible to reach every American with antitoxin doses through voting location distribution centers, but this was still the best possibility for widespread distribution. Compliance is not going to be very high."

"Why not?" Nicole asked. "Won't the media promote compliance?"

"People just don't trust the government," Director Ties said. "The Pew Research Center cites that only one in five adults trust the federal government, so how then could all of the adult population be convinced that they must immediately go to the place where they vote and pick up antitoxin for themselves and for their family members? That is virtually an impossible task for emergency planners to solve."

The Swiss team then chimed in, stating, "We can reach the entire cell phone population with an emergency text message from our Federal Council, which reaches more than ninety percent of all teenagers and adults and more than seventy percent of the entire population. Could the U.S. government use mobile phone networks to drive people to voting centers?"

"Yes," answered the director, "the president of the United States can issue a warning through the Wireless Emergency Alert System, but the system is voluntary and some consumers can block the messages."

"So, some people will not get the message?" someone asked.

"Yes," replied Nicole, "probably about ten to fifteen percent who will either ignore the alert, block it, or receive it but not pass it on to their children. But I have an idea for reaching them. My IT team is working on a powerful mobile phone gaming app. We are not ready to roll it out yet, but we will be prepared to do so in about one hundred and twenty days."

"One hundred and twenty days is not fast enough," Director Ties said. He then turned to face Nicole. "Organize your IT team and coordinate with the other overseas labs to meet a sixty-day goal on both the botulinum antidotes we need and the phone app."

I saw weight of these words come upon Nicole as she struggled to maintain her composure.

She then sat up, leaned forward, and said, "We will get it done!"

"I have one more question, Director," asked Lin from Singapore. "Do you suspect any other bioagents and any other countries that may be attacked? I am especially concerned about Asia."

"Understandably so, Ms. Lin. The other agent we are concerned about right now is Saxitoxin, and we have not picked up any actionable intelligence about any other target with the exception of chatter of a possible threat to China."

"For now, we need all labs to focus on producing as much product as possible and getting it distributed in the U.S. as fast as possible. We will contact Emergent BioSolutions and see how much antitoxin they can ship to us immediately and how much they can produce in the coming weeks. Let's get to work."

"And if it is Saxitoxin instead of Botulinum?" Nicole asked Director Ties.

"If it's another agent like Saxitoxin, for which there is no antidote, then we're in trouble; but no one believes Saxitoxin can be effectively weaponized at this time."

Susan turned off the video feed to the conference meeting as soon as they all left the room. I looked around at Susan, Julianna, Alan, and Christina. There was a depressed look on everyone's faces. Finally, Alan spoke.

"What else have you got, Susan?"

"I've intercepted online contact between Churgrill and two aerospace engineers, but I cannot access their actual dialogue. He would need them for only one thing—executing an attack from space."

CHAPTER 7

"WELCOME TO OUR LAB." DR. Keppler said with a warm smile as he extended his hand toward me. "I am so happy that you accepted our invitation to work as a lab assistant."

"This is a great honor for me. From a young age I dreamed about working at a lab like this where I can explore the universe."

"Then we already share much in common, Johann. For many years I dreamed of building a lab like this for the very purpose of space exploration and discovery. In this lab we are exploring galaxies and black holes and the remotest regions of the universe."

I could not withhold the joy I felt at that moment and Dr. Keppler, I surmised, could probably see that joy on my face.

"During the next several weeks, I want you to work with Tim McClellan. Tim is a Ph.D. student and lab technician who will show you how to work several important pieces of equipment. Learning is doing, so I will put you on a project as soon as you can master the essentials of calibration, measurement, and recording data. This Fall you will mainly be learning how to track and document the movement of space objects that we are already following."

"That sounds exciting."

"Once you learn how to do your job well, then we will proceed to another phase of work, probably in December, in which we will begin to teach you how to analyze data and make projections about future movements within prescribed statistical probabilities. We would like to see you put a minimum of fifteen hours per week, but you can work a maximum of twenty-five hours per week if your schedule allows you to do so. You also must maintain a minimum 3.0 GPA or higher to continue working here, so your coursework must be your first priority."

"I want to keep my GPA above 3.5, Dr. Keppler; I know the coursework is challenging but I love being here."

"That is one reason I hired you; I see in you great potential. I think you'll like Tim—he likes baseball, too. And I like the Cubs, although I'm a rather uneducated baseball fan."

"How did you know I like baseball?"

"How could I not know? Our university doesn't offer many athletic scholarships. Also, Coach Kevin Knightley is a personal friend. I commend you, Johann, on making such a tough decision. That is another reason I wanted you here. Coach and I talked about your great love for astronomy even though you are a naturally gifted athlete. We both knew you belonged here in the lab."

I sat there in Dr. Keppler's office and looked at the floor as a wave of emotion welled up.

"I knew I couldn't pursue two dreams with abandonment, so I had to let one go. Astronomy is my first dream; baseball is my first love."

I saw a slight smile come upon Dr. Keppler.

"If it is any consolation, my first love was hockey, believe it or not. I was born in Manitoba. My parents both worked at Lethridge University. I played hockey from age six through age eighteen. I even played in college at Boston College for a year until I had my second concussion. That's when I hung up the hockey skates and transferred to MIT."

"Serious?"

"Serious. Not that I was a pro prospect. But I was a pretty good college hockey player and we had a very good team when I played at BC. A couple of my close friends did make it to the NHL, but they're now retired."

"Did you ever second guess hanging up your skates?"

"Never. My second concussion was one of the best things that ever happened to me. It was like God himself smacking me in the head and saying, 'not hockey, I've got something much better.' Now I have this great lab and I love teaching. I wouldn't trade it for anything and I thank God every day."

"May I ask you something rather personal?"

"Yes, of course."

"Do you believe in a personal Creator?"

"It's hard to be an astronomer, Johann, and not believe, at least for me. There is simply too much design out there to deny a master designer. The more we explore, the more evidence we gain of extraordinary intricate design that simply could not be random. All serious astronomers now know there was a big bang—the instantaneous creation of the universe. And who orchestrated the big bang? Scientists don't know through science. You can know through faith, faith in randomness and meaninglessness or faith in design and purpose. I choose the latter."

A knock on the office door brought a conclusion to our serious conversation. It was Tim.

"Oh, excuse me, Dr. Keppler, I didn't mean to interrupt you."

"No, come in Tim. I want you to meet Johann, the new lab assistant I told you about. We are just getting acquainted."

"I am looking forward to working with you, Johann. Are you free tomorrow afternoon?"

"We are starting on Sunday?"

"Yes, if you are free. A friend is out of town this week and gave me his two tickets to the Cubs game. What better way to get oriented to Chicago? And we will have plenty of time to talk about the lab and the project I am working on."

I was delighted. Dr. Keppler smiled.

"I told you that you would like Tim. Have fun. I'll be boating and fishing on Lake Michigan with my two grandsons."

The next day, I thoroughly enjoyed the game with Tim. He had an app on his phone that measured the distance of every home run, and we had a contest guessing how far each home run went based on the trajectory of the ball. There were five home runs, and Tim won our contest, three to two.

I learned that the lab was doing much more than I had anticipated. Tim and his colleagues were conducting research on how lasers emitted from satellites orbiting the Earth could be potentially used to pulverize asteroids that might come too close to the Earth's gravitational pull. They were also experimenting with the use of various kinds of high energy beams that could be used to shield the United States from various types of calamities, including attacks from foreign governments such as electromagnetic pulse bombs, nuclear bombs, and chemical and biological warfare. Some of the projects that Tim alluded to were obviously military in nature and required special security clearance.

My first project was going to be basic research on how electromagnetic pulses could be used to alter the flight paths of any remotely controlled flying devices, whether airplanes or drones or satellites. I found out that the research would provide Tim's doctoral dissertation data, and that although I did need to be screened for this assignment with some type of security clearance, it would be basic academic research, not applied research for the U.S. government or private corporations.

I was aware of some of this ongoing research when I learned a few months ago that researchers were exploring how the International Space Station could one day be armed with a laser that could shoot down orbiting debris, or space junk. NASA researchers estimated that up to 3,000 tons of space debris reside in low-Earth orbit. This debris included old decommissioned satellites, bodies and parts from rockets, and pieces of wreckage produced by collisions involving larger objects. The potential harmful impacts from pieces of space junk that are the size of a dime on orbiting satellites was great, because these projectiles could travel at speeds on the order of 22,370 mph.

The research sounded very exciting to me so I could not wait to begin, but one of Tim's statements indicated that the value of such research in wrong hands was a great threat.

"Although we are doing academic research, we have to be very discreet about it. It must be carefully presented to the public and not everything we discover will be for public consumption."

———————————

My phone dinged at about 2:30 a.m. early Monday morning, loud enough to wake me. I had forgotten to silence it before falling asleep.

I instinctively picked it up off my dresser to see that Julianna had sent me a text and a web link. She had been up much of the night researching a story she had read on several news sites. I clicked on the link to a story titled, "China Builds Rocket-Launchers on Disputed Islands in South China Sea."

I had already read about China's rapid military buildup on the Diaoyu Islands in the People's Republic of China, also called the Senkaku Islands in Japan and the Tiaoyutai Islands in Taiwan. I recalled that all three countries claimed the islands but China began a rapid military deployment on the uninhabited islands in 2015 and 2016. One paragraph especially caught my attention:

> China continues to invest in military programs and weapons designed to improve power projection, anti-access area denial and operations in emerging domains such as cyberspace, space and the electromagnetic spectrum," said Abraham Denmark, deputy assistant secretary of defense for East Asia. The report to Congress reveals that China has added over 3,200 acres to the seven sites it occupies in the South China Sea during the last two years.

I knew that in these islands, China had excavated deep channels to improve access to its artificial and natural harbors. They also had constructed new berthing areas to allow access for larger ships and had built 9,800 feet runways. The Pentagon's annual China Military Power report documented all kinds of military building projects in these islands, including the construction of missile launch sites.

After reading the article, I sent a text to Julianna.

"Read article—very alarming."

She immediately sent an abbreviated reply.

"China denies hostile intentions. Claims all projects advance energy production and space research. Don't believe them. When U.S. Navy sent guided missile destroyer within twelve miles to investigate, China objected vehemently."

I then responded with a question.

"Can China reach Guam with missiles from these islands?"

"Yes," she texted.

She ended our conversation with, "Let's meet for soul searching on Mars @20:00. Christina has new info. Going back to bed."

———————————

I picked up a large pizza and made my way to Dursen Shoes. Julianna was waiting for me with Alan and Christina. Susan was invited, too, but was out of the country on an assignment for her employer. When I entered the *Eleutheria Club* lounge, I was greeted with measured smiles on solemn faces.

"Thanks so much for bringing pizza," Alan said as I plopped the pizza box on the table. "Julianna brought some beer for us, and soda for you."

She also flashed me a warm but reserved smile.

"More troubling news?" I asked.

"Let's eat first," Alan said.

"Can we eat and discuss? I have a tight window of time."

"We can as soon as Darrell arrives. He's on the way."

As we all grabbed some pizza and drinks, Darrell walked in.

Then Julianna and Christina began to describe what they had just learned about the situation on the disputed islands in the South China Sea.

"Our Taiwanese friends have picked up chatter online that China has built launch sites for satellites that can be armed with multiple types of weapons capable of carrying out chemical and biological attacks from space," Julianna said.

Christina explained more details.

"We also found out that they plan on informing the world that their new satellites are designed to gather data about space junk and to eliminate dangerous junk through lasers," Christina said. "But the primary purpose is to gain military superiority over the U.S., Russia, and European nations."

"This is an obvious national security threat," Alan said, a slice of pizza in hand. "If China secures weapons in space, it can use its lasers to immobilize our reconnaissance satellites and then launch attacks against the U.S. after we are blinded from monitoring their activities."

"What's worse," Julianna said, "is that if we are attacked chemically or biologically without warning, it would be nearly impossible to protect our citizens. We would not have enough time to move agents into the attack areas to treat people."

"That would be catastrophic," I said.

"I hope to learn more tomorrow," Christina said, "When I talk directly with friends from the *Jùlèbù Fāxiàn*."

"Who?"

"The *Jùlèbù Fāxiàn*."

"Is that our sister club that you and Darrell have mentioned?"

"Yes, they are another network like ours that operate in Taiwan. *Jùlèbù Fāxiàn* (我要走了)is roughly translated as *Discovery Club*. They have been closely monitoring the military development in the South China Sea in the Diaoyu Islands."

"You should come with me, Johann, I want you to meet them," Christina said.

"Did you all see the recent news conference by the vice president about the U.S. Space Force?" Alan asked. "The president has been talking about it in his public rallies."

"No, but I read the news. The U.S. will be investing billions of dollars to assure our military supremacy in space. It's looking good for my future employment."

"What great sage said, 'be careful what you wish for?'"

"John Cliché," I said.

"W.W. Jacobs," Christina argued, "from a horror story he published in 1902, and it's 'be careful what you wish for, you may receive it.'"

"I'm impressed." Darrell smiled. "I thought it was a Chinese proverb."

"My B.A. is in American literature."

"It's getting late friends, and many of us have work to do. Let's meet again Friday night at eight and see if we can figure out how to fulfill a genuine Chinese proverb."

"What's that?" Susan asked.

"The supreme art of war is to subdue the enemy without fighting," Alan said.

On the following day, Wang Shu Liang sent a coded text to Christina naming a time and place to receive a secure phone call. Christina contacted me and I met her at a table at an Italian restaurant on La Salle Street. She and I were just finishing our Lavazza coffee while looking through the plate glass window at the late morning shoppers strolling by when one of the servers discreetly informed Christina that she had a phone call.

"Thanks, Lizzy," she said.

Before rising, she enjoyed one last sip of the delicious drink. It was early afternoon in Chicago and just past midnight in Taipei. Christina and I made our way inconspicuously to a door around the corner from the seating area that led to a small back room office behind the kitchen to take the call.

"Are you alone?" Wang Shu asked.

"No, I have my friend, Johann, with me. He is a space junkie and member of the *Eleutheria Club*. He knows everything I know."

"We can't be too careful. And how was your cup of Lavazza coffee?"

"You know me too well, Wang Shu. I keep telling you we could make a lot of money in Taipei if we opened our own café."

Wang Shu laughed. "Let's table that idea for now. We need to get down to business," she said, her tone transitioning.

"Are you on a disposable phone?" Christina asked.

"Yes, but there are ways to trace these calls, too, if enough time is available and if you know what you are looking for. I don't want to put you or your friends at risk. I have a lot to tell you in a short amount of time. No more than ten minutes."

"Are our friends in *Jùlèbù Fāxiàn* all okay?" Christina asked.

"Yes, we are all fine but very concerned. We confirmed last night that a satellite launch is imminent in the disputed Tiaoyutai Islands."

"Why is the concern so high now? They have launched rockets from there before, haven't they?"

"Yes, but never with a deadly payload," Wang Shu said. "We suspect the next satellite they launch will carry a WMD."

"Why would the government be so reckless?" Christina asked.

"It's not officially sanctioned by CCP."

"What do you mean? It's a private satellite? I thought the whole complex was military?"

"It is. But a private entity is launching this satellite and the government does not know the entire payload; or if they do know, they are denying that they know," Wang Shu said.

"How can that be?"

"A big payoff. Money talks in China, too."

I wanted to ask questions but just listened as carefully as I could.

"Who is getting rich?" Christina asked.

"General Bingwen Tso and his close associates."

"General Tso as in General Tso's chicken? Is that some kind of code name?"

"That's his name—it has an important history," Wang Shu said.

"Please explain," Christina said.

"Long before the popular General Tso's chicken, there was the real person, Tso Tsungtang. He was a war hero who distinguished himself as a brilliant strategist during the Taiping Rebellion from 1850 to 1864, China's greatest civil war. Tso was both ruthless and legendary, pushing many of the rebels out of China to the U.S. Without General Tso, your Transcontinental Railroad would not have been completed until the mid to late 1870s. It was the emigrants from China that carried the heavy load of construction resulting in a completion in 1869, a pivotal point in American history. The hard toil of working on that railroad was far better than facing General Tso's troops in battle."

"And the chicken?" Christina asked.

"Ironically, the famous Hunanese battered and sauced chicken dish that bears his name was created by Peng Chang-kuei, one of the classically trained chefs of the Hunan Court that Mao Zedong caused to flee to Taiwan when the communists took over China. Peng created the dish to honor General Tso and its characteristics matched the physical and personality characteristics of the famous general—heavy, sour, hot, and salty. You do not want to get on the wrong side of General Tso."

"He sounds like the Chinese version of General Patton," I said.

"Good comparison Johann. He was revered in China as a patriot like Patton, and like Patton, General Bingwen Tso wants to see his own beloved country rule the world."

"Not uncommon," Christina said.

"There's more. Bingwen means master of arts."

"So that's important?" Christina asked.

"Yes. General Bingwen Tso is not only like his distant relative more than 160 years ago, but he is intelligent and cunning. He graduated at the top of his class at the Air Force Command College in Beijing, China's elite academy established in 1958 to train and educate air force officers, receiving his master of arts degree in 2012 with students from sixteen different countries."

"He must be young," Christina said. "How did he become so powerful?"

"The right heritage, the right connections, and the disciplined use of his considerable skills and knowledge," replied Wang Shu. "General Tso is a gifted leader who is in great favor with a lot of powerful Communist leaders, which is ironic since he is not known as a strong supporter of the communist party nor a fan of past Chinese leaders who forced China to implement Marxist ideas. He is much more of a nationalist leader who strongly advocates for reunification with Taiwan and rejects globalism and any cooperation with foreign entities that do not favor China."

"But listen, my time is up. I just wanted to alert you about General Tso. It was good to meet you over the phone, Johann. Give Darrell my special greetings and let your other friends in the *Eleutheria Club* know what is going on."

On Friday night Christina and I shared with the others at the *Eleutheria Club* our conversation with Wang Shu. After we finished, silence hung in the air like a paralyzing fog. Darrell waited a few moments and then cautiously interjected some levity, noting that he was hungry and he knew a place close by that made awesome General Tso's chicken.

Julianna was first to begin laughing and then we all chimed in. Chinese food sounded good tonight. We decided to follow Darrell's suggestion and eat out, think about things over the weekend, and then meet again during the week. Besides, we all had either work, school, or family responsibilities over the weekend and had taken a lot of time out of our schedules this week to meet. I had a long weekend of twelve hours of lab work to complete by Sunday night.

CHAPTER 8

JUST BEFORE LEAVING THE LAB on Sunday evening, after working long hours on tracking trajectories of various lasers from moving satellites, I discovered in my mailbox a sealed envelope from Tim. I was surprised to read that both Dr. Keppler and Tim thought it would be good if I attended the twentieth Annual Space and Missile Defense Symposium in Huntsville, Alabama, next year. Both of them had other travel commitments and could not attend, so they decided that I should go since some of the presentations would deal with satellite-based laser technology. The note gave me a link to an online forum where I could meet and chat with others who were planning to attend the symposium.

The following week out of pure curiosity, I decided to peruse the forum to learn a little bit about the attendees and their areas of research. While browsing, I saw a post from Nicole Jacobson. She shared that her research lab director had asked her to attend the conference and attend the sessions on biological space warfare threats. She couldn't know I was posting in the forum because I was not using my first name, but when I revealed my identity, she was delighted. She sent me a text.

"I didn't know it was you—sneaking around as Smedley."

"It's my middle name. Trying to keep a low profile," I said.

When I had first met Nicole that one night for dinner, after I found her personal journal, I had felt a bit awkward. I was intimidated as a sixteen-year old new undergraduate student talking to a Ph.D. graduate. I was pleasantly surprised when I learned that Nicole was nineteen, the same age as Angela. As we continued to communicate online and occasionally by phone, my infatuation for her dissipated. I had no idea if she had any interest in me beyond a professional relationship and felt stupid thinking about her. I hoped we could meet face-to-face again at the upcoming conference.

Then one evening Nicole sent me a text, "We need to talk ASAP. Confidential."

I set up a call for the following morning.

Lizzy came to my table at the cafe to inform me discreetly that I had a call from a Miss Nicole Jacobson. My first question to Nicole was if she was using a disposable phone.

"Not yet," she said, "but I need to bounce something off you." There was a noticeable change in her voice.

"You know that my team has been working feverishly with a network of other labs internationally to produce a certain antitoxin to prepare for a potential terrorist attack that our government is seriously worried about?"

"Yes."

"Yesterday, we had an emergency meeting with defense officials who told us to stop working on that antitoxin, but instead, switch gears and begin working on developing another antitoxin that does not yet exist."

"Was it recorded?"

"No, the cameras have been removed."

"What's going on?"

"We don't know yet, but I don't buy it. It just does not add up."

"You need to tell me more."

"For two months we have been producing Botulinum antitoxin. Now, we are told that the threat is Saxitoxin. There is no known antidote or vaccine for Saxitoxin."

"What is Saxitoxin?"

"Saxitoxins are commonly referred to as Paralytic Shellfish Poisons (PSPs) that are found in marine and freshwater microalga. When ingested by human beings, they function as neurotoxic alkaloids that block the entrance of sodium ions into nerve cells, which causes paralysis. Saxitoxins are studied in labs as treatments for nerve disorders, so they are potentially beneficial. However, they also can be used as biological weapons to kill people. Saxitoxins are the most lethal non-protein toxin. You need 0.2 milligrams of a Saxitoxin to kill a human of average bodyweight. It is 1,000 times more toxic than sarin gas. During the 1950s, the CIA used Saxitoxins for suicide capsules. Apparently, Francis Gary Powers carried a Saxitoxin pill on the tip of a hidden drill bit inside a silver dollar.

"It's a horrific way to die, and it is difficult to weaponize, which is why the experiments with it seemed to have tapered off in the 1960s. That is why I don't understand why now it is such a threat and why we are changing course so abruptly. In my opinion, the toxin we were initially concerned about is a far more likely biological threat."

"Do you think it's a diversion?"

"Do you mean is someone misleading us?"

"Yes. It could be a purposeful misdirection from a source that wants you to stop making the antitoxin you are now producing. How do you know that the new threat is more credible than the existing threat?"

"I don't. That's what I meant when I said I don't buy it. I am not convinced that the new threat is more credible, but I have no way to know. I am trusting my superiors and they are getting their orders from U.S. intelligence services."

"Maybe I can help you find out."

"You work at an astrophysics lab, Johann, not at the CIA."

"I know, but I have some good connections."

"A teenager with connections to intelligence agencies?"

Ouch, that hurt, I thought to myself, but I held my tongue.

I ended the conversation by telling Nicole I would see what I could find about recent terror threats and that she should do the same through her networks. I also reminded her that we both needed to be careful as to not draw attention to ourselves by directly asking too many sensitive questions.

I told Nicole, "You need to play dumb and ask indirectly and you should also get a disposal SIM card."

We decided that we should talk again as soon as we had new information to share.

———————

Two days after talking with Nicole, we had another meeting at the *Eleutheria Club* lounge in the basement of Dursen Shoes. This time Alan was out of town on a scouting trip to Canada, but Christina, Susan, Julianna, and Darrell all came. Before he left, Alan had asked Christina to lead the meeting in his absence.

"I have some critical new information," Christina said as we all took a bite of our calzones from Dominic's a few blocks away.

"I also have some new information," Darrell said.

"That makes three of us," I said with a mouthful of food.

"We do, too," said Julianna and Susan. "We intercepted some important conversations just last night."

Christina looked around. "I would first like to hear about the chatter you intercepted, Julianna," she said.

"As you all recall," Julianna began, "one of the networks we have been listening to has been following the activities of General Nicoli Sarkovsky, the high-ranking retired general and associate of the president of Russia. Susan was able to access a conversation in which Sarkovsky reported back to another close associate of the Russian president that biological agents produced in Russia had been secured from Iran and were being transported by a fishing vessel to Zamboanga City Harbor in Mindanao, the largest southern island of the Philippines archipelago. Zamboanga City is a Muslim stronghold in the Philippines and has secured arms shipments from Iran over the past ten years for the Abu Sayyaf, a Muslim terrorist group."

"Great work," Christina said.

"Well, I have to thank my old mentor, Kevin Mitnick, who helped us on this one," Susan said.

"Isn't the Abu Sayyaf the same group that was involved in the attack on a U.S. weapons lab in the Mariana Islands a number of years ago that then launched a biological attack on an airplane?" Christina asked.

"Yes," Julianna said. "It's the same group. They went underground after that attack as the Philippines' military launched a major campaign to wipe them out. Although several leaders were captured and hundreds were killed, they have re-emerged and are now in the kidnapping business. In July of 2016, three members of the Abu Sayyaf were arrested for kidnapping and extortion of ten Malaysians, nine

Europeans, and two Filipinos on Sipadan Island and six members of the religious group, Jehovah's Witnesses, in Sulu."

"Are they preparing to launch another attack?" I asked.

"No. It doesn't seem so. They have been hired to transport the biological weapons coming from Iran into the South China Sea in a fishing boat. No one will suspect a Filipino fishing boat operated by Filipino fishermen to be smuggling biological weapons. They will be able to evade military patrols in the South China Sea and will have an official fishing charter granted by the Beijing government to fish in the Scarborough Shoal, a small but strategic reef and fertile fishing ground 130 miles west from the Philippine island of Luzon."

Julianna pointed to an electronic map of these islands on her laptop, explaining, "If I enlarge this map you can see these islands."

"CNN news reported in September of 2016 that Beijing was reclaiming land on the Scarborough Shoal, which China calls Huangyan Dao. The Philippines' military then released images of Chinese ships it said were capable of dredging sand around the shoal. Of course, China denied that it was reclaiming land and said they were merely conducting law enforcement.

"Analysts have confirmed that the Scarborough Shoal is a strategic military foothold for China with its short distance to Subic Bay, the former American military base that U.S. Marines, ships, and planes have resumed using again under a new deal with the Philippines. China has blockaded the shoal since 2012 as part of its claims to almost all of the South China Sea, including islands more than 800 miles from the Chinese mainland, despite objections from the Philippines, Malaysia, Brunei, and Vietnam. Tensions have escalated during the past few years as China has reclaimed land in massive dredging operations in the Spratly Islands, turning sandbars into islands equipped with airfields, ports, and lighthouses."

"It would be a brilliant strategy to transport biological weapons onto the islands on a fishing vessel," Julianna said.

"Did they disclose in the conversation what kind of biological weapons?" Christina asked.

"No. They never stated the weapons. But they alluded to the fact that the Abu Sayyaf already had experience handling the agent, which can only mean it is Botulinum toxin. That is the agent they stole from the U.S. weapons lab in the Mariana Islands and that they used in the airline attack several years ago."

"Is Iran capable of producing the Botulinum toxin?" Darrell asked.

Susan answered, "In researching this weapon, I found out that there is some speculation that when the Abu Sayyaf stole Botulinum from the U.S., they sold some of these weapons to the Iranians for cash. Iranian scientists have been using the samples they purchased to learn how to produce them. U.S. intelligence affirms the Iranians are capable of producing their own Botulinum toxin, but it would be easier for them to purchase the toxin from Russia than make their own."

"I'm not sure I completely understand it," Julianna said. "The Chinese are quite capable of producing their own Botulinum toxin. I am not sure why General Tso would need weaponized Botulinum from Iran or Russia."

"Two reasons," Darrell said. "Plausible deniability and flexibility. My contacts in China have confirmed that General Tso is regarded by some political leaders as a loose cannon capable of pushing his own agenda without official approval from leaders in Beijing. He knows he could not access China's biological agents without great risk, as it would become known to many in the military. By secretly using biological agents produced in Iran or Russia, General Tso would have the option of launching either a preemptive strike or a retaliatory strike on the States. A retaliatory strike would of course be seen as justified by his leaders; but in the case of a preemptive strike, he would make sure that the Iranians had their fingerprints all over the attack and could then blame Iran. In either case, General Tso could prove to his leaders the weapon was Iranian, and Chinese diplomats could then state truthfully to the United Nations if an attack occurred that evidence would show no biological agents were used from China."

"Thanks Darrell," Christina said. "Johann, why don't you share next—what have you got?"

"I had a discussion with my lab director this week about China's recent activities in space. You all may recall Tim McClelland is my supervisor, a Ph.D. student who is writing his dissertation on shooting down space debris with satellite-based laser technology. Tim told me of a recent conversation he had with Dr. Keppler. Dr. Keppler was concerned that China's recent placement of more military satellites in space is causing the U.S. to shift its focus to military applications of satellite-based lasers and that Tim's doctoral dissertation research, including the research I do, could be co-opted for military purposes."

"Everything seems to be pointing toward China," Darrell said.

"But we have to be careful," Christina cautioned. "Remember from Sun Tzu's *The Art of War,* 'all warfare is based on deception.' We are being led to believe that China is gearing up for a biological attack on the U.S. from space. But this, too, could be a deception. And I have reason to believe it is."

"Why?" I asked.

"I've got some information on Atlas Churgrill," Christina said. "Remember that Churgrill was a former South African ambassador to the United Nations and he wanted to be president of South Africa. When he lost that bid, partly due to his father's refusal to support him, he turned bitter and began working with unscrupulous people to build a vast economic empire."

"How did you find out?" I asked.

"Friends in the State Security Agency in South Africa," Christina said. "Remember when I did my four-month Fulbright Fellowship there?"

We all nodded.

"Two of the professors I worked with had children working with the National Intelligence Coordinating Committee (NICOC). The director of the State Security Agency is a member of the NICOC and was familiar with Churgrill because of his past dealings with corrupt leaders in Mozambique, Qatar, Libya, and the United States. Churgrill is a billionaire who had become rich through his knowledge of and dealings with precious gems, energy resources, and rare earths, both legal and illegal. He has more recently been involved in acquiring pharmaceutical companies."

"So Churgrill's plot involving satellites and biological warfare is confirmed," I said.

"The NICOC doesn't know yet for sure," Christina said. "But I could discern that they are getting nervous. I did find out Churgrill has taken several recent trips to Winnipeg, Canada. That is one of the places Alan was planning to visit on his Canada trip right now. I don't fully understand his motives yet. We might know more next week when Alan returns."

I left our meeting with more questions than I had come with. What was Churgrill doing in Canada? What was he paying General Nicoli Sarkovsky to do? Was General Sarkovsky working with General Tso? The ride back to the Alper House on the L had my head spinning with so many possibilities. I could not take my mind off the many unanswered questions raised.

CHAPTER 9

MY CELL PHONE RATTLED ME awake at 1:30 a.m. I scolded myself for not having put it on silent. I looked at the number through my slightly blurred vision and recognized it—Alan was calling. I knew he was in Manitoba. Surely, he had forgotten he was in another time zone. But I wasn't thinking clearly. Winnipeg time was the same as Chicago time.

I answered with feigned enthusiasm. "Alan, you must have very important earth-shattering news since it's 1:30 a.m."

"Sorry, Johann, I couldn't get through to Christina or Julianna. I have important information to give you, and I might be in danger." Alan was practically speaking in a whisper.

I instantly sat up in bed and turned on my lamp stand light. "Where are you?"

"I am in the closet of my hotel room. I think it could be monitored with surveillance equipment. Even this cell phone conversation may not be private. I'm going to leave my hotel room and find a safe phone. But just in case you don't hear from me within the next hour, check your mail tomorrow. I sent you a letter by FedEx with next day delivery. It's coming to your lab."

The next hour seemed like ten. I waited patiently but had such intense anxiety I began to perspire profusely. As 2:30 a.m. approached

I felt mounting concern for Alan. But the phone call never came and I finally fell asleep, exhausted, just before 4:00 a.m.

Alan's letter came to the lab just before noon and I made sure I was there to pick it up. I knew he feared using my home address because of security reasons. Something must have frightened him greatly. I immediately contacted Julianna, Christina, and Darrell, and we arranged to meet to read the letter together.

I entered Dursen Shoes with trepidation. It had already been eighteen hours since we had heard from Alan. We all knew the day was coming when our lives could be at risk, but none of us were prepared for that day.

I opened the FedEx to reveal a three-page handwritten letter from Alan:

Dear Friends,

If you are reading this letter, I may be in captivity or injured. If I'm fortunate, I may simply be in hiding and unable to communicate. I don't mean to be melodramatic, but I had intended to talk with you by phone and have not been able to do so. This letter is my backup plan in case I could not contact you by phone.

As soon as I arrived in Winnipeg, I felt like I was being watched. It's like someone knew I was coming. I have tried to act like a complete tourist: I went to the Assiniboine Park Zoo, which was amazing, and to the Canadian Museum for Human Rights, to the Manitoba Museum and to the Winnipeg Art Gallery. I also visited the Forks National Historic Site. This is a wonderful town. But what I have learned is much too serious and consequential.

I was able to observe Churgrill's movements. He stayed at the Fort Garry Hotel on Broadway for three days and visited

Emergent BioSolutions Corporation twice. I was able to get close enough both times to listen to his conversation with several executives. He posed as a potential client interested in Emergent BioSolutions' manufacturing capabilities and said he represented a group of investors in southern Africa that had developed a product to treat side effects of chemotherapy, similar to episil, a product already produced by Emergent BioSolutions.

He asked many questions about their manufacturing capabilities with their existing products, including heptavalent botulism antitoxin, vaccinia immune globulin, and anthrax immune globulin, in addition to episil. What struck me was that he needed to know the production levels of the biodefense products. Why would this be so if he was interested in the manufacturing of a product like episil? Churgrill was very smooth, very sharp, and congenial. I could tell by the responses of Emergent BioSolutions executives that they were favorably impressed with Churgrill. He knows how to turn on the charm. Julianna, please research the company, which goes by EBS on the New York Stock Exchange. See if it is vulnerable to a hostile takeover.

After the meetings, I began to drive my rental car back to my hotel when I noticed a car that seemed to be following me. I was staying at the Four Points by Sheraton and was following a GPS I had brought with me back to the hotel. As I continued to survey the environment, at times I thought I was being followed by two cars. I became so concerned I decided to change my destination and head back to the Winnipeg Art Gallery, which was still loaded in my GPS. Fortunately, it was in the same general direction as my hotel. As I pulled into the gallery, I saw two cars pull into the lot behind me. I went into the museum and found a way to hide behind a door. I then bought a book, put my jacket and sunglasses in the bag given to me, and exited the museum. Instead of returning to my car rental, I slipped into a short taxi line and was able to enter a taxi just as I saw two men walk out of the museum and begin looking around. I'm sure they saw the taxi line but pretty sure they didn't recognize me. I had the taxi drop me off at a coffee shop close to the FedEx office and now I'm quickly writing out this letter.

I'm not sure if I should go back to my hotel or not and I need to get my rental car. I may simply cancel my room and then book another hotel. I believe someone knows that I'm here doing surveillance and that they are following me. I transferred what I recorded to the cloud and then destroyed my cell phone and purchased another disposable one. I could be in danger and will not try to contact you until I feel it's safe. I fear that I could be apprehended and might need to disappear for a while. Please pray for my safety.

Alan

We all sat silently in our chairs digesting the letter. I was the first to speak up.

"I have a gut feeling that Alan is laying low but is okay."

Julianna looked at me unsure. "I hope your gut is right, Johann."

Christina took charge, leading us with practical questions while putting emotion aside.

"Let's talk through who might have been following Alan. First, does it sound like he was sure about being followed, and if so, by who?"

"Yes, I am convinced he was," Darrell said. "I know it is easy to imagine that someone is following you; it has happened to me. But why would two people emerge from the museum and begin looking around? It's hard to imagine that."

"I agree," said Julianna. "He also felt two cars were following, not one. That also is harder to imagine."

Christina took us back to the second part of her question.

"Who would be following him? Were they with Churgrill, or someone else?"

I jumped into the conservation.

"I don't think they're with Churgrill. He had security with him. I think they would be with him or close by. Alan said he felt he was being followed after leaving his hotel and he was staying at a different hotel than Churgrill."

"Good analysis, Johann. I worked on a security detail when I was in the military, and we always stayed close by the diplomat we were guarding. I agree with you," Darrell said.

Christina pressed on.

"Could it have been U.S. intelligence? Perhaps the CIA, FBI, or other agents in homeland security?"

"Or, Christina, the South Africa State Security Agency?"

"Good point, Darrell."

"Surely Alan would not be in danger from intelligence agents from the U.S. or South Africa, would he?" Julianna asked.

"I worked for the government, so I am a bit jaded," Darrell said. "But I would not trust any government's intelligence agents, not even our own. They always have an agenda and can justify whatever they choose to do on the basis of national security. Alan should stay low and get out of Canada as soon as he can. What goes on outside of the U.S. is even worse than what these agencies can get away with inside the U.S."

Christina weighed in on Darrell's assessment.

"I am not quite as jaded as you are, but I wholeheartedly agree," she said. "We already know how corrupt our government has been during the past two decades. Our leaders have continually lied to the American people and justified all kinds of unconstitutional activities in the name of homeland security. Rogue agents in our FBI, CIA, and Justice Department have tried to overthrow the president. Anyone trying to uncover the corruption like Snowden and Assange have been vilified as treasonous and attempts have been made on their lives. Our government wants them locked away forever. Intelligence leaders don't want to be held accountable for their actions when they feel they need to cross the line into illegal activities. It apparently is not that difficult to justify sacrificing a few people to save many people. Alan is precious to us but expendable to our government."

Darrell looked thoughtful. "We are now the new generation of whistleblowers that could make a lot of enemies and we have to be more vigilant and more careful," he said. "We shouldn't have let Alan go to Winnipeg alone. I remember thinking this when Alan said he was going, but I didn't say anything. I could have gone with him."

Christina drew our conversation to a close.

"You are right, Darrell. But it's our fault collectively for letting Alan go alone. We need to be looking out for each other. Let's not ever make that mistake again and pray that Alan gets out of there safely."

I walked back to the L-station feeling depressed and looking over my shoulder to make sure I wasn't being followed. I had never done that before. I didn't like it. The idea that my own government could betray me was a hellish thought that was difficult to shake.

———————————

When I got home that evening, I picked up my mail and received another FedEx delivery, this one from Grand Rapids, Minnesota. I was not about to wait to open this one before our group. I ripped open the sealed envelope and was immediately ecstatic to see Alan's handwriting again. I consumed his letter in one bite:

Made it out of Canada safely. Two men followed me to border. Lost them at Baudette border crossing. They were delayed by agents. I hid out in the First Lutheran Church in Baudette till the danger passed. Left my rental car at the church, and the pastor is going to get it back and get a ride for me to Grand Rapids, MN. Plan to make my way to Minneapolis and then to Chicago. Will be home in two days but will call before arrival.

Assume you are under surveillance. I recommend you all leave Chicago residences and find other places to stay outside the city. Do a survey on Chicago residence to see if you are being watched. Leave all vehicles parked at residence and travel only by mass transit. Pay cash for all transportation. Cancel all credit cards and get prepaid visa cards at Target or Walmart. Get new P.O. boxes for all business mail. Get off the web completely with all devices you own. Access web only on public computers. Close all social media accounts, electronic banking accounts, existing cell phone accounts, etc. Withdraw all funds from existing bank accounts and open up new bank accounts with local credit unions with paper only bank statements to be sent to new P.O. Box. Stop all electronic bill paying and automatic deposits from employers—go back to receiving paper paychecks. I cannot stress this enough—YOU MUST GET COMPLETELY OFF INTERNET IMMEDIATELY. Meeting place at shoe store may also be compromised. Do surveillance to see if the place is being watched. Leaving here in an hour. Remember cash only. Will explain when I get there.

One more thing. Contact Dr. Stephen Monroe at the CDC and ask for interview. Tell him you are writing a research paper for University of Chicago course on bio-threats to U.S. Find out his thinking on Saxitoxin and Botulinum toxin attacks and potential antidotes and treatments. See you all soon. Stay safe.

Alan

My first instinct was to call Julianna, Christina, and Darrell and arrange a meeting. I immediately rejected the idea as unwise—I was unsure if we all had disposable phones or SIM cards. I could ask Mark to drive me but that also could be dangerous. I had to assume that I was under surveillance, which meant Mark's car could have had surveillance equipment placed on it. Alan said mass transit only and cash only. Fortunately, I had $500 cash stashed away in my closet.

I had to leave the Alper House without being seen. There were several doors in and out of the large complex. I reasoned that whoever might be watching me could not watch all the exits. I checked the back window of my third-story dorm room and realized there was a tree close by with a large enough tree limb to hold my weight, and that I could make it out that way if I had enough rope. I had some clothesline rope that seemed to be strong enough to hold my weight. I rejected that idea as another stupid one. Would there be any better way to draw attention to myself than to be seen climbing out of a window of the Alper House?

An idea came. Mark and I had recently purchased costumes for the upcoming Alper House Halloween party. If I slipped out one of the side doors in my costume, anyone watching would just assume I was heading out to another crazy student party. I would be unrecognizable dressed as Quasimodo. I turned our TV on and increased the volume just enough to hear it if you were at the door of our dorm room. I left a note for Mark explaining that I went home to see my parents.

I concluded that my disguise had worked as I surveyed the strange looks I received boarding a bus heading for the Harold Washington Library Center on State Street. Before arriving at the library, I made three stops. First, since I was still in costume, I went to a department store on State Street and purchased some Wranglers and a new shirt. After changing, I went to the Verizon Wireless store on State Street and turned in my old Samsung Note 8, explaining that I had just recently heard about it overheating. They replaced my phone with one that, upon my request, featured the use of disposable prepaid SIM cards and the Signal app. The feature would enable me to send private secured text messages with no SMS fees, create groups so I could chat in real time with all my friends at once, and share media or attachments with complete privacy. I knew that Signal worked through a server that never has access to any of my communication and never stores any of my data. It used an advanced end-to-end encryption protocol that provides privacy for every message every time. We all needed to get similar phones immediately, but I had to contact Julianna, Christina, and Darrell on their existing mobile phones.

I walked to the library nearby, got on a public computer, and sent each of them an email and text message instructing them to meet at our favorite reading place at 7:00 p.m. and to get there in a circuitous route, assuming that they might be followed. Everyone knew the place to meet was at the PN6000 library shelf in the Harold Washington Library, but anyone intercepting their text messages wouldn't know that. I was so thankful that we had set up an emergency meeting place in case we could not meet at the shoe store. The library was such a great meeting place because of its great size and many pathways, making it very difficult to be followed to a pre-determined location within myriads of bookshelves.

I then went to the post office on the corner of State Street and 21st Street and opened a post office box, prepaying for six months with cash. Next, I went to the Bank of America, withdrew the amount I had in my checking and savings accounts, and closed both accounts. I then went to the First Northern Credit Union on W. Monroe and opened a checking and savings account using my new post office box as my address. Next, I called my two credit card companies and cancelled my Visa and American Express accounts. I then went to the Target on State Street and purchased five $200 prepaid visa cards. I called the financial department at our lab and stopped electronic payments, asking that instead my paychecks be sent to my new P.O. box.

My goal was to get as much done as I could of what Alan had instructed us to do. I still had a few hours before our meeting, so I turned my attention to online security. First, I closed my existing Gmail account and opened a new one with a new and much more complex password. I then reset my laptop password with a much more complex one and protected it against break-ins using Pogostick. I then protected my laptop by disabling booting from a CD or USB. By altering the settings in my laptop's basic input/output system using the function keys, I password protected the BIOS so that no more changes could be made to it without entering the password. I then encrypted the hard drive using TrueCrypt, a free open source program which worked on my Windows XP system. Now I just needed to purchase a secure travel router like TP-Link TL-WR702N, which protects against malicious users connected to the same business center, hotel, or airport network that I might connect to through my laptop. TP-Link TL-WR702N provides an effective hardware firewall which helps keep my computer isolated from other users on the network. I used TrueCrypt again to encrypt all my USB memory sticks.

Within one afternoon I was able to close all my online accounts that may have been breached, secure my laptop and protect it from online attacks, and purchase a secure phone that I could use to send secure encrypted messages that could not be intercepted. I was able to set up a cash-based financial system that could not be used to trace my location. Hopefully, there was no surveillance technology attached to any of my possessions. I checked my clothing and belongings thoroughly, but there were too many places in my dorm room to hide microphones and cameras. I had to assume that my dorm room was not secure.

I finished all these tasks and still had more than an hour before our meeting time, so I decided to text Angela Farrentino from the library computer and asked her to call me from a public phone on my new cell phone number. We had formed a small study group of five among our freshman class and had been meeting about twice a week to help each other on class assignments and to study for quizzes and exams. Thus far, both Angela and I had made every meeting. My initial attraction to her proved to be a mutual liking, despite our three-year age difference. Angela's father, Vincenzo, a retired political leader, had a close friend who worked for the Centers for Disease Control in the Washington, D.C. office, and I had asked Angela to try and get some important information for me. I left the library and found a quiet bench in a shaded area and waited. Angela called and had time to talk.

"I wish you were here to watch the birds and squirrels play in the shade; it's a most beautiful sunny day."

"I'm in my dorm room working on a boring research paper."

"Things have become much more intense," I said. "Did you find out any information from your father's good friend?"

"Yes, but it's sensitive. I told my father I was doing research, which is true, but did not tell him about you. There are some things going on at the CDC office that are not right."

"I think we need to talk face-to-face. Can you meet me in thirty minutes at the Chicago library on State Street?"

"Yes, if I drop everything right now. Is there a reward involved?" Angela always seemed to be flirting with me with barely disguised innuendo. I could not resist finding out what she was thinking.

"Yes. Did you have something in mind?"

"Dinner and a movie. Or if you want to be exotic, a bike ride and picnic in Indiana Dunes State Park."

"Dunes it is." I felt a bit uneasy about going alone to the Dunes with Angela but knew it could be a lot of fun. It would be more like a date though, and I wasn't sure I was ready.

I found Angela perusing the books on the PN6000 bookshelf, sporting a white crochet lace overlay tank and a pair of curvy fit bootcut jeans with her black Franco Sarto Kacey leather ankle boots.

"You are a beautiful sight to behold among the books."

I tried to be complimentary but not too forward. She smiled.

"Let's find a quiet area to talk."

We slipped into a small study room. I had to suppress an unexpected rush of butterflies in my stomach. She was gorgeous. I held out her chair for her and then tripped over the leg. She didn't laugh and sat in the seat, while I fumbled my way to the seat across from her. Our age difference was constantly telling me I was way too young for her. It was the same insecurity I felt toward Nicole, but my attraction to Angela was different than my attraction to Nicole. I hoped that Angela had not sensed how clumsy I felt. The last thing I wanted was to create awkwardness between us. With all these crazy thoughts and feelings swirling, I forged ahead.

"Angela, I have some close friends that you don't know yet that I want you to meet. They are meeting us here at 7:00. There is so much that I would like to tell you but I can't right now. I need you to trust me even though you don't know why I need certain information."

"I trust you, Johann. But my father also trusts me and I cannot ever break that trust. He is in a precarious situation."

"I understand. We all are. What did you find out?"

"There was a threat of a biological attack, just as you told me a couple of weeks ago. My father's good friend was helping to coordinate the stockpiling of heptavalent Botulinum antitoxin. But then it all changed after meeting with his former boss, Dr. Weyant, who formerly led the agency's select agent program. Dr. Weyant is now a senior advisor in the Office of the Associate Director for Laboratory Science and Safety. Dr. Weyant hinted that his reappointment was a political decision. My father's friend is now working under Dr. Sosin, the acting director of the select agent division that is charged with developing regulations for hundreds of labs that work with select agents."

"Is that a good thing or a bad thing?"

"My father's friend was told by his new boss that the threat had changed and is now Saxitoxins, for which there is no current defense, and he is now involved in setting up safety for experiments with Saxitoxins as they search for antidotes. The work is dangerous because Saxitoxins are 1000 times more toxic than sarin, and 0.2 milligrams of Saxitoxin can kill an adult."

"This confirms what my friend Nicole Jacobson has been telling us."

"Who is Nicole?"

"A friend who works at a government biotech lab in Maryland."

"There's more. My father's friend said that he and several colleagues were mystified about the abrupt change in direction. No evidence was provided as to why Saxitoxins became a national threat. The U.S. experimented with Saxitoxins as a potential biological weapon in the 1950s and 1960s and found it too difficult to work with. There is no scientific literature to suggest a sudden breakthrough with weaponizing a Saxitoxin. This friend feels that somehow a political decision was made, and not a scientific one."

"Does he have any idea about why this change was made?"

"No, but he and his colleagues have been frustrated with the increased politicization of the CDC. You remember the whole Zika virus scare? My dad said much of that was political, as a number of scientists provided evidence that the head and brain deformities of babies born in areas where Zika existed were more likely caused by the pesticides used to eradicate the mosquitoes in those areas, and not by the virus itself."

"For what reason would they hide this?"

"Big pharma," Angela said. "Do you know how much money is in vaccines? Billions of dollars. Big pharma was salivating over a new

Zika vaccine. But first they need the CDC to validate the threat and ramp up the fear. Now of course they're pursuing a COVID-19 vaccine."

"The politics sound almost criminal to me," I said.

"It bothers my dad and his friend. It's not the first time politics trumps science; it happens all the time now."

"I know."

"And now I find myself as a science student that may end up one day in one of those political environments like my father's friend and I will not compromise my integrity as a scientist."

I immediately recognized that we shared the same concern, but it was dwarfed by another more powerful thought—the thought that Angela's passion for science was as strong as mine, a passion that substantially added to her attractiveness. I could not help giving her an affectionate look. She smiled back at me.

I looked at my watch and it was five minutes before 7:00; time to meet the others.

Julianna, Christina, and Darrell all made it safely to the PN6000 library shelf featuring books on journalism and mass communication. Susan was out of town.

"Before we get down to business, I want you all to meet Angela Farrentino, a close friend from the University of Chicago and part of my study group."

"Now I understand why you love going to your study group," Darrell joked.

"Angela, you are more beautiful than Johann has told us," Julianna said. "It's great to meet you."

"And I am sure you are also smarter than Johann has told us," Christina said.

"Now I know why Johann speaks so highly of you all," Angela said. "That's the nicest round of introductions I have ever experienced. I understand your need for complete privacy, and I don't want to interrupt your important meeting. Johann thinks what I have found out from my father's friend, who works at the CDC office in Washington, D.C., may be important to you."

Christina then took charge.

"Please know that whatever you share with us will be kept completely confidential. Neither you nor your father or his friend will ever be revealed as the source of the information you share with us."

Angela proceeded to tell us what her father had learned from his friend, about the political pressures he felt, and the conviction that there was something not right about the CDC's sudden change of focus from a potential Botulinum attack to a potential Saxitoxin attack.

"It is all making sense to me now," Julianna said. "I did the research that Alan asked me to do and confirmed that EBS is vulnerable to a hostile takeover on the New York Stock Exchange. Churgrill was in Winnipeg to assess the strength of the company and he has enough money to buy up their stock and become the majority shareholder. If there is a major biological attack with Botulinum, the value of EBS stock will sky-rocket."

"Your information is of great value," Christina said, turning to Angela. "If anyone discovers that you have worked with us, it may become dangerous for you, especially if you keep hanging out with Johann."

Angela looked at me and then responded, "He's worth the risk."

Her look was enough to make me blush; both Christina and Julianna noticed. After we all thanked Angela, she left our meeting.

"Johann, she likes you a lot," Christina said.

"She is crazy about you," Julianna said. "You need her to completely understand the dangers of being close to you."

"I like her but am so insecure about that kind of thing."

Julianna gave me an inquisitive look. "What kind of thing, Johann?"

"You know—romantic relationships. I'm legally protected from it. I'm not even seventeen until August," I said.

Julianna's eyebrows raised.

"We're just talking about getting romantically involved. You're certainly not protected from that."

"Romance knows no consent," Darrell said. "You need to tell her you're toxic."

"I think she already knows. We need to seriously consider adding her to our circle."

"Possibly," Christina said, "but it's unthinkable to consider putting anyone else in any more danger, especially given the ordeal that Alan has endured."

"You're right, as you usually are," I agreed.

"Usually?"

"Almost always." I laughed. "I promise to talk to her about it this weekend. We are going to the Dunes."

"Just the two of you?" Julianna asked. "You're getting involved."

"Can we move on from your romantic life and get to Alan's last FedEx?" Christina asked.

I took Alan's last handwritten letter carefully from the front pocket of my jeans and read it out loud. A long period of silence followed, and then everyone began talking at once.

I explained what I had already done earlier in the day.

"I can't believe you did all that in one day," Julianna said.

"I did, and I feel much more secure."

"Okay," said Christina, "let's all do what Alan has asked us to do immediately. Alan should be back soon."

"What about finding new places to live?" Darrell asked. "I'm living with my grandparents in South Chicago and am not sure where I could go."

"What about Downers Grove?" Christina asked. "We all have close friends there. The train is an hour from there to downtown Chicago."

"Great idea," Julianna replied. "We should all be able to find safe havens there."

"Not me." Darrell frowned.

"You can stay with me and my parents, Darrell, we have plenty of room."

"I'll look forward to that, Johann. Thanks."

We all left with much to do. I had to think of a good story to tell my parents without revealing how much danger we might be in. I knew more fretful sleep lay ahead, and that I needed to tell them what was going on.

CHAPTER 10

WHILE I TOSSED AND TURNED in bed at my parents' house, I could not stop thinking about Alan. We still had not heard from him since he had sent the letter from Grand Rapids, Minnesota. It should have taken a day to travel from Grand Rapids to Chicago. *Why was it taking so long? Was he okay?*

Then it occurred to me how stupid I was. Of course, he could not communicate—I'd cancelled my cell phone, I'd cancelled my Facebook and Twitter accounts, I'd cancelled my email account—there was no way Alan knew how to contact me. All of us had cancelled our old means of communication. Whatever was happening with Alan, he had no way of communicating with us.

Then I thought about how Alan had told us to go underground. So, he knew we would have new encrypted phones and new email accounts. We just had to sit tight and trust him. He could be simply waiting to contact us until he was sure that we had enough time to do everything he had asked us to do. I knew it was time to ask for Chief Ryan's help; we were getting in over our heads. We needed more than his guidance; we needed his protection.

Lying awake in bed, I got up and turned my bedroom light on. I thought I had heard the sound of a motorcycle. It was close to midnight. I decided to read a bit since I was still not very sleepy.

Darrell was staying in the large guest room in our basement and I was staying in the smaller guest bedroom, also in the basement. Our house was on a hill so the basement was the ground floor if you approached it from the back. It had two bedrooms, a large living, a small dining room and a full kitchen. It also had its own door so that it could be completely rented out as an apartment.

I was about ten minutes into my latest David Baldacci novel when I heard a faint knock on the basement door. My room was closest to the door so Darrell could probably not hear it. I quickly went to the downstairs closet adjacent to my bedroom and grabbed the twenty-gauge shotgun that my father kept hidden underneath the extra linens on the top shelf. I checked the empty chamber and then loaded two shells. The outdoor light was on and I could see one man silhouetted in the light just outside the door. As I peered through the window, I recognized Alan's New England Patriots sweatshirt. My heart leapt as I took a closer look and was able to catch a glimpse of Alan's face.

I excitedly, and yet quietly, opened the door and quickly let Alan into our home, immediately closing and locking the door behind him. I hoped that he had not been followed. Alan was grinning from ear to ear.

"You can put the shotgun down now, Johann; it's me."

He did not look like a scared man desperately on the run. We gave each other a long bear hug. Before I could speak, Alan whispered, "Don't worry, I was not followed here. We are going to be safe."

He knew exactly what I was thinking.

"Darrell is sleeping in our large guest bedroom." I pointed down the hallway. "My parents are asleep upstairs. We are all staying in Downers Grove."

"That's exactly what I thought you would do. Did you all complete the other things I asked you to do?"

"Yes, we are all underground."

"I know it must have sounded extreme, but the people we are up against are very evil and very resourceful," Alan said. "I had to lay low before returning. They were monitoring everything, even bus lines. Thankfully, I've met some very nice bikers."

"Bikers?"

"Yes. Have you heard of the CMA, the Christian Motorcyclists Association?"

"No."

"They have thousands of members in thirty nations. I met one of their leaders at a church. He connected me with a network of close CMA friends that gave me rides from Grand Rapids, all the way back here."

"What have we gotten ourselves into?"

"Let's wait until morning, Johann. I'm exhausted."

Alan helped me pull out the sofa bed in the living room and make it with the extra linens we found in the hallway closet. After a hot shower, he fell asleep quickly. It still took me another thirty minutes before I fell asleep, my last thought fixated on what we had gotten ourselves into and if we would get out of it alive.

Only a few hours later, I received my first encrypted text on my new phone from Angela. She was at a Starbucks coffee shop and was scared. She wanted me to come get her. Someone had followed her home, so she stayed at her girlfriend's apartment across the street from where she lived.

I rode my bike to the train station and took the train to a station close by. I met Angela at the Starbucks an hour later and worked out an elaborate plan to get back to the L system by entering the subway through a different stop. Stepping out of the shop, we hastily grabbed a taxi and followed our plan. We were confident that we had lost anyone that had been following her.

Angela told me on the train that when she had arrived close to home from the library, she felt like she was being watched. She immediately went to her friend's house and stayed with her. She had hoped she was not followed to the Starbucks this morning but did not know for sure. Before we left Starbucks, I sent a text to Chief Ryan's cell phone.

We took the train back to Downers Grove and arrived back home just past 8:00 a.m. My mom was cooking up a big Saturday morning breakfast for everyone who was now congregating around our dining room table. Christina, Susan, and Julianna had just arrived.

"One more guest," I said to my mom with a big smile as I brought Angela into our home.

"Welcome, Angela. We have plenty of food—scrambled eggs with cheese and mushrooms, Canadian bacon, whole-wheat pancakes, fresh Kona coffee and juice."

"Wow," Darrell said, "I'm glad I'm staying here. It smells just like my grandmother's cooking."

"I take that as a big compliment, Darrell," my mother said.

After a hearty breakfast, my father initiated the conversation I knew we had to have. There was no way to protect my parents now. We had to tell them something. There was no way we could keep them in the dark, yet the more we told them, the more at risk they would be.

"Okay, let's all move to the large TV room downstairs and leave the clean-up for later," my father said. "Then you can explain to Mom and me what this is all about."

"Dad, Chief Ryan needs to be a part, too. I invited him over."

"That makes two of us," my dad said. "He'll be here soon."

We all decided that it was a good time to take bathroom breaks and get coffee and tea refills. It was going to be a long meeting. We heard a car pull up to our home, and then our front doorbell rang. My dad went upstairs and came back down followed by Chief Ryan.

He took off his hat as my dad introduced him.

"Let me introduce to you a good friend and our town's chief of police, whom most of you already know, Chief Joshua Ryan. Chief Ryan, these are Johann's friends from Chicago. Johann, can you introduce them?"

"Chief Ryan," I said. "I think you know a bit about our *Eleutheria Club*, mostly alums from Avery Coonley."

"Yes, I've heard some good things," Chief Ryan said.

I stood up and walked with Chief Ryan to each of our members, introducing them by name and their occupation. Chief Ryan smiled warmly at each person, grasping their hand in a firm handshake before walking to the next in line.

"Finally," I said, turning toward Angela who stood in the back, "This is my good friend Angela Farrentino, who was born and raised in Sorrento, Italy, and is a student with me at the University of Chicago."

As Angela shook the Chief's hand, I added, "She is one of the primary reasons why I am currently acing my exams in physics and chemistry."

"I'm afraid that Johann is a bit too modest," Angela said. "I doubt that I'm contributing much to his academic achievements."

Angela gave me a playful look and smile that I'm sure my mother picked up on.

"Since you were all about to explain what is going on," my dad stated, taking charge of our meeting again, "I thought that Chief Ryan should also hear about it."

Alan was the first to speak. "Mr. and Mrs. Oberhausen and Chief Ryan, I serve as the current president of the *Eleutheria Club* and was away in Canada for a week. As a group, we have not had time to meet and to discuss some very recent events. Could you give us thirty minutes to meet without you so we can plan a clear and accurate presentation to you? It's very important, as I believe things will get very muddled and perhaps confusing if we don't."

"I am fine with that," my dad replied, "are you in a time crunch, Chief Ryan?"

"Not at all," the Chief responded. "I have a golf game this afternoon but I could always move the game to another time or day."

Once our group met together, I shared that I felt like we were getting in over our heads now that our lives were being threatened. To my relief, everyone agreed. We then heard from Alan the details of his trip to Canada, and then we planned our presentation. When we reconvened, Alan asked me to speak first.

"Mom and Dad, Chief Ryan, we are in a very difficult situation trying to fully explain to you the predicament we are in. Right now, I'm concerned that my life is at risk as is Alan's, Julianna's, Susan's, Christina's, and Darrell's. We have national security information that our own government may or may not know. We fear that enemies of the U.S. know that we have recordings or documents they don't wish us to possess. Recently, Angela met with us and was followed back to her home last night in Chicago. Even though she does not know what the rest of us know, her life may now be at risk. Alan was followed in Canada by two men he believes were professional agents.

"If we tell you everything we know, then your lives may also be threatened. We do not want to put you in danger. That is the last thing we want to do. To complicate matters even more, we have strong reason to believe that certain individuals within our U.S. intelligence services may be compromised. We do not know who we can trust. We even fear harm from U.S. government agents. At this point we do not know who is following us or who had planted surveillance devises in our residences in Chicago, which prompted us to temporarily leave the city. All we know is that we can trust each other and that we have to keep following our leads as new information emerges."

"May I respond?" Chief Ryan asked.

"Yes, please do," replied Alan.

"I believe you all are doing the right thing in letting us know what is going on. We understand your predicament and appreciate your concern for our safety, but we can't help protect you unless we know what this is about. Any criminal organization involved in creating national threats would already have the resources to track down all of your parents and other family members. They probably know we are meeting right now. You will not be able to fight against foreign agents or rogue agents within our government without professional law enforcement helping you. You should remember that my father was the former Deputy Superintendent of Police, head of counterterrorism for the city of Chicago, and was instrumental in stopping the terrorist attacks against the Sears Tower and the Nasdaq stock exchange several years ago. My father is retired but still well-connected to people he completely trusts; I have those same connections in our intelligence agencies, and I help lead the Joint Terrorism Task Force in the National Counterterrorism Center."

"I believe what Chief Ryan is plainly telling us," my dad interjected, "is that you need to share with others you can completely trust and who have the resources to help you. That is the best way to protect us and yourselves."

"That's exactly what we concluded," Alan said. "Let me pick up where Johann left off."

For the next hour Alan explained how they had first intercepted a recording between General Nicoli Sarkovsky and Atlas Churgrill. As Alan spoke, we were all flabbergasted by how much information Chief Ryan seemed to already know. When Alan shared how the small group of them had hacked into a CIA communication network, Chief Ryan asked, "And how many of the twenty-one members of your *Eleutheria Club* were present when you heard this conversation?"

"You know about all the members of our club?" Alan asked in surprise.

"Oh yes, and many of your exploits. Remember, our town is a relatively medium-sized one, around 50,000, and people like to talk. It is my responsibility to know what is going on."

"There were four of us present: me, Susan, Julianna, and Christina," said Alan. "We told Johann because of his knowledge of satellites and his research on satellite-based lasers, and we told Darrell because of his military background, language expertise, and connection to military leaders and diplomats from China and Taiwan. Only six of us know about the planning of a WMD attack on the U.S. that the U.S. would blame China for, bringing the two countries into war. Angela is learning this for the first time."

"What about the intelligence agent who recorded this conversation?" Chief Ryan asked. "Do you know his name and does he know that his network was hacked?"

"We don't know the identity of the agent or what he or she knows," Alan replied.

"I do," said Chief Ryan to the shock of everyone present.

"How do you already know so much?" asked Christina.

"It's my job to know. I work for the citizens of Downers Grove, and thus I work for your parents. What is the greatest concern of your parents? You are. I already knew about your great job at CBRE in Chicago, Christina. I know about your work, Johann, with Tim and Dr. Carlson in the Astronomy and Astrophysics Lab at the Kavli Institute. I also know about your study group."

I looked at my parents and saw their great admiration for their friend.

"I also know about your study group at Northwestern, Julianna. I can say your parents are all proud of you doing well in Chicago and staying out of trouble, until now, that is. I have checked up on your work for Microsoft, Susan, and they love you, even though you have this ongoing fascination with hacking into secure networks."

"Chief Ryan, we have all wished many times we never heard that conversation, but how did you know we heard it?" Julianna asked.

"A friend of mine, I'll refer to him as Enrico Mariuchi, is a CIA agent; our fathers worked together on anti-terrorism interventions. Enrico was informed of a security breach through a computer server in the Chicago area. The hackers had to have been very sophisticated and bright to break through the protections set up by the CIA. Knowing that I was the chief of police here, but with many contacts in Chicago, Enrico called me and asked me to try and track down the hackers. I naturally knew the profile of hackers are usually young, in their early twenties or younger, and I knew the smartest young people in our community attended the Avery Coonley School. Once I found your secret club, it was easy to deduce who the culprits were. Do you have any idea of the legal ramifications for hacking into a CIA network?"

None of us could reply.

"And then getting Nicole Jacobson to let you into her network at her facility in Silver Spring? That could have landed both you and Nicole in jail."

"Not just any jail," Christina said, "Probably life in ADX Florence."

"Where?" I asked.

"ADX in Florence, Colorado, or Supermax, the Alcatraz of the Rockies. It's the most awful maximum-security prison in the U.S. where they send spies and traitors."

I could see the color run out of my mom's face.

"Don't worry, Katarina. No charges will ever be brought against these kids. The CIA will never admit that their network has been hacked by a Gen Z hackers' club. Also, they already know you were anonymously forwarding good information to U.S. intelligence agents."

"Who were you targeting?" my dad asked.

"It's a long story," Alan replied, "but not the CIA. We thought it was the Foreign Intelligence Service."

Chief Ryan's reprimand was not finished. "Also very dangerous behavior, I might add. Did it ever occur to you that the CIA would be masquerading as the SVR in order to penetrate their networks?"

"We didn't think of that," Susan said.

"None of you thought through what you were doing. Nonetheless, the CIA is using this breach to their advantage as you have brought the cockroaches out of the woodwork. The CIA now knows much about General Nicoli Sarkovsky, Atlas Churgrill, and General Bingwen Tso, the launch sites on the disputed islands in the South China Sea, planned satellite warfare, and threats of biological attacks."

We all felt some relief.

"Unfortunately, there is still much to learn. Is the biological threat Saxitoxin, as our government now believes, or Botulinum toxin, or something else? Where will the attacks occur and when? How will they be launched from satellites? Is there a similar attack being planned against China?"

"What should we do?" Alan asked.

"You need to stay on this, and we must now work closely together. You are going to need to trust me completely. We are now all in this together."

"There is one more thing, Chief Ryan," Alan spoke up. "While I was in Winnipeg, I found a device in my hotel room. I believe it was placed there by someone either working for Churgrill or following him. Through the device, I was able to electronically find a way back into the surveillance network of whoever planted it. I can now monitor the network."

"What have you found out?"

"That Churgrill has been feeding someone in the NSA information about a Chinese attack against the U.S. using a weaponized Saxitoxin."

"But you think it's misinformation?"

"Absolutely. Emergent BioSolutions Corporation makes the heptavalent Botulinum antitoxin. They don't make a Saxitoxin antidote. There is no biodefense product to treat Saxitoxin poisoning."

"Why do you think Churgrill was visiting them?"

"He wants the company," Julianna replied.

"Exactly," confirmed Alan.

"That's my conclusion as well. In addition, one of our intelligence agencies is likely compromised by one or more agents bought off by Churgrill or Sarkovsky. From now on, you can no longer pass on information to your contacts. Everything must go through me. And because Johann is the youngest and a freshman in college, he is perceived as the least likely threat, so I will use Johann as a communication hub to the *Eleutheria Club*. I may not be able to communicate directly with all of you, so I will always let Johann know what is going on and he will keep me informed. Is that clear?"

"Yes, sir," we all replied.

Chief Ryan was now in charge. My dad squeezed my mom's hand and she smiled. Chief Ryan sat up, lifted his chin, and looked around the room like an army captain assessing his troops. For the first time I began to grapple with the fact that we were fighting for our own survival.

CHAPTER 11

AFTER TWO WEEKS OF CAREFUL surveillance by Chicago's counterterrorism task force, Chief Ryan gave us the all clear to continue to meet at Dursen Shoes. He also cleared us to return to our residences in Chicago but recommended that we stay in Downers Grove if we felt safer there. We had all been paranoid about being followed, but there was no evidence that our residences were under surveillance. Angela may have been followed home, but we could not know for sure.

Alan had been definitely followed. We learned later from Chief Ryan that an Emergent BioSolutions security guard had registered the license plate number of Alan's car when he was surveilling the complex and they traced the car to his name. Churgrill's security professionals found out Alan was a computer programmer. They then broke into his cell phone and traced one of his calls to the TD Ameritrade office in downtown Chicago. He was calling Julianna at work to see if they wanted to have lunch together. Fearing Alan was working for someone who also was interested in investing in the company, Churgrill had two men follow Alan. After Alan lost them at the U.S. border crossing, he continued to lay low. He also created a new narrative that he was investigating Emergent BioSolutions because his company was considering using their services. The narrative also included presenting Julianna as Alan's girlfriend, who just happened to work at a trading company. These constructive narratives, disseminated via social media, were successful in ending the intense surveillance Alan had experienced.

I decided to stay at my parents' house another couple of days and then returned to my dorm room in the Alper House. I was relieved to hear that Mark did not notice anything unusual while I was gone and that no one came around asking for me other than a couple of friends in the building.

I returned to class on Monday as if nothing had happened, trying not to be pre-occupied with thoughts of a national disaster due to a biological attack on the nation. My courses were all going fine, without any problems, and more importantly, my lab experiences were getting more and more challenging and exciting. By working with Tim, our satellite-based laser simulations were making continual improvements each week. We had now reached a success rate of seventy-nine percent regarding the removal of space junk.

On Friday evening, Tim told me that Dr. Keppler wanted to meet with us and a couple other people on Saturday morning. Tim had a bad feeling about it and said he knew what it was about.

"I saw a couple of high-ranking military guys come to the office on Tuesday morning," Tim explained. "I'm afraid that we are going to be tasked with some kind of military project."

I had a hunch I knew what the project would be but kept quiet.

"There is more and more news out of the South China Sea," Tim continued. "There is fear they are going to create some kind of new space threat, and the U.S. military wants us to be ready."

"What does this mean for your dissertation?"

"My dissertation will be fine. We have already collected more than enough data for my dissertation. It may slow down my writing, but I am nearly finished with the statistical analyses and reporting of results. I just don't want to end up working for the U.S. military. We are still far too willing, in my view, to intervene in other countries where we don't know what we are doing and what the final result will be."

"I could not agree with you more, Tim. I'm a pacifist at heart and I think any kind of military action must be a last resort when our national security is truly threatened."

I exchanged a glance with Tim. I knew I would enjoy working with him.

Tim nodded at the paperwork before us. "We need to start working on our presentation now," he said resolutely. "Dr. Keppler wants us to present a thirty to thirty-five-minute PowerPoint presentation to the two people he's bringing to the meeting, on space lasers and their ability to shoot down things in space."

"Who are they?" I asked.

"Military intelligence officers," Tim said.

"I'm ready to work," I said.

I tried to muster some enthusiasm. During the next three hours, we put together a pretty good presentation for our meeting the next morning. We included three months of data showing the steady increase of our successful hit ratio, and also prepared vivid video simulations of our satellite lasers knocking out various types of space junk at different altitudes moving at different speeds. Tim suggested that we brainstorm a number of questions that we should anticipate and discussed how we would answer them. We considered the important information that we would need about potential military targets as compared to space junk in order to create a viable defense system, and the increased security that we would need for such a project.

Just before we finished our work near midnight, Tim received a warning on his computer that someone was trying to breach our firewall and get into our laboratory mainframe computer. We had recently installed a Mira BlueGene/Q Power BQC 16C 1.60GHz custom mainframe computer like the one at Argonne National Laboratory in Lemont, Illinois, also operated by the University of Chicago. The system is nearly impossible to hack into because of a security system that functions like IBM's resource access control facility on their z/OS and z/VM operating systems. However, our great security systems did not mean people still did not try to breach them. We thus took added precautions by keeping all our original data on hard drives that were completely offline and not accessible through the Internet or through any kind of wireless technology. If our system ever got hacked, we would not be in trouble.

"Can you trace where the hack is coming from?" I asked.

"Our IT experts gave us a program that tracks attempted breaches and organizes them out in weekly reports," Tim said. "Most of the hackers are from China and Russia and are likely funded by their governments. We should probably bring the last few months of security reports to the meeting tomorrow."

We were about to leave when the power went out in the building and the emergency generator kicked on. Then we heard breaking glass near the front entrance—someone was breaking in. Tim called 911 on his cell phone and we scrambled to a back-exit door. We both ran through a parking lot and made our way to a bus stop to get to our homes as fast as we could. My hand was shaking as I scanned my bus pass.

Tim sent me a text after he got off at his stop: "Called police and Dr. Keppler to report the break-in. The police should be there now. Be careful getting back to your dorm and I'll see you tomorrow at 9:00 a.m. That will give us some time to get our act together before our 10:00 a.m. meeting."

The bus and train ride back to the Alper house was stressful and I was just beginning to calm down when I received an encrypted text message from Darrell. It was close to midnight and I was dead tired and still shaken by the break-in into our lab. Darrell wanted to meet as soon as possible. I explained how tonight was out of the question given my exhausted condition, so we arranged to meet at a café near my lab before my meeting with Tim.

I awoke in the middle of the night with my hand over my mouth. I had been having a nightmare that two people were trying to make me drink poison. I was covering my mouth to protect myself while a woman was trying to pull my hand off my mouth. A much larger man had a vile of poison that he was trying to pour down my throat as I was pinned to a bed. It had been so real I found myself coughing violently and raced to the bathroom to drink some water.

After calming down, I was able to go back to sleep, though I was getting more concerned each day about my personal safety. Why did I continue to have nightmares of people trying to kill me? Was this an omen? A warning? I didn't know. Nicole didn't know how to stop her nightmares either. I decided that I needed to talk to Angela about it. Maybe she could help both of us.

I slept soundly for the rest of the night and rose refreshed. The coffee shop was a fifteen-minute walk and Darrell had picked out an outdoor table in a quiet area of the back courtyard. He was wearing white shorts, a blue blazer, and a blue White Sox baseball cap with designer sunglasses. He looked more like a University of Chicago football player than a professional interpreter. I joined him with my large coffee and blueberry scone and could see the anxiousness in his body language.

"My friends in Taiwan gave me some important information last night," Darrell began.

"They intercepted a conversation confirming the delivery of special cargo on a Filipino fishing vessel out of the port of Zamboanga in Mindanao, southern Philippines. That is consistent with the previous information we had heard. Part of that cargo was Botulinum toxin that had been shipped from Iran. The shipment was arranged by Churgrill and was being transferred onto a Chinese ship at the Scarborough Shoal. General Tso was personally taking possession of the shipment and making payment in cash for it. More importantly, General Tso was taking the toxin to the Diaoyu Islands."

I sat there in silence, trying to take in all the information and make sense of it. Darrell explained more.

"This confirms our suspicions that General Tso is preparing to launch a biological attack from space."

"Against who?" I asked.

"It is probably against the U.S. They dare not attack Russia at this time. Except for our president, they believe our leaders are currently weak, pre-occupied, and indecisive regarding our foreign policy. We are not prepared for this."

"Would China attack us?" I asked.

"We don't know. We know General Tso would attack us, but we don't know if the CCP has sanctioned such an attack."

"What about the Saxitoxin threat?"

"It must be a diversion; disinformation spread by China. The Chinese clearly have Botulinum toxin. The CCP is pushing another narrative that the real threat is Saxitoxin, for which there is no defense."

"There also is another important narrative coming out of China. My friends in Taiwan have been picking up a lot of chatter about a biological attack on China from the U.S."

"That's ridiculous. That's not even credible. How could they believe that?" I asked.

"They don't think like we do. They think the U.S. wants to economically and militarily dominate them and that the U.S. will do anything to slow down their economic and military growth. My friends said the Chinese believe if an attack would come that the U.S. would orchestrate it and then completely deny their part. It will be made to look like someone else is responsible, maybe an attack by terrorists. They are not sure if it will be officially sanctioned by the U.S. government."

"This reinforces the original CIA recording we intercepted. You remember the end of the conversation between General Sarkovsky and Churgrill?"

"Could not forget it," I said. *"China will blame the U.S. and the U.S. will blame China."*

"It's all making sense now. Churgrill is orchestrating a biological attack on the U.S. and on China and is manipulating intelligence information so that each country will blame the other."

Darrell clasped his hands, raised them to his face, and lowered his chin.

"And if the attacks are big enough, it could escalate into a major war that neither country wants."

"We have to stop this," I said.

Darrell sat quietly deep in thought.

"We need a strategy."

"We also need Chief Ryan," I said. "He and his father have a lot of experience fighting international terrorists and they have many personal friends in the intelligence services."

I looked at my watch having lost sight of the time.

"It's ten till 9:00, I have to run to my meeting. Maybe we can meet either tonight or on Sunday."

"I'll see if I can get everyone together," Darrell said. "I'll get the bill." I left the coffee shop and began a slow jog toward the lab office a few blocks away. I could see police cars out front and realized they were investigating the break-in last night. They would want to interview me and Tim.

As I got closer to the building, I spotted a HAZMAT truck and what appeared to be an FBI HMRU outside the building. As I slowed down my jog, I realized the break-in was not a random act of vandalism or attempted larceny. Something much bigger was going on. I wondered what they had found.

Dr. Keppler and Tim were standing outside the front entrance to the William Eckhardt Research Center, the building that houses our lab, waiting for me along with several police officers, FBI officers, and the military officers we were scheduled to meet.

As soon as he spotted me, Dr. Keppler moved quickly with Tim to greet me.

"We have a change of plans, Johann," said Dr. Keppler. "The break-in you and Tim reported last night just before you left the building involved a hazardous agent. We are not sure what it is but the FBI HMRU are doing tests now and our building is completely off-limits. Both the FBI and local police want to talk with you. They have their hands full now so they have agreed to interview you and Tim after our meeting. Let me introduce you."

We walked over to greet two distinguished looking men.

"Johann, let me introduce you now to General Donald Cumberland, the U.S. Army's deputy chief of staff, the Army's chief intelligence officer, who has come from Fort Belvoir, Virginia."

"Pleased to meet you," I said, looking up at a tall man built like an NFL quarterback with deep blue eyes and sandy blond hair.

"Thank you, I've heard a lot about you." His voice was warm.

Then, turning to his right, Dr. Keppler said, "Johann, this is General David Welsh, the chief of staff of the United States Air Force, who works at the Pentagon."

"I am also pleased to meet you, General."

I looked at eye level into the face of a man about the same age and physical build of my father, but my height.

"We are thankful that Dr. Keppler has made you both available to assist us," General Welsh said. "We need to find a private and secure place to meet."

"We can go to the Quantum Café," Tim suggested.

"Not secure enough," General Welsh said.

"I know a very private secure area of the Joseph Regenstein Library across the street," I said. "They have private study rooms on the fifth floor big enough to give our presentation and there are usually very few people around."

Both generals agreed that should work well.

Dr. Keppler parted company to return to the police to assist them and I escorted the two generals along with Tom to the fifth floor of the Regenstein Library. We found the perfect room in which to meet. It had three solid walls and one wall with glass windows that we could cover with inside curtains for privacy. General Cumberland took an electronic box out of his briefcase and scanned the room, explaining that it could detect any electronic surveillance in the environment. The room was clean.

Tim set up his laptop and micro-projector and set it on the study table in the room, projecting it on one of the solid white walls. General Welsh took charge of the meeting.

"What we are about to share with you we have kept confidential."

"General," Tim said, "Dr. Keppler briefed us on the sensitive nature of our discussion. We will guard the information vigilantly."

"We have both read your preliminary research. We know that you have been developing the capability to destroy space junk with satellite-based lasers, and we have reviewed your longitudinal data and understand that you have increased your successful intercept rate to seventy-nine-and-a-half percent."

"We just exceeded eighty-five percent this week. We will show you in our presentation."

"That is great news, Tim," General Welsh said. "We've been doing extensive reconnaissance over the South China Sea during the past two years."

General Welsh then turned to General Cumberland and added, "General Cumberland has been overseeing that work."

"What we have found is missile sites and evidence of satellites being prepared for space," Cumberland explained. "We believe the satellites will have military grade lasers capable of disabling our communication systems. We must protect ourselves against such an attack."

"We need your help in developing a satellite-based laser defense system that can disable or destroy military-based satellites that may try to attack us," General Welsh said. "Can you do this?"

"We can," Tim and I answered in unison without hesitation.

"How soon?"

"How soon do you need it?"

"Yesterday," General Welsh replied.

"Then we will get on it right away."

"Great," General Welsh replied. "Now show us what you've been doing."

Tim turned on the projector and for the next thirty minutes, he explained to the generals our research, providing visual simulations of the satellite-based lasers we had developed and how we were able to destroy space junk with them.

"How do you know this will work?" General Cumberland asked.

"We are going to test it in a couple weeks, General. Our very own satellite-based laser system is being launched in ten days at Cape Canaveral. As soon as it's in place, we will begin destroying space junk."

I read the facial expressions of both generals. They were pleased.

CHAPTER 12

AFTER TIM AND I WERE interviewed by the police about the break-in, I took the train back to my dorm. Shortly after finding a seat I received a call from Nicole. It had been nearly a week since we had talked. The L was quite noisy so I told her I would call her back and that it might be an hour as I had to find a safe place to call.

I noticed a woman who boarded the train when I did; she seemed to be keeping an eye on me. She looked to be in her mid-twenties with short blonde hair and a familiar face. I just could not place her, but I was sure I had seen her before. My suspicions appeared to be proven valid as she exited the same stop that I did, although I realized that could be a complete coincidence. It was not my regular stop. I decided to exit the train, walk around the station, and get back on the train going in the same direction. I got back on the station platform nearly where I exited and saw her from the corner of my eye. She was following me.

I was very tempted to circle back around behind her and then come up to her from the back and startle her by inviting her out for a cup of coffee. Nevertheless, I vetoed my own idea as too risky since I had no idea who she was and how she might react. I decided instead to lose her. I stepped onto the next train and pretended like I was about to sit down. Just before the doors closed, I jumped off and ran for the nearest exit. I knew the area well and decided to take a bus the rest of the way home. I decided to make my call from a local café, where I could see if the woman following me had caught up to me.

Convinced I had lost her, I purchased a cappuccino and called Nicole. I felt good about having the chance to talk with her again. Not because we were trying to solve a serious problem; it was something different.

Nicole's voice was noticeably strained when I reached her by phone. "Are you okay?"

"Barely. I've slept a couple of hours a night all week. I now understand why sleep deprivation is a form of torture. My team has been working around the clock with two other research groups, one in Switzerland and the other in Singapore, to develop a vaccine for Saxitoxin. I have read dozens of case studies of people who have been poisoned by eating crabs, blue-green algae, and blue-ringed octopus. These paralytic shellfish poisoning (PSP) cases have given me no insight thus far into understanding how to develop a vaccine. What I need to find is a positive deviant not susceptible to PSP who can consume all the marine dinoflagellates he or she wants."

"What is a positive deviant?" I said, never having heard of the term.

"It is someone who is not affected in the same way by the same conditions or environment as everyone else is."

"Okay . . ." I still did not understand.

"Let me explain it another way, Johann. Suppose you go to Tropical Smoothie with four friends and you all get strawberry smoothies. During the next month all four of your friends get sick with a hepatitis A infection. In fact, out of nineteen people who had strawberry smoothies that day at the restaurant, eighteen get sick, everyone, except for you. In that case, you would be the positive deviant. You ate the tainted strawberries from Egypt, as the epidemiologists discovered in the Tropical Smoothie incident, but you did not get sick. Something in you likely protected you. That would make you a positive deviant."

"How are you going to find the people who eat bad shellfish and don't get PSP?"

"That's the challenge. I need to go to where there have been outbreaks of PSP."

"Where is that?" I asked.

"Western Samar in the Philippines or the Patagonia Chilean fjords."

"Wow, sounds exotic, can I come?"

"No, it won't be fun. We are under immense pressure. This is dead serious. Do you know what it is like to die from Saxitoxin poisoning? It's brutal. Within ten minutes after exposure, you will feel numbness or tingling of the lips, tongue, and fingertips. The numbness will then spread to the neck and extremities and muscles will begin to fail. Simple things like picking up a glass of water become difficult to accomplish. Then you will feel nauseated and may begin vomiting, but that is not the worst of it. If you have ingested a lethal dose of Saxitoxin, you will then progress into respiratory distress and muscular paralysis. You will struggle to breathe. Every breath will be a battle to stay alive, but you will eventually lose. You will die of respiratory paralysis or asphyxia respiratory failure."

"It sounds like torture."

"It is, and the powers that believe that the U.S. is going to be attacked with Saxitoxins have no protection against it. Can you imagine the chaos and panic this could cause?"

As I began to process what Nicole was explaining to me, I began to understand why a Saxitoxin attack had created more concern than a Botulinum attack. I knew we already had an antidote to Botulinum, although we did not have enough to protect everyone. But I could see how a major Saxitoxin attack would be devastating since the government would seem powerless and unable to protect the American people.

"When we talked last, you said you did not believe the real threat was Saxitoxin. You had a gut feeling that it was a diversion. And now?"

"Totally confused. I just don't know anymore, but I have no choice in the matter. We have reassigned all resources to developing a Saxitoxin vaccine. But enough about my crises, how are you?"

"Someone's following me, a woman in her mid-to-late twenties. I have no idea who she is or whom she works for, but she seems professionally trained. I have no doubt she could incapacitate me in a short amount of time. She looks totally buff—I just hope she's not a professional killer."

"There you go again with your fantasies of someone trying to kill you. Remember, they are bad dreams. I have them, too, but no one is trying to kill me. You are one of my most paranoid friends, though not the only one."

"No, this has nothing to do with my occasional nightmares. A woman followed me down the street, into the subway system, and onto the train. I lost her by quickly jumping off the train just before the doors closed and running out the exit as fast as I could."

"Maybe you should not sleep in your dorm room tonight."

"I'm thinking the same thing. I'm walking back to my dorm now but I am feeling uneasy."

"Where else would you stay—back to your parents?"

"My lab supervisor, Tim, has offered me his comfortable couch if I ever needed a quiet place to sleep after a long night in the lab."

"Be careful and whatever you do, Johann, text me when you get to a safe place."

———————

Tim was very gracious to let me use his home. He had gone away for the weekend to visit his parents in Minnesota, so there was no need to contrive a story to cover for the real reason I did not want to stay in my dorm room. He was already becoming concerned about his security since accepting General Cumberland's request to work on a military project. The last thing I wanted to do was to freak him out by telling him I was being followed.

I decided to spend the entire day at Tim's place doing homework and then preparing for my dinner meeting with the *Eleutheria Club*. Chief Ryan had contacted my parents and he had requested to meet with us.

Coincidentally, my physics class required me to read two chapters on satellites and a recent article on satellites and national security. The focus of one of the chapters was developing a space shield to protect us from asteroids, meteors, comets, and harmful space debris that might penetrate our atmosphere. I also spent a couple of hours on our project for General Cumberland, discovering that our existing laser technology had many offensive capabilities but few defensive ones. Thus, despite General Cumberland's description of our project as defensive in nature, I conjectured that we had much work to do to expand the overall capabilities of our satellite-based lasers.

That evening, I was diligent to make sure I was not followed on my way to Dursen Shoes for our meeting. Everyone made it safely. It was the first time that Chief Ryan had joined us since our meeting at my parents' house and he was our first invited police officer ever to join us in our official *Eleutheria Club* meeting place. I did not see any sign of the woman who had followed me as I walked into the shoe store.

Julianna, Christina, and Alan were already there when I arrived. After warm greetings and even warmer hugs, we heard a knock on the door and saw that Darrell and Chief Ryan had arrived at about the same time. Chief Ryan had a serious look on his face and Darrell had his typical happy-go-lucky demeanor as if he did not have a care in the world. It was as if they had come from two completely different worlds. Not long after entering our private clubroom, Alan opened the meeting and asked Chief Ryan to share with us.

Chief Ryan, already an intimidating presence due to his reputation as a former Army Ranger and local hero who nearly lost his life fighting al Qaeda terrorists at the Sears Tower sixteen years ago, stood up. His tall body was still sculpted like a warrior, although his wife's great cooking and a slowing metabolism had added ten pounds. He wasted no time in getting down to business.

"I received information yesterday from two of my close friends working for two different intelligence agencies, one in the U.S. and one in Israel."

Everyone stopped munching on snacks, put down whatever they were drinking, and came to complete attention, focusing on Chief Ryan.

"The U.S. is in imminent danger from a biological attack from China and China fears a biological attack from the United States. The Chinese may not wait to be attacked. They may be poised to launch a preemptive strike unless someone can convince them that the U.S. has no intentions of attacking them."

"Why do they think the U.S. is going to attack them?" Susan asked. "We have no history of launching a first strike."

"What about Iraq?" Chief Ryan asked. "And our first use of atomic bombs in Japan?"

"I concede your point, Chief Ryan. But it's hard to believe the U.S. would ever strike first again with a weapon of mass destruction," Susan said.

"The Chinese don't find it hard to believe; they don't trust us. We allowed the Russians to invade Manchuria during World War II, even though we knew the Russian soldiers would rape and pillage and murder thousands of Chinese citizens in their path, just as the Japanese had done. We just looked the other way because we were pressing the Japanese hard for an unconditional surrender. President Truman and our military leaders wanted Hirohito and all of Japan to fear the threat of a brutal invasion into Japan by Russian troops from the west and American troops from the south and east, so they looked the other way, not holding the Soviets accountable for their policy of Red Terror, which inflicted horrible atrocities on the people of Manchuria."

"That was more than seventy years ago."

"To the Chinese," Darrell explained, "seventy years is like yesterday. They have a very long-term view of history, and they don't think in terms of decades. They think in terms of centuries. If I may continue?" He turned toward Alan and Chief Ryan, who nodded their approval.

"When Christina and I checked in with our friends from *Jùlèbù Fāxiàn* in Taiwan, they told us they also believed a high ranking general in China was saber-rattling about an impending U.S. attack and the need for a preemptive strike against the U.S."

"We have triangulation," I said.

"What do you mean?" Susan asked, turning toward me.

"In the math world in which I live, triangulation is the process of determining the location of a point by forming triangles from known points. In sailing and ship navigation, triangulation is used to chart one's location by mapping the lines and angles to two or more known points that can be seen off in the horizon. But in the social sciences, it is getting information from two or more methodologies to confirm your findings."

"And in the intelligence community, when we have two or more sources of information in agreement," Chief Ryan said, "we have triangulation, which means a high probability that the information is accurate."

"But we still do not know the motivations behind this," Alan said. "It goes back to the first conversation we intercepted between Atlas Churgrill and General Nicoli Sarkovsky. They want to start a major war between China and the U.S."

"Are we sure that an attack would come from space?" Julianna asked, turning toward Chief Ryan. "Aren't satellite-based weapons still in the distant future?"

"Take a look at this recent *Worldwide Threat Assessment Report* published in February of 2018 by the director of national intelligence."

Chief Ryan produced a copy of the report from his briefcase.

"Let me read from page thirteen."

> Both Russia and China continue to pursue antisatellite (ASAT) weapons as a means to reduce U.S. and allied military effectiveness. Russia and China aim to have nondestructive and destructive counterspace weapons available for use during a potential future conflict. We assess that, if a future conflict were to occur involving Russia or China, either country would justify attacks against U.S. and allied satellites as necessary to offset any perceived U.S. military advantage derived from military, civil, or commercial space systems. Military reforms in both countries in the past few years indicate an increased focus on establishing operational forces designed to integrate attacks against space systems and services with military operations in other domains.

"The report confirms what we already know, that our U.S. national intelligence agencies have a growing concern about space-based weapons and have been closely tracking Chinese and Russian satellite activities."

I realized my role in stopping this threat could take center stage.

"The president, the State Department, and Homeland Security think the threat is the biological agent Saxitoxin," continued Chief Ryan. "The CIA and the Defense Department are not sure; they think it is more likely to be a Botulinum toxin. Others fear it's a new biological or chemical agent that we don't know about."

"And what do you think?" Alan asked.

"We already have strong evidence that Botulinum was delivered to the Chinese, so I don't believe it's a new agent. I especially fear Botulinum since it almost killed me in the Sears Tower attack many years ago."

We all sat there in silence for a while. It seemed like a long time but it had probably been only a minute or so when a deafening explosion knocked us all down to the floor.

My hearing immediately went out as did the lights. I was instantly engulfed in blackness and began coughing as thick dust filled the room. I was completely disoriented and trying to get my bearings when I felt someone grabbing my arm and pulling me in the direction of where I remember an escape tunnel existed. I began crouching down low and followed whomever was leading me. I could hear muffled sounds but could not make out the words spoken. I instantly remembered the last time I had experienced this kind of hearing loss. I had been in a men's bathroom in Chicago when someone exploded an M-80 in a urinal. I was washing my hands at the sink. The hearing loss frightened me.

Whoever was pulling my arm did not let go. I felt myself stepping over debris on the floor, which I could not see because of the thick dust and loss of electricity. When we reached the tunnel, I tripped over something, felt my head slamming into the ground, and then lost consciousness.

CHAPTER 13

"JOHANN, WAKE UP; JOHANN, WE have to go."

I opened my eyes and looked into Julianna's face and said, "I'm okay," although I could not hear myself clearly.

"Can you hear me, Julianna?"

"Yes, but I have a substantial loss of hearing. What matters right now is getting out of this tunnel to safety." I could barely understand, but at least my hearing was returning.

"How are the others?" I asked.

"Everyone survived with slight injuries and is ahead of us except Chief Ryan, who is right behind me. He wanted to make sure everyone was out before him."

As I looked back, I saw Chief Ryan scramble up close behind Julianna. He had seen me fall and had a look of deep concern on his face.

"That looked like a strong smack on the side of the head," he said, inspecting my scalp. "I can't believe there is no bleeding."

"Just a mild concussion, Chief, I guess some brain cells just bit the dust."

"Fortunately, you have plenty to spare; now if that had been me, I would be in serious trouble." He smiled at me, looked around at the others, and asked, "Does anyone need help getting out of here?

He waited until everyone responded with a *no*.

"You guys look like tunnel rats," Chief Ryan said, smiling a second time.

"I hope we have a greater life expectancy," Darrell said.

"Me, too," Chief Ryan said, "let's get out of here."

Alan was the first one out of the tunnel, which fed into an underground cavern that was part of the city's old drainage system. The city had replaced the old system of tunnels with a new deep tunnel system, a massive $3.6 billion project that was the largest public works project in Chicago's history. The city had laid 130 miles of new tunnel, boring into rock 150 to 350 feet below the surface.

I noticed some blood on my hands as I emerged into the cavern, which had some light coming in through grated openings that reached the street level. I was still somewhat in a daze as we followed the cavern into an older drainage system that led us into an overflow drainage outlet in the North Branch of the Chicago River. It seemed like we were walking on our hands and knees for a couple of hours. Alan kicked the grate open when we reached the end of the outlet, which opened into a heavily wooded area along the river, well-concealed from the public.

When we crawled out of the old drainage pipe, I could see how ravaged we all were. Alan's face was completely covered with dust, and blood was dripping down his right arm. Julianna's white blouse was covered with dirt and blood; her hair was severely matted and both of her knees were bleeding through her white pants. Christina looked like a zombie from *The Walking Dead*, with all kinds of cuts and gashes on her face and hands. Susan and Darrell looked like they had fared best, until Darrell showed me the piece of glass embedded into his right thigh. He needed that glass removed as soon as possible.

Chief Ryan, who was behind me the whole way, was closest to the door through which the blast wave came through. He had a sizable welt on the right side of his head where the door had hit him after being blown off its hinges. Other than a few bruises, minor cuts, and some pain in his neck, he was in good shape. My head ached, my knees were sore, and my ears hurt, but I was thankful to be alive. We all realized how fortunate we were that none of us were seriously injured. We sat silently on the riverbank in the heavy brush while the realization was sinking in that someone had tried to kill all of us. After a couple of minutes of contemplation, Chief Ryan gathered our focused attention.

"Listen carefully, everyone. I do not want to ask this, but it is critically important. Is everyone sure that you were not followed tonight? We do not know what caused this explosion. It could have been a natural gas leak. It could have been a truck carrying explosive material. It could have been a bomb planted inside. The answer to this question determines our future course of action."

As I thought about my journey to our meeting, I watched everyone replay their own journeys to the shoe store in their heads. No one had any suspicion that they had been followed. Alan then turned to Chief Ryan, and asked hesitantly, "Chief Ryan, did any other person know that you were coming here tonight?" Chief Ryan thought carefully and then replied, "Yes, my secretary knew. I called her before coming here to check in on activities in the office. She asked me where I was and I told her that I was on my way here. But I don't know why she would tell anyone else."

"Unless someone called her and asked where you were?" Julianna said.

"I'll find out."

Chief Ryan then rallied us to get up and suggested we make our way to a hospital outside of the city to make sure we were okay. However, we could not be sure that the culprit might realize that we escaped when no bodies would be pulled out of the rubble by the rescue teams combing the blast site. Would they come after us in a hospital? We all thought, yes, they would. Everyone went back to their homes, too afraid to go to a hospital, with the exception of Darrell. I took him to his primary care physician, who removed the piece of glass and gave him stitches in his leg. He came back to my house with me. My mom was away and my dad at work. We cleaned up, put on Neosporin and bandages over our smaller cuts and scrapes, and quietly slipped into bed early, leaving a note for my dad on the kitchen table.

I laid awake on my bed, exhausted but trying to make sense of the frenetic events and unexpected storm that had engulfed me during my first semester at the University of Chicago. My recurring nightmare of someone trying to kill me was becoming true. Miraculously, no one had been killed. Besides Darrell, only Chief Ryan had a serious enough injury requiring a doctor. He had a piece of wood removed from the back of his neck where he had felt pain after the blast, but fortunately it was a minor wound. I drifted off to sleep.

My dad awoke me abruptly at about 3:15 a.m. "We've got to leave now," he said. "Darrell is already up. Get dressed, quickly pack some clothes, toiletries, your phone charger, laptop, and what you need to live on for a week in your backpack. We are going to leave in five minutes."

Chief Ryan was out front waiting for us in his Range Rover. He had called my dad earlier and told him we were all in danger. I was glad my mom was out-of-state at a women's conference; this would have freaked her out. Immediately after Dad, Darrell, and I climbed into Chief Ryan's vehicle and he'd started to drive, we heard a helicopter from afar flying toward our neighborhood. Chief Ryan cut the lights and turned down a country road that took us out of town. The sound of the helicopter remained in our neighborhood as we sped away in the dark. About three miles outside of town, Chief Ryan pulled off the road onto a small dirt path and put on his low beams. I saw an old barn ahead. When we pulled up to it, Chief Ryan jumped out with haste and unlocked the door. He kept the low beams on as he drove the Rover into the barn. Then we all heard it—the chopper was heading our way. Chief Ryan turned off the lights and turned off the car as my dad and I jumped out to close the barn door. It was completely closed by the time we heard the chopper coming down the road. As we waited in darkness, we could see flashes of a large search beam panning the countryside. Our hearts were pounding as the chopper seemed to hover in place not far from our location. *Were they friends or enemies? Had they come for us? Had they seen the dust we had stirred up? Had they seen the lights?* The chopper circled back around, heading back the way it had come, back toward town.

Chief Ryan whispered, "We need to get out of here soon, but not until they stop searching for us." I could discern in his voice his ambivalence about who these people were.

I asked, "Who do you think they were?"

"I suspect either CIA operatives or special forces."

"So, we are running from them?"

"We are avoiding them because we don't know what their intentions are and there could be people in our security forces who are compromised or even rogue forces at work. They also could be loyal patriots who have been told that we are the bad guys that need to be stopped."

That was the last thing I wanted to hear.

"So, we can't trust anybody?"

"We can trust each other and we can trust our good friends who we know love us and would lay their lives down for us."

"Don't be dismayed," my dad said. "If God is with us then it doesn't matter who is against us. We will be protected."

"It seems that everyone is against us, Dad."

Before I could say more, Chief Ryan put his hand over my mouth. We all heard a car traveling fast down the road. Just as we had feared, it turned down the dirt road and was heading toward the barn. We could hear it but could not see any lights. Instead of pulling up to the barn door, the vehicle pulled behind the barn and stopped. We heard two car doors open. At least two people had found us. The four of us started looking for places to hide in the small barn.

All of us dived behind bales of hay that lied close by. *Sometimes our instincts fail at the most critical moments,* I thought, realizing hay bales offered no protection from bullets. We heard a gentle knocking on the back door of the barn and heard the soft voices of two women.

Chief Ryan jumped up, knowing that no commando force would be knocking on the door. Darrell followed close behind. Chief Ryan unlocked the door and opened it, relieved to see Julianna and Susan standing in the moonlight with sheepish grins.

"How did you track us down?" Darrell whispered.

"It wasn't hard once we broke into the tracking device on your Range Rover," Susan answered as they turned toward Chief Ryan.

"The helicopter was tracking my car," Chief Ryan said, realizing what was happening.

"As soon as we got your coordinates, we electronically disabled the device which is probably on your car," Susan said. "Or else that helicopter surely would have found you."

"I had my car detailed just a few days ago. Someone put a tracking device on it and must have tracked me to Dursen Shoes. I am so sorry, I almost got us all killed."

"I know we are all exhausted," Julianna said, "but we need to watch the Nasdaq today. It could be a big day."

"We might as well stay here. This barn and the house nearby belong to my grandparents who are overseas for a month. That's why I drove here. There are plenty of beds and three full bathrooms, so we can all get some hot showers and get some rest. The Nasdaq doesn't open until 9:30 a.m., so let's get some sleep."

We all were awakened by the smell of bacon. Chief Ryan was cooking up a big breakfast of bacon, eggs, and waffles. We were just finishing breakfast when Julianna began setting up her laptop to follow a certain stock on the Nasdaq, EBS. She turned the TV onto CNBC's *Squawk on the Street*.

The stock exchanges would be opening with great uncertainty for the day, according to the early market watch analysts from CNBC. It was the last Monday of October following a volatile week, and traders were hoping things would calm down, but worried about more sell-off. The Fed's decision the previous week to increase interest rates a full percentage point to head off inflation had sent the markets into a tizzy. The market had large fluctuations, with the DOW dropping briefly below 28,000 before bouncing up to 28,007 before the closing bell on Friday. The Nasdaq followed in suit, dipping below 8000. Everyone was holding their breath to see if Monday would bring more downside.

I received an unexpected call from Angela. She told me her brother Angelo had contacts in South Africa who had put surveillance cameras in the home of Churgrill's chief financial officer, Ethan Krugar, in Hout Bay, Cape Town.

I did not understand the value of what she was saying.

She repeated herself, explaining that one of her brothers worked in counterterrorism in Italy. He had been tracking Churgrill for months.

"Why didn't you tell me earlier?"

"I couldn't," Angela said. "My brother had to find out who you are first and then check out all the members of the *Eleutheria Club*. Chief Ryan gave him assurances."

I had many more questions for Angela, including how her brother knew Chief Ryan, but the markets were opening in minutes.

"I'm watching Krugar now on my laptop on a live feed from my brother," Angela said. "He's on his computer and is closely following a financial network on television."

"Stay on the phone Angela and tell us what's going on. I'll put you on speaker."

"Got it," Angela said. "Krugar has two computer monitors. One is on some kind of trading site and the other is showing the price of EBS on a graph."

The financial commentators on Bloomberg expected a five to six percent market drop. The sell-off began immediately and gained momentum quickly. By 9:45 a.m. EST, the DOW had dropped 467 points; by 10:30, it had dropped to 27,540. The Nasdaq dropped more than 150 points. The graph on EBS showed the stock had dropped to $52.27 per share, still well above its fifty-two-week low.

Krugar picked up his cell and made a call.

We could not hear the other party on the call.

"Yes. Are they shutting it down?" Krugar asked.

After a long period of silence, Krugar said, "Okay, if EBS hits $52, then buy if it creeps up from there. If it keeps dropping, wait till it hits $50. If it doesn't drop to $50, then buy if it reverses upward."

More silence.

"Yes, buy the float," Krugar said, "which should be 3.7 million shares. I transferred $200 million into the account which will cover up to $54 per share. Call me when it's done."

Krugar ended the call.

"I have to go, Johann," Angela said. "I'll call you back in ten minutes."

As soon as Angela ended our call, Julianna filled in the missing pieces to help us understand what was happening.

"EBS dropped to $50.07 per share," she said. "Then it shot back up to $51.75 and rapidly climbed to $62.00 per share."

"Somebody purchased a lot of shares of EBS," Julianna said.

"Churgrill," Chief Ryan said.

We all understood what had just happened but waited for confirmation from Angela's brother.

Angela called. "It's done. Churgrill's CFO bought 3.7 million shares of EBS for $50.07 per share. He's now the major shareholder of EBS."

CHAPTER 14

THE LAST TWO MONTHS OF my fall semester were a blur of activity. The false news stories and coroner's report that Chief Ryan orchestrated indicating seven people had been killed in an accidental gas explosion at Dursen Shoes while playing cards in the basement had temporarily taken the heat off of us. We created a new *Eleutheria Club* meeting place in Downers Grove under the watchful eye of Chief Ryan, but our surveillance capabilities were greatly reduced while we carefully rebuilt our network. I did my schoolwork and lab work as we waited to see how I could be helpful. I was so exhausted and sick by finals week in mid-December, I feared I would need to be hospitalized for an unrelenting bronchial infection. I could not stop coughing regardless of what medicines I tried.

Despite my condition, I helped my team in physics solve the problem we had been given to prevent a comet's catastrophic collision with Earth within budget and within the time frame specified. That project was worth half our grade and Dr. Schroeder jubilantly gave all of us A's on the project, explaining that we were the first class to completely solve the problem he presented at the beginning of the semester. The fall semester was soon ending, and I found out I was receiving two A's and two A-minuses for my final course grades in four of my classes. My final grade for PHSC 12600, however, was not posted. I received an email from Dr. Schroeder, who had become my favorite professor, to come see him in his office.

I knocked on the door quietly, wishing that I did not have to meet with Dr. Schroeder to hear what I presumed must be bad news about my final exam score.

"Come in," a jovial Dr. Schroeder said. "Have a seat."

I looked around the office and was captivated by the many brilliant photographs of new galaxies that had been discovered in the past thirty years.

"Johann, I called you in for good news, so relax. You received a one hundred percent average in PHSC 12600, a perfect score. That has never happened before and I have been teaching this course for twenty-four years. Congratulations."

"I have absolutely loved this class and feel like I have learned so much from you."

"I asked a close friend to send you an invitation. It is a surprise, but it will come soon," he said.

I entered the office fearful; I left it elated.

Two days later the invitation that Chief Ryan had orchestrated arrived in the form of an overnight letter delivered by FedEx.

I opened it and read quickly, registering the words, "I would be delighted if you could visit me next week during your winter break at the Keck Observatory in Hawaii. Dr. Keppler and I will cover all your expenses for you and a companion to travel with you."

The invitation was from Dr. David Bolen, a distinguished professor at the University of Hawaii's Institute for Astronomy and close friend of both Dr. Schroeder and Dr. Keppler. Dr. Bolen was working at the Keck Observatory tracking the DR_{34} asteroid that would be passing relatively close to Earth (about 166,000 miles) on February 25.

Fortuitously, Darrell had found out from his Taiwanese friends that there was another reason for an additional member of the *Eleutheria Club* to come along, too. So, with approval from Dr. Bolen, I asked Darrell to join me on the trip.

Recovering from bronchitis, I thought the eighty-degree Hawaiian sunshine was just the kind of break I needed. Darrell and I flew into the Kona airport on December 17 in early afternoon, picked up our four-wheel drive Jeep at National car rental, and traveled to the Hilton Waikoloa Resort. Our $350 per night room was the result of an act of generosity by Professor Keppler, who had many points built up in his Hilton Honors account. He wanted us to have a good rest after two long plane rides and a long layover at LAX.

Before leaving Waikoloa, we made good use of our morning planning session watching whales from our beach lounges just off the western shore. We retreated to a quiet area of the shallow lagoon adjacent to the waterfalls and the dolphin sanctuary. As we watched the dolphins glide effortlessly through the water, I was amazed at their extraordinary navigation abilities. They could turn on and off their echolocation system, which makes them supreme hunters, when they don't need it, giving their brains a rest. They also must have liked Waikoloa where they needed only half a brain to live. It seemed ludicrous to me to believe that their perfect design for ocean living was a result of millions of years of evolution, since we were using all the brain power we could muster to design navigation systems in space that were not as good as the natural systems of dolphins. Their advanced surveillance system had to be by brilliant design, not by blind chance.

Darrell looked refreshed relaxing by the pool, and I felt rested for the first time in months. I felt fairly confident that no one was following us or planning to blow us up on the Big Island. Focusing around me, I forgot the desperate situation we were in. Children were swimming and following large tortoises in the lagoon, vacationers were sitting in beach chairs in the sand soaking up the sun, engrossed in their novels. Others sat up in their chairs, taking in the whole scene. They didn't have to look too far. Even the few normally glued to their cell phones seemed to limit their technology addictions and engage in lively conversations with strangers around them who had converged at this paradise cove from different states and different regions of the world.

As for me, I was enjoying a few moments of tranquility, like one of the teenagers on the paddleboards riding confidently through the shallow lagoon, knowing there were no waves that could disrupt his enjoyment. I began to think about my last camping trip with my parents to Yosemite Valley, but my quiet reflections were abruptly interrupted by Darrell's reminder that we needed to get going soon. My expression must have changed immediately.

"Don't worry, Johann, we are going to figure this thing out."

I loved Darrell for that. He was always positive, even in the bleakest situation.

"I'm just thinking of all these innocent children and families who are carefree and happy and the horror that would be unleashed from a biological attack," I said.

"I know."

"How did we get here, Darrell? Did God put us in this position or is this some kind of cosmic destiny that we cannot control or stop?"

"Maybe a little of both," he said.

"I wanted to be a hero on the baseball field growing up. I have no idea how to be a real hero."

"Just be yourself, Johann. You are not God, so it doesn't depend on you, or on me; we just need to do our part."

"But how could God allow such devastation? What if we fail?"

"God has a lot more resources than just us."

"He better."

Darrell's last statement helped me to relax a bit. I knew not everyone was motivated by money, greed, and power. I had seen too much real love and good will in the world.

While relaxed, I dosed off.

When I awoke, Darrell was working on his laptop computer.

"Are you ready to work after your long nap?"

"How long was I sleeping?"

"About an hour."

"Yeah, I'm ready, and thanks for listening; I just needed some emotional release."

"While you were off sleeping in la-la land, I received some updated information from my friends in Taiwan."

"So, what's the news from your friends?"

"They recovered encrypted communication from a military ship docked at the Tiaoyutai Islands. They confirmed that one of the military IT specialists on the ship was corresponding with Huang Tai Simonnes, a University of Hawaii graduate student."

"This doesn't confirm Chief Ryan's suspicion that he is a spy, does it?"

"Not necessarily. He is a real student working on his Ph.D. in Astronomy, and his contact could be a friend or relative. But it doesn't look good."

"You mean he could be a graduate student also working for the CCP?"

"Yes, China has planted Ph.D. students all over the world who are working for the government. Some of their best computer minds are active hackers exploiting vulnerable data bases."

"So, what is our goal with Huang Tai Simonnes?"

"What we need to do is befriend him and earn his trust. Then, to find out if he is spying on us."

"And if he is?"

"Then we try and change his mind by letting him know the stakes and appealing to his conscience."

"And if he has no conscience?" I asked, not wanting to know the answer.

"Then we'll help him to develop one," Darrell said.

"Hopefully."

Darrell's friends in Taiwan had uncovered his background. *Huang Tai* was his given name but Simonnes was his adoptive name. His parents had been missionaries in Shanghai and adopted him at two months old from an orphanage, but he grew up in southern California. His biological mother was battling breast cancer when his father died in a construction accident, so she gave her baby up for adoption. Although his mother had a younger brother, he was working with the Chinese military in rural Tanzania and she could not reach him. His mother died a week after she brought him to the orphanage. She saw her son as a bright star in the sky, so she named him Huang Tai, meaning very bright, shiny and luminous.

Andreas and Anniken Simonnes, the Norwegian missionary couple who ran the orphanage, knew the mother and her dire situation. They decided to adopt Huang Tai. The process took a couple months, but they had him from one-week old, They later immigrated to California with Huang Tai.

Darrell's friends explained that Huang Tai's adoptive parents were able to contact Huang Tai's uncle in China after they had returned to California. After Huang Tai and his uncle corresponded by letter for ten years, his uncle invited him to return to China to pursue his college education. Huang Tai, obsessed with finding out more about his cultural roots, returned to China supposedly at age sixteen—although we think he was younger—to live with his uncle and attend Peking University in Beijing. By that time his uncle was already a high ranking military general.

"Do you think we can work with him?" I asked.

"His uncle is a real patriot who loves China. He has advocated for peace throughout his storied career. Huang Tai adores his uncle and knows the U.S. is not evil. He very much loves his adoptive parents who are still in close touch with him. Also, we don't even know for sure if he is a Chinese agent."

"How old is he?"

"His passport claims he's twenty-one, but he looks much younger. He's probably just a kid like you."

I smiled and felt better about the whole thing.

"Let's review our plan."

Darrell took out his notepad.

"Huang Tai is working at the Keck Observatory forty hours a week on a funded astronomy project to measure the spectral distortions of space debris, which affects our ability to locate exact positions of objects in space. He is a brilliant mathematician, a child prodigy. He is now working on math equations that predict how to adjust navigation systems based on the density of space debris and other penetrating objects such as fragments from meteors, comets, asteroids, and the like. He also has knowledge of space lasers and has studied the effects of space debris on laser-guided objects."

"That sounds like some of the work we are doing at the University of Chicago."

"That's our common ground, Johann. You know Huang Tai's professional language and passion; I know his Chinese language and culture. Together we can form a strong connection with him."

"In one week? Is that long enough?"

"Any longer and he may get suspicious. It will need to be long enough."

Just as we finished our conversation, a strange man walked up to us. He was not dressed in pool attire. He looked like an armed security agent.

"May I have a word with you?" he asked, looking at both of us. "In private?"

The three of us walked to a quiet secluded area away from the pool and began to chat.

"I'm agent Michael Brown," the man in his mid-twenties said, "and I have been assigned to you by the Joint Terrorism Task Force to watch your back. Chief Joshua Ryan sends his warm greetings."

"Do you understand what we are doing here?" Darrell asked.

"Yes, I have been briefed; I will be close by, but you will not see me."

"Thank you, Agent Brown," I said. "We can use all the help we can get."

"I want to put a tracking device on each of you. It is undetectable so your friends at the Keck Observatory will not be aware of it." Agent Brown then gave us each a wristwatch.

Darrell and I decided to leave Waikoloa that same morning with an hour to spend whale-watching on the western shore. We found two empty lounge chairs under a small grove of palm trees growing adjacent to the shore lined with jagged lava rocks. As we scanned the ocean with our binoculars, we spotted two whales less than half a mile offshore. They seemed to jump out of the water and shoot their waterspouts in unison, like synchronized swimmers. We watched them for twenty minutes as a mongoose scampered across the walkway in front of us and birds ate sunflower seeds strewn around our lounges.

There was a gentle wind this morning and a light surf. The warm temperature and slightly veiled sunlight through thin clouds made a perfect morning. I was reluctant to leave the scene and venture towards the cold barren slopes of Mauna Kea.

I began to completely let go of my apprehensions as we climbed the road to Mauna Kea. It was lined with miles and miles of lava rock, mostly broken into large chunks, with groves of short rugged trees and bushes interspersed, growing out of the lava. I could understand why NASA once considered the slopes of Mauna Kea as a training ground for the moon landing.

When we reached the summit, we drove past nearly half a dozen observatories. We saw the sign for the Keck Observatory and turned off the main road onto Mauna Kea Access Road. A short distance down the road, after passing the Subaru Telescope on the right, we observed the twin shells covering the two telescopes. We parked adjacent to the main building in a partially concealed area. Dr. David

Bolen, the University of Hawaii astronomy professor, was there to meet us.

Dr. Bolen immediately took us into his office where Huang Tai was waiting for us for an orientation meeting. We introduced ourselves and Huang Tai grasped my hand eagerly as I offered my handshake. He leaned forward and said, "I would like to make some American friends."

I immediately spoke without thinking, "I would like to be your friend."

Dr. Bolen looked pleased, and said to me and Darrell, "You will have access to one of the most powerful means of exploration on Earth. The telescopes must be treated with extreme care and respect. There is nothing comparable to these telescopes. Thus, we check everything we are doing not twice, but three times. Mistakes can be costly.

"Your access will be limited and controlled," Dr. Bolen continued, "as we have thirty-two researchers using them on seventeen current projects. Some of the greatest astronomical discoveries in the world have been made through these telescopes, including the research that declassified Pluto as the ninth planet in our solar system."

Huang Tai and Darrell chatted in Mandarin while Dr. Bolen and I became acquainted. He knew my work in Chicago and seemed to know many of my professors as friends. I could see Dr. Bolen's passion for astronomy. I doubted that he knew our real intentions for being there.

As we collected data together, Huang Tai warmed up to us. He asked us a lot about various NBA players he followed, like soliciting our opinion about whether or not Lebron James would bring another championship to the L.A. Lakers. He shared with us his great love

for Kobe Bryant, telling us he cried when he retired in 2016 and then
again when he died in the helicopter crash. He also loved American
films, especially fantasy adventures like the *Lord of the Rings* trilogy.

Near the end of the week, Huang Tai invited us to his small apartment for dinner. He lived on the western outskirts of Hilo off of
Saddle Road, about a fifty-minute drive from the Keck Observatory.
We brought food with us to help cook, as Darrell had worked in his
parents' restaurant for three years in California and was handy in
the kitchen. We were surprised to learn that Huang Tai had also
worked in a Chinese restaurant for a couple years as a teenager in
Chino Hills.

We had a sumptuous meal of Shanghai chicken and rice, stir-fried
vegetables, and Tom Kha Gai. Huang Tai was pleased as it reminded
him of his days back in Chino Hills. After the meal we shared some
drinks, and Huang Tai's reserve gave way to his desire for friendship.

Darrell took the leap of faith and told Huang Tai there were
forces in our nation, and likely in his nation, too, that were moving
our two countries toward a military conflict.

Huang Tai responded by stating that this was common knowledge. He shared how his uncle, who had now advanced to the rank of
a three-star general in the People's Liberation Army, had briefed him
of such threats.

"We are greatly concerned about this," Darrell said. "Would you
be surprised to learn that some evil men want to start a space war
between China and the U.S. to satisfy their own greed?"

We both noticed that Huang Tai flinched and seemed disturbed
by the question.

"Our governments will stop such attempts," he said.

Darrell pressed on. We were now fully committed to a risky conversation.

"But what if our governments were deceived? What if they were being fed lies against each other?"

"Then such evil men must be stopped at all costs," he said.

I took the full plunge.

"Huang Tai," I said. I gave him direct eye contact. "We are both blessed with great gifts. We both have had a love and aptitude for science from a very young age. We both love our countries. We both have adoptive parents whom we love and who are proud of us. We need to work together as friends to prevent evil men from pushing our countries into war. We know you may be a government agent, but that is not our concern as we understand your loyalty to China, your birthplace. We have knowledge of an evil plot against our countries and we need your help to stop it."

Huang Tai sat up in his chair and was clearly alarmed. He thought intensely and looked down for a couple of minutes. He then looked up and said, "I will help you stop such evil men, but I must tell my uncle."

We had expected this.

"We ask that you and your uncle will protect our identities," Darrell said.

"You have my word."

Huang Tai was deep in thought. I imagined he was trying to make sense of things.

"I was told you both were government agents," he said.

"We are not working for the government." Darrell paused. "We are private citizens that are helping individuals within our government to stop this plot."

"Can you share with us who you are working for? We will not give anyone this information, but we need to know so we can establish trust with each other."

Huang Tai then shared with us for the next half an hour how he had been recruited into a twelve-month cyber-security program and then sent to the University of Hawaii with government support. He didn't know much about the agency he was working for; he knew the cyber-security unit was overseen by the Ministry of State Security. Even his uncle did not know much about the inner workings of this secretive intelligence agency. His uncle did know the director of the cyber-security group Huang Tai was working under, but he believed that he was a man of integrity who would not risk the life of Huang Tai needlessly.

Huang Tai then looked us both in the eyes and whispered, "Our friendship cannot be known."

"Liǎojiě [Understood]," Darrell responded in Mandarin. "Our lives are now in your uncle's hand."

"My uncle is a good man, a trustworthy man. I will tell him you are my friends and he will protect your identity. He is a man of his word."

"It's late," I said. "We should go."

"Why not sleep here tonight? I have a couple of comfortable futons, and plenty of hot water for showers."

"Thanks Huang Tai," Darrell replied. "We accept. I hate driving in the dark, especially in strange places."

———————————

The next morning, we left Huang Tai's apartment early and drove back up the mountain. About ten minutes after we turned onto

Mauna Kea access road, we all heard the unmistakable sound of a helicopter approaching from the rear.

"That's strange," Huang Tai commented, "helicopters are rarely allowed to fly up here. This is restricted airspace."

A hail of bullets hit the dirt road immediately in front of our Jeep. Darrell instinctively swerved off the road, which prevented us from being hit. As the chopper circled back around, Darrell gunned the four-wheel drive toward a large road grader sitting off to the side of the road that might offer some protection. We exited the car as quickly as possible and dived under the road grader just as another round of bullets began hitting the dirt close to us. We buried our faces in the dirt and covered our heads with our hands, praying we would survive. Then we heard two rifle shots coming from behind us. Someone was shooting back.

CHAPTER 15

AS WE CRINGED IN FEAR, we heard the helicopter engine sputter. We looked up and saw smoke coming from its engine. The chopper plummeted toward the ground as it disappeared over a hillside. We heard an explosion and saw a plume of smoke rising from where the helicopter had crashed. Darrell and I both deduced where the bullets had come from—Agent Brown. We did not see him or any other vehicles on the road.

"What happened?" Huang Tai asked in a semi-state of shock. "Were they trying to kill us?"

"They were trying to kill me and Darrell. They have tried before."

"Who is trying to kill you?"

"We don't know," Darrell said. "We only know that they are evil people involved in a plot to push our countries into war."

"I heard rifle shots. Did they bring down the helicopter?"

"Yes," Darrell replied, "good people did that; one very good person."

We checked our Jeep; the spare tire in the back had been hit by a couple of bullets and was flat. The back bumper also had taken some bullets. Then we noticed several bullets had penetrated the inside through the doors of the Jeep. We would have been shot if we had stayed inside.

We received a call from the Keck Observatory.

"I heard an explosion, Darrell, what happened?" Dr. Bolen asked.

"I think they had to move a large boulder to fix the road. It was no big deal—just a little gunpowder, I guess, but it has delayed us."

Dr. Bolen seemed to be satisfied. We were still rattled.

When we reached the Keck Observatory, we all did our best to act as if nothing had happened. We dropped off Huang Tai, gathered our belongings, and said our good-byes to Dr. Bolen and his staff. Huang Tai walked us out to our car.

"You can trust my uncle. I will talk with him tonight."

"Cell phone conversations can be monitored and recorded by the NSA," Darrell said. "Are you going to use Skype?"

"No," Huang Tai explained, "I have access to a virtual private network online that is out of the reach of the NSA and other government agencies. It is a secure network out of China that provides videoconferencing. It will be safe."

"Remember what I told you," I reminded Huang Tai. "Tell your uncle that you have placed your life in our hands, and we are now placing our lives in his hands."

"I will; he will guard your lives and protect you with his own, just as he has protected me all these years."

"If your uncle agrees, I will arrange for you to receive an invitation from the Kavli Institute for Cosmological Physics to conduct research with us. We can work together to stop this threat."

"I would love to come and work with you, Johann. We will be in touch soon."

Darrell and I drove back down the mountain toward Kona, deep in thought and not saying much. I knew we were both thinking about whether we were doing the right thing. We took a great risk in trusting Huang Tai, but he also took a great risk in trusting us. Had we compromised ourselves? Had we put our friends at risk? What if Huang Tai's uncle would not protect us? We didn't even know his uncle's identity. Neither of us verbalized these unanswerable questions, but I could feel their presence during the quiet ride from Mauna Kea.

I broke the silence.

"We have to tell our friends."

"I know, as soon as we debrief Chief Ryan. But we have to protect Huang Tai and we cannot reveal that he has an uncle in the Chinese military, except to Chief Ryan. We don't know anything about his uncle, not even his name."

"I've been thinking about that, too. But I understand why Huang Tai cannot reveal his identity."

"You know without Agent Brown we might be dead."

"I've also been thinking about that. Are there any more assassins coming after us?"

Within a few seconds of my question, we heard another helicopter heading up the mountain coming toward us. I could see the fear in Darrell's eyes as he looked around for cover. There was nowhere to go for safety. We were out in the open. I closed my eyes and thought to myself, *maybe it ends here right now.*

The chopper had closed to within 300 yards from us; I could see the pilot and it appeared to be a police helicopter. Darrell pivoted our car enough for us to see the big white lettering on the side of the fuselage. We both blurted out loud at the same time, "Police!" The Kona police department had dispatched a helicopter from the Kona airport to check out the reports of a helicopter crash and explosion on Mauna Kea. I waved to the pilot in great relief and I looked over at Darrell who was perspiring profusely.

"I know, we have to resist paranoia," he said.

"I thought we were going to die, so I am worse off than you."

"Let's go into Kona, get a nice table near the water at the Royal Kona Resort Hotel, and have a couple of drinks and a nice meal. We can talk more about going to the Diaoyu Islands."

We made our way to the bar near our Kona hotel and Darrell ordered both our Virgin Royal Hawaiians.

"Tell me more about your friend John and how he can help us."

"He teaches script and screenwriting at the University of the Nations Kona campus and travels all over. He knows a lot about the Diaoyu Islands because two years ago he visited these islands while scouting shooting locations for a film he was working on. We have a few hours to hang out at the beach. We can go snorkeling in Kahaluu Beach Park and we'll ask John to join us for dinner."

The Kona weather was perfect and it was a calm day for snorkeling.

We arrived during happy hour at Bubba Gump Shrimp Co. and managed to get a table with a great ocean-view close to the water.

John Fraser arrived a few minutes later, dressed casually in a tank top, shorts, and sandals. His 6-foot 3-inch 185-lb frame was well-defined, giving him a muscular athletic appearance. Although he was lean, he was not lanky. His auburn hair was shoulder length, clean, and glistening in the sun. Both arms sported colorful pictures, created by talented tattoo artists.

He gave Darrell a big warm hug before greeting me.

"John, I want you to meet Johann, a very close friend. We have gotten into much trouble together."

"Those are some of the best friendships," John replied as he gave me a firm handshake. "Any friend of Darrell's is a friend of mine; I hope I can be of assistance."

"Thanks."

"So, you want to go to the Diaoyu Islands? That's a tough journey."

"We don't want to go as much as we need to go," I replied.

"Don't expect to get a visa from China. You do realize how dangerous it is now?"

"But you went," Darrell said.

"Yes, I went two years ago when the Chinese were just exploring the island. They gave me permission to scout out the island as a shooting location as long as I showed them each night all the film I shot each day and then produced a copy for them."

"How many days were you there?"

"A short time—just three days and two nights. They are pretty small islands. We visited four of them during our scouting trip."

"And how did your filming go?"

"It took us six months to secure our funding, and during that time, things changed and we were denied access to the islands."

"So, they initially said yes, and then later said no?" Darrell asked.

"Yeah, we were disappointed. But they did direct us to some other islands nearby that we did end up using for our film. The Chinese general in charge of the islands was very helpful to us."

"Do you remember his name?"

"Oh yes; it would be hard to forget. General Bingwen Tso. Yes, as in General Tso's chicken—the same spelling."

"What was he like?"

"All business and driven, like a man on a mission."

"But you said they were nice to you?"

"They were respectful, maybe because I'm a filmmaker," John explained. "The soldiers shared many meals with us. Several of them could speak English and they loved to talk with us about the NBA and the NFL and the president. We were surprised to find out that they liked Trump, since he had taken such a strong stand against China in trade and what they were doing in the islands. I think they liked his bravado, but you could tell they feared displeasing General Tso."

"And how did General Tso treat you?" I asked.

"Very cordial and proper. He provided his assistance whenever we needed logistical support and he made sure we were comfortable. I would not say he was friendly, but he was helpful. When we contacted him six months later, he did apologize that he had to inform us that using the islands for our film was no longer possible. Then he helped us to find an alternative filming location. He seemed to care about our movie and he asked us a lot of questions about our digital film cameras and their capabilities. I kind of liked him, despite his dark side."

"Dark side?" I asked.

"I cannot put my finger on it, but I saw it several times in his eyes, a kind of steely determination and distance. Several times I felt as if he was looking through me and it made me very uncomfortable. I felt that he harbored some dark secrets."

"That's what we are afraid of. And that's why we need to go. We have information indicating they are planning a rocket launch next week."

"How will you be able to do that without an invitation? It's heavily guarded."

"We are hoping you can help us John."

"Do you know how to dive?"

"Yes, we are both certified," I replied.

"Then I think there is a place where you could swim ashore undetected underwater," John said, as he pulled a map out of his back pocket.

John then spread the map out on the table and showed us the small cove hidden by rocky cliffs where he thought we could swim ashore.

Darrell and I both nodded. "It's a perfect spot," Darrell said.

"Indeed, it is. We were going to film a scene there. Because I saw it as an obvious security risk, I never showed it to General Tso. It was an original part of the island whereas most of the island is flat. But you can't get caught," John warned with a more somber tone, "I would not mess with General Tso."

"Will you come with us?" Darrell asked.

"I'm married now with children. I don't know. I'll have to talk to my wife."

After finishing dinner and saying our good-byes for the evening, we left the restaurant and made our way to the beachfront area nearby where we could talk.

"We need Agent Brown to come with us," Darrell concluded as we walked along the beach.

"We also need John Fraser," I concluded. "He knows the landing spot and he knows how to work cameras."

"I was thinking the same thing, Johann. Four of us in a dinghy with diving and camera equipment, I think we could manage it. We just need a watertight canister to protect the digital film camera equipment underwater."

"Now let's pray that Agent Brown and John both say yes," I said.

Just as we concluded our conversation, a stranger dressed in dark clothing and wearing a hat approached us on the beach. As he came closer to us, we were relieved to recognize it was Agent Brown.

"I need to get you out of here immediately," Brown said. "Follow me now and keep your heads down."

CHAPTER 16

AGENT BROWN LED US ALONG the beach and then under a dock where he untied a small dinghy hidden under the dock by a piece of black tarp. We climbed in and slowly motored away from shore in the dark as quietly as possible.

"Just stay down low and don't talk. I'll explain later."

After thirty minutes of slow travel away from land, the surf significantly increased and waves began to break over our dinghy, soaking us all with sea water. Darrell and I began to fear being capsized but Brown reassured us that the dinghy would safely take us to our rendezvous point.

"There it is," he shouted over the waves.

We looked up and could see the outline of a small yacht. As it came into full view, it looked to be forty to fifty feet long. We circled around to the back of the boat where there were boarding areas close to the water.

After climbing aboard, Darrell turned to Agent Brown and asked, "What about our bags and personal belongings packed in the trunk of our car rental?"

"Those are already on board."

"What about John Fraser? We need him," I said.

"I know. He will join us tomorrow."

"Where are we going?" Darrell asked.

"Our island trip has come together quickly. My agency picked up some chatter indicating it was best if we left Kona."

Darrell and I looked at each other in disbelief.

"It's probably not what we think. We are simply taking extra precautions. We're taking a short trip to Hilo to fly you out of here."

Neither Darrell nor I bought Agent Brown's de-escalation. He acted as if we were in real danger the moment he met us on the beach. I was glad we were now safe on a yacht.

"Who owns this yacht?"

"A friend," Brown said. "Just enjoy it. We will wait here for your friend John in the morning. He has to talk with his wife tonight."

———————————

When we awoke early the next morning, we felt much better. Darrell received a text message from John confirming that he was coming, and Agent Brown received clearance from his agency to accompany us on the dangerous journey. John was a certified diver and experienced underwater photographer with more than 200 dives. I felt more secure now that I was surrounded by professionals.

After sailing to Hilo in good weather, we traveled directly to the Hilo airport and flew to Honolulu to catch a China Airlines flight to Taipei. We were picked up by two members of the *Jùlèbù Fāxiàn,* who drove us directly to a yacht club in the Tamsui District of New Taipei City. We then boarded a massive *M33 Explorer Mondo Marine Mega Yacht* for our trip to the Diaoyu Islands.

The yacht, called the *Sorrento Explorer,* appeared to be like any other multi-million-dollar yacht of the rich and famous seen cruising across the Mediterranean. We all knew that was not the case, though. The captain, Demetrios Jarvis, was a friend of Chief Ryan through Demetrios' cousin, Winnifield Jarvis, a former National Security Council member and an expert on biological terrorism. Demetrios was a stout, well-built Greek man in his late fifties, just short of six feet tall with curly salt and pepper hair. He had a square jaw, two large dimples on both sides of his face and a small one on his chin that gave him a warm smile. His personality was jovial and he did not talk like a sailor. Profanity was not in his speech, unless it was in other languages we didn't understand, since he spoke Greek, French, Spanish, Italian, and Portuguese fluently. I suspected that he knew how to handle himself in terms of defending himself. I would later learn that he had served for five years in the 32nd Marines Brigade "Moravas."

Darrell and I stayed in the same room that evening and Agent Brown stayed in an adjacent room. I rose early the next morning just before dawn and came out on deck to watch the sun rise.

"Aye—we have another early riser on board," a voice beckoned from behind me as I looked out over the water from the wooden banisters.

I turned around to see Captain Demetrios Jarvis smiling at me.

"I am a very blessed man, Johann. Good things happen to those who rise early. I worked with my father in the shipping business for twenty-five years in Greece and had to rise early every morning. I first met my wife, Nannetta, at the Port of Cinque Terre, Italy, early in the morning on the dock at the Paradiso Hotel. Neither of us had slept well and we both decided to get some fresh air on the dock and enjoy a cup of coffee at sunrise. One casual conversation led to a dinner together that evening, followed by twelve months of rendezvous throughout the Mediterranean when my shipping business and her fashion business put us in the same country at the same time."

"You are a long way from home, Captain," I said.

"Indeed, we are. During the past year we have been hired by a large company for sailing trips in and out of the Philippines," Captain Jarvis said. "I do miss the Mediterranean. We will return home after this last trip."

"Is your wife still in the fashion business?" I asked.

"Yes. She is as busy as ever, not just modeling but also managing a team of models throughout the world. She loves the work. Fortunately, she can conduct much of her business on board. You will meet her tonight at dinner along with our two daughters."

"That is very kind of you, Captain, to invite us to dinner. I will look forward to being with you and your family."

Captain Jarvis sailed in a northeasterly direction into the East China Sea, making good time on the first day off our voyage. He wanted to make sure we reached the vicinity of the islands at least two days before the scheduled rocket launch.

In the evening, Darrell, Michael, John, and I met with Captain Jarvis, his wife Nannetta, and their two daughters, Isabella and Michela, in the ship's luxurious dining room. The oval table could comfortably seat twelve, so we had plenty of room. When Nannetta and her daughters walked into the room, they appeared to be three sisters. At first it was difficult for me to pick out Nannetta, as her skin tone and quality was that of a woman still in her twenties.

When Captain Jarvis introduced his wife and daughters, they seemed to all recognize my slight embarrassment in not knowing who the mom was, and Nannetta received it as a great compliment.

The proper way to respond was to admit my surprise, which gave them all a good laugh.

"I apologize, Isabella, but I guessed that you were the mom."

"Don't feel bad, Johann," John said, "I thought Michela was the mom."

"Gentleman," Captain Jarvis said, "it happens all the time. Most people who see us together at a restaurant think it is so nice of me to take my three daughters out to dinner."

Agent Brown was quiet but his nonverbal communication revealed sparks were flying between him and Isabella.

The Chateaubriand with pan jus served with truffle fries and buttery mixed vegetables was better than I had ever had anywhere, and even better than my mom's Chateaubriand dinner, which was delicious. The waiter who served us gave the adults a choice of aged Barolo wine from Italy or an aged Médoc Rouge from France while I enjoyed natural spring water. The meal was concluded with creamy homemade gelato and coffee or tea.

The first hour of table conversation was light-hearted and fun, with lots of laughter about how Nannetta exchanged clothes and identities with Isabella and Michela and about all the hilarious missteps in John's latest feature film production.

Then Captain Jarvis turned the conversation serious.

"Gentleman, we know that you are embarking on a dangerous mission during the next several days. We want you to know we deeply appreciate what you are doing and pledge our support and complete confidentiality. None of us work for the U.S. government and although we are not Americans, we are here to help you and support you. I have many close friends who have entrusted you to me. Everyone on this yacht, and I mean everyone, is trained in self-defense and in the use of weapons, and we have ample firepower on board should we need it. Our yacht flies under the Greek flag and we are officially on a holiday fishing expedition; of course, we understand that you are looking for a different kind of fish when we sail to the Diaoyu Islands. We can be expected to be intercepted and boarded by Chinese authorities who will search our vessel, severely scold us for being in what they claim to be Chinese territorial waters, and then will accept our generous gift to General Bingwen Tso as we make amends for our grievous mistake."

The plan was not complex. We had a few days of travel and planning before we reached the area. During that time, I had numerous intriguing and stimulating conversations with the captain, his wife, and his two daughters. They were one of the most unique and most talented families I had ever encountered.

After reaching the islands and doing practice dives with our equipment, the evening for our mission was upon us. The captain's underwater night vision equipment was better than expected and the night vision goggles on shore also gave us superb visibility. My scuba mask was a little too tight at the beginning of our first practice dive, but after I loosened the strap, the leaking stopped.

Captain Jarvis kept the yacht far enough offshore to be out of sight from the island where we chose our launch site. We left the yacht just after sunset. The seas were calm and the weather clear. It was a good omen. We took a dinghy with a quiet motor to about 200 yards offshore on the less guarded side of the island. There, we put on our diving equipment and swam underwater to shore, bypassing the offshore electronic sensors designed to intercept vessels coming to the island. Once on the island, we made our way to approximately

100 meters from the launch pad. John set up his camera to record the rocket launch with his nighttime, high-definition digital camera. The launch was scheduled at 11:00 p.m., according to the information intercepted by the Discovering Club, if the weather stayed clear as forecasted. Agent Brown was heavily armed and provided reconnaissance, Darrell would listen to the conversation and I would record it with long distance microphone equipment, ironically made by Northvision Technologies in China.

The dive went just as planned. Our arrival on shore was undetected. We all had rehearsed a narrative that we were shooting scenes for a feature film in case we were apprehended and interrogated. None of us had much confidence that our story would save us from imprisonment. We made our way quickly to the perimeter of the air base over some very rough terrain just below where we landed under complete coverage of large rocks and dense foliage. No security forces would expect a breach of defense from the rocky terrain below. Climbing carefully up the hillside, we positioned ourselves in the dark just outside the electrified fence. The wires were set apart just far enough for John's camera lens to peer through. We calculated that we were now within 300 meters from the launch pad but adequately protected by large boulders. If anything went seriously wrong with the launch, we knew we could be in danger.

I set up my microphone carefully, pointing it toward the command center. It was a cool night as expected, but there was a crack in the window to let fresh air into the crowded room, enabling our mic to pick up and record the conversations in the room. Twenty minutes after we completely set up, we saw General Tso enter the room. We then saw soldiers loading materials onto the rockets on the launch pad. Their

HAZMAT suits, protective gear, and extreme caution confirmed our intelligence that they were carrying biological or chemical weapons.

"How is the video recording?" Darrell asked.

"It's fine," John answered as he followed the action on his monitor.

"What about the audio recording?" Darrell asked me.

"It's good," I replied, "crisp and clear, especially when the wind dies down."

"Is there any way to confirm the payload?" I asked Darrell.

"We have tried but only a few people know that information. We aren't even sure that the Chinese leaders in Beijing know what is on that rocket. General Tso knows and a couple of his confidants. The president of China might not know."

"What about using remote sensing equipment to detect biological and chemical agents?"

"We weren't able to bring those assets with us and we are too far away."

Just then General Tso began to speak, and we all stayed silent so Darrell could quietly interpret what he was saying as I recorded him from a distance.

"This is a very proud day for China. In thirty minutes, we will launch our superior satellite technology into space that will be able to defend against the aggressions of any nation. China will never again suffer from the dictates of the United States, Russia, Korea, Japan, or Europe. We will be respected as a world superpower. We will dominate the last and final frontier of space. We will be second to none."

When he finished speaking, a thunderous roar of clapping followed. The countdown then began with T minus fifteen minutes to launch. The launch pad was completely cleared as General Tso and the other leaders watched in the command center. John moved the camera from filming the command center to filming the Launchpad. We all inserted earplugs to protect our hearing from the deafening sound of the rocket launch. I could imagine the gleam in General Tso's eyes as he watched the successful launch of China's first space weapon of mass destruction. The ground around us shook with such force that we felt like we were in an earthquake. Although small rocks and gravel fell on top of us, we had chosen our position well and were protected from the blast. As I watched the rocket fly higher with a trail of white following close behind, I knew the launch had been successful. We heard the men cheering and imagined them opening some select bottles of liquor to celebrate.

As fast as we could, we packed up our equipment and silently left the launch perimeter. We wanted to get out of there as soon as possible but also were contemplating the gravity of what we had just witnessed. None of us spoke a word to each other as we dived underwater and swam back to our dinghy, following a guideline we had laid under the water. We safely made it back to the yacht, fully expecting to be intercepted as we left the area. We arrived back at the yacht just after midnight.

Captain Jarvis informed us that because the Chinese were celebrating the launch, they had sent out no patrol boats that evening. Using no motors, he sailed the *Sorrento Explorer* out of the area, traveling under full sail toward international waters, which we reached by early morning. We were a full sixty miles into international waters, sailing toward the Philippines, when we were intercepted by a Chinese military gunboat. As expected, they boarded our vessel and asked us about our business and why we were sailing in such a dangerous area where pirates roamed. We explained our voyage and feigned ignorance about the pirate danger. When the discussion became a bit heated, Captain Jarvis asked about General Tso and noted his authority to monitor and oversee the oceangoing vessels in the region, even in international waters. This inquiry obviously pleased the Chinese captain, who graciously accepted our apology for sailing in waters that might require a rescue from the Chinese Navy. Captain Jarvis then offered a gift of five canned hams, five cured pork roasts, ten cans of candied sweet potatoes, and ten bottles of red wine to the captain and his twelve-man crew for their concern about our welfare, which they graciously accepted. Captain Jarvis then gave the captain a special package of expensive perfumes, whisky, and cigars to be delivered personally to General Tso. This gesture surprised the captain.

"Captain, do you know General Tso?" asked the Chinese captain in English.

"We met in Hong Kong years ago when we were both training in martial arts," Captain Jarvis replied. "He is an extraordinary person. Please give your general my best regards."

The Chinese captain bowed slightly in respect toward Captain Jarvis, who returned the bow. It was the perfect gesture.

"I wish you safe passage to the Philippines," the captain said. "Be careful when you reach the Philippine Sea. You should be able to outrun any suspicious vessels, but don't let them get too close."

"Xièxiè chuánzhǎng," Captain Jarvis replied in perfect Mandarin. "Nǐ hé nǐ de nánrén bǎochí ānquán."

Captain Jarvis then said in English, "There are six bottles of whisky in the case. Please give General Tso five bottles and let him know the whisky is a twenty-one-year-old Balvenie Scotch whisky of very high quality. The sixth bottle is for you, Captain."

"Xièxiè chuánzhǎng," the Chinese captain said as a big smile came across his face.

I was amazed at how skillfully Captain Jarvis took control of the whole situation, turning the Chinese captain from a potential adversary into a helpful person by wishing them good will and giving them respect.

As the gunboat departed, the Chinese soldiers came on deck to wave good-bye, and we returned the gesture, also wishing safety for them. I was struck with how reaching out in good will can turn potential adversaries into friends. It made me even more determined to prevent an impending war between the U.S. and China.

I left the deck hopeful, concerned, and exhausted. China had positioned an unknown WMD on a satellite; but somehow, I felt encouraged that the tense situation could be resolved between our two countries.

CHAPTER 17

MICHAEL WOKE ME ABRUPTLY OUT of a dead sleep at 4:00 a.m., along with John and Darrell.

"We have trouble. Get dressed and come on deck immediately. A pirate boat is chasing us, and we need to take action. It's a large vessel and we cannot outrun it."

I slipped on my clothes as my heart began racing. I knew the south Asian pirates in these waters were ruthless. I heard the first shots fired and knew we were in a dangerous fight for survival. By the time I climbed up on the deck, Captain Jarvis was shouting out commands to keep down. I could hear automatic gunfire but none of the bullets were reaching us—yet. Lying on my belly, I crawled closer to Captain Jarvis who told me exactly where to find automatic weapons below. He instructed me to stay below with his wife and daughters and to ask Nannetta to lead them all into the safe room and to lock the door. I began to move toward the stairway just as I saw Agent Brown climbing up the stairs shouldering an RPG-7. I knew that weapon had a range of 500 meters and could shoot an explosive at a velocity of 295 meters/second.

I wanted to watch him in action, but knew I needed to obey the captain. I went below as I heard the gunfire get closer. I quickly found Nannetta, Isabella, and Michela emerging from their rooms and told Nannetta her husband's orders. She led us down a hallway and through a hidden door under a rug that revealed a stairway to a lower cabin on the engine room level of the ship. The four of us climbed down the stairway and into the secure room. I lowered the door in the floorboard, making sure the rug on top kept it hidden.

I grabbed one of Isabella's hands and one of Michela's hands, squeezed tight, closed my eyes, and prayed quietly for the safety of everyone on deck. Annetta followed my lead and led us in reciting the Lord's Prayer. Just as she finished, we heard a loud explosion. I hoped that Agent Brown had just successfully launched a grenade into the pirate vessel, setting it on fire. Shortly thereafter we heard a second explosion and correctly deduced that the pirate vessel was now sinking. We all opened our eyes and breathed a sigh of relief. Michela made direct eye contact with me and smiled in a way that caused my heart to start racing. She stirred a passion in me that I was not used to nor was I sure how to handle. I maintained my composure, pretending nothing had happened between us, trying not to alarm Nannetta.

Captain Jarvis came to my rescue, knocking on the door and letting us know it was safe to come out. He immediately wrapped his strong arms around Nannetta, giving her a long embrace. He also hugged his two daughters.

Once on deck, we could see smoke off in the distance on the starboard side of the yacht. The pirate vessel had come to within 400 meters of our vessel when Agent Brown blew it out of the water. What was left was rapidly sinking and there did not seem to be any survivors.

"Excellent work, Agent Brown," Captain Jarvis said. "I'm buying you all dinner and drinks when we get to Manila. Now let's get out of here."

After several more days of safe sailing, we made it to the Manila Yacht Club adjacent the Metropolitan Museum and found a mooring for the night. Captain Jarvis insisted on taking us all out to dinner at a restaurant with great seafood that was walking distance from the harbor. After a delicious meal of fresh mahi-mahi, smoked salmon, shrimp, lobster, and clams with rice and seasoned vegetables, I intended to turn in for the night but instead I ran into Michela on the way to my cabin. We started talking and before we recognized the time, it was 2:00 a.m. when we said good night. We discovered we shared many interests.

Despite a short night, I was surprised how rested I felt the next morning. Nannetta called us all together for breakfast before we went our separate ways. John, Darrell, Agent Brown, and I had a late morning flight back to Honolulu where we would bring the digital footage that John had taken. Agent Brown was then assigned to carry the digital film drives from Honolulu back to Chicago and deliver them to Chief Ryan. Chief Ryan would carry them to the FBI lab in Quantico to be inspected and analyzed. Darrell and I were asked by Chief Ryan to rest in Honolulu for a day. Captain Jarvis and his family would be sailing back to their home in Greece.

After Nannetta spoiled us with a special Filipino breakfast, we all gave each other warm embraces and Isabella and Michela had tears in their eyes as we said our goodbyes. As our taxi waited to depart the yacht harbor, Captain Jarvis looked me in the eyes and said, "Johann, I know young love can come and go as emotions change quickly over time, but my daughter is obviously stricken by you. Even though you are young, you are growing into a mature young man and will one day catch up in terms of your emotional intelligence. In case Michela has fallen for you, be careful not to crush her heart. Be gentle as you see what might become of your friendship. If you decide to keep in touch and pursue closer relations, always respect and honor her. If you do, you will always have my love and respect."

I deeply appreciated his words of affirmation. He handed me a handwritten card from Nannetta to be read later on the plane. We began a wild taxi ride through the streets of Manila on our way to the airport as we all wondered about our futures, but especially me with regard to one of the beautiful Jarvis sisters.

Our flight to Honolulu was relatively uneventful. I began to psychoanalyze my romantic feelings for Nicole, Angela, and Michela. *Was it even a healthy type of attraction, or was I too young?* I remember my parents warning me to beware of sexual advances by older women, especially teachers, as there were a number of incidents covered in the news about teenage boys who had been seduced by female teachers. I kept thinking about all the female teachers in jail in the U.S. for sexual encounters with teenage boys they had as students. My romantic encounters all involved women several years older than me. I took some solace in knowing the teachers in these stories were usually in their mid-to-late twenties and thirties, and none of my romantic interests were teachers and none were older than nineteen.

I felt closest to Angela. We had a strong and growing friend-ship. Michela was a short one-week encounter; I hardly knew her. In Nicole's last conversation with me, she asked if we could arrange to stay in the same conference hotel so we could spend time together. I thought that indicated she wanted a deeper relationship with me. I seriously doubted if I was even old enough to handle a romantic relationship with any of them. I was too young, though I found it nearly impossible to put my awakened passions back to sleep.

At that moment I was so ready to exit this confusing, awkward phase in my life with hormones and emotions running wild.

I had been waiting for the right moment and felt that now was the right time to read Nannetta's card. It was early morning and everyone on the plane was sleeping. I opened the card carefully, noticing the sweet perfume on the card, and I read these words by the light of my phone:

> Dear Johann,
>
> You are a sweet young man and both my husband and I have a high regard for you. We are deeply impressed with your willingness to face personal danger and great sacrifice in order to stop a potential catastrophic war. We are aware that our daughter Michela is struck by your engaging personality and handsome physical appearance. She has previously been deeply hurt by two young men that she had loved. Both had pursued Michela for their own reasons, leading her into months of depression. We therefore ask you that if you decide to pursue a closer relationship with Michela, be especially careful not to lead her into an emotional attachment if you are not serious about her. I don't mean to be presumptive, as you are still quite young, but I know she thoroughly enjoyed her time with you. If you both decide to pursue your friendship, then go slowly and be a true friend. You both still have much growing up to do. I have seen so many young teenagers in Europe ruined by their premature and irresponsible relationships. Both my

daughters have been too intimate with their previous boy-
friends and I don't want them falling into the same mistake
with you and Agent Brown. Regardless of what direction
your relationship with Michela might take, we wish you
safety and true success and contentment.

Sincerely, Nannetta Jarvis

Now both Captain Jarvis and his wife Nannetta had given me
their affirmation and exhortation to be careful with their daughter.
I needed to send Michela a text message but decided to wait until
we arrived in Honolulu. I needed to make her understand the reality that I could be dead soon, given the threats on my life. At the
same time, it was a natural impulse to want to have close relationship with another beautiful young woman who deeply cared about
my wellbeing. I saw John's emotions toward missing his wife and
children and I saw Darrell's emotions toward missing his girlfriend.
I wanted that, too.

I fell asleep and awoke to the captain announcing that we would
soon be landing at Honolulu International Airport. Aware that Agent
Brown was now carrying our valuable film, we were all very alert when
we departed the plane and picked up our luggage in baggage claim.

When we exited the airport late that morning, John's wife,
Elizabeth, was there to pick him up. She invited Darrell, Agent Brown
and me to join them for dinner at her sister's home in Honolulu. We
were keenly aware that if certain people knew the nature of the
raw footage of digital film that John had recorded, he and his family would be in great danger. We therefore decided to lock up the
SDHC memory cards in a Bank of Hawaii safe deposit box until Agent
Brown was ready to fly back to Chicago the following evening.

We had many exciting stories to tell at Elizabeth's sister's house and kept Elizabeth mesmerized by what she considered to be our tall tales. We thanked her for the mashed potatoes and gravy, baked chicken, asparagus, and cabbage salad dinner. To top it off, she made her famous coconut crème pie with tea and coffee. We had to restrain ourselves from accepting her offer for a second piece of pie; it was so delightful.

It was good that we locked up the film, because the following morning we learned that two men came to John's house in Kona looking for him. John was meeting us for breakfast at the time, still in Oahu, and Elizabeth, who had returned to Kona the next morning, was meeting their children at the Kona airport. Two neighbors told Elizabeth about the suspicious visitors after they returned home from the airport. Elizabeth reported the incident to the local police after discovering the men had forced their entry into their home and searched it illegally. When she told John about the break-in, he was baffled, as he did not tell anyone about his trip the Diaoyu Islands other than his family. Someone had obviously discovered his film work there.

Later that afternoon, John discreetly arranged to meet with me, Agent Brown, and Darrell on Lanikai Beach on the Kailua side of the island for a picnic lunch. We arrived from different directions and made sure we were not followed. After learning about what happened at John's house, we had to assume that we could be under surveillance and that someone might be trying to prevent us from bringing the digital film to Chicago. We decided to contact Chief Ryan and have him meet Agent Brown at the O'Hare airport in Chicago so he could travel with Chief Ryan to Quantico. Chief Ryan agreed that this was a good plan. Now we just needed to get it from the Bank of Hawaii to the Honolulu airport the following day. Drawing from his vast network of trusted law enforcement professionals, Chief Ryan phoned a close friend in Honolulu and arranged for two private security professionals to escort us to the bank and then to the airport.

At 9:30 a.m. on Saturday, I travelled alone from our hotel to the bank with a small suitcase. Shortly after my taxi turned left from Bishop Street onto Queen Street, a car pulled in front of my taxi and forced us to pull over to the side of the road, blocking us in. Then another car pulled in back of us and two men quickly got out with weapons drawn and demanded that the taxi driver open the trunk. He complied. The men opened my suitcase and took out the metal case that I had put in there from the bank. When they opened the metal box, shock fell across their faces as they looked at bags of Kona coffee and cans of macadamia nuts that I was bringing to Chief Ryan and his wife, Niloa, as a gift.

Before they could react, four patrol cars from the Honolulu police department arrived on the scene with an 8-member tactical police force with heavy weapons. The men in both cars were disarmed and placed under arrest. While this was taking place, Darrell and Agent Brown entered the Bank of Hawaii at 10:00 a.m. and withdrew the memory cards from the safe deposit box where they had been placed. The police escorted them in a marked police car directly to the airport. Our plan had worked perfectly.

Brown boarded his United Airlines flight for Chicago with the digital film in his possession without further incident. Darrell and I returned to our nice hotel rooms at the Outrigger Waikiki Beach Resort, appreciative that we had another day to relax before our next trip.

———————

Chief Ryan called me to let me know he reached the airport safely after a harrowing trip.

"You might say I faced some unexpected challenges," Chief Ryan said. "I realized that I was being followed from the police station in Downers Grove. I was in my police car on I-88 with one of my deputies when four men in two vehicles attacked us. The bullets could not penetrate our protected glass but a few did pierce the metal frame of our police car. I realized we were in deep trouble. While my deputy took the risk of returning fire, hitting the front doors of both cars, I called in reinforcements. Two state cruisers reached our location quickly and the four men decided to withdraw their attack. They disappeared quickly as soon as they exited I-88. When I arrived at O'Hare, I was still rattled and wondering who else might be waiting for me besides Agent Brown."

I heard him gasp on the other end of the phone.

"Someone's coming now," Chief Ryan said. He then disconnected.

CHAPTER 18

WHEN DARRELL AND I BEGAN our secure Skype meeting with Chief Ryan and Alan, we both recognized he was not himself.

"Are you okay?" I asked.

"I'm still a bit on edge," Chief Ryan said. "I ended our call, Johann, because when I exited my police car at the curbside for departing passengers, I saw from the corner of my eye a man and woman approaching me very rapidly and I thought I was in danger. It was only Alan and Christina, and I was so glad to see them."

"Did you meet the FBI agents?" Darrell asked.

"Not yet, but Alan and Christina said they were waiting in the terminal."

"Chief Ryan, we need to update you on some recent intelligence that we have acquired before you go through security," Alan said.

Seeing that Darrell and I were fine and in good spirits brought a smile back to Chief Ryan's face.

"I trust your trip to the East China Sea and to Manila went well without incident," Chief Ryan said.

"Yes, due to the extraordinary work of Captain Jarvis," Darrell answered.

"I trust you met his beautiful wife and two beautiful daughters?" he asked as nonchalantly as he could with a sparkle in his eye.

"Yes, he has a wonderful family," I said. My futile attempt to act disinterested amused Chief Ryan.

"Indeed, they are wonderful, and Captain Jarvis gave me a full report of your activities."

"I enjoyed our time together," I said, wondering what Captain Jarvis had said to Chief Ryan.

"Don't be worried, Johann. I put in a good word for you."

That meant that Captain Jarvis had been asking about me, and perhaps Michela also was asking about my trip. I remembered I had completely forgotten to text her to let her know I had traveled safely back to Honolulu.

"Thank you, Chief," I said.

I sent a quick text to Michela to let her know I was safe and to tell her how much I appreciated her kindness and the great hospitality of her family. I didn't let her know about the danger we faced in Honolulu though.

Alan then took control of our meeting so he could update Chief Ryan.

"Chief Ryan, we cannot thank you enough for getting involved with us. When we first stumbled across the conversation between General Nicoli Sarkovsky and Atlas Churgrill, we had no idea what we were getting into. We have been careful not to widen our circle of those entrusted with the sensitive information we have obtained. Now, there seems to be a number of unknown people who know about the information we have been intercepting and who regard us as threats to their plans. We don't know if it is foreign entities or our own intelligence agencies who have put us under surveillance and who have made attempts on our lives. It could be both, of course. We are simply an intelligence gathering club with no authority. We are not trained government agents. It is a miracle that none of us have been killed yet."

Alan then asked Darrell to share some new information.

"Our latest information came last night," Darrell said. "Our friends in Taiwan have confirmed that Chinese authorities are worried about General Tso. A few generals have referred to him in intercepted communication as a dangerous person. They also confirmed the missile launch from the Diaoyu Islands that we filmed of them putting a WMD into space. Huang Tai also confirmed the same information from his uncle."

"When are you planning, Darrell, to meet Huang Tai's uncle?"

"Soon, Chief Ryan. Huang Tai is setting up a meeting for me and Johann to meet him and his uncle. We plan to travel to Hong Kong in two days."

"You both will now have a third person to travel with," Chief Ryan explained. "I have asked your friend, Angela Farrentino, to meet you in Honolulu and then travel with you to Hong Kong and China. She speaks Mandarin and her cousin knows one of the people you will be working with in Hong Kong. She will be arriving in Honolulu later tonight and will explain further."

———————

I fell asleep shortly after dinner and awoke in my room at the Pacific Beach Hotel to the vibration of my cell phone beside my bed. *Who would be calling me this late?* I thought.

A name appeared with the number, *Angela Farrentino.* My heart leaped.

"Angela. I just heard the good news. Where are you?"

"Hi Johann, I just landed in Honolulu."

"It is so nice to hear your voice. I thought you were coming much later."

"I arrived on an earlier flight and I'm on my way to my hotel. Do you remember my brother, Angelo, who works with Italy's counter-terrorism surveillance team?"

"Yes, I remember you telling me about him."

"He just learned that our whole research group at the University of Chicago has been under surveillance by some very dangerous criminals."

I immediately sat up in my bed. We had known that we were under surveillance, but we did not know by whom.

"Why would Organized Crime be following our research group, Angela? We are a bunch of college students."

"College students working at a top research lab doing experiments on intercepting objects in space."

I thought about the two previous attempts on my life. First, the bookstore meeting and then in Hawaii, when someone tried to shoot me from a helicopter coming back from Mauna Kea. If it wasn't for Agent Brown, Darrell and I would likely both be dead.

"I didn't sign up for this craziness when I came to the University of Chicago to study astronomy."

"I know Johann, but we must stop this plot. Are you alone?"

"Yes. Darrell is nearby in another room, but we both agreed to sleep in. Do you have your Hong Kong ticket?"

"Yes, I have it. I asked Chief Ryan if I could join you because I speak Mandarin. My brother believes some of the people following you may be Chinese agents. I'm concerned that you and Darrell may be in danger in Hong Kong."

"Darrell knows Hong Kong very well, Angela. He was born just outside of Hong Kong and lived there until he was eight. He returned there for four years when he went to college at Hong Kong Baptist University. He also has a younger sister who still lives there."

"I know you completely trust Darrell. One more thing, Johann. My brother is picking up chatter in Rome about an impending attack on the U.S. by China from space."

"Everything is now in motion that makes that possible, Angela. That's one of the reasons why we must go to Hong Kong and then to China. I'm glad you are coming with us."

"I will meet you and Darrell at nine in the morning for breakfast, in the lobby of your hotel."

As I lay back in bed, I started to drift off to sleep again. It was late, so I set my alarm to 7:45 a.m. Surprisingly, I slept through the night without any interruptions.

I awoke, startled by a knock on my door. I looked at the alarm clock next to my bed; it was 7:00 a.m. I knew it wasn't Darrell, and it was too early to be room service. I realized that I had nowhere to run and nowhere to hide. We were on the twelfth floor of the hotel. Whoever it was, the person wanted in my room and there were always ways to get through locks. My mind and heart were racing; I needed an escape plan now. I looked at the lock on the door to see how hard it might be to pick. Then I heard a second gentle knock and a woman's voice saying my name. I looked through the small peephole in the door, which I had completely forgotten about. I was both shocked and relieved. Standing outside my door was Angela.

I immediately opened the door and said, "You are early Angela; I thought we were meeting at nine." Angela responded by closing the door behind her with her right hand, locking it, and grabbing the back of my neck with her left hand, drawing us together as she passionately kissed me. Her passion was intense, and she did not stop kissing me. In fact, she seemed to have no intention of stopping.

My head was spinning as I realized Angela's intentions. I pulled away, so stunned that I could not speak, and Angela placed her hand over my mouth when she saw that I was struggling to say something. She leaned in to kiss me again.

We did not let things get out of control, but I did feel happiness, satisfaction, and guilt all in one; fortunately, we had not done anything which I would have regretted.

"What in the world was that?" I asked.

"Just something I have wanted to do for a while."

I hastily made my way to the bathroom and showered quickly while Angela made some coffee. After my shower, I sat on the side of the bed in my jeans, holding the fresh cup of coffee Angela handed me, frowning as I thought through what had just happened.

"What's wrong, Johann?"

"I wasn't ready for that Angela. That was so intense, and I don't know what I'm doing and I don't know if this is all right."

"Is it the age thing? We are only two and a half years apart in age."

"I don't know, Angela—why do I still feel like this is not right? I mean, my mind is saying *no* but my body is saying *yes*."

"Maybe in your upbringing, Johann, you were conditioned to feel guilty about expressing your feelings. In Italy where I grew up, most teenagers begin enjoying and exploring their romantic passions by the time they are fifteen. It may be simply the cultural differences between our two countries."

She looked at me tenderly and added, "Don't feel bad or ashamed by your feelings."

I gently kissed her on the forehead. "I need to think about this before we ever get passionate."

"I guess I was a bit aggressive the way I came through the door. In Italy, expressing such passion is common. I will try to be more sensitive to you."

As Angela prepared to leave, I unintentionally added some fuel to the fire she initiated.

"One thing I have no confusion about, Angela, is your sheer beauty. Regarding that, I have great clarity."

She kissed me.

"You have to go now, Angela; Darrell could awaken at any time and come over to my room."

She kissed me again before leaving, and right then my alarm rang. I turned it off.

What just happened? I wondered.

———————

Darrell met me in the hotel's restaurant. Angela was waiting for us. As we discussed the situation in Hong Kong over breakfast, Darrell agreed that having a beautiful, intelligent, Mandarin-speaking woman with us would be a distinct advantage. Angela had managed to reserve her ticket to Hong Kong on the same flight as me and Darrell.

As the plane took off and reached cruising altitude, I settled into reading a book because I seldom was able to sleep on a plane. Then a deviously playful thought came into my mind. The plane was not full; it was a long trans-Pacific flight at nighttime, and a perfect opportunity to play a practical joke on Angela. I wrote a quick note and dropped it in Angela's lap on the way to the bathroom near the back of the plane.

Angela opened the note to read: "I'm on a scouting trip."

On my way back to my seat, she handed me a note. I opened it and read, "I'm game if you are."

Oh no, I thought, *does she think I'm serious or is she just playing along and she gets that I'm joking?*

Angela fell asleep, along with everyone else on the plane, as far as I could see. The lights were turned off and everyone settled into a sleeping position, except me. I pondered my stupidity. I knew it was wrong to be joking in the context of what had just happened between us at the hotel. Somehow, I still miraculously drifted off to sleep.

At 3:30 a.m. I awoke; Angela was gently shaking me.

I felt terrible about what I had done. "You do know I was joking, right?" I asked.

She looked at me with an expression I could not read but said nothing.

"I apologize, Angela, I wasn't serious."

"That's what I thought but I wasn't sure," she said.

The two middle seats beside her were empty, so I asked her if we could go back to her row and talk. When we sat down, she grabbed my arm and leaned toward me.

"I'm sorry, Angela. It was a stupid joke. As much as I would like to, I cannot get physical with you. Not you or anyone. It's just where I'm at. I'm not ready for it, and I'm just playing with fire I have no business playing with."

"I understand, Johann. I had hoped that you were joking around with me."

I sat up surprised.

"Really?"

"Yes," she said.

Angela gave me a sweet smile. It was a different kind of smile than she had ever given me before. It was a kind and pure smile. Angela took my hand in hers, looked into my eyes, and began to share her heart with me in an open way. She appeared to be completely vulnerable.

"I'm sorry," she said, "that I was so aggressive this morning. I came on so strong and I have realized that I made it nearly impossible for you to say no. I've been thinking deeply about that and I realized that deep down I feared that you would reject me. I've been attracted to you for a while and was just waiting for an opportunity. I covered up my fear of rejection with assertiveness. I put you in a vulnerable situation, and I knew it was wrong. Wrong for both of us. I've gone too far too many times."

Tears were now rolling down both her cheeks.

"I need to grow up before I or someone else gets hurt. I've been far too risky in my behavior in the past."

I gently wiped her tears away with my thumbs and kissed her on the forehead.

"That is one of the bravest things I've seen you do, Angela. It takes a lot of courage to become vulnerable and share your weaknesses so honestly."

"I don't think I've ever been this honest with anyone," she admitted.

"I'm so sorry for my bad joke. It was a stupid thing to do."

"I forgive you; let's put it behind us."

"You are beautiful, Angela, but beauty is complex; there's an inner beauty in you. You are going to become an amazing woman when your inner beauty catches up to the quality of your physical beauty. Our physical beauty fades away; but not our inner beauty."

"No guy has ever told me that, Johann. It's your kindness and innocence that attracts me to you. You are unlike any other guy I've been with. You don't have a hidden agenda. I'm not sure if you understand this, but the fact that you resist getting physical makes you even more desirable."

"I still have my free will," I said, "which is why I owe you another apology. I should've stopped you in my hotel room this morning, but I didn't. I wanted you when wisdom was shouting no in my ear, and I couldn't put my finger on what was wrong until I saw that it was my own selfishness. I wanted to enjoy you, but you are not mine to enjoy. My parents have always taught me that sex is one of the most beautiful gifts that God gives to a husband and wife, and if you try to take that gift before you are married, you spoil it by wasting it on others. I realize how backward and old-fashioned that sounds, but I believe them. My dad told me it's like uncorking a fine wine before it is fully fermented. We were beginning to go down that road and that was my fault, too."

"I'm sorry, Johann, that's been my road for several years," Angela said.

"Our whole generation is messed up because there is so much sexual brokenness and very few among those in our generation understand the gift that sex is," I said. "I know many people in my university would laugh at me saying this, but sex has been devalued. Our generation thinks we can have sex with whomever we want whenever we want and that we will then be happy. Instead, we are depressed. We are drinking the cheapest wine of sexual pleasure, the dregs at the bottom of the barrel, because we don't know about waiting for the best wine we can have in marriage. Then we wonder why marriages don't last, why people aren't happy, why we have the greatest opioid epidemic in history, why children are abused, why families break apart, and why suicide in our generation is sky-rocketing."

"I've seen the brokenness in my own life," Angela said.

"I don't want brokenness. I'm fighting for something better. When I get to the point when I can look into a woman's eyes and say, 'I love you,' I have to be ready to also say, 'I am willing to lay down my life for you.' I know this sounds like I'm in the dark ages of chivalry, but that's what I believe real love is about; there is so little of it in the world. I know my parents have that love. It has kept them together and happy for thirty years. That's what I want."

Angela place her hands on my shoulders and said, "I want that, too. I've always dreamed about being married to one man who would be my best friend for the rest of my life. My parents' infidelities almost destroyed our family, but they were sorry for what they did and they changed. They have been faithful to each other for twenty years now and their life together is beautiful. I want a faithful husband with whom I can have a close family with children and grandchildren to love, care for, cook for, travel with, and laugh with."

"We can have an authentic friendship," I said. "That's what I want with you, not a physical relationship that is superficial. Let's let our passions subside and focus on being authentic with each other. I'm willing to do that if you are."

"I'm ready for that," Angela said. "I've never had that before."

This time I gave Angela a big warm hug. Tears streamed down her face again. There would be no airplane mischief to write about in my journal tonight, and I was perfectly happy with that; in fact, greatly relieved. I had been close to the fire, and once again, somehow, I was protected from making another big mistake.

———————————

I was excited when I heard that Dr. Briggand would be working with Alan and Chief Ryan on reviewing the film we had taken of the rocket launch. She was one of the most respected scientists at the CDC and provides consultation to the FBI's Scientific Response and Analysis Unit. She had been on the scene of every major disease outbreak in the United States for the past twenty years, including the West Nile Virus, Anthrax, Ebola, the Zika Virus, and COVID-19.

When the wheels of our plane touched down in Hong Kong, I read a long text message from Alan and Chief Ryan. They had been at the FBI lab in Quantico, along with Dr. Briggand, reviewing the digital film footage we had recorded in the South China Sea. When they reached the point in the digital film where the soldiers were loading the WMD in the rocket, Dr. Briggand saw something important. She noticed that the HAZMAT suits being worn by eight of the soldiers were not a heavy rubber or polyvinyl chloride, or Tyvek (high-density polyethylene fibers) or Teflon. Those materials were used to protect against chemical agents.

Instead, she saw that the soldiers were wearing fully sealed systems that appeared to be over-pressurized. This done to prevent contamination even if the suits were damaged. The suits also sported air purifying respirators with full hoods. They were clearly wearing level C protection against biological agents.

Given the amount of materials that they saw loaded, the text read, *Dr. Briggand doesn't see how the agent could be Saxitoxin. She believes it's most likely Botulinum.*

Chief Ryan concluded his text by saying we now have overwhelming evidence that Botulinum is in the Chinese WMD; so Nicole Jacobson was right. They made a mistake when they stopped production of the heptavalent Botulinum antitoxin.

CHAPTER 19

DARRELL, ANGELA, AND I WORKED our way through immigration and customs and retrieved our luggage without any problems at the Hong Kong International Airport. Darrell's sister, Anna, was there to greet us. We had decided to let Anna arrange our housing, since we didn't want to be found, and she decided to rearrange the furniture in her two-bedroom apartment on Bowen Road in the mid-levels of Hong Kong Island so that she and Angela could sleep on beds in her master bedroom and Darrell and I could sleep on comfortable futons in the guest room. The apartment was spacious, with 1600 square feet, and on the twenty-fourth floor. It featured a beautiful view of Hong Kong Harbor and of the city.

We had learned from Darrell that Anna had been living in Hong Kong for five years working as a financial analyst and vice president of new acquisitions at the HSBC International Banking Center on Queen's Road in the Central District. She was paid very well, more than $200,000 per year base salary, and she loved her job, which required extensive international travel.

"This place is beautiful, sis!"

Darrell was ecstatic as he took in the view of the financial district and Hong Kong Harbor.

"Wait till you see the view at night, Darrell. Hong Kong sparkles like a jewel, and of course it is the great jewel of the Orient."

"And you are right in the middle of it, sis—I am so proud of you!"

"And how are you, Darrell—what crazy thing are you mixed up in now? Are you still doing international consulting or professional interpreting for the government?"

"It's a long story, sis. But let me give you the gist of it. Some very bad people are trying to start a war between China and the U.S. for their own profit, and we are trying to stop it."

"What? That's serious, Da kine!"

"We know—and the bad guys have a lot of money and we don't know completely what they are financing. We only know about one rogue Russian general and one businessman from South Africa who are trying to create a biological war."

"Maybe I can help?"

"Anna, you are already helping enough by housing us. I am not sure what more you could do given that Hong Kong is currently in political turmoil."

"Well, I do know a few things about following money flows, uncovering hidden transactions, and researching the financial holdings of wealthy people—stuff like that. I am sure you are familiar with the phrase, *follow the money?* That's much of what I do for HSBC and all the other leading banks and commercial investment companies around the world that we deal with."

I looked at Darrell and it seemed as if the lights were turned on in his brain. I verbalized what I guessed Darrell was thinking.

"You could be of immense help, Anna, if you could investigate the financial holdings and transactions of General Nicoli Sarkovsky, a high-ranking retired general and associate of the Russian president, and Atlas Churgrill, the South African businessman."

"Johann is right. I should have thought of asking you earlier, but I guess I just wanted to keep you out of this," Darrell added.

"My company has some extraordinary resources," Anna said. "We publish our financial holdings in public reports that we make available online. Four years ago, we reported $48.0 billion in revenue and $19.3 billion in adjusted profit before tax. We are even richer now. We have 4,400 offices in seventy countries and we have close working relationships with both law enforcement and intelligence agencies throughout the world. You can scarcely imagine what can be done with these kinds of resources, and fortunately the CCP is leaving our bank alone for now."

"How did you become so big?"

"It's a long story, Johann."

Angela then jumped into the conversation.

"I know much of the story. Could I try, Anna, and you fill in the missing pieces?"

"Please do, Angela."

"I'm fascinated by the history of HSBC. In the early years it made much money through the opium trade with China. In 1929, it was registered by the Banking Commissioner of Hong Kong as *The Hong Kong and Shanghai Banking Corporation Limited* and incorporated in England and Wales. In the 20th century, HSBC Limited purchased hundreds of banks, financial institutions, and investment companies throughout the world. By 2014, HSBC had become the fourth-largest bank in the world by assets (with $2,670 billion), the second largest in terms of revenues (with $146.50 billion), and the largest in terms of market value (with $180.81 billion)."

"Excellent summary, Angela."

"Now I'm embarrassed," Darrell said, "let me just humble myself now and admit in sackcloth and ashes that I didn't know that my flesh-and-blood sister was a VP for one of the world's largest banks."

"Apology accepted, brother." Anna laughed, adding, "but it gets even better. This next bit of information is not to leave this room. I have great favor right now with the leaders of my company . . . Stuart Oliver, the Group Chief Executive of HSBC, wants me to be his future daughter-in-law. His son, Jonathan, and I have been dating for two years now, but his son still likes his independence too much. However, our relationship is strong and we are mutually committed to not date any other people as we contemplate marriage in the future.

"His father is a man of great integrity, and we completely trust each other. He allows me to access any resources that I need when investigating the financial activities of any company or any individual that we may be dealing with anywhere in the world."

"Wow, you are blowing my mind, Anna, I've been negligent in keeping up with you. That is going to stop right now."

"I will have to talk to my boss and Jonathan as soon as possible about all of this. I can assure you that HSBC Limited wants continued peace and even stronger relations between China and the U.S., so it's completely in the company's best interest to do whatever it can to stop this evil plot designed to plunge these countries into a destructive war."

"Our first need is security for us while we are here in Hong Kong," said Darrell.

"It already has been arranged. My security head, Chen Sīkòu, is extraordinary and has his team ready. Also, I want to officially hire you,

Darrell, along with Johann and Angela, as part of my investigative team. Our lawyer will have your contracts drawn up tomorrow with the terms, provisions, and appropriate compensation. You can sign and notarize them in my office tomorrow morning. This will allow me to officially assign security agents to you, who you should know are among the best agents in the world. They will ensure your safety in Hong Kong and China until this investigation is concluded, which I will determine."

"Anna, we cannot thank you enough," Angela said.

Darrell rose and gave Anna an extended embrace. I could see tears welling up in Darrell's eyes.

"I love you, Anna, please forgive me for not being involved more in your life, and for not telling you enough how much I love and appreciate you."

I was elated to see Darrell reconnect with his sister in this way. I looked over at Angela through the tears in my eyes, and I saw she also had tears. We had witnessed a beautiful family reunion. In that moment, I felt a new connection with Angela, something much deeper than we had ever experienced. We both felt it. I also knew at that moment that I needed to clearly communicate to both Michela and Nicole that I could not pursue any romantic intentions toward them. My feelings toward Angela were growing, and I knew that I could have such feelings for only one woman at a time in my life.

My thoughts were interrupted by a call to Anna's phone. She picked it up and greeted Chen, the head of our security detail. He explained that assailants were on the move and that we should all change location ASAP.

"It's time to go to Lantau Island," Anna said. "I'm officially going on vacation, and I'm inviting all of you to join me."

Ten minutes after we exited Anna's protected condominium high-rise in a taxi with Chen, we learned that two men arrived at the security entrance to the building to ask about Anna.

"She has officially gone on vacation," the guard told the men.

The two men reached inside their coats to grab hold of their weapons. "Do you know where she is going? It is urgent that we reach her before she leaves Hong Kong."

"No," the guard said. "I do not know her whereabouts. She never discloses to me or any of the other security agents where she is going for vacation."

Both men realized their vulnerability and that the security window was more than likely bullet-proof. Showing no emotion or concern, the men released hold of their weapons and one of them pulled out a business card with his company name and cell phone number. He handed it to the head security guard under the window.

"Thank you. Please call me if you receive any additional information regarding where I can find her."

Chen monitored the entire conversation during our taxi ride to the Lantau Ferry through a camera in the corner of the security booth.

"The two men have left your building and are on their way to the airport to try and intercept you there. I will make sure to send them on a wild goose chase at the Hong Kong airport. We will have you booked on five different flights to five different continents within minutes."

Chen then made a quick call on his phone and the diversion setup was completed.

"That's one of the many attributes that I appreciate about you, Chen, you are always so creative in the way you do your job."

"Thank you." Chen spoke with professional courtesy but revealed a subdued smile, knowing Anna's compliment likely meant a bonus at the end of the month.

"It's an honor for me to be trusted to implement creative solutions to meet your needs."

"I like you Chen, I can see why my sister speaks so highly of you," Darrell said.

"Oh, you are seeing the tip of the iceberg, my brother, regarding Mr. Chen's capabilities; you'll see."

Chen did his best to subdue another smile.

Sailing from Central Pier No. 6, we decided to take the slow ferry to Lantau Island, which took about an hour. As we passed Green Island on our left and Kau Yi Chau Island on the right, I was reminded of how beautiful Hong Kong was when you got away from the city and out into its many islands, which most foreigners failed to visit. I recalled how my parents told me about going to Lantau Island in the 1980s before the bridge was built. The only way to get there had been by a slow public ferry or private boat. Mostly local people would take the ferry to enjoy Hong Kong's best beaches, which were relatively unknown to tourists. Food on the island was so inexpensive that you could have a multi-course meal at one of the restaurants on the beach for less than $5.00. In those days you could follow the *Hong Kong $20 Per Day* guidebook. As we slowly made our way between Sunshine Island and Peng Chau Island, the underwater visibility increased, so I leaned over the rail to watch the fish, and I spotted some white herring and mackerel swimming several yards below the surface. There were several Chinese junks not far from us doing some family fishing, but I didn't see any commercial fishing vessels.

A speed boat in the area closed distance and seemed to be heading directly toward our ferry. It was within fifty yards of our vessel when another boat approached from the west and intercepted it, cutting off its path to our ferry. Then I saw a man in the intercepting boat stand up with a rocket-propelled grenade launcher on his shoulder. The man was one of Anna's security guards. The other speedboat quickly turned around and retreated. The man did not need to fire the weapon. Anna pretended not to be alarmed, but I could see that she was slightly shaken.

I tried to make light of the clearly dangerous situation, commenting, "for a moment I thought I was in a Stanley Tong film."

Anna smiled slightly and responded wittingly.

"My security team is the best; and Tong is a great director."

The remainder of the trip to Lantau Island went without incident. It was beautiful, boating between several of the smaller islands among the 261 islands in the Hong Kong archipelago. On Lantau we found a small private beach area connected to a restaurant with tables, chairs, and canopies sitting in the sand just off the water.

"Not too long ago you could order a six-course meal of some of the best Chinese food in the world at this restaurant for the price of a coffee," Chen said.

"That's what my parents told me, Chen," I said. "They loved this place."

"When were your parents in Hong Kong, Johann?"

"They came here for their fifth wedding anniversary. Before I arrived."

"My parents used to bring our family here for the day and they would hang out at this restaurant for hours," Chen said. "Back then it was just a little grass shack but the food was better than you could find in any of the expensive Chinese restaurants in Kowloon City or the Central and Western Districts of Hong Kong Island."

"You were spoiled, Chen," I said while still consuming some Har Gow. "This is some of the best food I've ever had."

Anna looked over at me and smiled. I hoped that she was relieved that we were all relaxed and having a good time. I also wondered if hidden beneath her smile was a deep concern that the organized and well-funded crime syndicate they were now encountering was obviously willing to kill them. As we all relaxed and enjoyed the sunshine, warm water, gentle breezes, and good food, we all knew we had to talk about the elephant on the beach.

Our conversations dissipated as I could see that Darrell, Angela, Anna, and Chen were all deep in thought.

I did not want to be the first person to address the obvious, but I decided to do so anyway.

"We need a plan," I said. "These bad actors are not going away, and they want us dead."

"Anna, I'm sorry to put you in grave danger," Darrell said. "This is why I hesitated to get you involved."

"I've been here before, my brother. These are not the first bad guys I've had to deal with and we deal with the CCP every day. I am confident Chen and his team can handle our security needs now that they know who they are dealing with. I'm sure by now they have already tracked down the boat owner or rental company used by those who tried to attack us. They probably also have taken the fingerprints from the entrance area of my condominium building and run them through an online data base to identify them."

"Correct on both accounts," Chen responded with a clear voice of confidence. "I've received two text messages in the past thirty minutes, confirming that my team has identified the men who tried to attack us and that warrants are now being processed by a magistrate for their arrest and interrogation."

"Chen, you never fail to amaze me with your proficiency."

Chen smiled and said, "HSBC compensates me well and I want to keep this job."

Darrell then proposed that someone needed to go to mainland China, or perhaps the New Territories, and arrange to meet with Huang Tai Simonnes. We explained who Huang Tai was to Chen and Anna, both curious for more details.

"It's probably too risky for him to come to Hong Kong," Chen said after we finished. "He would be monitored closely by Chinese security forces because of the time he spent in Hawaii."

"I agree," said Darrell.

"I feel I need to stay here in Hong Kong to provide security for Anna," said Chen, "but I recommend that one of my assistants go to China with you. Her name is Melissa Tang. She is a very bright, articulate, twenty-four-year old specialist on my team and she has a unique skill set. Her father was an independent locksmith who assisted the most powerful triad gang in Hong Kong for years through his personal friendship with one of their founders. So you might say that Melissa grew up in the business of breaking into things. She's also a martial arts expert and has won numerous martial arts competitions."

"I will go, too," I responded. "I have a good relationship with Huang Tai. We connected in Hawaii while working together at the Keck Observatory, and I believe he and his uncle will trust me."

"It will be especially dangerous for Americans," Chen said. "It is different than being here in Hong Kong. China is still a communist country with an autocratic government that doesn't allow basic human freedoms and rights as in the U.S. You can be arrested and interrogated harshly based on mere suspicion."

"I understand. But I have a valid reason for visiting my friend Huang Tai. Chinese authorities could confirm that we worked together at the Keck Observatory. Also, I know that Huang Tai's uncle, Colonel General, would provide the necessary covering for me. I hope that they would be less concerned about me than they would about you, Darrell, since you have strong Taiwan connections and understand the language."

"I think he's right," Chen said, looking over toward Darrell and Anna.

"What about me?" Angela asked. "Wouldn't it be kind of strange for a sixteen-year old American to be traveling with a twenty-four-year-old Hong Kong martial arts expert? I think it would be less suspicious if I was traveling with Johann from the U.S., and if we hired Melissa to take us into China both for tourism and to visit Huang Tai."

"And how would you know Melissa?"

"My twenty-five-year-old cousin is a martial arts competitor, and she has competed all over Asia. It would be natural for my cousin to know Melissa."

"What's her name, Angela?"

"Joanna Farrentino."

"Her name sounds familiar to me. Perhaps Melissa and your cousin may have competed in the same competition. Let me find out if that is the case."

"If Melissa knows my cousin, wouldn't it be good for me to go?"

"Yes, it would," Chen said.

Anna and Darrell agreed.

Then I remembered Chief Ryan said Angela should join us in Hong Kong because she would have a connection to someone here that we would be working with. I wondered how he knew about Melissa and Angela's cousin.

Our return trip to Hong Kong Island was uneventful. Anna thought it would be better for us to stay at Le Méridien Cyberport in the Southern District for the evening. She said that the hotel manager was a personal friend and the hotel's security staff was exceptional. We needed a secure place to finish planning our next actions.

"You will not be disappointed," Chen said. "But I have to go now. I will meet you there tonight."

"I've often housed important associates of my company in Le Méridien Cyberport during their visits to Hong Kong. The hotel is also situated away from the hustle and bustle of the Central District. I'll make a call now."

A warm smile came across Anna's face as she wrapped up her phone conversation with her friend Alexandre Martin, the current manager of the hotel. A special suite in the hotel was available and Alexandre would give it to Anna for a heavily discounted price, along with a second deluxe ocean room.

"You are in for a treat. I was able to book the Deluxe suite where you and I will stay Angela," she said, and then turning toward me, "and I booked the Bayside Premiere suite for you and Darrell. Both suites are amazing."

Amazing was the correct word. When Darrell and I walked into the luxury 945-square foot Bayside Premier suite, we looked out to a stunning sunset over the South China Sea. The floor-to-ceiling windows flooded the room with shades of pink and orange. I immediately recognized the self-contained workstation with wireless high-speed Internet access. The flexible, well-designed working space, complete with docking stations for iPods and iPhones and Internet radio with international channel access, gave me a new vision for where I wanted to read, write, and study for a long time.

Exploring the suite even further, I walked into the deluxe bathroom featuring a granite tub, rain shower, and glass wall overlooking the harbor.

"I could take nice, long, hot showers in here," I said to Darrell, Angela, and Anna as they walked in behind me.

"Come see our room and we'll relax and enjoy the rest of the sunset."

Anna then led us to the Deluxe suite.

"This is my favorite suite," she said as we walked into 800 square feet of luxurious living. The light-filled suite was furnished with modern pieces in a sea-inspired palette to reflect the stunning 180-degree bay and ocean view. Like our suite, beautiful rays of red, yellow, and orange sun beams enveloped the room. I could see that it also provided the latest in new technologies, including laptop, iPod, and mobile phone docking stations with high-speed Internet access, a DECT phone, and a 42-inch plasma TV.

The forward-looking glass and chrome bathroom provided a spacious walk-in rain shower and upscale amenities, including a Soothing Corner where an infusion of stimulating essential oils wafted across the space. A stand-alone roll top bathtub overlooked the sea. Like our suite, the room offered a flexible working space with floor-to-ceiling windows. The suite had a homey feel, which I quickly discerned was why it was Anna's favorite.

After the adults helped themselves to the elegant wooden cabinet filled with high quality wines and liquors, Anna proposed a toast.

"To our health, safety, and overcoming evil with good," she declared with a resolute tone as she raised a glass of fine red wine.

I raised my glass of soda water and repeated the words aloud, adding, "and may we find God's grace to succeed."

We then sat down on the comfortable sofas and peered out over the South China Sea as we watched the sun set. It was peaceful, yet somber. We all knew that difficult days were ahead.

Our peace and serenity were broken by a phone call to the DECT room phone. Anna answered and listened, without saying a word as she had been instructed. The call ended without Anna uttering a single word about who had called, but her face revealed the gravity of the message.

"We must begin planning now. Time is running out fast."

CHAPTER 20

Aᴨᴨᴀ Iᴍᴍᴇᴅɪᴀᴛᴇʟʏ sᴇᴨᴛ ᴀ sʜᴏʀᴛ text message before relaying any more news to us. The CIA had contacted her bank president to confirm that she was to work on the accounts associated with General Nicoli Sarkovsky and Atlas Churgrill. As we already knew, the agency had been conducting surveillance on the two men.

"My boss gave the agent my location. The agent told my boss there was now a contract for my death by a professional assassin who was flying into Hong Kong from Ukraine and that I needed to expedite my investigations into the financial dealings of these two men."

"Was one of the men who came to your condominium the assassin?" Darrell asked.

"I don't know. Chen will know or will find out soon."

We decided to order room service for dinner and begin planning immediately. I texted Huang Tai and to my great relief, he responded quickly. He was visiting a friend at the Zhejiang University of Technology in Xihu, Hangzhou. We decided to meet nearby at the Zhejiang Art Museum on the southeastern shore of West Lake. Anna contacted our hotel Air France travel agent, who was able to book our flights into Shanghai Pudong International Airport. The agent was able to secure three business class seats for me, Angela, and Melissa on a flight leaving tomorrow in the afternoon.

Chen had already talked with Melissa that evening about taking me and Angela into China. She agreed and had begun packing her bags immediately. As we planned, the phone rang again, and we all tensed up as Anna answered it. She was told our food was ready and was being delivered to our suite. One nice security measure of the hotel was that room service to the suites did not require opening the door for a hotel employee. Food would be delivered on carts with large sterling silver pans heated with sterno canisters. An indoor monitor to two hallway cameras was available in each suite to ensure that no one would be present in the hallway when the door was opened to retrieve the food.

Darrell opened the door slowly, confirmed visually that the hallway was empty, and wheeled in our dinner.

In spite of the weight of our concerns, we enjoyed a great assortment of Chinese and European entrees and French desserts, almost as delicious as the food on Lantau Island. After dinner, Anna expressed her only regret was that we could only enjoy our suites and the great amenities of Le Méridien until noon the next day, when we would have to depart for the airport. It was a regret we all shared.

Our after-meal enjoyment and brief relaxation came to a halt after an unusual knock on the door.

"It's Chen. He texted me on the elevator and that is his signature knock."

There was plenty of food left for Chen so we urged him to have dinner first before continuing with our planning session. Chen was hungry and grateful.

By midnight we had finished talking through in detail every person's course of action for the next four days. Chen, Anna, and

Darrell would stay together in a safe place in Hong Kong while I would travel with Angela and Melissa to the West Lake region of China. We agreed that all of us would reconvene back at Le Méridien in ninety hours.

———————————

I awoke late the next morning after a great night of sleep. I had slept nearly eight and a half hours without interruption. Our room phone rang at 8:00 a.m. Anna was calling to invite me and Darrell to come over to their suite for breakfast and to tell us that Melissa would be joining us.

Melissa Tang was even more striking than I had imagined. When she entered the Deluxe Suite, she brought an air of confidence with her. She was a physically striking young woman with beautiful long brown hair flowing down her muscular body. At age twenty-four, she had already been an athlete for eighteen years and it clearly showed. We all could see how her chiseled frame would be intimidating to any competitor. She had a strong countenance and an easy-going laid-back smile that was disarming. I instantly had a good feeling about her.

After a splendid breakfast was delivered to our suite, we needed to give Melissa a thorough orientation. Chen opened the conversation by asking Melissa to share a little bit of her life story so we could get to know her.

"Well, I am twenty-four years old. My parents were both accomplished athletes and they wanted me and my siblings to follow in their footsteps. I began learning martial arts at age five and entered into my first competition at age eight. Since then I've earned many awards, including two first place awards at the U.S. Open Martial Arts Championship in New York City. Last year I stopped competing and I now privately mentor young women in martial arts, and I work for HSBC's security team when Mr. Chen needs me."

"Tell them about your locksmith experience," said Chen.

"I began working with my father in his locksmith shop at age ten. By age fifteen, I could open just about any lock made, so my father sent me out to assist some of his clients. One client in particular, Mr. Shan, was a close friend of my father's. Mr. Shan, at the age of nineteen, had founded one of the major triad gangs in Hong Kong. He always loved me and protected me and my whole family. To this day I am greatly respected among all the triad gangs because of Mr. Shan, and no gang members have ever given me any trouble. I think that is enough about me, what about all of you?"

During the next hour, Angela, Darrell, and I shared extended biographies of our lives to Melissa. Her nonverbal behavior revealed that she was a focused listener who took in as much as she could so that she could effectively work with us. I felt a shot of encouragement knowing that she was joining us.

We shared with Melissa what our mission was in going into mainland China, who we were meeting with, what we needed to accomplish, and what were the potential dangers. When we were finished, Melissa looked a bit stunned.

"This is way over my head. You are talking about preventing a major war that likely would involve weapons of mass destruction that could kill millions and millions of people. I've never been involved in something this big."

"None of us are ready for this, Melissa. Look at me, a mere sixteen-year-old college student from Illinois with no training at all facing any kind of criminal, trained assassins. I might as well be the teenage shepherd boy David facing the nine-and-a-half-foot Goliath. But here I am. If God allowed me to be here in this situation, then He must have a plan to get me through this."

"Johann speaks from the heart, Melissa," Darrell said. "None of us would choose to be here, but if we don't do everything in our power to stop these people, then who will? The U.S. government is very distrustful of China and is trying to figure things out; China is very distrustful of the U.S. and can be drawn into a conflict with the U.S. through deception."

Just then Melissa begin smiling, almost laughing, which seemed very odd.

"Did I say something funny?" Darrell asked, dumbfounded.

"No Darrell, I'm so sorry; it's my warped sense of humor. Just as you were talking, the lyrics to the verse of an old Bob Dylan song entered my mind. Please continue."

"Now I'm curious. What are the lyrics?" I asked.

"Yes I'm stuck in the middle with you / And I'm wondering what it is I should do / It's so hard to keep this smile from my face / Losing control, yeah, I'm all over the place / Clowns to the left of me, jokers to the right / here I am stuck in the middle with you," she half-sang.

"I'll be the clown," Angela said, raising her right hand.

"I'll be the joker," I said, matching her enthusiasm.

Melissa burst out laughing, as did the rest of us. The laughter dissipated the tension in the room.

"Well then, my only choice is to also put myself under providence. Count me in," Melissa said.

Chen exhaled a big sigh of relief. He told us later that he could not compel Melissa to join this mission if she was not willing to do so. He had never compelled any employee in his security company to risk their lives for anything they did not believe in.

The team was now complete.

———————

Our flight to Shanghai was very pleasant. We had good comfortable seats in business class, decent food and drinks, no turbulence, and an on-time arrival. It did cross my mind what had happened the last time that Angela and I were on an airplane together. It was a turning point in our relationship. Angela and Melissa sat side-by-side and used the time to develop their friendship. I noticed that Melissa warmed up to Angela very quickly. The two of them acted as if they were life-long friends.

As the plane taxied to our arrival gate, the head stewardess made an announcement that rattled us.

"Will Melissa Tang please identify yourself?"

Melissa raised her hand and the stewardess came over to her for a private conversation.

"After we deplane, please follow me as there is someone who wants to see you."

"We'll pick your bag up, Melissa, and meet you in baggage claim," Angela said, trying not to be alarmed.

Angela then turned to me and whispered, "Johann, please get all our bags and we'll meet you in baggage claim. I'm going to follow them." I watched her follow the stewardess and Melissa, disappearing as the crowd of departing passengers blocked my view. I shrugged and began pulling down our carry-ons from the overhead storage bins.

While waiting in baggage claim of the Shanghai airport, I sent Darrell a text confirming our safe arrival. Darrell replied, telling me that he and Anna had delayed their check-out from Le Méridien Cyberport to give Chen adequate time to deal with the assassin who had been sent to kill Anna. Alarmed, I called Darrell and he explained to me what had happened at Le Méridien.

He said that Chen's security team spotted a man in the bar adjacent to the lobby who fit the description of the suspected assassin. Chen walked into the bar, sat next to the man, and began a conversation with him. They both had a direct line of sight to the checkout desk and Chen knew this was important because the hotel required a face-to-face checkout and that they held the passports of all guests in a locked safe assigned to each room until the bill was paid in full and checkout was completed.

After ordering a drink and continuing with his small talk, Chen told the man sent to kill Anna outright that he was providing security for her. When the assassin reached for his gun, Chen put his hand on his arm and asked him to look at the red dot on his chest. Chen told him he could live if he accepted a generous offer of 10,000 euros in cash to walk away and tear up his contract. The assassin agreed.

"Why did Chen pay him off like that?" I asked.

Darrell then explained to me all the problems that would arise from a shooting in the hotel lobby. Also, Chen was able to access his phone during the encounter.

"How?" I asked.

Chen told me that after he gave the man an envelope with twenty crisp 500 Euro banknotes, the man asked him why he spared his life. Chen told him killing was terrible for business and that his business was security, not killing.

Chen then asked the man to text to him his contact information for future reference. When the assassin sent the text message to Chen's mobile phone, Chen saw the assassin identified himself as TB12, creating another opening for Chen.

As I listened to Darrell, I wondered why he was giving me all this detail.

"TB12," I said. "What opening?"

Chen apparently told the assassin, "You know your name is trademarked by NFL quarterback Tom Brady?"

"I've been using his system," the assassin said. "And Brady has not complained."

Chen lifted up his glass of brandy to the man and said, "Live to fight another day, TB12."

Sufficiently distracted by the conversation, the man never suspected that while sitting side-by-side, Chen had activated a surveillance program on his mobile phone that, through their common Wi-Fi connection, had downloaded all the incoming and outgoing phone numbers made on TB12's mobile phone during the past twenty-four hours. The program functioned with mobile phones that are within ten feet of each other once they have been connected through a text message. TB12 quietly disappeared.

"So, Anna is safe?" I asked.

"Yes," Darrell said. "Anna never did actually go to the checkout desk. The manager had already checked her out while this drama ensued in the hotel lobby. We are both being driven now by one of Chen's security officers to a private home in Hong Kong. Do you want to say hi?"

Darrell handed his phone to Anna.

"Hi Johann, I'm fine," said Anna. "I heard your concern for me and want you to know how glad I am that you are here with us."

I could pick up the emotion in Anna's voice and knew she was scared, despite her assurances. I also knew not to acknowledge the fear.

"Where are you going?" I asked.

"To the mid-levels area of Hong Kong Island where Chen's aunt and uncle live. Chen said it's the safest place now and that his aunt and uncle love hospitality. We'll all meet there. Be safe in Hangzhou and we'll talk again tonight."

Darrell then came back on the phone. "Have to go—let's connect again soon."

Just as Darrell ended the call, I spotted our luggage on the conveyor belt. I took it off and looked around. There was still no sign of Angela and Melissa. I checked my watch. They had been gone twenty minutes.

I could sense fear creeping into me, and not just my mind. I could feel it in my gut. It was palpable and paralyzing. The fear became stronger as I waited, but I knew not to call them. They could be in the immigration hall.

I looked at my watch again. It had been thirty minutes since I had seen Angela and Melissa. The luggage terminal was thinning out as people were leaving the baggage area, but there was still no sign of

Angela and Melissa. Just as I was wondering what to do next, Angela sent a text message to me.

"Melissa went with an agent to the airlines lounge. I followed them and asked an airlines agent for a membership application so I could stay in lounge. I can see Melissa talking with a man."

I texted back to Angela, "Got luggage and am waiting at bay number 6."

After a grueling forty-five minutes of waiting with the luggage, my phone vibrated and overwhelming relief came over me. I checked the number and it was not Angela or Melissa, but Chen. He called to assure me Darrell and Anna were now safely with his aunt and uncle. I told Chen what was going on with Angela and Melissa and that they still had not come to baggage claim. He assured me that his associates in Shanghai were trustworthy and they would be there soon.

"You know I trust you Chen."

"Yes, I know," Chen said. "Darrell is here and wants to talk to you."

"Hi Johann, we are on Bowen Road on Hong Kong Island. Chen is lending me his secure Blackphone. Do you have a few minutes to talk?"

"Yes," I said.

"Chen's aunt and uncle have a beautiful home surrounded by dense trees and foliage, so we're safe from visibility from the road. We arrived through a small, curved driveway lined with brick walls and overhanging bougainvillea that descended into an underground parking garage. We walked through a thirty-yard underground passageway secured by a series of heavy metal doors that were opened with an app."

"Sounds like a fortress," I said.

"It is. Chen's uncle retired from a military career, but he still has a powerful influence on Hong Kong government affairs. He has been trying to negotiate a peaceful resolution to the ongoing conflict between Hong Kong and China. His wife was born in China, and she is a close cousin to the wife of the president of China."

"How long are you staying there?" I asked.

"Not long enough," Darrell said. "When we arrived, Chen's aunt led us into a stunning parlor with high ceilings, classic molding, marble pillars, large oriental rugs, late nineteenth century wall paper, wooden furniture, and sixteen-foot windows adorned with beautiful full-length, hand-made drapes that touched the floor, revealing an overwhelming visual display of an exquisite Victorian home. After introducing herself as Elizabeth, Mrs. Sīkòu welcomed each of us with tangible gracefulness.

"When Chen's uncle entered the parlor, Mrs. Sīkòu introduced her husband Charles. He filled the room with strong authoritative presence that we all felt. He welcomed us with a genuine, unrehearsed greeting and warm hospitality, telling us to relax and rest. He knew from Chen the challenges we faced. He shared with us that he was a former commander in The Royal Military Police, the corps of the British Army responsible for the policing of army service personnel. They provided a military police presence in Hong Kong during the years of British rule. At the age of eighty-one, Mr. Sīkòu is still physically fit; he has a commanding aura."

"I wish I was there," I said.

"Chen and the rest of us urged him to tell us stories from his days as a commander in the RMP with other 'Redcaps,' as they were known, because of the scarlet covers on their peaked caps or scarlet-colored berets. He obliged, noting that the Redcaps were greatly respected in Hong Kong by both the British and Chinese and were known for their courage, professionalism, and integrity. Reflecting on the current conflict, he said, 'we would never fire on the people we were sworn to protect.' I believe him."

I then heard, "Dinner is now served, follow me."

"Have to go," Darrell said. "After dinner we'll connect again."

Several minutes went by as I sat there quietly. When I looked up from my phone, I noticed many hushed conversations and concerned looks on people's faces in the baggage claims area as they viewed their phones. It was clear to me something major was going on. I tried but could not get Internet access on my phone to find out what was happening.

My frustration level was rising rapidly when I received a text from Darrell.

"Large explosion in Hong Kong. May be a bomb blast. Don't call; I'll call you."

———————————

After ten more minutes of agonizing worry and looking into the anxious crowds, Angela sent me another text.

"We are on our way—be there soon."

When they entered the baggage hall, I knew they could see I was emotionally distraught.

I wanted to immediately move the attention from me.

"Are you both okay?" I asked. Melissa looked like she was close to tears.

"Yes, I'm okay," she said. "In the lounge I met with a friend of Mr. Shan, a very powerful man in Shanghai. My father had shared with Mr. Shan about my trip and Mr. Shan did some checking around and asked his friend to come to the airport and meet me to warn me of a threat to my life. Mr. Shan's friend, who did not give me his name, has arranged for one of his own security professionals to follow us while we are in China in order to protect us from any harm. He gave me a photograph of the agent and said his first name is Jin."

"Everything is fine now," Angela said, attempting to ease my obvious concern.

"Everything is okay," Melissa repeated.

"Everything is not okay," I said. "A short while ago, I noticed many hushed conversations and concerned looks on people's faces as they viewed their phones. I tried in vain to access the internet from here but couldn't. Then Darrell sent me a text from Hong Kong about a bombing."

"What kind of bombing?" Melissa asked.

"He didn't say but said he would call us."

"We need to exit this baggage area," Melissa said, "and then I can access the Internet."

When we cleared customs and entered the reception hall, there were police everywhere; the airport was in a state of a high security threat.

Melissa could barely speak as she watched the news footage on her phone of thick clouds of smoke billowing in the Hong Kong night above Tsim Sha Tsui.

"What's going on?" Angela and I asked.

"A bomb has gone off in Hong Kong," she said. "It appears to be a terrorist attack."

"Where?" I asked.

"One block from Tsim Sha Tsui subway station. That is one subway stop from my parents." Melissa was in tears.

"Thank God, they are calling me now," she said as her phone began vibrating in her hand.

We traveled by taxi to the Shanghai train station to catch the bullet train to Hangzhou. I received a phone call from Downers Grove shortly after purchasing our train tickets.

"Yes, I'm fine, Dad," I said. "I'm at the Shanghai train station waiting for our train to Hangzhou. Angela is with me but Darrell is back in Hong Kong. He called my phone and he's fine. Angela and I are with Melissa Tang, who is escorting us on our trip to meet a friend and to do some sightseeing."

My father knew the real purpose of our trip and that this wasn't it, but just in case my secure Blackphone was being surveilled on the mobile phone network in China that I was using, I had to speak in coded language.

"Have a good time sightseeing with your friends. Your mom says hi. Lucie says hi and that she misses you. Let me know how you are doing and when you return to Hong Kong."

"I will, Dad, thanks for calling."

After my conversation, Melissa asked us to completely turn off our phones and to store them in protective cases that she had brought with her.

I explained to Angela and Melissa what my father had communicated.

"We have to contact Chief Ryan."

"How come?" Angela asked. "I could hear your father but did not hear him say anything about Chief Ryan. And who is Lucie?"

"He said it in code. Lucie is our dog. My dad is telling me Chief Ryan is missing me, meaning, he wants me to contact him."

"Wow," Melissa said, "I thought we were the only strange family that communicated with code words."

"Darrell told me that we must assume all our electronic communication is being monitored. I'm keeping my phone off when I'm not using it."

"Even when our phones are off," Melissa warned, "our conversations in China can be monitored. That's why I keep mine in a special protective case when I'm not using it."

"Our phones use encryption," I said, "and have disposable SIM cards."

"The cyber-technology here is so good that even encrypted systems are not safe. Our phones are not secure or protected against surveillance."

"I've been talking to Darrell on several calls already," I said.

"Yes, but those were incoming calls from Hong Kong. There is a way to get those calls through without surveillance with certain encrypted phones like Darrell's," Melissa said.

"I can't keep track of it, Melissa, but Darrell is calling me now."

"Go ahead and connect," Melissa said. I greeted Darrell.

"Did you listen to our Marco Polo message and are you in a private area where there would be no hidden listening devices?"

I repeated the question and Melissa affirmed that we were in a safe place.

"Not yet and we are," I said.

"Are your other phones in Melissa's protective case?" Darrell asked.

Melissa nodded her head affirming that they were after I repeated that question.

"Yes."

"Good. You can put me on speaker so Angela and Melissa can hear. Okay, after dinner, the table conversation drifted to a discussion of the perceived ongoing conflict between the U.S. and China over the Diaoyu Islands. They all agreed of the dire need of everyone in Hong

Kong to do whatever they could to help resolve their conflict with China peacefully. If conflict broke out between the U.S. and China, China would seize the opportunity to take over Hong Kong militarily in the name of national security. Their freedom here would evaporate," Darrell said.

"What do Charles and Elizabeth Sīkòu think about this?" Melissa asked.

"Commander Sīkòu told us, 'Just as the British and Chinese worked hard together to bring us a peaceful transition of Hong Kong from a former British possession back into the sovereignty of China, so our American friends and Chinese leaders must work hard together to resolve this conflict peacefully and strengthen their global partnerships and friendship.' They are clearly caught in the middle of this conflict with direct ties to the president of China but with staunch loyalty to the people of Hong Kong," Darrell continued. "They also have many American friends.

"After several cups of tea and some traditionally baked lianrong mooncakes, we retired for the evening but then the second bomb blast occurred," Darrell said. "We immediately arose, left our rooms, and went to the veranda where we had been eating earlier. Facing Hong Kong Harbor and Kowloon, all we could see was thick smoke rising from the area of Tsim Sha Tsui. We could hear the sirens. Chen confirmed through his security contacts that a large car bomb had exploded in front of the Peninsula Hotel, a famous tourist destination. It was another terrorist attack."

After the call ended, we sat in silence together.

"We still have not talked to Chief Ryan about all these recent events," I said.

"I think before contacting him, we need to find out how to make a secure call to the U.S.," Angela said.

We all agreed.

"Melissa, let's have another look at that security man, Jin Liu, so we will be able to recognize him," Angela said.

Melissa took out the photo. They knew that Jin was personally known and highly recommended by Mr. Shan, the life-long friend of Melissa's father, and that Jin was described by Mr. Shan as intelligent, multilingual, and an exceptional security agent.

"He is quite handsome," Melissa said, not intending for everyone to hear her spontaneous assessment.

"I noticed," Angela said.

"Let's hope he can protect as good as he looks," I said, not caring about my sloppy grammar.

"I have a feeling he is quite capable of defending himself and us," Melissa said.

"I hope you're right," I said. "Before we make our way to the station to catch our bullet train to Hangzhou, let's do some shopping. We have some time to kill."

Angela gave me a curious look.

"What do you have in mind?" she asked.

"You'll see."

CHAPTER 21

JIN LIU WAS TRYING TO do his job well, but he could not understand what we were doing. He had followed us to the Jiangzhenlao Department Store, a fifteen-minute taxi ride from the airport. We all went to a ladies' clothing department for older women. First, we purchased canes and purses. Then, we tried on women's clothing but for much older women, including me. After purchasing our outfits, we purchased makeup and then disappeared into the restrooms. We emerged looking like three women in their eighties. Jin almost panicked, thinking he had lost us, until he realized what we were doing. Then his facial expressions turned from concern to amusement. We had just made Jin's job much easier as we would not be moving fast as three older ladies.

In our disguises, we waited for our bullet train on the very crowded platform, knowing that Jin was not far away and would be coming with us. We had only ten more minutes until the train arrived when two young men suddenly came up behind us. One stumbled into Melissa, distracting her, while the second man grabbed her purse and began to run. Instinctively, Melissa ran after the second man.

While we were frantically looking through crowds in all directions trying to figure out where Melissa had run to, she caught up to the purse thief as he turned a corner and entered a dingy hallway. The first man arrived shortly behind Melissa, dumbfounded that an old woman could move that fast. She was trapped in a dead-end hallway between the two thieves with only one exit door to a janitor's supply closet.

The two purse-snatching thieves closed in on Melissa but were hesitant, realizing she could not be an old woman. This gave Jin time to catch up to them from behind, but before he could react, Melissa brought the thief holding her purse to the ground with a strong kick to his left knee. The other thief tried to put her in a choke hold from behind, but she quickly slid toward the floor and flipped him over her body onto his back, and then came down hard on top of him with her elbow striking his sternum. Both of them cried out in pain and Melissa grabbed her purse.

Jin backed off into the small crowd that had quietly gathered, amazed at how quickly this old woman had subdued the two attackers. The crowd began clapping and Melissa smiled, uttered a couple of lines in Chinese to the onlookers, and disappeared into the subway crowd on the platform just before the police arrived. Jin was both relieved and impressed. This woman he was sent to protect could obviously protect herself.

Fortunately, after Melissa returned to the platform, we were able to board the train before the police could locate Melissa through the eyewitnesses at the scene. Melissa knew eyewitnesses could blow her cover as an old woman, but she had no choice though, because her mobile phone and identity papers were in her purse.

While on the train, I retrieved my phone to listen to the Marco Polo message. I put in my earphones to watch and listen in private:

Hi Johann. Greetings from the Jumbo Floating Restaurant in Aberdeen, where we are enjoying dinner. Anna, guess where Chief Ryan wants us to meet him?

I don't know, Rome? Paris?

No, Istanbul.

Awesome. I've always wanted to go there.

Chief Ryan wants you and Angela to come to Istanbul as soon as you return to Hong Kong from China. You can bring Melissa too if she would like to join us. Then guess where we are going, Anna?

Cairo?

No, we are then all going to Malta.

Why Malta? I know HSBC is there.

We'll see.

It's also on my must-see list.

We'll see you all in a few days.

I contemplated the video message and had the same question as Anna, "Why Malta?" Immediately I turned off my phone and put it back into its protective case. I needed to talk to Chief Ryan. We now had thirty-six hours to do our business in China before he would be traveling to Malta.

While on the train, we ditched our disguises and changed into business casual. We all had to use our phones again and risk a surveillance breach in order to arrange our travel to Malta. Fortunately, the train had good Wi-Fi for that. We arrived in Hangzhou without further incident. Although we knew that Jin was somewhere on the train with us, we didn't know at the time that he was hiding close by, monitoring our communication with some very sophisticated high-tech equipment. He knew we had to speed up our plans in China.

Our bullet train had arrived in Hangzhou around noon. We quickly found a taxi willing to take us to the Zhejiang Art Museum on the southeastern shore of West Lake. Melissa, who had been looking for Jin, was the first to spot him when he stepped off the train.

Neither Jin nor any of us realized that some unwanted company was following both of our taxis. Jin's taxi sped up and pulled beside us. Jin's taxi driver rolled down Jin's window on the passenger side and our driver did the same. When our taxi driver rolled down the window, Jin's driver shouted in Mandarin, "We are being followed."

Our driver said, "Follow me."

We sped past them and accelerated, dangerously passing cars and trucks until we abruptly pulled into a parking garage, drove up the fourth floor, parked and turned the car off. Remarkably, the taxi behind was able to follow and Angela voiced what we were all thinking, "These are no ordinary taxi drivers." We learned later the two drivers were part of Jin's security team.

After twenty minutes of waiting quietly, Jin received a text message indicating those who had followed did not know our whereabouts and had left the area. Jin impressed me as a well-trained professional. He turned to us and said kindly in fluent English, "Thank you for your patience and I apologize for the unusual driving. We were being followed but the threat is now gone."

Angela smiled and replied in Mandarin, "Thank you Jin, we feel safe in your hands."

Jin was taken aback that Angela could speak good Mandarin.

Melissa then smiled at Jin and repeated what Angela had said for added emphasis.

We arrived at the Zhejiang Arts Museum confident that we were alone. Just after we entered the building, Huang Tai and his uncle, who we code-named General Hu, stepped out of the shadows to greet us in the lobby. I knew it was not culturally appropriate, but I gave Huang Tai a very warm greeting, grabbing both of his forearms with my hands. After making brief introductions to each other, General Hu suggested that we go on a walk together toward the Leifeng Pagoda, which was not far to the south of us.

Huang Tai turned to me and said, "Please share your concerns with my uncle."

"I have heard much about you from Huang Tai," I said, "and I am greatly honored to meet you."

"I am also honored," Melissa said.

"As am I," Angela added.

"We are all here, General, because Huang Tai is my friend, and I trust him. Huang Tai assures us that we also can completely trust you, so we put our lives in your hands."

"You are wise to trust Huang Tai," the general responded in very good English. "I will do everything I can to protect you."

"There are nefarious forces, General, that are seeking to push the United States and China into a dangerous military confrontation," I said. "We have learned in the last few months that both of our countries are contemplating the use of WMD's from satellite stations. We are all private citizens that learned about this threat accidentally through the advanced surveillance techniques of a private club outside of Chicago."

"Yes, I have heard of your *Eleutheria Club*. You are quite an impressive group of young people, similar to my nephew Huang Tai."

We were all a bit stunned, but then, we should not have been surprised that the general was able to find a great deal of information about us.

The general saw our facial expressions and chuckled, adding, "I suppose you know that in China we have pretty good surveillance capabilities. We know quite a bit about your activities."

"Then you must know, General, that although we are young and inexperienced, our intentions are good. We do not want our two nations to be destroyed by a war; we want our nations to be friends."

"That is what Huang Tai has told me, and I do believe him. That is why I was willing to meet with you. Can you tell me what you know about this impending conflict?"

As we continued to walk south along the lake, I started with the conversation we intercepted between Atlas Churgrill and General Nicoli Sarkovsky. General Hu listened attentively until we were finished. We then all stopped walking and waited for his response.

The general sighed deeply and then responded, "Everything you have said I believe is true. Huang Tai has provided evidence to convince me that we now have the satellite technology to successfully launch a biological attack from space. A close confidant has confirmed that General Tso has recently armed a satellite with biological weapons. Many of our diplomats believe war with the U.S. is inevitable for many reasons, especially because of our recent trade wars as we each fight for global economic domination. Our leaders believe the COVID-19 pandemic is the beginning of war between our countries. I do not agree with this position."

Angela looked for encouragement from General Hu. "How do we stop this?"

"It is difficult to stop this momentum. If I begin to exert my influence to a degree that I am perceived as challenging General Tso, I could be arrested, imprisoned, or even executed. General Tso is much more powerful than I am. There are many other generals and national leaders who oppose war with the United States, but General Tso has the ear of the president of China. However, the president is rumored to be reluctant to favor a pre-emptive strike but would not oppose a retaliatory strike."

I then explained how this could take place.

"Our sources, General, suggest that China will be attacked with biological or chemical weapons from a third party in an attempt to frame the U.S. as the attacker, so that your president will be given no choice but to attack the U.S."

"And how might this third party accomplish such an attack?"

"We believe it will take place through a Russian satellite."

We all began walking again in silence as we contemplated the dilemma of preventing a world catastrophe. We soon reached the Leifeng Pagoda and looked upon the magnificent structure. General Hu broke the heavy silence.

"This original pagoda was built in 975 AD during the Five Dynasties and Ten Kingdoms period, at the order of King Qian Chu of Wuyue. Our ancestors built this structure to celebrate the birth of Qian Chu's son, born to Queen Yu. The original Pagoda was an octagonal, five-story structure built of brick and wood on a brick base. During the

Ming dynasty, Japanese pirates burned the pagoda during an attack on Hangzhou, suspecting the pagoda contained weapons. Over decades of abuse and neglect, the entire structure collapsed in September of 1924. This was a difficult time period in China. Seventy-five years later, in October 1999, at the end of one of the greatest periods of economic development in China, the provincial and municipal governments decided to rebuild Leifeng Pagoda on top of the ruins of the old one. The new pagoda opened in October 2002. It is a new century in China, one filled with hope for a bright future and in which our children, grandchildren, and great-grandchildren can thrive in peace. We cannot let this peace and economic blessing be destroyed by unwise men who are controlled by fear. I am afraid that the leaders of the older generation have already made too many reckless decisions."

The general looked into my eyes with steely determination.

"And how do you believe, Johann, that we can stop this plot to push our countries into war?"

"We must stop the retired Russian general who wants to be the next president of Russia and a South African billionaire who wants to be the next president of South Africa. They are both powerful men with a shared hatred toward our two countries. We must expose them and stop this planned biological attack."

"It may be up to the young people like you, Johann and Huang Tai, and like you, Angela and Melissa, and your friends, to stop this war. I will do all that I can to help you, but you will need to find a way to destroy the armed satellites."

"Huang Tai and I can create a laser system to incapacitate any space weapons and neutralize an attack, but we need the coordinates in space of the Chinese satellite with the WMD."

"I understand. It will be difficult to get this information, but when I do, it must be delivered face-to-face. I cannot risk using any electronic communication."

General Hu finished his last statement giving direct eye contact to me and Huang Tai. When he finished, I looked toward Huang Tai and we both exchanged glances. We knew it was up to us; we had to find a way to destroy the threat.

Huang Tai and Jin accompanied us safely back to the train station in Hangzhou without incident. We were relieved that other than initially being followed from the railway station, there were no security threats. Perhaps the threat against Melissa was thwarted when we lost the people following us, thanks to Jin's quick response and knowledge of the parking garages nearby.

Just as we sat down on the bullet train from Hangzhou back to Shanghai, we noticed everyone staring intently at their cell phones. Melissa asked a passenger nearby what was happening and was told a third bomb had exploded in Hong Kong, this one at the Star Ferry terminal on Hong Kong Island. Initial casualty reports were in the hundreds. I could see the waves of shock and fear sweep through the passengers. Hong Kong would certainly be on edge when we returned.

CHAPTER 22

OUR LONG FLIGHT BACK TO Hong Kong on Cathay Pacific from Shanghai was eerily quiet. Certainly, many were concerned about possible family members, friends, and relatives who could have been injured or killed in those three bombings. We were relieved to learn that Darrell and Anna had already left the island and were en route to Istanbul a day ahead of us. Our concern was for Melissa's family and friends.

Nearly 70,000 passengers a day travel by ferry back and forth across Victoria Harbour from Kowloon to Hong Kong Island. Melissa said her father travelled on Star Ferry four to five times a week and her mother at least once a week.

I reached across the aisle shortly after take-off and grabbed Melissa's hand to reassure her, but we both knew her parents could have been in harm's way and she had to wait an agonizing three hours before she could contact them. As soon as our plane touched down in Hong Kong, Melissa powered on her phone and called her father. Her mother answered—they were at the Hong Kong Seventh Day Adventist Hospital.

"Is Dad all right?"

"Yes, he's okay honey, but one of your father's friends and co-workers was severely injured in the blast at Star Ferry, and your father is quite upset. We are here in the waiting room while he is undergoing surgery to remove shrapnel from his body. God protected your father, as he left an hour earlier than normal on the ferry. He could have been on that pier if he had taken the ferry on his usual schedule."

Melissa exhaled a sigh of relief as tears streamed down her face. Angela grabbed her hand as our plane taxied toward the terminal and pulled into the gate.

Melissa was torn between wanting to accompany us to Istanbul and feeling the need to stay with her family. We convinced her to stay with her family in Hong Kong and to check up on her friends until things calmed down. We had no knowledge whether the bombings had anything to do with the plot to push the U.S. and China into war, but it had an opposite effect as the U.S. government was the first nation to offer its assistance to China. Our travel from Hong Kong to Istanbul was thankfully uneventful. While Angela and I were quietly sipping cappuccinos at a coffee shop near our gate in the Istanbul Havalimani Airport, a man with a cup of coffee and Danish pastry came to our table and asked if he could sit in one of the two empty chairs. We acquiesced, responding to him as if he was a stranger. The man was Chief Joshua Ryan. Five minutes later, at the table next to us, two others sat down with their cappuccinos and café lattes. I glanced over and saw Darrell and Anna enjoying their drinks with some light snacks.

After sitting quietly together for about ten minutes, we heard what sounded like automatic gunfire in the adjacent terminal. Emergency sirens went off for about ten seconds, but quickly shut off. We did not leave our table as we waited for police instructions. When the police came, they said they were just doing some drills and instructed us to stay and carry on as if there was no incident. We were able to board our flight thirty minutes later, after enduring a second intense security check, which included fifteen to twenty prying questions as to why we were going to Malta. After we each communicated tourism fifteen to twenty different ways, which was partially true, we were allowed to board. We heard no more automatic gunfire and assumed that whatever was going on had been a minor incident, but we did notice the tense looks on the faces of all the security personnel we encountered. The airport was too risky of a place for Chief Ryan to explain to us the primary reason why we were traveling to Malta, so we remained in the dark as to the main reason for our trip, beyond tourism.

Our two-hour flight to Malta was pleasant. The farther away from Istanbul we flew the better I felt. Arriving at the Malta International Airport near Luqa, we took a cab to the San Antonio Hotel in Bugibba, not far from St. Paul's Bay. After checking in to our hotel, we all went for a mile walk south on Qawra Road along the Qawra Coast, past Malta's beautiful aquarium, to the Luzzu Restaurant, right on the water facing east. Chief Ryan was unusually tight-lipped during the walk and turned around several times to make sure no one was following us. The large brick walkway, ranging from ten to twenty feet wide, provided plenty of open space so that it would be easy to see if anyone was following us. It was a beautiful sunny day, about seventy-two degrees, and a bit breezy. We sat on the terrace at the restaurant facing the dark blue Mediterranean Sea. Chief Ryan and Darrell ordered cold Cisk Excels, a local lager beer; Anna and Angela each ordered a flavored latte, and Chief Ryan ordered a coke for me.

After relaxing in his chair, donning a new pair of fancy sunglasses, wearing stylish tan khaki pants, a red polo shirt, comfortable

Italian loafers, pouring his cold Cisk Excel into a glass, Chief Ryan looked both extraordinarily cool and relaxed.

"Okay," he said looking at us with a crooked smile. "You have been amazingly patient waiting to hear why I abruptly pulled you out of Hong Kong to travel to this piece of rock halfway around the world."

"Whatever the reason, we are glad to be here as tourists and no longer in Istanbul," I said.

"Yes, that was tense in Istanbul," Chief Ryan said. "You all did an excellent job during those security interrogations. I did not feel free to say anything about this trip other than tourism until we got here. But before I begin, I need a full debrief of your trips to Hong Kong and China."

"That'll take some time."

"Hey, we're in no hurry, Johann." Chief Ryan was relaxed, enjoying his favorite local beer.

During the next ninety minutes, we recounted all the major events that had taken place in Hong Kong and China, with all of us chiming in and contributing to the stories.

Chief Ryan listened carefully, and although he barely interrupted us with questions, he jotted down two pages of notes. When we had finished, he then summarized for us.

"Did I miss anything?"

"We saw a beautiful pagoda on West Lake," Angela said, trying to add some lightness.

"And the bullet trains in China are wonderful," I said.

"I am glad you did not forget those important details," Chief Ryan said. "It cannot be all bad news."

I wanted to elaborate. "You are right, Chief Ryan. It isn't all bad news. We now know exactly what we need to do because what we have learned on these trips confirms the strategy of this nefarious group we are up against."

"I agree, Johann. Continue your analysis."

I laid out all the facts we had learned.

"I may be redundant here, but we know a great deal. Anna confirmed that Atlas Churgrill was moving large sums of money through his accounts at HSBC. She can get the details while here in Malta. Anna also believes that Sarkovsky is receiving funds from Churgrill here in Malta. We know these deposits are most likely for the purchase of a biological agent from Iran with components from Russia. We also confirmed through General Hu that General Tso had successfully armed a satellite space station with biological weapons. We know that the rocket launch was successful, based on the film analysis of the rocket launch. We also know the biological agent is confirmed to be Botulinum, which many others in our intelligence agencies also have concluded. We know that Churgrill's company now controls the Canadian company that manufactures the antidote to Botulinum poisoning. Thus, Churgrill will make hundreds of millions of dollars if there is a major biological attack with Botulinum because the U.S., and perhaps others fearing an attack with Botulinum, will need to purchase the antitoxin from the company he now owns the majority share of stock, Emergent BioSolutions. We have confirmation that the threat of a Saxitoxin attack was disinformation sent to government agencies in order to curtail the production of the Botulinum antitoxin HBAT. We also know that Churgrill knows that we are zeroing in on him and his nefarious plot because he has hired professional assassins to kill us. We know that inside China, it will be nearly impossible to stop a biological attack on the U.S. if China believes it is being attacked by the U.S. We know that before China can attack us, we must destroy its satellite-based weapons' station in space or immediately destroy any WMD it may launch."

"Excellent summary, Johann, but there is something important I do not fully understand. The CDC oversees the manufacture of our own supplies of antitoxin in the U.S. Why would the U.S. need to purchase antitoxin from EBS in Canada?" asked Chief Ryan.

"We don't have enough. My friend Nicole Jacobson, who works at the Naval Medical Research Center in collaboration with the National Biodefense Analysis & Countermeasures Center, told me the U.S. will need to purchase more than 100 million doses of the Botulinum antitoxin from EBS in Canada to meet its need.

"But there is something I don't fully understand," I continued. "It is clear to me that Sarkovsky wants to be the next president of Russia and disdains both the U.S. and China, so his motivation is clear and he will make a lot of money from the stock in EBS Churgrill gave him, from which he can fund his political ambitions. Churgrill, in contrast, is already a billionaire and although he wants to be president of South Africa, I don't fully understand his motivation for doing this."

"That has always puzzled me, too, Johann. Last week the CIA received information from the National Intelligence Coordinating Committee in South Africa that enabled them to complete his psychological profile. We learned that Atlas' father was hard on him from a young age, no matter how hard he tried to please his father. When Churgrill became the South African ambassador to the United Nations, it was a proud moment in his life. His father, however, publicly criticized him for introducing a United Nations resolution to ban all military satellites in space, a position openly rejected by the

U.S., Russia, and China. The Chinese and American ambassadors made Churgrill look foolish, and Churgrill's father felt he had humiliated himself. When Churgrill ran for the presidency in South Africa, his father felt he wasn't ready and would not publicly support him. His father was a wealthy businessman and former member of the South African Parliament, so his lack of support was devastating both professionally and personally. Something snapped in Churgrill."

Angela looked at Chief Ryan.

"My brother, Angelo, agrees. He has been following Churgrill's activities in Italy now for more than a year and believes Churgrill is unstable."

"If your brother is correct, Angela, then I believe Churgrill is deeply emotionally wounded and very dangerous. He is out to prove his father wrong."

After another thirty minutes of discussion, I asked Chief Ryan to address our biggest question.

"Why are we here in Malta, Chief Ryan?"

"Because we all needed to be together to plan our next steps and Anna needed to come here anyway to investigate Churgrill's banking activities, and we need to talk to a high-ranking ex-military general who lives here. Can you think of a nicer place to rendezvous?"

"No, sir," we all replied.

"I see three immediate courses of action needed. First, we still do not know the details of how Churgrill and Sarkovsky plan to attack China from space and blame it on the U.S. I believe the general we are going to see soon may help us in this regard. Second, we must accelerate the development of a defensive satellite-based system in space to destroy any WMD that can be launched from a satellite.

"Johann," Chief Ryan said, turning to me, "you will need to spearhead this effort. You can get Huang Tai and others to help you. Third, we need to ramp up manufacture of the HBAT antitoxin and its distribution to key metropolitan areas throughout the U.S., just in case our other plans fail and we are attacked."

"And fourth?" asked Anna.

"Do you have a fourth action plan, Anna?" asked Chief Ryan.

"I do. We need to plan when we will visit the 'must see' places while we are in Malta."

"I agree, Anna; we need to make time for that," Chief Ryan said. "But first, we must meet a retired Russian general, and second, we must put surveillance on the Bugibba branch of HSBC. That is the big reason why you are here, Anna."

"As for me, I hope I'm here for tourism."

"Nice try, Johann; your presence is also strategic. The retired general we are meeting with was one of the foremost experts in the country on the capabilities of Russian satellites. I need you to ask him the right questions. He moved here because he no longer trusts the Russian president or the Russian government."

Sitting up in my chair and leaning toward Chief Ryan, I asked earnestly, "How well does this Russian general know General Nicoli Sarkovsky?"

"Very well. And he also knows Atlas Churgrill."

Chief Ryan finished his beer and then grinned broadly. "Before laying out our strategies, I saw a case of gelato on the way in. Let's go get some."

I picked out one scoop of Amaretto and one scoop of Biscotti, two flavors you won't find in the U.S. Anna and Chief Ryan picked out equally exotic flavors. We returned to the balcony and sat in the shade with our glass gelato dishes, intending to delay the melting process so we could all enjoy our double scoops very slowly.

Chief Ryan revealed more of his thinking.

"Here's the deal. Nicoli Sarkovsky was a rival to General Mikkail Suberov, the man we are going to see tomorrow. Sarkovsky pushed Suberov out of power, although he still has some favor with the president. The Russian president allowed it because Sarkovsky is funneling money to him by giving him a cut of illegal deals, which the president turns a blind eye to as long as he receives a cut. Suberov has warned the president not to trust Sarkovsky, and he doesn't, but the Russian president will take in $20 million on the Sarkovsky-Churgrill deal, and he has been in on many other deals of similar magnitude."

"So, it sounds like payback time."

"I think so, Johann. General Suberov feels that now is the time to pay back General Sarkovsky for forcing him to leave his role as a top advisor to the president and to leave Russia because of concerns about being forced to compromise his integrity."

Anna felt uneasy.

"Does my boss in Hong Kong know I'm here?"

"Yes, he knows."

"Twenty years ago, both Sarkovsky and Suberov purchased homes in Malta with funds provided by the president of Russia as thank you gifts for their loyalty. The president has learned that rewards are just as powerful as punishments. Rewarding loyalty, he discovered, produces even greater loyalty. There are very few people who have turned on the Russian president. Even after General Suberov left Russia, the president sent his personal security to make sure Suberov and his family were protected and comfortably moved out of Russia, originally to Prague. Suberov then later decided to move permanently to his winter home in Malta."

"Does Sarkovsky come here often?"

"Yes, is my guess," Anna answered. "I bet he is laundering money through his local HSBC branch here in Bugibba."

"You nailed it, Anna—it is speculated to be up to $20 million per year, all through one small HSBC branch not far from our hotel."

"Wow. I knew the banking laws were very liberal here. I just did not ever expect that much money coming through one branch would not attract some attention," Anna said.

"I anticipate it is hidden in the very large transactions for the whole country," Chief Ryan speculated. "But I am sure you will be able to figure it out while you are here."

"This gelato is wonderful," I said. "I like this place."

"I knew you would, Johann. Wait till the boat ride tomorrow."

"I thought General Suberov lived here?"

"He does—just on a different island, a smaller and more private island."

The steady breeze began to develop into a stronger offshore wind.

"The famous winds of Malta are upon us. Let's walk back to the San Antonio Hotel and enjoy the ocean vistas on the way."

Upon entering into the San Antonio lobby, the hotel concierge spotted us and told us there was a man in the coffee shop who had been waiting for us. We had not told anyone yet of our arrival in Malta, not even General Suberov. We were very hesitant to meet a stranger given the many attacks on our lives. We walked toward the coffee shop with great apprehension.

CHAPTER 23

CAUTIOUSLY ENTERING THE LARGE COFFEE shop adjacent to the lobby of the San Antonio Hotel, we could see that it was not heavily crowded. It seemed like a good place to talk. An older man left his seat and approached us. He was not intimidating. He introduced himself in English as Martino, and with a strong accent, explained that he was a local fisherman and friend of General Suberov. He said that he would take us in his fishing boat the following morning to General Suberov's home, which was on another island. Then he drew directions that we could follow to reach the dock where he would meet us tomorrow.

I asked Martino how he knew we were here.

"General Suberov knows," he said in broken English smiling. "He knows many things."

Chief Ryan smiled. "Yes, that's exactly what the general had told me. He said, 'I will know when you arrive.'"

———————

At 7:00 a.m. sharp, Martino was waiting on the dock for us about a half mile walk from our hotel. His sturdy but heavily weathered thirty-two-foot fishing boat with twin engines was tied up beside him.

"This is the Maltese Falcon."

265

A proud smile came across his face, but I doubted if he had ever read the novel.

As if he was reading my mind, he turned to me and said, "I like that movie very much."

Martino was a man of few words but was obviously a very hard worker and we could all see from the way he moved things around his boat that he was very strong for his size. He had a welcoming disposition and a gentle smile. At first, we didn't know how to read him, but then grew to like him. We all offered our services to him as our boat captain. He gave us all a very warm smile and began giving us all simple duties to carry out with very gentle but clear commands. It was a joy for us to help him and it was not hard to discern that Martino was a kind man.

The sea was a bit choppy, but not enough to upset our stomachs. One reason Martino had wanted to leave early was because the wind was forecast to be calmer in the morning. It was also a good time when there would be the best security, as not many boats would be out at that time and thus, we would be hard to secretly follow. When we reached Gozo Island, we travelled along its southern shore before entering a bay near San Lorenz. We entered into a cove with a private fishing pier and dock that was hidden from view. A beautiful golden retriever came running down the dock to greet us. He was wagging his tail furiously and barking, obviously happy to see Martino.

Martino and Brady, the golden retriever, led us off the dock and up a heavily wooded trail to a patio behind a beautiful two-story house that was nestled in the trees. Sitting in a chair in front of an outdoor fireplace, sipping coffee, and reading the International Wall

Street Journal, was General Mikkail Suberov. He rose and greeted us heartily as if we were old friends.

Martino and the general spoke with each other briefly in Maltese, and then the general thanked Martino in English for bringing us here safely. We also thanked Martino before he departed for a real fishing trip. General Suberov immediately took the role of a gracious host, asking us to be seated and asking his wife, Leyla, if she would bring out a fresh pot of coffee with cream and sugar, fresh fruit, and cinnamon rolls that she had made that morning. After we were all comfortably seated, the general asked that, before we discussed the important business at hand, we first each introduce ourselves in a more in-depth manner. He said he would begin, which helped to put us all at ease.

When he had finished, we were all taken aback by the authenticity with which the general had shared about his life. He talked about the heartbreaking loss of his twenty-one-year-old son, who gave his life to rescue two of his comrades during a military operation against terrorists in Chechnya.

He also shared about the loss of his wife's parents, who died of sickness and malnutrition due to lack of food during the Stalinist purges of the Jewish city in which they lived. He shared how he had risen in rank rapidly and how he was in the right place at the right time to protect the president of Russia from some competitors who were trying to destroy him before he rose to power in the SVR. He shared his grief and sadness for his country, which he believed had gone astray when it embraced communism during the Bolshevik Revolution instead of developing into a representative republic like other European nations. His greatest fear was that the Russian president would miscalculate and risk nuclear destruction in conflict with the West. He shared happy times that he and his wife had enjoyed recently with their two daughters, two great sons-in-law, and six grandchildren who lived in Switzerland and Italy.

Chief Joshua Ryan shared next, following General Suberov's example with more personal information, much of it that I didn't know. I knew my father and Chief Ryan were friends, but I did not know that he considered my father to be among his closest friends. I also knew his father was the head of counterterrorism for the city of Chicago and that Chief Ryan was among the security officers that fought against the terrorists in Chicago, but I never understood the full extent to which he was a hero who saved many lives during the Sears Tower attack. I also did not fully understand the authority Chief Ryan had been given by the Secretary of Homeland Security through his position on the Joint Terrorism Task Force, partly because of the close friendship the Secretary had with Chief Ryan's father.

Anna then shared about herself. Although I had learned much about Anna through our many conversations, I did not know that she'd dreamed of becoming a concert pianist, but that her dream was crushed through a freak injury to her right hand, which was caught in a car door when she was nine years old. Although her hand had healed, the ligament damage greatly reduced her flexibility and speed. She never was able to fully recover the brilliance she had shown on the piano from a very young age.

Darrell then shared his brief biography after his sister's. We had been friends for long enough, I did not expect to learn something new, but I did. I knew Darrell was born in Tao Fong Shan in the New Territories of China to the west of Hong Kong and that his family immigrated to Taiwan when he was eight years old. I also knew that his father then took a job at a hospital in Illinois when Darrell was fourteen, which brought Darrell to the Chicago area. Because of Darrell's fluency in English, Mandarin, and Cantonese, after he had served in the Air Force for four years, he had become a professional interpreter for the U.S. Citizenship and Immigration Services in Chicago. What I didn't know was that Darrell had always wanted to be a licensed commercial pilot, but his impaired eyesight prevented him from being an Air Force pilot where he had hoped to gain the flying experience he needed to pursue a career with United Airlines, the company he had preferred because they fly throughout the world.

Angela then spoke. As she shared about her life growing up in Italy with a mother who was a model for Versace and a father who had served four terms in the Senate of the Italian Parliament, I could better understand her socially liberal upbringing. She disclosed to us that her parents had been married for decades but seemed to have each had their dalliances, at least according to the paparazzi. She was never sure what was true and what was simply rumor and speculation. Their family was surrounded by important people and for the most part, worldly people, during most of her life until her parents purchased a vineyard in a small village in Tuscany after retiring from politics and the fashion industry. It was in her last few teenage years when she and her brothers, Stefan and Angelo, developed a close bond with their parents. Now she was very close to her parents and brothers and was especially bonded with Angelo.

Angela shared with the group that she had unique interests. She enjoyed painting but also loved physics and astronomy. She said her parents would always tell her that their family had da Vinci in their blood line. They felt that the University of Chicago would be a perfect place for her to pursue her interests in art, science, and astronomy. The more I learned about Angela, the more I understood why I was deeply attracted to her.

I was the last one in our group to share. General Suberov was surprised to learn that I was only sixteen. He thought I was eighteen or nineteen, close to the age of his son when he had died. As I shared, I had an intuitive sense that something I said reminded him of his son. I knew he liked me and it made me feel drawn to him. It was strange, since I never anticipated having such positive feelings about a Russian general that I knew little about, but he exhibited many fatherly qualities. He had a hearty laugh and did not hold back when he thought something was funny or stupid.

It was a brilliant strategy of the general to give us time to share about our lives for it helped us all feel very comfortable with each other. The general then called his wife, Leyla, who shared briefly about her life and the lives of their children and grandchildren. She was a strong and yet gracious woman, and she obviously loved her husband. Interestingly, she had also developed and maintained a close relationship with the ex-wife of the president of Russia.

We were just about ready to talk business when General Suberov asked us all to be quiet.

"I hear something," he whispered.

He opened up his laptop and his cameras verified what he had heard, a drone was above their home, positioned to allow others to listen in on our conversation. He put his finger across his lips, motioning to us that we should all remain silent. He then took steps to neutralize the threat. His jamming devices were excellent—the drone above was cut off from all visual and audio communication. General Suberov then accessed a home security application and launched an attack against the surveillance drone by a small predator drone about the size of a locust. The predator drone found its target quickly and completely destroyed the intruder. Now we could communicate without interference or concern, but to be on the safe side, we moved our meeting to the general's secure underground office facility.

He addressed all of us, preferring to speak in Russian. His wife Leyla interpreted into English.

"Thank you all for sharing something very precious from your lives. We have all suffered the loss of that which we have greatly valued, some more than others. We are here to prevent millions of people from losing their lives. Evil men are trying to ignite a major war between the United States and China for their own personal gains. One of the men, Nicoli Sarkovsky, I know very well. He is ambitious and dangerous and wants to be the next president of Russia after the current president leaves that post. The Russian president is already one of the richest men in the world, having milked billions of dollars from the Russian people, so his ambitions are to hold onto power and create a great legacy for himself. The president is using Sarkovsky for his own purposes and Sarkovsky knows this. He also knows the tables can turn quickly if Russian weapons were ever used to kill millions of Americans, which would create the opening for Sarkovsky to seize power."

The general then turned his attention to Churgrill.

"Atlas Churgrill is a complex and disturbed man, and also brilliant. He doesn't need money; he wants recognition and respect. He also has political ambitions. He failed once at the South African presidency and has vowed not to fail again to prove his father wrong. Now, he is perceived as a legitimate businessman, though one with a sordid past. Those who know him understand he is a driven person. God help us if we don't stop these two men."

He paused and waited for questions. I couldn't help myself from asking, "Do you believe in God, General?"

"Yes, but I'll believe in Him more if He helps us to stop this evil, because it's going to take a miracle. We have much work to do and we need to work right through the Christmas season. The danger is imminent."

I had completely forgotten about Christmas.

The next six hours were a blur. Our plans were not that complicated, but we must have developed a half dozen contingencies for every planned action. General Suberov would use his considerable network in Russia to find out where and when an impending terrorist attack on China from space would be carried out and how this attack would be blamed on the U.S. Through her connection, Leyla would work to see what dates the Russian president was planning to use the Palace on the Idokopas Cape, their summer home on the Black Sea. The general knew the president would strategically be there during the time of an attack on China to remove all plausibility that he or Russia had anything to do with it. This would also help to verify the timing of the attack.

Anna was going to go to the HSBC Bugibba branch and access their financial records to document the suspected tens of millions of euros that Sarkovsky and Churgrill were funneling through HSBC. Chief Ryan would work through his contacts in U.S. intelligence agencies to confirm increased threats from China of a biological attack on the U.S. Angela would work through her brother to aggressively use

INTERPOL to follow the movement and activities of Atlas Churgrill, who also was a person of interest trafficking weapons between northern Libya and southern Italy.

Darrell was going to work with his network in Taiwan to see if they could penetrate the cyber defenses of China's satellite network to determine the coordinates where China was posed to launch a biological attack in retaliation for a perceived U.S. attack. I was going to return to Chicago and invite Huang Tai to work with me in the Kavli Institute for Cosmological Physics to develop a laser system that would destroy any biological weapons in space, either before or as soon as they were launched. For me and Angela, we had to both postpone returning to the University of Chicago in January for the spring semester. We were not happy about having to temporarily stop our education plans.

After our planning was completed, we emerged from the general's secure underground office and planning facility to enjoy dinner in the large gazebo outside with a beautiful view. Leyla made lamb chops with mint jelly, roasted potatoes, grilled vegetables, fresh local Grouper steaks purchased at the fish market in the late morning, and several Russian deserts, including Pastila.

Just as I was taking my last bite of Pastila, as we watched the beautiful sunset, we heard the faint sound of a boat coming into the bay. General Suberov immediately called his security detail as the boat seemed to be coming toward us at a high speed. I could barely make out the boat as it turned into our cove when I saw a bright flash emanate from the boat and heard the clear sound of a rocket propelled explosive heading toward the gazebo. There was no time to do anything but to dive for cover as far away from the gazebo as possible. I jumped into nearby bushes about ten feet away and buried my face into the ground and covered my head with my arms.

Holding my breath, I waited for the destruction of the gazebo, I heard the blast on the other side from where I was lying. I thanked God the explosive had sailed just over the roof structure and landed far enough away from us that no one was injured by the explosion. Before the perpetrators could launch a second projectile, General Suberov's weaponized drone, which one of his security personnel controlled, had launched its explosive into the speedboat in a counterattack, damaging it heavily and starting a fire. The boat retreated immediately with thick smoke emanating from it until it exploded just after it left the cove.

———————

Shortly after we arrived back at our hotel, I received a call from Susan. She was at the new meeting place of the *Eleutheria Club*.

"Johann," she said after telling me how much she missed us, "tell Chief Ryan I am very happy with the new surveillance equipment he purchased for us. I was able to intercept two calls made by Atlas Churgrill from the back deck of his home in Coffee Bay on the wild coast of South Africa."

"You penetrated his mobile phone network?"

"Yes, crystal clear, and I recorded his conversations."

"Excellent," I said.

"The first call was to General Sarkovsky's home in Malta. And the second one to his stockbroker. I am sending the two audio files encrypted via Dropbox. Tell Chief Ryan he needs to listen ASAP. Have to run, Johann. Be safe!"

We convened in Chief Ryan's hotel room back in the San Antonio hotel and listened to the audio files together. Chief Ryan clicked on the first file and kept the sound low so that we all had to huddle around his laptop to hear.

"Good evening, General."

"Good evening, Mr. Churgrill."

"I need an update on the execution of our plans; our opponents are beginning to quickly piece things together."

"The Chinese successfully loaded their WMD on their weather satellite. Our satellite launch is confirmed for tomorrow night. The weather will be perfect. The payload has already been loaded and only a few people close to the president know about it. Of course, the president officially knows nothing about it. None of the space scientists have any idea about the Botulinum on board."

"How much Botulinum?"

"What we had agreed on. There will be enough toxin on our weather station to kill millions in China and there is enough toxin on the Chinese satellite station to kill millions in the U.S. The catastrophe in both countries will be quite substantial."

"When will the attack be initiated?"

"Once we launch the satellite, it will take six hours for it to reach its docking station but a couple of days to complete the docking. Once it's in place, then we need to set up our command and control center in Malta and complete some testing to make it fully operational."

"So next month's target date is still on track?"

"Yes, as long as the long-term weather forecasts hold and a high-pressure system settles over eastern China. Any low-pressure systems will fundamentally interfere with effective delivery and dispersion, so we need clear weather. It looks like God is on our side this time."

"All those poor souls that think their great militaries will protect them from attacks will have a rude awakening. They should have listened to me when I warned them at the United Nations. But we will save most of them with our antitoxin."

"Indeed, you will, Mr. Churgrill, and the Chinese and Americans will thank you and pour billions of dollars into your company. What a great irony."

"Yes, but only after the U.S. and China pummel each other. They are nearly at war now over the COVID-19 pandemic. I still have one lingering question, General. How do we know the quality of the toxin? I don't trust the Iranians."

"As we have previously discussed, the biotoxin in both WMDs is produced with oversight by Russian scientists. It has been thoroughly tested and I have scrutinized the test results. Iran has assured me that the toxin will do its work and the president said our intelligence has verified this."

"Yes, I know. Will the president be resting comfortably in his summer home while China and the U.S. are threatening to annihilate one another?"

"Yes, he will. The president feels both vindicated and pleased."

"Is he convinced he can prove the toxin did not originally come from Russia and that there is no definitive means by which the Chinese or Americans can trace the attack from a Russian weather satellite?"

"Yes, he is one hundred percent convinced of this. The weather satellite will strategically pass in and out of the orbit of one of America's most important surveillance satellites—the one that has long been believed to carry weapons that can be launched from space. Our engineers have arranged it so that the Chinese will trace the attack back to the Americans."

"Good. I will be here until it is time to go to Malta. Keep me informed."

As we listened to the recording, I could imagine Churgrill picking up his glass and making a toast to Sarkovsky.

Chief Ryan said, "Let's listen to the second call before we discuss what we've heard." He then clicked on the next audio file.

"This is Ethan Krugar."

"Churgrill here. How much is EBS trading for?"

"It closed Friday at $57.02 per share."

"Good. It's creeping up slowly as we planned but not fast enough to raise suspicion. I want to make one more purchase tomorrow."

"Are you sure you want to risk scrutiny? You already own fifty-three percent of the company."

"I know, but I want seventy percent of the company."

"Wow, another seventeen percent will make big news."

"I realize that, but we will announce we are close to a major breakthrough on a new AIDS vaccine."

"I didn't know EBS was diversifying into AIDS vaccines."

"We're not, Ethan, but the public needs a good reason to explain my purchase."

"Is that legal?"

"As long as I have the intention of developing such a vaccine or acquiring the development from others and feel we will make a breakthrough in short time, the government cannot prove otherwise."

"Isn't it a big risk putting so much money in one stock?"

"The value of EBS is going to rise dramatically."

"Why?"

"You ask too many questions, Ethan. Let's just say because of an accident. Just do your job and don't worry about anything else."

"I'll call Botha early and get the trade set up. Do you want me to sell another stock to help generate the purchase funds?"

"Yes, sell all my social media stock."

"All of it?"

"Yes, all of it. Social media stocks are going to run into government interference very soon and then those stocks will take a beating. That should generate enough funds for the EBS purchase."

"I agree. I guess I'll sell my social media stock, too, and invest in EBS."

"You are beginning to smarten up, Ethan. I just might keep you on my payroll."

After a long pause when the audio file ended, Chief Ryan initiated the discussion.

"These conversations just confirm what we have already pieced together. Churgrill now has tighter control of Emergent BioSolutions.

What we have to do now is stop the plot and secure the evidence to put these two men in prison for the rest of their lives. What is new is that Churgrill plans to come to Sarkovsky's home here in Malta, probably to avoid any scrutiny after the attacks. "

I spoke out the obvious.

"If we can't stop the scheduled launch of the Russian satellite, then we will have to intercept those weapons in space."

Angela looked directly into my eyes.

"Or millions could die."

I could not read her eyes to know what she was thinking. I hoped it was more hope than fear. We all left Malta with heavy hearts but strong determination to fight this plot that would unleash horror across the U.S. and China.

CHAPTER 24

WHEN I ARRIVED BACK IN Chicago, I was overjoyed that Huang Tai was waiting for me at the airport. I felt confident that together we would be able to develop a successful laser system capable of destroying any biological weapons in space.

As we were waiting for my baggage at the O'Hare Airport terminal, I received an urgent text message from Anna asking me to call her. I decided to use a public pay phone and called her immediately at the phone number she had given me.

"Hi Anna, we just landed. Are you okay?"

"Yes. One of my HSBC security officers just confirmed that Churgrill moved large sums of money out of his HSBC account in Malta to purchase more EBS stock, as we expected. But what troubled me during our surveillance of Churgrill's stockbroker was that one of our agents heard him telling someone on the phone that the stock was going to rise dramatically because of an accident. Churgrill said the same thing in the audio recording, too."

"What accident?"

"We don't know."

I had been continually fearful that a planned attack might be coming soon, but such an attack would not seem to be an "accident."

I then immediately thought about the production centers in the U.S. and abroad that were producing the Botulinum antitoxin.

I explained to Anna, "If something happened to those production centers producing the Botulinum antitoxin, EBS would have a corner on the market."

"If your hunch is correct, you need to tell Nicole Jacobson and Chief Ryan immediately."

"I have to go now," I said, "but stay in touch, Anna, and be careful."

Huang Tai saw the heavy concern etched on my face as I picked my bag off the conveyer belt.

"I have to make two more calls Huang Tai; I'm sorry for the delay."

Huang Tai nodded.

Nicole picked up the phone and sounded pleasantly surprised.

"Are you at work, Nicole?"

"Yes. We've ramped up production of HBAT and we are working day and night."

"You and all your colleagues need to evacuate your building immediately."

"What? We need to leave the building? We can't stop production."

"Yes, you need to get out of there now! You are all in danger! Get out of the building and away from it. Trust me, Nicole. There is a credible threat to destroy your lab."

"There are seventeen of us working in here right now."

"Pull the fire alarm, Nicole, and get everyone out. Don't return until the building is searched."

It was a radical thing to do; I hoped she trusted me enough to do it.

I heard the alarm ringing.

"Okay, we are getting out!"

"Get out and get away from the structure. I will ask Chief Ryan to call you immediately to explain what is going on."

I later learned that Chief Ryan called Nicole to make sure she had left the building. Just after Nicole said hello on her phone, a series of loud explosions interrupted their conversation and their connection was cut off. Chief Ryan could not tell whether she was inside or outside of the building. He told me that he had no time to think, as he had to immediately warn the biotoxin production labs in Switzerland and Singapore. As Huang Tai and I left O'Hare airport in a police car that Chief Ryan had arranged to pick us up, I was in a stupor and sick with worry and with questions I could not answer. *Was the threat real? Had I overreacted? Had the building been bombed? Had Nicole gotten out? Did I put people at risk by delaying her operation?* I made repeated failed attempts to contact Nicole. There were no answers and we had no time to monitor the news. Huang Tai did not know what to say to console me but realized he needed to get me functioning again. We had to do what Chief Ryan did—think about what we had to do.

"We can only change what we can control." Huang Tai was seeking to break my inability to cope with the uncertainty I felt. It worked. Somehow, I knew I had to focus on what I was doing. Nicole would call when she could, if she could. I could not dwell on the what-ifs.

The police took us directly to Chief Ryan's own home, which now was protected by a 24/7 security detail. He arranged for me and Huang Tai to stay in his basement, which was a fully furnished two-bedroom apartment with its own kitchen, living room, and study. About five minutes after our arrival Nicole called my cell phone. My hand was shaking when I picked it up.

"Nicole, are you okay?"

"Yes, we all made it out. The building imploded, sending smoke and debris billowing into the air, less than ten minutes after we vacated it. All of us got out safely. It was completely destroyed. Johann, thank you! You saved our lives!"

Nicole was weeping as she spoke. "I can't talk now but tell Chief Ryan. He called me when the bombs detonated and we were cut off. I will call later on a secure phone."

When I looked up from my phone, Huang Tai was staring at me, reading my facial expressions. "She's okay, isn't she?"

"Yes, she's safe. But the building where they had been making the Botulinum antitoxin was destroyed."

"If we do our job right, Johann, there won't be any need for those antitoxins. We just need to destroy those payloads before they ever reach the Earth's atmosphere."

I looked at Huang Tai with a renewed determination and confidence.

"That is exactly what we are going to do Huang Tai, and I am glad we can do it together. We will save both our countries from this nightmare. I have to let Chief Ryan know Nicole and her colleagues are safe."

After two more attempts, I was able to reach Chief Ryan with the only good news of the day. He was so relieved he could not talk as emotion overwhelmed him. He barely whispered, "Thank you—will see you in the morning at home."

———————————

We didn't hear Chief Ryan come home but he was at the breakfast table at 8:00 a.m. the next morning. We all ate together and talked about sports as if nothing bad had happened yesterday. In the middle of our sports discussions, Chief Ryan said, "I did reach the labs in Switzerland and Singapore in time. I have arranged an unmarked police car with two officers to drive you each day to and from our home in Downers Grove to the Kavli Institute in Chicago." That was the only business we discussed.

Huang Tai and I began working twelve to fourteen hours a day at the Kavli Institute. We had a number of problems to overcome in order to create a viable means for emitting a powerful laser. We initially considered the possibility of using the International Space Station. We could launch a defensive weapon stored there. The challenge was that the International Space Station operated through a consortium of countries, including Canada, Japan, the Russian Federation, the United States, and eleven member states of the European Space Agency. It would be too difficult to build a powerful space laser that could be used as a weapon with full cooperation and secrecy of all those countries.

If we built our weapon on a new space station, it would take months to put in place and it would be fixed in one orbit. If we built it as a mobile object that we could control from the ground, it would have to be large enough to house a powerful laser but small enough to be mobile with a small fuel supply.

We met Colin Murphy and Sarah Anderson, two NASA engineers from the NASA Ames Research Center sent to collaborate with us. We spent a couple of hours discussing the dilemma and trying to figure an answer. In the middle of this, an idea came to me.

"What if we used a U.S. weather satellite as the site for housing our laser but then built small mobile space platforms with powerful mirrors that could change the trajectory of the lasers?"

Huang Tai immediately understood.

"We could then control the mobile platforms from the ground," he said.

Colin and Sarah also understood, both realizing that their facility in California would be the perfect place to build the laser and its mirrors.

"We have all the tools to do it," Colin said. "Then we simply attach the weapon and mobile mirrors to the next weather satellite to be launched."

"We just need a ride on the SpaceX Falcon nine rocket launch at Vandenberg," Sarah said.

"I like your idea, Sarah, about hitching a ride," Colin said. "Have you ever been to the Ames Research Center, Huang Tai?"

"No, I've always wanted to go there."

"Same for me," I replied.

"It won't be all work. We will take you to all kinds of fun places," Colin said.

"What Colin means," Sarah explained, "is that he will take you to his favorite pubs in Mountain View and Los Altos."

"Hey, we are proud of our pubs with great food, some of the best wines and beers, and the most beautiful and most intelligent women from many countries who enjoy the company of bright young engineers like myself."

"I think I am getting sick to my stomach," Sarah said. "Please ignore the foolish babblings of my colleague."

We all knew we were spending precious time engaged in frivolity, but we all needed the tension relief. We still had a complex task ahead of us in creating and testing high-powered optical coatings.

Furthermore, creating an adequate power supply for the lasers presented another great challenge we had to overcome. We knew that China and Russia already had the laser technology to damage and incapacitate our satellites in space. We needed more powerful lasers with mobility to destroy a biological weapon launched from space. Adding more solar panels to harvest energy from the sun was problematic and storing energy was also problematic. Energy conversion technologies, such as harnessing decaying energy from the plutonium-238 radioisotope, were still in the experimental phase. Likewise, energy storage options were not sufficient. Although we had four electric energy storage options available, including batteries, regenerative fuel cells, capacitors, and flywheels, none of those options provided enough storage capacity. We needed time to test and experiment with various options in space, but there was not enough time to do thorough testing. We had to build a powerful laser that theoretically we knew would work without knowing through experimentation first.

We left the Medici Restaurant on 57th Street in the car that Colin had rented, encouraged but sober, knowing the formidable challenges we had ahead of us. We all felt it was one of the best brainstorming experiences of any of our lives.

On the way back to our lab at the Kavli Institute, I received a text message from Chief Ryan:

> Singapore bomb squad has successfully defused three bombs at biotech production facility. We traced bombs to Iran. Everyone OK. Zurich lab also damaged by explosion but not destroyed; everyone escaped unharmed. Police had shoot-out with two Iranian terrorists. Both were killed. Watch your backs.

I erased the message, turned off my phone, and looked out the backseat rear window.

A black SUV with tinted windows was directly behind us. As we turned a corner, it turned with us. I was beginning to feel panic again.

"Colin, we may have company following us."

Colin instinctively stepped on the gas but not before I recorded the license plate. We ran through a late yellow light that turned red just as we entered the intersection.

We immediately heard a siren glaring behind us as a police car began to pursue us. We were all relieved. The black SUV drove by just as we were pulled over by the police. We told the police we thought we were being followed by a black SUV and rushed through the intersection because we felt we were in grave danger. After making two calls, the officer verified who we were and escorted us to the lab, telling us, "From now on, do not travel anywhere without a police escort, including walking or driving to a restaurant for lunch." The officer also encouraged Colin and Sarah to return their car rental and to not travel without a police officer for the remaining length of their stay in Chicago.

After returning to the lab, Colin and Sarah were visibly disturbed.

"What was that all about?" Sarah asked. "Were we in danger?"

I had to tell them the truth. "Yes, anyone who works with us is in danger. There have already been two attempts on our lives. Some very powerful people would like to see us gone."

"What have you done to get yourselves on a hit list?" Colin asked. He was visibly angry.

"It's not what we've done; it's what we are about to do. By the way, you and Sarah are also on their list now. You need to watch your back at all times."

Our intense conversation was interrupted by the ringing of the phone on my desk in the lab. I picked it up, relieved to hear Chief Ryan's reassuring voice.

"I am sorry you were followed, Johann. We have arrested two South Africans based on the license plate you provided. It was a stolen SUV. They are being questioned now by the FBI."

"Chief Ryan, can I put you on speaker phone? Huang Tai, Colin, and Sarah are here with me."

"Yes."

I placed my phone on my desk, and Chief Ryan continued.

"We are concerned that the men who followed you in the black SUV may have had training in the use of explosives. Just to be precautionary, I have sent a bomb squad to your lab to sweep the building and have appointed two permanent canine units to guard the entrances. C-4 plastic explosives were recovered at the biotech labs in Singapore and Switzerland. We must assume your building is a target, so we also are guarding your lab building, Colin and Sarah, at Ames."

"Thanks, Chief Ryan," I said. "We may just decide to hang out here day and night until we finish our work. We'll order takeout deliveries."

"And miss my wife's cooking?"

"You are right, we couldn't do that. But would it be too much to ask that Colin and Sarah join us for dinner?"

"I'm way ahead of you, Johann. My wife is already expecting all of you for dinner tonight, and every night until they leave. For security reasons, I have checked you out of your hotel in Chicago, Colin and Sarah, and checked you into a new hotel a mile from our home in Downers Grove. From now on, you will all be under police escort and they will have added security at your hotel. I'm not comfortable with you spending your nights in Chicago."

"We are very grateful to you and your wife," Sarah said.

"We have exciting news, Chief Ryan. We think we have a breakthrough idea," I said.

"And you are all going to California to execute this idea at Ames?" Sarah sat up with a surprised expression.

"How did you know?" Sarah asked. "We didn't tell anyone yet."

"I get paid to know these things Sarah. I'll pick you up at 6:00 p.m. sharp."

We worked for the rest of the evening when we experienced a power failure in our building. We knew something was not right when we saw through a window that other buildings in our area had power. We locked up our computers and decided that we needed to leave through the emergency exit.

Just as I closed the metal trap door that led into the underground tunnel, a concussion grenade landed above us. The thick metal plate that hid the emergency exit dulled the explosion, and yet we instinctively covered our ears, too late, to protect us. I pulled up the heavy steel plate that provided a second barrier from the bottom side of the trap door and securely locked both plates. We had two heavy-duty atomic beam flashlights with us to guide us through the tunnel on our hands and knees.

"Where are we going?" Huang Tai asked.

He was in a bit of shock trying to make sense of what was happening. I tried to reassure everyone

"We are safe," I said. "This tunnel leads us under Ellis Avenue to the Mansueto Library building across the street. A janitor told me it will take about twenty minutes to make our way through the tunnel."

"Who is trying to kill us?" Huang Tai asked.

"I don't know. Chief Ryan will track them down."

Colin and Sarah were both silent until we exited the tunnel through an unlocked wall exit into a utility room in the library basement.

After looking at Sarah, Colin said, "I'm ready for California."

We decided to leave the utility room just in case the tunnel was discovered. As soon as we exited the utility room and entered into an office area down a hallway, I found an office desk phone and called Chief Ryan to let him know where we were. We heard sirens everywhere and assumed the William Eckhardt Research Center building that housed our research lab and the Mansueto Library building where we had fled to had both been closed by police. We dared not go upstairs into the large glass dome area where there would be no place to hide.

Chief Ryan was about five minutes away from our lab by car when the power was cut to the building and it was attacked. The rapid police response did not allow the four intruders to do much damage. They tossed two percussion grenades, shattering some of the glass in our lab, but they were unable to destroy our most important equipment. After hearing the police sirens and seeing that we had abandoned the premises, the attackers fled. Our procedure of locking all our laptop computers in a hidden vault in the storage closet had saved us great loss.

We made our way to the Joseph Regenstein Library and went to the second-floor reading rooms where we had prearranged to meet Chief Ryan in case of an emergency, room 205. We assumed the library would be reopened soon. Chief Ryan arrived shortly after us and quickly updated us on the situation. What he said shocked us.

"My intelligence contacts believe Russian-trained professional killers from Chechnya and Ukraine, South African paramilitary, and Iranian agents are working together to eliminate threats that interfere with the plot to draw China and the U.S. into armed conflict. We believe they have learned about your research to create space-based laser weapons. You all were the primary target in this attack."

A shudder went through my body. *How many attacks could I survive?* I wondered.

There was more troubling news.

"What is more disconcerting is that the Chicago police force is concerned that someone within the police force is compromised and may be feeding these criminals their information. Although we have neutralized the threat for now, I think you should leave Chicago as soon as you are able and complete your work at the Ames Research Center, ahead of schedule."

I looked over at Huang Tai, Colin, and Sarah. They were dirty from crawling through the tunnel, shocked by the attack, weary, and ready to get out of Chicago.

"Can you finish your work at the Kavli Institute in the next three days?"

We all looked at each other. "It depends on the damage to our lab," I replied.

"None of your equipment was damaged."

"Then we can probably finish in three days," I said. The others agreed.

Chief Ryan then led us to a library exit that took us out to where his car was parked. We traveled to his home, tucked into a secluded residential area very close to the Avery Coonley School. As we walked in, a wonderful aroma of a homemade red pasta sauce with meatballs and sausages, along with fresh Italian garlic bread heating up in the oven, greeted us. We were a mess.

Niloa Ryan greeted us warmly and said, "After you shower and clean up, I have Caprese salad with fresh homemade mozzarella made from fresh curd and with tomatoes and sweet basil from our own garden waiting for you as an appetizer. Just come to the kitchen when you're ready."

The meal was more delicious than the best Italian restaurant I had been to in my life. I had not had a better red sauce or more tasty Italian meatballs anywhere. The Rigatoni was cooked to perfection and the Romano cheese was freshly grated from a block that must have just arrived from Italy. Though we had no capacity to eat a dessert, we managed to consume a scoop of traditional spumoni ice scream with a cup of cappuccino.

After a long discussion with Chief Ryan, he drove Colin and Sarah to the Esplanade Lakes Doubletree Hotel to check them into their rooms and get them settled. That gave me and Huang Tai a chance to talk with Niloa as we helped to clean up after the meal.

Niloa told us that she had learned how to cook during the summer that she had spent working for her Aunt Seraphina and Uncle Joe, who owned an Italian restaurant in New York City. Seraphina and her brother Joe had helped their parents with their restaurant in Calabria in southern Italy. Although her Aunt Seraphina's father had never been involved in law enforcement, her grandfather had been a police detective in Italy. Niloa then recalled to us a frightening event that she had witnessed in their Brooklyn restaurant.

"This is where I first learned about standing up against terrorists. When my aunt and uncle owned their restaurant in New York, there were no Islamic terrorists in Brooklyn, but there was another kind of terrorism. Some men would come to business owners and threaten them with violence if they did not pay protection money."

"The Italian mafia?"

"That's what they were known as, but to my Uncle Joe and Aunt Seraphina, they were the local terrorists giving Italians a bad name. My uncle refused to give them protection money, of course, so they threatened him and beat him up twice. Then they crossed the line and threatened to harm my Aunt Seraphina."

Huang Tai said he had heard similar stories about Chinese gangs threatening Chinese restaurant owners in California.

"What did your uncle do?" he asked.

"Not what I expected, Huang Tai. Let me tell you what happened as I remember it. My uncle invited the mafia leader who had been threatening him to his restaurant for a big Italian meal, free of charge. The mafia leader arrived with two big men to assure that my uncle would pay up. After the meal ended and they had consumed several bottles of fine Italian wine, my uncle came out of the kitchen with a loaded twenty-gauge shot gun and placed the barrel into the chest of the mafia boss, who froze in fear. His two accomplices did not dare move after he pulled the shaft of the gun toward him to load the chamber.

"My uncle said in Italian, so there would be no miscommunication, 'Do you see the gentleman reading the newspaper on the table across the room?' The mafia boss looked across the room and spotted him. 'He is the chief of police. And do you see the man eating a meal with two men in the adjacent table?' The mafia boss nodded. 'They are the leading FBI agents in this city. They are both welcome to eat here any time, free of charge, and they are my protection. Capisci?'

"They nodded. My uncle put the weapon away and graciously served them tiramisu.

"I had been cooking at the time but one of the waiters told me what was going on, so I came out of the kitchen and witnessed the entire confrontation. That was the last time that anyone in our family was ever threatened by the mafia."

"So, you learned to not be intimidated," I said.

"Bullies don't go away on their own," Niloa said. "My husband and I have already faced Islamic terrorists. All bullies thrive when they are not confronted and stopped. Terrorists are nothing but extreme bullies seeking to impose their beliefs upon others, trampling over people's God-given freedoms to peacefully follow their own beliefs. The way to overcome them is to resist them with greater force."

"That's been my experience, too, in China and in California," Huang Tai said.

"I think it is true of human nature," Niloa said.

Just as we finished cleaning the kitchen, a house alarm began buzzing just loud enough for us to hear on the inside of the house.

Niloa immediately checked an HD security camera monitor under the kitchen cabinets.

"We need to go to the basement now." She spoke with urgency but great composure. "There are intruders on our property."

Huang Tai and I quickly followed Niloa to the stairs and she directed us down to the basement level adjacent to where we were staying. The basement had a large security room with equipment. It also featured an underground entrance from the garage. We entered the security room and Niloa closed and bolted shut the heavy metal door behind us.

In the surveillance room, we watched on one of the monitors as two men dressed in camo followed along the perimeter of the property looking for a way to climb over or break through the high security fence. We then heard three shots ring out and saw the two men flee.

Niloa received a text from her husband, who had received the same security alert on his phone and through an app had also seen the two men seek to invade his property. Fortunately, Chief Ryan had exceptional security systems in place to protect him and his wife and guests. It seemed to be less than a minute until two police cars pulled into the driveway to make sure everything was fine. They had fired the shots. The security system at Chief Ryan's home was directly connected to the city's police headquarters a few miles away. One of the patrol cars had seen a suspicious car leaving the neighborhood hastily and was able to record the license plate number with its dash-cam.

Five minutes later, one of Chief Ryan's prime investigators traced the license plate to the Avis car rental company at O'Hare Airport. The rental contract revealed a false driver's license and a stolen credit card had been used to secure the rental, and that the car had not been returned yet. An APB was released to find the car and the two men in it.

CHAPTER 25

AFTER ARRIVING AT HOME AND joining us in the surveillance room downstairs, Chief Ryan turned on a monitor linked to a surveillance camera that his officers had placed in the hotel lobby. We all watched as two terrorists entered the hotel; one took the elevator to the second floor.

Chief Ryan told us that while driving home as fast as he could, he had called the two police officers he had dispatched to guard Colin and Sarah at the hotel to warn them of a possible attack from the two men who had tried to enter his property. He also called for backup. One of the officers was stationed in the hotel lobby while the other officer stayed in the second-floor hallway adjacent to the stairway where the front desk had officially checked them into a room as a decoy. In actuality, Colin and Sarah were staying in adjacent rooms on the fifth floor.

The first bullet fired on the second floor hit Officer Doug Scott square in the chest, near the center of his Cordura bulletproof vest, knocking him backwards and onto the hallway carpet, while the second bullet glanced by his right shin, creating a surface wound. As Officer Scott was falling, he retrieved his weapon, a Beretta 92C, and returned fire, placing three bullets in the shooter's right hand, immediately knocking the gun out of his hands. The shooter had not anticipated encountering the state's top police marksman. One of the bullets also pierced the gunman's upper thigh and brought him to the ground. Just as the gunman was reaching for his second handgun, Officer Scott shot two bullets into his other hand, blowing off his left thumb and totally incapacitating him. Scott disarmed him and quickly headed for the stairwell to help his partner in the lobby.

Scott's partner, Captain Dana Pruitt, was the second woman to achieve the rank of captain in the Downers Grove Police Department. Scott found her lying face down in a pool of blood just outside the lobby entrance. She had been shot once in the leg and once in the head and was unconscious, but the bullet had grazed across her right temple. Scott could see that she had returned fire. The high capacity magazine for her Glock 19 was empty, still in her left hand. She had fired all fifteen rounds before being shot in the head. The would-be assassin, assuming that his partner was dead, had tried to escape in his rental car, leaving a trail of blood. He did not get far. Pruitt had hit her target with seven bullets. The gunman was found less than a mile away in a ditch, having driven his car off the road. He had bled to death.

The second assassin that had been incapacitated by Officer Scott on the second floor was interrogated by the FBI. He and his partner were Russian-trained assassins from Chechnya. They had both entered the U.S. from Canada on tourist visas using fake Greek passports.

Colin and Sarah told us later that they did not hear the confrontation in the hotel three floors below, since all the weapons fired used suppressors to reduce the sound. They did hear the police sirens. What disturbed Chief Ryan was the professionalism of the gunmen. This attack represented the seventh encounter of one or more members of our *Eleutheria Club* with professional assassins from several different countries. Churgrill and Sarkovsky had access to an extensive network of trained assassins. I wondered again how much longer we could thwart such attacks before they succeeded, but I dared not pose the question aloud.

I awoke at 4:00 a.m. struggling to breathe. Somehow, I just knew someone was trying to poison me. My heart was palpitating and my sheets were drenched in perspiration. I began convulsing, but then realized it was only a nightmare. It had been several months since the last one. The nightmares were as frightening to me as the real attempts on my life because I could never figure out who was trying to kill me and why. I tried to shift my thoughts by thinking about what Niloa would make us for breakfast. It worked. I was able to fall back asleep.

I rose early and decided to go upstairs to the kitchen to get some bottled water. Chief Ryan was in his library and reading room, talking quietly on the phone. I stayed in the kitchen drinking my water until he finished the call, and then went into the room to say hello.

"How did you sleep, Johann?"

"Other than a bad dream of someone trying to kill me, I slept fine."

"Both you and Silvia Bershenko are having the same nightmare."

"Who is Silvia Bershenko?"

"The woman I was just talking to in New York. She also is having nightmares about someone trying to kill her. She told me her late husband's fatal brain aneurysm two weeks ago was fresh on her mind, as were the secret bank accounts where he had been receiving $75,000 monthly payments for "consulting services" as an aeronautical engineer and scientist. She then found hidden documents that explained exactly what he was doing for that money from a retired Russian general and a South African businessman."

"Sarkovsky and Churgrill?"

"Her husband, Andrei, had not mentioned their names to her, but she found them in his cell phone messages. Because he had been diagnosed with Alzheimer's disease for more than a year, she was never sure if her husband's interactions were delusional or genuine. He told her he was working on a project to help protect their beloved homeland, Russia, from a potential attack from space."

"It obviously was them!" I exclaimed.

"When Silvia reminded her husband they had lived in the U.S. for ten years, he had taught as a distinguished professor at MIT for seven years, and that they both had become American citizens," Chief Ryan said, "he responded as if he had forgotten who he was. She strongly suspected that it was her husband's rapidly deteriorating mind that had been manipulated by these two men, and she feared it was for nefarious purposes."

"So, she called you?"

"No, she called a friend in Boston, Natasha Calabrese. She was afraid that if she called law enforcement, they could confiscate her money and property as an accomplice to whatever her husband was involved in, and maybe even put her in prison. She didn't know who to turn to or who to trust, so she called a trusted friend whose husband was in law enforcement."

"Who is Natasha Calabrese?"

"Natasha Calabrese is a violinist from Kirov, Russia, who is now playing for the Boston Symphony Orchestra. Natasha's husband, Michael, works in the Boston office of the FBI."

"Do you know Michael?"

"Yes, he is a good friend who works with me on the Joint Terrorism Task Force. Michael called me immediately after talking with his wife about her phone conversation with Silvia, who shared about her husband's recent death and why she needed help. His wife said Silvia was fearful for her life and didn't know what to do. Natasha offered to come to New York with her husband so they could help Silvia sort everything out about her husband's affairs. Michael knows the terrorism threat we have been working on and thought I should call Silvia immediately. He was right."

"Can she help us?"

"Yes."

"Did she know what he was doing for Sarkovsky and Churgrill?"

"I don't know. That's what we have to find out, Johann. Michael and Natasha are traveling to New York tomorrow to stay with Silvia in her Long Island condominium on the water."

"That sounds great to me."

"Well, I'll tell you what it's like. I need to get there as soon as I can. She may be in danger."

"I hope you're staying for breakfast."

"Of course. I seldom walk away from my wife's cooking. And you should catch another couple of hours of sleep, Johann. That's what I'm going to try to do."

————————————

I took Chief Ryan's advice, got some more rest, and awoke at 8:00 a.m. to the pleasant smell of bacon. Niloa was cooking up a full breakfast for us: Canadian bacon, scrambled eggs with spinach, mushroom, and cheddar cheese, buttermilk blueberry pancakes, and Kona coffee. Chief Ryan picked up Colin and Sarah from their hotel and brought them home for breakfast.

They entered the kitchen as I eyed a crispy piece of bacon.

"How did you sleep?"

"Like a baby," Colin replied.

"So, you awoke hungry several times? That's how babies sleep," Sarah said.

"Then I did not sleep like a baby; I slept like a log," Colin replied.

"Well, I did sleep like a baby. I awoke at about 2:00 a.m. to sirens. I looked out my window and saw several police cars and an ambulance. Someone must have had a heart attack, I figured. Then I awoke to the sound of birds chirping outside my window, and again to the sound of the garbage truck backing up to empty the large trash dispensers behind the hotel. When my alarm rang at 7:00 a.m., I was just in the early stages of the sweetest sleep. Why is the best sleep always just before you have to get up?"

"I think you got plenty of beauty rest given your appearance this morning."

Sarah blushed visibly but with a smile, acknowledging Colin's compliment.

"You should sleep like a baby more often if it causes you to wake up in such a jovial mood."

"Aren't you in a complimenting mood," Sarah said. "You should sleep like a log more often."

As we were all enjoying the breakfast Niloa had lovingly prepared, Chief Ryan received a text message from Michael Calabrese. He confirmed that he wanted Chief Ryan to meet him in New York as soon as possible for a follow-up meeting with Silvia Bershenko. Niloa looked sad.

"Why do they need you, honey?" Niloa asked.

"Because a friend of mine may have stumbled upon a scientist involved in helping Atlas Churgrill and General Sarkovsky. This scientist recently died of a brain aneurism, and my friend and his wife are going to meet with his widow and they want me to come for a follow-up meeting. I need to leave later this morning."

Chief Ryan turned from his wife and asked me, "When will you finish your work at the lab?"

I looked over to Colin and Sarah but they were engaged in their own little side conversation. "I think we can finish in a couple days," I said.

"I hope you can, Johann. I'm giving all of you extra security for the rest of your time here. I want you to continue to stay here at my home. There will be a 24/7 security detail watching the house. Hopefully there are no more troublemakers out there."

Chief Ryan decided to drive us to Chicago before leaving on his trip to New York. On our way to the Kavli Institute, he received a call. The conversation sounded intense and concern etched across his face.

"That was from Michael Calabrese," he said after hanging up the call. "Silvia Bershenko fell asleep early this morning on her outdoor couch and was awakened by the sound of something striking the sofa close to her head. When she turned her head, she noticed a small hole in the couch. Instinctively she laid down flat on the couch when she heard another sound. It was a second bullet from a long-range rifle that would have killed her if she had not moved. She quickly rolled off the sofa and onto the covered floor of her lanai, out of sight of the shooter. She knew someone had to be shooting at her from a boat in the ocean. Fortunately, the ocean was not calm, or the first bullet would have killed her."

We assured Chief Ryan we would push ourselves to finish as soon as possible. Instead of traveling immediately back to California, we agreed to Sarah's recommendation that we first visit Dr. James White, a professor and fellow at the Center for Astrophysics and Space Astronomy at the University of Colorado whom she had worked with for two years while earning her doctorate in Astrophysical and Planetary Sciences. Dr. White had more than two decades of experience in developing space instrumentation and in monitoring rocket payloads, and he had graciously adjusted his busy schedule so he could spend time with us to review our research before we applied it to building lasers at the Ames Research Center.

The unexpected change in our schedule was fortuitous, as Chicago's counterterrorism task force had discovered another attack was made on the Kavli Institute on the last day we were scheduled to be in the building. Although the attack was carried out, no one was in the building at the time and the police quickly intercepted the three gunmen who carried out the attack, which did damage the lab where we had been working. It was as if an invisible force was protecting us every time we were in harm's way. I had lost count at how many times we escaped injury or death.

Dr. White was of immense help. He showed us why our calculations were slightly off as to how our measuring instruments would change within certain atmospheric conditions. These adjustments were critical to our understanding of how to create a computer program that would constantly adjust the trajectory of our lasers and angles of our mirrors as atmospheric conditions changed.

Our visit to the University of Colorado had delayed our scheduled arrival in California by one day. Sarah, Colin, Huang Tai and I were now concerned about security after hearing from Chief Ryan about the attack on the Kavli Institute. We wondered about any planned attack on us in California.

Chief Ryan immediately put in place extra security at the NASA Ames Research Center. All entrances and exits into the facility were heavily guarded by the time we arrived, helping us to feel more relaxed. Instead of traveling back and forth to the facility from a hotel, we decided to stay there for the duration of our project. We hastily converted office space into makeshift bedrooms, sleeping on comfortable futons. We had good shower facilities with clean bathrooms—we were content. Several excellent restaurants nearby delivered food to our facility. The arrangement enabled Sarah, Colin, Huang Tai and me to devote twelve hours a day to our project. At that pace we believed we could complete our task within eight to ten days.

Our enthusiasm fueled our feverish work schedule. Huang Tai ordered chicken wings and house-fried rice twice a day and drank copious quantities of Ginseng Tea. Sarah and I subsisted on salads and Italian paninis from a local deli, while Colin lived on Five Guys burgers and an occasional salad. We had to thoroughly screen all the food preparation and delivery drivers to make sure no one was tampering with our food. It seemed crazy that we had to take such precautions, but there had already been too many attempts on our lives. The work was challenging and not terribly exciting in a creative sense. We had to painstakingly test everything we were doing at least twice, and then figure out how to overcome each failure. We understood theoretically that our laser tests in the controlled laboratory should indicate how the lasers would work in space, but there were always lingering doubts in our minds because we could not test them in space until we had completely built them and put them in place.

While the four of us worked at Moffett Field, absorbed in our own project, I realized how increasingly difficult it was to keep track of our friends now dispersed throughout the world. I wondered what Anna had found in Malta as she uncovered the cash flows of Sarkovsky and Churgrill. I knew Darrell had left Chicago and was traveling to Taiwan to meet with his contacts there and hoped he would be safe, traveling alone. I had not heard from Nicole regarding her progress in Maryland producing Botulinum antitoxin after her lab had been destroyed. I also had not heard from Angela since she had sent me a brief text to tell me she was traveling to Florence to meet with her twin brother. Chief Ryan was on his way to New York to meet with agent Michael Calabrese and Silvia Bershenko. Then I wondered how my family and friends were back in Downers Grove.

I felt that everyone connected to me was at risk. There was the possibility of moles in our own government. Although we were working under the radar of Chief Ryan, and most of our intelligence agencies did not know about us, someone was doing excellent surveillance on us and always seemed to know our next move. I knew I had to completely put these concerns out of my mind in order to do my work but struggled to do so. I talked with Huang Tai about how he was doing emotionally and he told me he was dealing with the same anxieties. He was especially worried about his uncle, who had many enemies among the hawkish military leaders in China. Although his uncle had the respect of the leader of China, some of the leaders directly under the Chinese president were not strong supporters of him.

We decided we needed to go to a movie to break the tension. We chose to see the Star Wars movie featuring Han Solo, an older movie that had returned to a local theater. Again, security was our primary concern. How could we leave the facility undetected, just in case we were being watched? Colin created a brilliant plan. We made arrangements with

Mountain Mike's Pizza in Palo Alto to send a delivery van to us, making sure the delivery driver was a male close in size and age to Colin. When the delivery van arrived, the driver and Colin changed clothes and Huang Tai, Sarah, and I got into the back of the van and laid down out of sight. We then drove to Mike's Pizza and picked up a customer's order. After leaving on another pizza run, we made sure no one was following us and drove to the Century Cinema 16 in Mountain View. After the movie, we returned to Mike's Pizza, picked up another order, and returned to Moffett Field to pay the driver for his time and to give him his delivery clothes back. The scheme worked flawlessly.

Although I did not particularly think the movie was that good, both Huang Tai and I got some good ideas about the use of laser weapons during the film. We realized we both had underestimated how the use of mirrors could extend the distances of laser beams without losing much power. We stayed up that night brainstorming about how we might apply what we had been thinking about during the film. Even more importantly, all four of us sensed a new exhilaration as we pushed hard toward our goal.

After three hours of sleep, we were all awakened by the sound of an explosion. It shook our building and I wondered if it was another terrorist attack. I reached for the lights but there was no electricity. I began looking in the dark for my SIG Sauer P365 pistol, while listening for footsteps coming toward us. It was impossible to hear anything but the shaking of our building. The bomb must have been powerful, I thought. I heard Colin speaking with a loud voice, "Earthquake— get down on the floor and pull your futon on top of you!"

Earthquake! I thought. *Of course.* I had read that some earthquakes begin with what sounds like an explosion, but I had never been in an earthquake before. I was immediately relieved that it was not a terrorist attack. Nobody was going to come running down the hallway with guns blazing, seeking to kill us. The shaking I could tolerate. Other than a couple of books and lamps falling on top of our futons, we were all unharmed. The earthquake had lasted for twenty-seven seconds, which I found out is a long time for an earthquake. I had no sense of how big the quake had been, but knew I needed to get some more sleep to face whatever challenges lay before us regarding damage to our equipment. I cleared some debris from my futon, mostly some books and plaster, climbed back onto it, and fell asleep.

Colin woke me up at 7:00 a.m. I looked around our room with my flashlight and it was trashed. Everything was on the floor but we still had a roof over our heads. I slowly got dressed and stumbled my way into the small kitchen where we made coffee and breakfast every morning. The power was still out but our gas stove was working fine.

"No gas leaks?"

"Not here," Sarah replied. "But there are lots of big gas leaks throughout the Bay Area."

"And lots of big fires," Colin added. "San Francisco and Oakland both."

"What about the whole region?"

"More than forty fires have already been reported in San Francisco and more than seventy fires in Oakland," Colin replied. "The quake was a 7.9, or possibly 8.0 on the Richter scale. The whole region must be devastated."

My relief quickly turned to anguish as we listened to the emergency radio Colin had found in our lab. Authorities were estimating at least 1,000 deaths. Dozens of buildings, freeway overpasses, and bridges had completely collapsed. It was far more destructive than the Loma Prieta earthquake that killed sixty-three people and injured 3,000. Fortunately, it hit very early in the morning before heavy traffic and before most people were at work in high rise buildings.

The good news we learned that day was there was little damage to our equipment. We had emergency generators for power. The biggest challenge was going to be food and drinking water, since all the restaurants would be closed for at least a week. Cell towers were down so we could not communicate with our phones. Fortunately, we discovered the Internet was still operational so we could communicate via Skype and other video chat services.

What I saw on the Internet was disheartening. Every news site showed mile after mile of utter destruction with smoke billowing into the sky from hundreds of fires. Dozens of helicopters dropped fire retardant and water on the large building fires that were unreachable with standard fire-fighting equipment. I realized that all the resources in the U.S. would now be focused on the search and rescue and recovery efforts of communities stretching from San Francisco through Santa Cruz. I could not afford to think about how much energy and attention might be diverted from our national efforts to stave off a forthcoming biological attack, which the public had no knowledge of, yet it would be far more deadly than the earthquake that had just struck California.

Putting my hands on my face, I silently prayed for the injured and those still trapped in rubble. I prayed that our small team at Moffett Field, which could not afford to divert any attention to those suffering around us, would be able to keep working. I prayed that we would be mentally prepared for the possibility of big aftershocks, big enough to bring down more buildings.

My prayers were interrupted by a collective gasp in the room. I looked up to the lab computer monitor we were watching and saw the tsunami warning in large letters at the bottom of the screen along with the alarming words "up to eight feet." I immediately thought about the 2011 Japan earthquake, which created tsunami waves that reached run-up heights of an estimated 128 feet at Miyako City and traveled six miles inland in Sendai, flooding a large area. Sarah saw the obvious concern on my face and then reminded me the San Francisco Bay area had never experienced a large tsunami.

"The earthquakes here, Johann, are not in subduction zones like in Japan. If it was the San Andreas Fault or the Hayward Fault, the two plates do not slide over one another but instead, they would slide past each other horizontally. Unless this earthquake was an unknown fault in the ocean, the risk of a sizable tsunami in the Bay is minimal."

That information removed me from a panic mode, but it failed to put me at ease, since we were sitting on a very flat piece of land about a mile from the San Francisco Bay. However, even a small tsunami in the Bay could flood our buildings. We had to consider immediately whether to move our equipment to higher ground or not.

Just as I voiced this concern, Lieutenant Commander Brian Fields, sent from the executive officer's office for Moffett Field, entered our lab. He wanted us to know they were placing a two-foot high wall of sandbags around our building, as they expected some minor flooding from the Bay.

"The earthquake was centered along the Hayward Fault slightly North of Oakland. The greater threat of flooding is Alameda and

Oakland, not here," Lt. Fields explained. "Have you been able to assess any damage to your equipment?"

Colin responded that our initial assessment indicated no substantive damage.

"That's good news. The president wants to know immediately. He called Commander Jenkins fifteen minutes ago."

"Are you saying POTUS called?"

"Yes. The president knows exactly what you are working on here and directed us to use all resources available to protect your work."

When Lt. Commander Fields left the lab, none of us could speak. Up until now, we believed our mission and work was known only by the executive director of the National Counterterrorism and Security Center (NTSC) in Washington, who was a personal friend of Chief Ryan, and by the director of NTSC.

We learned later that concern about Russian interference into our security agencies had reached such a fever pitch that Chief Ryan did not know who could be trusted as heads of our intelligence agencies and who might be compromised in the office of the president. We were no longer working in the shadows—the president had likely been briefed by the director of national intelligence. Any moles in the National Intelligence Agency or in the president's office could know exactly who we are and what we are doing. We needed to speak to Chief Ryan immediately, but he was with Mrs. Silvia Bershenko on Long Island.

The wall of sandbags around our building was just completed as water from the Bay approached. How much water was coming we could not see. We then braced ourselves as the first aftershock rocked our building again—a 6.4 earthquake.

CHAPTER 26

ΔΠΠΔ CONTACTED ME BY SKYPE as soon as she heard about the earth-quake on the news as she passed a television in the lobby of her hotel. She had very little time to talk, as she had another appointment with the head of HSBC in Malta.

"Are you secure, Johann?"

"We're safe and our lab has minimal damage."

"The earthquake news is all over Europe. The fires look devastating."

"I know. It looks bad out there, but we are away from the city."

"My research at the Bugibba branch has confirmed that tens of millions of euros were being funneled in and out of the bank by Sarkovsky and Churgrill, with many electronic transfers from Russian and Swiss accounts. I also discovered transfers to Libya and Italy. The cash flow records have all the markings of organized crime."

"I bet Angela and her brother are finding out more of what Churgrill has been doing in Europe," I said.

"They are, and as soon as I finish my meeting with Geoffrey Goodlaite, the president of HSBC Malta, I'll call you."

I went back to work and an hour later Anna called again. She had met with Goodlaite in the Paranga at the InterContinental Beach Club at InterContinental in St. Julian. He had arranged a private se-cure area where they could enjoy brunch and talk privately.

"After explaining what I had discovered, Johann, Mr. Goodlaite was obviously embarrassed and apologetic. All he could do was put his head down and say, 'I missed something big,' obviously disappointed in himself."

"Did you have to turn him in?"

"No, not at all. First of all, I don't do any enforcement work or hiring or firing, only investigations. I told him, 'It's not your fault Geoffrey. These transactions were cleverly buried in all your national transactions. The reports you see do not break down the individual branches.'

I then told him who should have reported these irregular transactions, explaining, 'There are only two people who should have known about this—the manager at the Bugibba branch and auditor in your office who sees all the detailed reports. I suspect they are both compromised and likely are on Sarkovsky's payroll, since he has a residence here.'"

"How will you catch these people?"

"Probably cars, jewelry, and travel."

"What?"

"I asked Mr. Goodlaite if he had seen the cars these two employees were driving these days, explaining to him that although it was painfully obvious, I have discovered in previous investigations that most women receiving illicit funds take expensive trips and buy jewelry, and most men take exotic trips and buy expensive cars. Goodlaite, who was still kicking himself for not discovering the transactional irregularities, had never thought about these materialistic indicators of theft or fraud."

"What did you tell him to do to catch them?"

"I told him to do absolutely nothing, because he must not tip either one of them off that he even suspects malfeasance. In fact, I asked him to give them each a slight portion of company stock for their long-term commitment to HSBC. It will be interesting to see if they keep it or trade it for another stock that they believe will benefit them even more than HSBC."

"Brilliant scheme, Anna."

"Yes, Goodlaite figured out that I had a certain stock in mind, but he didn't fully understand the legal ramifications."

"What are they?"

"In 2017, the U.S. expanded investigations and enforcement actions by the U.S. Securities and Exchange Commission and the U.S. Department of Justice of foreign nationals involved in potential illegal insider trading. Since both bank employees have business interests in the U.S., I will let the U.S. government know about our internal investigation and we will let U.S. law enforcement take care of the two employees. If they cannot prosecute, I am sure their friends in the EU can."

"That would be very helpful if we could get them to provide more information."

"Yes, it could work to our advantage. Goodlaite was terribly concerned that this incident would ruin his career at HSBC. I assured him it would not after I reported his cooperation and assistance in this matter to my superiors."

"You're a good leader, Anna; you protect your people."

"Thanks, Johann. I need to spend another couple of days here to finalize my investigation and to complete my written report. Also, I plan to meet with General Suberov and his wife one more time."

When I talked to Anna again just before she left Malta, she told me that on the last day of her stay, she decided to walk early in the afternoon to St. Paul's Bay, a three-and-a-half-mile walk from her hotel. She'd arranged to meet General Suberov and his wife at Pepe Nero in St. Paul's Bay that evening, a new dinner restaurant featuring Maltese fish and steaks that had just opened in 2016.

On the way to the bay, she stopped by the memorial to St. Paul on Triq San Franġisk, overlooking St. Paul's Bay, contemplating his improbable journey to the island of Malta. She told me she was encouraged that Paul had escaped death many times, just as we had. It was a complete miracle that he survived the journey. The Romans were trained to execute the prisoners in their charge before abandoning a ship. Paul was a Roman prisoner who should have been executed, but he told the Roman commander an angel appeared before him and all 274 passengers must abandon the ship and swim to shore, and that if they did, none would be lost. The centurion in charge prevented his men from killing Paul and the other prisoners. Paul's ship was run aground and was broken up by the waves in a fierce storm. Any one of these waves, laden with debris from the ship, could have killed Paul, but miraculously, though weakened through prolonged fasting, he was able to swim safely to shore.

She then recalled the third miracle that occurred. When Paul picked up a piece of wood to put it into the fire that he was standing near, along with the other shipwreck survivors, a poisonous snake bit him. The local inhabitants of Malta recognized the snake and expected Paul's hand to swell immediately, followed by necrosis and death. When Paul did not die, the locals believed he was supernaturally protected by the gods, and they revered him. Anna told me she could not help but wonder how she had been supernaturally protected from harm on multiple occasions. She wondered to what extent her life now had taken on some divine purpose in Malta, through circumstances she was not controlling. It was the first time she began to seriously think about her life in that way, that she had a greater purpose and destiny that transcended herself.

I told Anna that was a profound revelation to consider. I then asked her about her dinner with General Suberov and his wife.

"Leyla spotted me as I approached Pepe Nero and jumped out of her seat and greeted me with a big hug. General Suberov also greeted me warmly. I was so welcomed by them."

"I read about that restaurant in an advertisement and I want to go there!" I said.

"After a sumptuous dinner of octopus in garlic, Tegamino seafood, roasted potatoes, and Caprese salad, Mikkail and Leyla turned off their cell phones and put them in a lead box which was placed in a secure area of the restaurant. They asked me to do the same.

General Suberov leaned toward me and said, 'I have confirmed Sarkovsky has hired Russian and Chechen paramilitary and a former Soviet scientist living in the U.S. I have some names but not the name of the scientist. I also confirmed they want to provoke a war between China and the U.S. by setting off a biological attack in China and blaming it on the U.S.'"

"So, he reconfirmed what we already know."

"Yes, but then Leyla said that the president of Russia is aware that Sarkovsky is trying to get the U.S. and China into an armed conflict, but he doesn't know the details and doesn't want to know so he can maintain plausible deniability. He despises Sarkovsky but will not stop him, since such a conflict would weaken China and the U.S. and help Russia."

"What else?"

"I explained to them that this was all making sense to me because I confirmed Sarkovsky was using his second home and residency in Malta to move large amounts of money from Russia, Libya, and South Africa into his HSBC bank in Bugibba and then into private Swiss bank accounts. I also told them he had received large amounts of money from South Africa from Atlas Churgrill, who was also moving large amounts of money in and out of his HSBC accounts in Malta. Some of these funds are going to a nonprofit refugee relief organization in Italy, which is a front for a human trafficking organization operating in Libya and southern Italy. We can prosecute Churgrill for this operation. In addition, I told them Churgrill had purchased large amounts of stock in the Emergent BioSolutions Corporation through his broker in South Africa, and that he had firm control of the company, which specializes in producing antitoxins."

"So, you now have the hard evidence?"

"Yes, and General Suberov was able to quickly understand the plot."

"I'm not surprised."

"He told me if a biological attack occurred on China, China would need large amounts of antitoxins, and if an attack occurred in the U.S., the U.S. would need large amounts, too. Churgrill would control a large percentage of those antitoxins."

"The general is sharp," I said.

"He also said Churgrill wants more than money, because he already has lots of it. What he craves is validation and respect. Also, Leyla then said that Sarkovsky wants to rule Russia."

"It sounds to me like they pieced together in a couple hours what it took us months to understand."

"I know. They arranged additional security for me. One Russian and one American former special forces military officer, who have formed their own private security company here in Malta, are now protecting me."

"I'm so glad about that. I need to go," I said, "the water is coming up. Pray that the tsunami in the San Francisco Bay does not flood our lab."

"Tsunami! There's a tsunami coming?"

"Just a small one in the San Francisco Bay. We'll be fine. Just call me once you get back to Hong Kong and keep in close contact with Chief Ryan."

"Stay safe."

"You, too. And whenever you can, check on Angela. I haven't heard anything since she arrived in Italy. We'll talk again soon," I said.

After the call, I felt better about Anna's safety but apprehensive about Angela's well-being. *What was going on in Italy?* I wondered.

I went to bed with water on my mind. It was hard to sleep because I could hear the water surrounding our building, but I did eventually. I had the best dream ever. I dreamt that Angela and I were cruising down the Grand Canal in a Venetian gondola. I awoke thinking how wonderful that would be and whether it would be possible given the reality of the threat of a biological attack, the threats on my life, and my haunting dreams of being killed before I had a chance to experience such joy. I felt a rush of emotion sweep over me. I wanted to be free and safe in the most romantic place in the world, and a few years older, with a beautiful Italian woman that I loved. I also had clarity on another dream, too, a dream that I lived in a more peaceful world where evil was subdued and where selfishness, hate, and brutality were deviations from normal life rather than common behavior.

Reality quickly overtook my musings. I looked outside and could see that the seiche created by the earthquake had submerged Moffett Field with four inches of water. The Swiss French word literally meant "to sway back and forth." *That's probably what I had felt while asleep,* I thought. I remembered reading that seiches could occur far away from the epicenter of an earthquake, such as the case of the February 2010 Chile earthquake that produced a seiche on Lake Pontchartrain, Louisiana, to a height of six inches.

I looked at my watch—it was 6:15 a.m., which was 11:15 a.m. in Florence. Angela was there working with her brother, Angelo. I could see them sipping late morning cappuccinos in one of the many coffee shops that surrounded the Duomo.

I was wide awake now so I decided to send her a text.

"Hi Angela—awoke with you on my mind. How are things going?"

To my surprise, she responded two minutes later with an encrypted text. "Have been very busy. Making good progress on Churgrill. The man is very powerful and evil. Managed a global crime syndicate of drug trafficking, prostitution, and human trafficking, mixed with many legitimate businesses. Has plenty of money. Has been selling off the illegal businesses and building a political organization with international leaders. He wants the South African presidency."

I just texted her one word, "Wow!"

Angela then replied, "My brothers are gathering evidence to support his arrest and prosecution in Italy. He could come here. He likes to visit Florence to meet with European leaders. Angelo will need overwhelming evidence because Churgrill has many powerful friends in European parliaments and banks. Anna's research at HSBC in Malta will greatly help."

"You talked with her?"

"Yes, she filled me in on everything she found out in Malta."

"Do you have good security?"

"Yes. My older brother has successfully prosecuted influential organized crime leaders for the past fourteen years. He and my father know how to protect our family. What about the earthquake?"

"Devastated our area but our lab is fine with minor flooding from the Bay around our building."

"Yes, I heard about the seiche in the Bay," Angela replied.

"Need to go now. Stay safe. Am going to catch more sleep before work," I texted.

As I lay on my bed, I tried to recapture my dream of me and Angela in a gondola on the Grand Canal.

I awoke at 6:34 a.m. to a new shaking. It was just another aftershock, this one a 5.7.

"We have a problem," Colin said to me after I crawled out of bed and walked into the kitchen. "The water keeps rising and these aftershocks are not helping the situation. We might have to move our equipment."

"I'm ready," I said. "I just need to give Chief Ryan an update."

I called Chief Ryan while he was walking to the platform in Grand Central to take a train to Islip, New York. Michael and Natasha had arranged to meet him at the Southward Ho Country Club on Montauk Highway in Bay Shore, not far from where Mrs. Silvia Bershenko lived.

"Good to hear from you, Johann, let me call you in a few minutes; I'm getting on a train now."

I grabbed a cup of coffee, made some toast, and waited. Colin came back into the kitchen with good news. "Commander Fields just told us the water rise is slowing down and will soon stop. We can continue working here."

Then Chief Ryan called me and I told him everything I had learned from Anna and Angela.

He told me Natasha and Michael had arranged to pick up Mrs. Bershenko at her home and drive her to the Southward Ho Country Club, because they were unsure if her home was a safe place to meet since at least one assassin had tried to shoot her from a boat while she sat on her lanai couch facing the ocean. He wanted to talk with me later that night by Skype.

As I waited for the day to end so I could hear about Chief Ryan's meeting, I had a premonition that he was in another dangerous situation, but this time I had peace that he would be protected. Huang Tai, Colin, Sarah, and I helped the men outside our building add one more layer of sandbags to raise our wall of protection another eight inches, and then we returned to work. There was now nearly two feet of water surrounding us but it seemed to be leveling off as Commander Fields had told us. Relieved that we did not need to move our equipment to higher ground, our team made good progress on our project.

Just after lunch, I received a perplexing text message from Silvia Bershenko.

This is Chief Ryan on Silvia's phone. My phone was damaged. Call the Suffolk County Police Department on Long Island—let them know there has been an armed attack at the Southward Ho Country Club. Then call the FBI office on Pinelawn Road in Melville, New York, and tell them the same. Let them know that Michael Calabrese and I are hunkered down at the scene with an important witness we are protecting.

I made the two calls immediately. I received no more messages from Chief Ryan for the rest of the day.

The four of us worked until late before eating dinner. The only food left in the pantry of our kitchen was four cans of sardines packed in olive oil, one large jar of peanut butter, one half a loaf of bread, and three cans of baked beans. There also was a nearly full jar of popcorn and enough butter in the refrigerator to make a panful.

Huang Tai and I ate the sardines and Colin and Sarah made peanut butter sandwiches. We then all enjoyed a panful of popcorn. We were happy to hear the news at the end of the day from Lt. Commander Brian Field's office that the water rise had stopped.

Just as we finished our meal, I received a call from Nicole. I picked up my phone as both fear and hope battled to overtake my emotions.

"Hi Nicole, are you okay?"

"Yes, I'm exhausted but safe. We have relocated our operation to another building, but we had to halt the production of Botulinum antitoxin until we could get set up again. How are you?"

"I am nearly exhausted, too, working twelve-hour days on creating a defense system. Your work was interrupted by a bomb, and my work was interrupted by an earthquake."

"You're in California?"

"Yes, at the NASA Ames Research Center at Moffett Field. The San Francisco Bay came to our doorstep after the earthquake, but we sandbagged our building so our work could continue and fortunately our equipment was not damaged."

"Bottom line, we have enough antitoxin now to protect about half our population in the event of an attack. We will need to get the rest from a private company in Canada. However, if any other countries are attacked, they will be buying from the same company and the company may not have enough. It's a precarious situation."

"Then we will just need to succeed so that no one is attacked."

"Those are my thoughts exactly. Your team has to succeed."

Nicole ended the call as she had to run to another important meeting. I still had no word from Chief Ryan in New York after his text message asking us to call for help, and he was not able to answer his damaged phone. It was too late to wait any longer, I had to get some sleep.

CHAPTER 27

WHEN CHIEF RYAN CONTACTED ME the very next day on his new phone, I then understood why he had been out of contact. He was generous with the details of his retelling of his time with Michael Calabrese, Natasha, his wife, and Silvia Bershenko, and would not leave anything out. I was able to relay the phone call I had with Chief Ryan to Huang Tai, Sarah, and Colin with the same detail, equipped, too, with an audio file that Chief Ryan had sent over once we hung up. I gathered everyone together and explained what had happened in New York.

"When Michael and Natasha escorted Mrs. Bershenko into the private dining room of the country club for lunch," I said, "Chief Ryan could see that she was visibly shaken. He knew that her husband had died, and now his whole career was in question. She needed comfort and support, not interrogation. He told me that he was so glad he had done his homework in studying the life of Andrei Bershenko; there were many good things he could say about him. Michael introduced Chief Ryan to Mrs. Bershenko, and then he offered his condolences."

"Who are Michael and Natasha?" Huang Tai asked.

"Michael is an FBI agent and his wife Natasha is a violinist. They live in Boston."

"And Silvia Bershenko is the wife of a Russian-America space engineer?" Sarah asked.

"Correct," I said, and continued on.

"Michael told Silvia he was deeply sorry that they were meeting for the first time under such difficult circumstances and that he couldn't imagine the pain of losing a spouse. He then told Silvia that his investigation showed that her husband was an American hero. He told her about the many things he did to help the United States that most people did now know about. He assured Silvia that whatever she had found that does not make sense would be interpreted in the light of the outstanding person that her husband had proven to be."

"How did she respond?" Sarah asked.

"Chief Ryan said Silvia immediately began to weep. She said that she felt so ashamed and worried that he may have done something wrong. She told us, 'I know he was a good man. I know he loved this country, he loved MIT, and he loved his students. It's just that he had not been in his right mind during the past eighteen months of his life. The Alzheimer's disease he suffered from was so devastating he could not make good decisions.'"

"That's important," said Colin, interrupting my story. I nodded and continued on.

"Natasha and Michael assured Silvia that they were there with Chief Ryan to help, and that whatever they found out, they would protect the reputation of her husband and would also keep her daughter Margarita safe."

"Where is her daughter?" Sarah asked.

"Silvia told them she was studying at the University of Bern in Switzerland. She had come to the U.S. for a brief visit last week for a private memorial service, but she had to return to Switzerland for her final exams. Chief Ryan told me Michael made a quick call and sent an FBI agent to Bern to protect Margarita."

"Then what?" Sarah asked.

"Then Silvia opened the briefcase she had brought with her and withdrew some important papers, including bank deposit slips and hard copies of emails and text messages her husband had downloaded from his laptop computer and mobile phone. She explained that the week before her husband died, he had given her several file folders and asked her to hide them in a safe place. She was somewhat alarmed by his sense of urgency, but he told her they were simply financial documents that would not be needed until they filed their income taxes in March."

"Were they?" Colin asked.

"She decided to look through the files after her husband died. After seeing bank deposits she did not know about and emails and text messages from people she didn't know, that's when she said she called Natasha."

"What did they show?" Huang Tai asked.

"Chief Ryan and Michael looked through the documents and started to ask probing questions and recorded their conversation," I said. I then opened the audio file from my computer and played it as Huang Tai, Sarah, and Colin crowded closer around the table.

"Is PNC Bank the bank you regularly use?" agent Michael Calabrese asked.

"No. Our checking and savings accounts are at the First National Bank of Long Island. I don't know of any accounts at the PNC Bank."

"According to these statements," Chief Ryan said, "you have a checking account with $15,480 in it and a savings account with $245,000 in it at PNC Bank, of which you are the sole beneficiary."

"In addition," Michael added, "during the past year, this account has received six deposits of $200,000 for a total of $1.2 million dollars. These funds were then transferred into your TD Ameritrade brokerage account."

"Did you know about the TD Ameritrade account?" Chief Ryan asked.

"Oh yes. Andrei loved to trade stocks, bonds, and ETFs. It was his hobby. He made some good trades and some bad ones, but a lot more good ones overall. He used to tell me about them all the time."

"Did you realize he had accumulated more than five million dollars in his trading account?" Chief Ryan asked.

"He always said that was the goal, Chief Ryan. Andrei said once he had built the account up to five million dollars, that me and Margarita would be able to be financially independent for the rest of our lives. He said he needed to achieve this just in case anything ever happened to him."

"What about life insurance?" Michael asked.

"He didn't believe in it; he simply did not trust that a company would pay what they promised and said they always had loopholes. Once he said to me, 'I could just hear one of the insurance agents explaining how sorry he was that I had passed away on a cruise and that the policy did not cover loss of life while boating.' It made me laugh but it explains why he wanted to make us financially independent."

"You can be thankful, Silvia, that he certainly succeeded in doing so. But we do have to investigate the sources of the recent six payments of $1.2 million dollars that you did not know about," Michael said. "May we make copies of these banking records?"

"Yes, of course."

We heard shuffling papers, which we assumed was Silvia placing the folder of text messages and emails on the table.

"Please look through these, I downloaded these from his personal computer and mobile phone," she said.

The recording went quiet as they reviewed the documents.

Agent Calabrese said, "It appears that your husband was being forced to do some things he objected to. Throughout these message exchanges there are veiled threats against both you and your daughter."

We could hear Silvia began to weep softly.

"We know this is difficult," Chief Ryan said. "What do you think was going on Silvia?"

"I think these men were using my husband and pressuring him to do research for them," Silvia replied without hesitation.

"I think that is a fair assessment," Michael said.

"Did your husband ever mention to you the two men mentioned in these exchanges?" Michael asked.

"No. But I found two names in his cell phone that he was communicating with—General Sarkovsky and a Mr. Churgrill."

"It appears that Churgrill made the deposits into your husband's PNC Bank account and that Sarkovsky gave your husband the research tasks that he needed to complete in a kind of consulting contract worth $1.2 million," Michael explained.

"That's what I concluded as well."

"Did your husband mention that he was doing some consulting?" Chief Ryan asked.

"Yes. He did say he had one large contract that involved his assistance in helping to place a communications satellite in space for a private company."

"Did he explain any details about this project?"

"No, I'm sorry that he did not. He had worked on many similar consulting contracts, so I did not think much about it until his sickness progressed. Then I wondered how he would ever finish the contract."

Michael then asked, "But he did finish?"

"Yes, about a week before his death he told me he had finished and that the launch was successful. But I remember something very peculiar that he said when he told me this. He told me he did this not only for our future, but also for Russia."

"Had he ever said anything like that before?" Chief Ryan asked.

"No, never; that is why it stood out to me. I realized that whatever he had been contracted to do, he had been convinced that it would help Russia. It was as if it was his patriotic duty. That is when I became suspicious that he was being manipulated."

"It's getting near dinner time, gentlemen. Soon this place will be filled with people. It is also beginning to get dark," Natasha said.

"If it is all right with you, Silvia, could we meet one more time for breakfast tomorrow morning?" Michael asked. "I think we could wrap things up."

"Yes, that would be fine. Please come to my home. I have two spacious guest bedrooms. I would like you all to come stay with me this evening. I will cook you a very fine breakfast in the morning and then we can finish our conversation."

"Chief Ryan stopped the recording," I said, "but just as they were about to leave the private room where they were meeting in the Southward Ho Country Club, there was a power failure. Chief Ryan told me that thunderstorms were in the area, but they had not seen or heard a lightning strike and were alarmed, wondering if it was an attack. He said they crawled on their hands and knees toward a back exit that was hidden behind a curtain on one side of the room. After exiting and quietly closing the door, they entered a storage area and looked for a place to hide, just as they heard guests screaming."

"What happened?" Sarah asked.

"Chief Ryan told me that while hiding in the storage room with Michael, Natasha, and Mrs. Bershenko, he spotted an external door that exited the back of the building. The four of them quickly made their way to the door, heartened that they had heard no gunfire. They quietly exited the building and ran across the dirt path to a storage building that housed the club's electric golf carts. They quickly made their way to the east side of the building, which kept them out of sight from the main clubhouse where the intruders may have been looking for them."

"Then what?" Huang Tai asked.

"They then walked to the backside of the storage building where they found two golf carts on chargers. Michael checked them and they were fully charged. He unhooked them and they quietly drove them away from the clubhouse and into a heavily wooded area between the eighth and ninth fairways, with Silvia riding with him while Chief Ryan took Natasha in the second golf cart. They positioned themselves in the woods to be safely out of sight. That is when Chief Ryan sent me a text message to call for help. As they nestled into the trees and quietly waited, they could hear the police sirens as a police swat team and the FBI hostage rescue team descended on the premises. All roads and exits were securely blocked.

The two gunmen tried to escape onto the golf course but were quickly captured near the eighteenth green. Fortunately, they did not try to take any hostages. The FBI later confirmed that both men were from Chechnya but had received training from a terrorist military camp in Libya. Because the clubhouse became a crime scene, they were invited to come to the FBI office in Melville to complete their interview with Silvia Bershenko the following day."

"That's an incredible story," Colin said.

"Chief Ryan said he'll call me again tomorrow to give us an update."

With everyone up to date, we ended our conversation. We'd had an excellent workday, one without any interruptions. We all went to bed before 9:00 p.m., all completely exhausted.

CHAPTER 28

CHIEF RYAN CALLED ME EARLY the next morning as he was on his way to the FBI office in Melville. He wanted to pick my brain about key questions that would be important to ask Silvia Bershenko regarding her husband's consulting work.

"We've already had quite an exciting day," Chief Ryan said. Late last night when we arrived at Silvia Bershenko's home, we were concerned about the security threat. The elevator had key-only access to her floor, which was good security. When Michael walked out onto her back lanai to inspect the bullet holes in the sofa, he realized that not only could a high-powered rifle attack be launched from a boat on the ocean, but also a rocket-propelled grenade attack could be carried out which could destroy Silvia's entire home and any evidence that was still there. Michael immediately called his office to arrange for a Coast Guard patrol to guard the stretch of ocean that could be used to launch an attack."

"Were you attacked?" I asked.

"No, thanks to Michael's diligence. Johann, we are going to finish our interview with Silvia today," Chief Ryan said. "I specifically need your insight on what questions I should ask her about Andrei's knowledge of space satellite technology. Fortunately, Andrei Bershenko kept excellent records of all that he was doing, greatly enhancing the questioning process. Even as Alzheimer's ravaged his mind, he attempted to record his daily activities. It's clear to us from his notes that during the last eighteen months of his life, he was told his work would directly protect Russia and would not hurt the United States, repeated lies that Sarkovsky and Churgrill fed him."

"So, he was not complicit in this plot," I asked.

"We don't believe that he was," Chief Ryan said. "Andrei believed he was protecting Russia from a Chinese attack. He helped to determine the exact place in space where a Russian weather satellite could be placed in close proximity to an American military satellite, so that the trajectory of any weapon launched from the satellite could be traced back to the American satellite. With two satellites in close proximity, it would be possible to conclude that an American satellite launched an attack rather than a Russian weather satellite. It was a clever, deceptive maneuver that only someone as bright as Andrei Bershenko could orchestrate. He was led to believe that if the Chinese attacked Russia, the U.S. would believe their satellite was being attacked and would thwart the Chinese. It is clear he had no knowledge of the WMD that was going to be placed on the Russian satellite. Bershenko was convinced that he was developing a system only to protect satellites in space. If he'd known, he likely could have uncovered the danger that his work could be used offensively but was unable to do so."

"Ask Mrs. Bershenko if she would help you to find any of her husband's scientific papers or notes," I said.

"That's an excellent question, Johann. Also, Bershenko was an MIT professor with many scientific publications and with a long record of helping the U.S. space program. We will try and contact some of his closest colleagues, too. I may want to call you at the end of our interview. Will you be available?" Chief Ryan asked.

"Yes," I answered.

Two hours later Chief Ryan called and put me on speaker phone. They had taken a lunch break and were wrapping up their interview with Mrs. Bershenko at the FBI facility.

Chief Ryan asked me, "Do you have any questions, Johann, for Mrs. Bershenko?"

"Just a few questions," I said. "Mrs. Bershenko, did your husband ever mention to you any locations where these men were that he was working with?"

Silvia paused and thought about it. "I only remember South Africa, and possibly Malta. I'm not positive, but he might have mentioned Malta. It stood out to me because I didn't know exactly where it was."

"I have one last question," I said. "Silvia, you said yesterday that Andrei told you the launch was successful. What do you think that meant when he said that to you?"

"I believed he must have been talking about the satellite he was working on," Silvia said. "He's worked on a lot of satellite projects and has mentioned satellite launches many times."

"Thanks Johann, please stay on the call. Well, that's it for me," Chief Ryan said to Silvia. "I believe we have all the information we need."

"That is all for me, too," Michael Calabrese said. "And thank you again for leaving all this information, the computers, and the cell phones here. This information will be safe with the FBI and kept private and confidential."

"I completely trust you," Silvia said.

"Let me just confer briefly with my colleagues and then we will be on our way, Michael said. "Natasha will take you to a reception area to get some fresh coffee and some snacks."

Michael and Chief Ryan then debriefed with two other FBI agents who had observed and recorded the entire interview with Silvia, with me still listening on the call.

"I asked Silvia if we could do a final sweep of her home when she goes on vacation with my wife to Tuscany," Michael noted, "and she has agreed. If there is any additional evidence there that may be useful, we should be able to find it."

"We still need to find the exact location of the Russian satellite," I said.

"Understood," said agent Calabrese. "I do think we need to continue to protect her residence against attack."

"We will make that happen," one of the agents replied. "We have already talked with the local police about it."

"If anything turns up in the final sweep regarding weaponizing a satellite and its location, will you all let me know?" I asked.

Chief Ryan responded first, "We will."

Agent Calabrese also replied, "We'll let you know if we find anything, Johann."

Chief Ryan thanked all the agents and ended the call. He followed with a short text to me.

"Thanks Johann, I'm heading home, we'll talk again soon."

———————————

Shortly after my call ended with Chief Ryan, I received a text from Darrell indicating that he had safely landed at the Taiwan Taoyuan

International Airport in Taipei and entered the country without any difficulties. Darrell sent me a secure audio message:

> "Hi Johann, we were all relieved that there was no vehicle following us from the airport, but as a precaution, my friends had worked out an elaborate scheme. The car they were driving was borrowed from another friend who was a police officer. They pulled into a popular fast food restaurant with a long drive-thru, then quickly got out of the car while they were in line on the back side of the building, hidden out of sight from the street and from three sides of the building. They got into another vehicle waiting for them close by with another driver, and then the police officer friend exited the second vehicle and got into his own car that was in line in the drive through lane. If anyone had followed them from the airport, they would be waiting for a car which no longer was occupied by three men, but by one man who was a police officer."

I stopped the audio. While listening to Darrell's account I could not prevent my memories of the many times my parents used to do such antics on long road trips when they wanted to switch drivers. My homesickness was always nearby.

Darrell's mission was to work with his network of friends in Taiwan to penetrate the cyber defenses of China's satellite network and to determine the coordinates in space where China was posed to launch a biological attack as retaliation for any U.S. attack. If we had that information, we could program our laser weapons to destroy any satellite loaded with biological weapons before or soon after they were launched. He wanted me to eventually talk with his friends about it. I clicked on the audio again.

"I told my friends that first, before any business, I had a craving for homemade noodles. They took me to Lao Shan Dong Niu Rou Mian in the Wan Nian building in Ximen. New to me, but not to my friends, the restaurant had been serving handmade wide noodles since 1949, and the Jia Chang Mian I ordered was indeed the best noodles I would ever taste. When we arrived, another friend, Cheng-han, was already waiting for us. During the meal, my friends began asking me technical questions that I could not answer, so I'm going to contact you later by Skype so you can directly talk with my friends and explain the system that you and Huang Tai are working on, and what you know about the Chinese weather satellite that General Tso had placed a payload of biological weapons on before its launch and placement in space."

Since I loved Chinese noodles, I made a mental note to one day return with Darrell to Lao Shan Dong Niu Rou Mian and enjoy a bowl of Jia Chang Mian.

While waiting for Darrell's Skype invitation, Darrell sent me a secure email to prepare for our conversation. I opened it and read his personal note:

"Before our Skype meeting Johann, I want to share a couple of important things. Cheng-han is a close friend who had also been a close friend of my parents when they all went to school in Boston together.

After completing their degrees, my father and Cheng-han both had to leave the city they had grown to love. My father took a job at the Northwestern Memorial Hospital in Chicago, where he became a leading cardiologist, and Cheng-han returned to Taiwan to work in the aerospace industry, where he served as Chairman of the Taiwan

Aerospace Industry Association for ten years. Cheng-han and I have a very close connection through my father.

During our dinner tonight, Cheng-han said to me, 'I miss your parents so much. I have many friends but none like your father. I know I told you before, but we were as close as brothers. I can't imagine how much you miss them.'

I said to Cheng-han, 'One thing that gives me some degree of comfort is that they died doing what they loved—helping the poor on a medical mission trip. I think they had gone on at least a dozen such trips throughout the world. It gave them great joy.'

He told me they both had such big hearts and that he saw that in me, too, and that our parents' greatest gifts to us was their giving hearts. Cheng-han reminded me to guard my heart and not to become jaded and cynical by the injustices of this world. He also reminded me that my parents taught me the meaning of true philanthropy and how to believe the best in others.

I'm telling you all this for two reasons, Johann. First, you can completely trust Cheng-han. He would never put you or me or any of our friends at risk. Second, if I make it out of this crisis, never let me be cynical like I have been in the past. I want to make my parents proud of how I live and die."

I sat there thinking deeply about what Darrell had said. There was more email to read but I had to stop. The words of Cheng-han were as much for me as they were for Darrell.

Darrell had sent the email from a secure facility in the basement of a travel bookstore in the Da'an District called the Zeelandia Bookshop. Darrell recalled later that when he first entered the store after hours, he saw travel-related memorabilia everywhere, including map-decorated walls and souvenirs picked up from bookstore patrons from their past travels. The staff were known for helping visitors find the travel books they needed to plan their next adventure. The store even hosted a secret travel club, which Darrell knew was very much like the *Eleutheria Club* in Chicago. The name of their club, *Jùlèbù Fāxiàn,* was created by the Chinese word for club, *Jùlèbù,* and the Chinese word for to find or to discover, *fāxiàn.* It was the perfect name for a secret club meeting in the basement of a travel bookstore whose mission was to find and discover that which is *Yǐn* (hidden).

I then read the rest of Darrell's email.

> We would love to have this facility in the U.S. The basement of the Zeelandia Bookshop is as large as the first floor, providing a spacious five-thousand square feet of workspace. Cheng-han gave me a personal tour. It was not difficult to see that the financial resources of the club's members were substantial, as this facility had some of the most sophisticated technology in the world. During the tour, I met many of the technology experts that were working there to track down the coordinates of the Chinese satellite carrying Botulinum toxin. I thought to myself, I'm not sure why you would need me or my friends. You have such outstanding people and technology.

> I already knew my good friends, Cheng-han and Chih-wei, were IT specialists. They are more than specialists. I would call them IT geniuses. Before coming here, I knew very little about *Jùlèbù Fāxiàn* and I did not completely understand the great pool of extraordinary technological talent here in Taiwan. Chih-wei Tsai began working at age sixteen for Taiwan Semiconductor Manufacturing Co. (TSMC), ranked the seventh leading technology company in the world. After twenty years of advancing in the company to a VP

position, he retired from TSMC very wealthy at age thirty-six. Although Chih-wei is still a consultant to the company, he launched his own company in 2016, specializing in the rapidly growing cryptocurrency financial sector.

Wang Shu Liang, another close friend, also worked with cryptocurrencies as VP of development in Chih-wei's new company. He was especially valuable as a partner to Chih-wei because of his fifteen-year career with Fubon Financial Holding Co Ltd., which made 224 billion Taiwanese dollars (about U.S. $7.3 billion) in revenue in 2018. Wang Shu learned the IT sectors in insurance, securities, commercial banking, and life insurance.

Cheng-han told me their greatest need was for human intelligence within China's military. When I told him about you and your friendship with Huang Tai Simonnes, whose uncle is a colonel general in the Chinese People's Liberation Army, Cheng-han knew that I needed to go to China. Cheng-han also told me that it was unlikely that they would be able to retrieve the exact location of China's weather satellites, particularly the one with a WMD. He said someone needed to go into mainland China to obtain the coordinates from a high-level military commander. That's part of what Cheng-han wants to discuss with you on Skype.

I thought about the predicament. It was too dangerous to try to bring Huang Tai to Taiwan. I could communicate directly with him from my research lab at the NASA Ames Research Center. Cheng-han and his friends didn't know me or Huang Tai, but they knew Darrell, so there was no one better prepared than Darrell for bringing us together. I also concluded that the most logical person to go to China to meet with Huang-Tai's uncle was Darrell.

When the Skype call came on my screen , I was thoroughly prepared. After short introductions and a mutual exchange of honoring each other, we rapidly entered the heart of the discussion, which was going to Huang Tai and asking him to put us in contact with his uncle in China.

"That will not be easy," I said. "Huang Tai is already risking his life and he could be executed for treason in China if his work with me in Chicago and California became known. Huang Tai's uncle has already placed himself at risk protecting Huang Tai and providing him with information. He could be arrested and executed through the efforts of a rival general. Cooperating with the Americans is a grievous offense, but cooperating with Taiwan, a perceived renegade republic that China sees as its own, is especially grievous. If this became known, the president of China would have no choice but to imprison and execute one of his favorite generals and his nephew."

"Cheng-han and I have talked at length about these risks," Darrell said. "We don't see any alternatives."

"Can you convince Huang Tai to trust Darrell?" Cheng-han asked me.

"I will have to," I said. "I don't see any other way to stop this impending catastrophe. We can intercept these weapons in space if we have the location of the launch satellite."

"We must also discuss this with Chief Ryan," Darrell said.

We concluded the Skype call with an agreement on how to proceed. I would talk to Huang Tai about arranging a meeting in China with Darrell. Darrell would prepare to travel into China with Melissa and Jin assisting him.

CHAPTER 29

HUANG TAI AND I WERE nearly finished with our work and collaboration with Colin and Sarah. We had a couple more simulations to run before we were ready to talk with Darrell and his friends again in Taiwan. First, we simulated incapacitating the Chinese satellite-based launch of biological weapons. Both tests were successful, achieving a projected 99.85 percent accuracy score, meaning that if we were able to simulate 10,000 tests, in 9,985 of those tests we would completely destroy the target and that in the remaining fifteen cases, we would heavily damage the target and likely incapacitate the weapon. We tested destroying deployed WMDs with our mobile laser satellite that would be controlled from the ground and achieved similar results.

Next, we simulated an attack on a Russian-based satellite system, which has different technology and exhibits different properties in space from the Chinese systems. Our results were very good but not great. Our two tests yielded an accuracy average score of 97.75 percent, meaning for every 10,000 laser system attacks on a Russian satellite, we would have a direct hit 9,775 times and a partial hit 225 times. What was disappointing was that there was an estimated 1.5 percent probability that five of the 225 partial hits would leave the satellite damaged but still operational. It was a very low probability but one that we wanted to eliminate. We felt confident that if any weapons were deployed from any satellites in space that we could navigate to them and destroy them with our lasers.

The sense of urgency was reaching an intensity that was palpable. The four of us could physically sense that our space research involved a life and death situation for millions of people. We also knew that the simulations were testing the accuracy of our space lasers in a laboratory setting and that we still had to launch our system into space and maneuver it to within close proximity to the Chinese and Russian satellites.

While Huang Tai and I were discussing our future needs and Colin and Sarah went searching for some dinner, my phone buzzed. Chief Ryan gave me the signal that he would call me in two minutes. I prepared for the call using my encrypted phone application and put him on speaker so Huang Tai could listen with me.

"We have much catching up to do Chief Ryan, are you safe?"

"Yes, I just arrived in Chicago and I'm waiting for my ride home. First, give me an update on your laser weapon satellite tests."

"A 99.85 percent accuracy score for the China satellite and a 97.75 percent accuracy score for the Russian satellite."

"These are excellent. Can you improve the Russian satellite hit statistics to above 99 percent?"

"Yes," answered Huang Tai, "I believe we can."

I was not as confident but I knew Huang Tai must have an idea about this.

"Good. I am so proud of both of you in what you have accomplished in a short time. I know that you still need coordinates for the location and the flight path of the Chinese satellite that holds the biological weapons payload."

"Yes, as soon as possible," Huang Tai said.

"Second, I know you also need confirmation that a biological weapons payload was delivered to a Russian weather satellite, and that you also need the specific coordinates and flight path of that satellite."

"Yes. After we have these confirmations we can deploy our satellite-based space lasers into orbit and place them within striking distance of these two biological weapons. There is also a crucial third piece of information that we need. We do not know for sure how these biological weapons would deploy. We know that Nicole and her team in Maryland are working on this issue with the Department of Defense's Chemical and Biological Defense Program and with the National Biodefense Analysis and Countermeasures Center. We can speculate based on past weapons' systems."

"Check," Chief Ryan replied. "Go ahead and speculate."

"We will," I said.

"Darrell, Melissa, and Jin are traveling into China to meet with Huang Tai's uncle. When Darrell returns to Taiwan, he should be able to confirm the Chinese target, coordinates, and flight plan."

"Yes, I have been in contact with Darrell since he arrived in Taiwan," I said.

"I will coordinate with the FBI office in Long Island to confirm the Russian target, coordinates, and flight plan. They are working on getting this information."

"What can I do?" I asked.

"Please confer with Nicole in Maryland to ascertain the most plausible types of delivery systems for these weapons. Also, check on Angela in Italy. Natasha Calabrese and Silvia Bershenko should be arriving there soon."

"I will. I haven't heard much from her since she's been there. I'm a bit concerned."

"She had a lot to do. Also, we are coordinating with NASA a launch of your laser systems from Vandenberg Air Force Base as soon as possible," Chief Ryan said. "My ride is here, have to run."

"Did you record?" Huang Tai asked after Chief Ryan disconnected. "That was a lot of info."

"Yes, I got it."

Shortly after the call ended, Colin and Sarah returned with food. We played Chief Ryan's phone message for them while we ate and then began to brainstorm as Chief Ryan had encouraged.

Colin opened the discussion.

"In the past, biological weapons have been designed to explode 35,000 feet above the Earth. The E96 cluster bomb, developed by the U.S. military in the early 1950s, was a 500-pound biological weapon designed to deliver an anti-personnel or anti-animal biological agent. The bomb contained 104 four-pound E48 submunitions that would fan out once detonated. The submunitions were clustered into an E38 cluster adapter that was designed to generate an aerosol cloud in the shape of an ellipse."

"How big?" Colin asked.

"Big enough to kill tens of thousands of animals, and people."

"What about the United Nations ban?" Sarah asked. "And pass me some more sweet potato fries, Colin."

Huang Tai then jumped into the conversation, stating, "Although the United Nations' Convention on Cluster Munitions 'prohibits all use, stockpiling, production, and transfer of Cluster Munitions,' adopted in Dublin in May 2008, not even the 108 signatories may completely be relied upon to keep their word about not developing these types of weapons given the real threat of biological weapons from space."

"I remember that President Richard Nixon officially ended the U.S. biological weapons program in 1969," I said.

"Really, Johann? You weren't even born yet," Sarah said.

"I learned it in tenth grade history, Sarah, when you were probably paying more attention to the boys in your class than to American history."

Sarah started laughing and said, "Guilty as charged."

It seemed like it had been weeks since we had laughed. It was good to hear someone laugh again.

"To elaborate," I said, "Nixon did end the program, but prior to his 1969 declaration, the U.S. created the E133 cluster bomb. The bomb weighed 750 pounds and held between 536 and 544 E61 bomblets designed to disperse an aerosol of a biological agent such as anthrax."

"So that is very old technology," Sarah said.

"It is," I said, "but we must realize that this same kind of technology could be used today, even though it is officially banned."

"I agree with that," said Huang Tai. "I would not be surprised if China has that technology. So, what is the U.S. doing now?" he asked, turning toward Colin.

"Officially, the U.S. Biological Defense Research Program today is strictly defensive," Colin said. "It has both medical and non-medical research objectives that focus on developing physical and medical countermeasures to protect all Americans from the threat of modern biological warfare."

"But the U.S. defensive position does not prevent other countries from developing offensive biological weapons from space," Huang Tai said.

"I agree with Huang Tai," Sarah said, "We must assume that not only China, but other nations are developing biological weapon capabilities in space."

"The next thing to consider is if we are employing the best strategy to protect populations from these weapons," Colin posed.

"I have a strong opinion about that," I said. "I think we are. At the Kavli Institute, I learned of five basic defense strategies implemented by our government to protect against space warfare. First, there is the long-duration orbital ASAT (anti-satellite weapons) program called *farsat*. It involves an orbital interceptor that is launched into a storage orbit for an extended period of time. When it is needed, it can be activated and maneuvered to monitor, engage, or even attack another satellite or space station. The ASAT may be standalone system or covertly placed on or in a 'mothership' satellite."

Sarah seemed to be glued to what I was saying.

"Are these in place now, Johann?"

"Not to my knowledge. I doubt that any country has these in place."

"I agree," Huang Tai said, "with regards to China, I do not think China has these capabilities yet."

I continued.

"The second defense strategy is called nearsat. In this defense system, the interceptor is either an independent satellite or part of a 'mothership' that is placed into orbit in close proximity to the target. The nearsat must be kept in close proximity to the target until it is commanded, from the ground, to either monitor or incapacitate the target satellite. The lethal radius of the attack mechanism determines how closely the nearsat must follow the target. Our planned laser-based system fits best into the nearsat strategy."

"I agree with your conclusion, Johann," Colin said. "We have worked on developing both farsat and nearsat systems here at the Ames Research Center, but we have found nearsat systems to be more feasible given the high costs of maintaining space stations and platforms."

"And the other three?" asked Huang Tai.

"The other defense strategies are space mines, pellet rings, also called fragmentation rings, and space-to-space missiles. In brief, space mines are put into orbit to navigate into the flight path of a target satellite and then detonate upon impact. Fragmentation or pellet rings are relatively small, non-maneuvering objects that are strategically dispersed from one or more satellites in order to create a protective Earth-orbiting ring. Satellites that attempt to fly through the ring will either be destroyed or severely damaged.

Space-to-space missiles are rocket propelled ASAT interceptors launched from an orbiting carrier platform in order to destroy a target satellite. These systems are expensive to deploy and difficult to maintain once set in orbit."

"Does the U.S. have these systems in place?" Huang Tai asked.

"That's beyond my security clearance, Huang Tai," I said.

Colin and Sarah also did not know for sure but doubted that we did.

"One fact we do know is other than what we are doing now, these strategies require years of preparation to put into place. Because of the imminent threat, we have weeks or perhaps only days and not years to put a defense system in place."

"Yet we have known this was coming for eighteen years," Colin said. "We just did not respond fast enough."

"Are you referring to Grossman's book?" I asked.

"Yes. Have you read it?"

"It was required reading in one of my classes at the University of Chicago."

"Did your professor agree, Johann, that Grossman accurately identified the threats in space from both China and Russia?"

"He did. My professor believes that space warfare is the most direct path for the Chinese regime to compete with the United States militarily. The Chinese see space as the ultimate high ground."

"That's true," Huang Tai said. "I was specifically taught that in China. One of China's national goals is to achieve space supremacy."

"Do you think China has achieved that goal, Huang Tai?"

Huang Tai thought about it for a while, and then said, "I don't know, but I guess we will find out."

Colin's last question stayed with us for a while. We all headed for bed wondering if China was ahead of us.

CHAPTER 30

THE FOLLOWING MORNING, DARRELL CALLED me just before boarding his plane in Taipei to travel to Hong Kong to meet Melissa and Jin.

"How is Taipei?"

"Home of the best homemade noodles in the world."

"You had some more, didn't you?"

"Of course."

"I told you I'm coming with you one day."

"I know. Is Huang Tai ready to talk to me?"

"As soon as he swallows the large bite of pancake in his mouth." I handed my phone to Huang Tai, who gave Darrell a detailed physical description of his uncle and a short biography of his life.

"He sounds like an amazing person."

"He is. Melissa, of course, will recognize my uncle, but I wanted you to be able to spot him, too, in a crowd. You will like him."

He handed my phone back to me while taking another big bite of the pancakes I had made from a box of old batter I had found.

"What are your plans?" I asked.

"We decided that the safest way to meet with Huang Tai's uncle is to travel with a tour group. We chose the three-day in-depth Shaolin Kung Fu Tour offered by China Discovery as the perfect tour for them. Since both Melissa and Jin have martial arts training, the tour would make sense to anyone conducting surveillance on the three of them."

"That sounds like fun, Darrell."

"I know; I'm looking forward to the tour. We worked out a meticulous plan with Huang Tai's uncle to camouflage our interaction. We will take a Cathay Dragon flight from Hong Kong to Zhengzhou, China, where they will begin the three-day tour. On the first day, our tour group would visit the Shaolin Temple in the morning, the origin of Shaolin Kung Fu, and will watch a Kung Fu show there in the afternoon. In the evening, our group will attend the Shaolin Zen Music Ritual and then watch a large-scale outdoor Kung Fu performance for tourists."

"I want to come, Darrell. I so enjoyed my last trip."

"General Hu has arranged to meet a close friend, a retired military leader who lives in Dengfeng, which is located at the foot of Mount Song, one of the most sacred mountains in China. The city, renowned as a spiritual center of China, is commonly visited by those who come to meditate and pray. General Hu and his friend also plan to visit the famous Gaocheng Observatory together and offer prayers at the Shaolin Temple."

"That's one of the most famous monasteries in China. And martial arts centers."

"I've always wanted to visit this place, Johann. After General Hu's friend leaves the temple to go home, he intends to accidentally run into our tour group while watching both the afternoon and evening Kung Fu shows, providing ample time for him to talk with me and Melissa while Jin provides security. General Hu is going to don a Boston Red Sox cap to make him easy to spot in a crowd."

"His English is excellent, too. He has a very strong presence. When you see him, give him a special greeting from me," I said.

"I will. On day two of the tour, our tour group will learn Kung Fu for two hours in the Shaolin Temple, while General Hu will have breakfast with another friend, a former teacher now retired in Dengfeng. Our group will then visit Songyang Academy to feel the atmosphere of class learning in ancient China, and the oldest Buddhist pagoda—Songyue Pagoda. General Hu will again mingle as a tourist with our tour group at the pagoda and then plans to later join us at the Zhongyue Temple. General Hu will travel back to Zhengzhou in the early evening."

"And on the third day of the tour?" I asked.

"On day three, as our tour group travels back to Zhengzhou in the morning, General Hu plans to speak to a class at Zhengzhou University of Aeronautics on cyber-warfare security as a guest lecturer. After the lecture, he will have one last meeting with us at the airport."

"That is an excellent plan; well thought out, and hopefully safe."

"Even if anyone is watching us, it would be difficult to discover our interactions and Jin and Melissa will be watchful for potential lurkers nearby."

We ended our conversation feeling good about the China trip. I knew Darrell was concerned about the many crazy hours we were working. But we still had more tests to do to increase the hit rate on our Russian satellite simulations. Also, I still needed to confer with Nicole about the Botulinum delivery systems and to check on Angela before getting some rest. I decided to check on Angela first.

————————

"Johann!" Angela said after taking my call. "I was just going to call you. I have had a very crazy week. It is so good to hear your voice."

"It is so good to hear you, Angela; I was getting a bit worried."

"It took me a long time to get here, Johann. I stopped to visit some friends in the Netherlands, and then my original flight to Italy was cancelled because the plane I was scheduled to take had mechanical problems. I stayed an extra day in Amsterdam."

"How is your brother, Angelo?"

"He's amazing, Johann. He is on his way to pick me up now. I can't remember if I told you, but he is one of the smartest people I know. He graduated from senior school, like high school in the U.S., at age sixteen. He then was admitted into the Scuola Superiore Sant'Anna, the highest ranked academic institution in Italy, where he studied forensics, criminal justice, and surveillance. He graduated at the top of his class at age nineteen and was immediately recruited by the Polizia di Stato, Italy's national police force, to work in counterterrorism."

"He sounds like he's as smart as you, Angela."

"I can't wait to see him."

"You haven't seen him yet?"

"No, I had other places to go. I just landed in Florence and picked up my luggage."

"He's in charge of counterterrorism now?"

"Listen to this, Johann. My father told me that in Angelo's first six months on the national counterterrorism police force, he was responsible for uncovering and stopping seven major terrorist attacks, including two in Rome that would have potentially killed hundreds of people. Within his first year he was moved up in rank and asked to help oversee Italy's international terrorism surveillance and monitoring program to track suspicious individuals and groups."

"So, they moved him up the chain of command."

"Yes, he now has the responsibility of one much older, yet he has the respect of those on his team because he is an exceptional listener and is constantly conferring with them. I see him now. Angelo!" Angela shouted as she spotted her bother waiting for her after she cleared immigration at the *Peretola Firenze.*

"Angela!" I heard her brother shout. "Welcome back to Florence!"

"I have to go but will call you in a few minutes." Angela ended the call.

I imagined in my mind the scene that unfolded, with Angela's brother running toward her and the witnesses in the airport confusing them for lovers. Then after falling into one another's arms, I could see them embracing with warm hugs and kisses on the cheek, not the lips, informing all the onlookers that they were brother and sister. I could almost hear them both talking so fast it would be difficult for any spectator to make any sense of what they were saying.

When Angela called me back, I asked her to describe their reunion. It was almost exactly as I had imagined.

"We're on our way to the Brandolino restaurant and I will call you from there," Angela said before leaving the airport. "My first order of business is to my meet my parents and older brother Stefan for lunch. The Brandolino is our favorite restaurant. It is close to the Duomo and partly owned by American friends. Besi, the manager and also an owner, will be waiting to seat us at our reserved table in the back. I'm sure it will be a raucous family reunion."

"I wish I was with you now," I said.

"Me, too. I'll call you again soon. I want to introduce you to my family."

When Angela called again, she said hi and immediately put her phone on speaker. I could hear loud laughter in the background. I heard someone say, "Sorry for all the commotion, Besi. Our whole family has not been together in more than a year."

Then I heard Besi respond, "No commotion at all, this is what our restaurant is all about."

Angela attempted to quiet everybody down so she could introduce me to everyone.

"Johann, I am going to introduce you to my family. I'm here with my father, Vincenzo, my mother, Carla, my oldest brother Stefan, my twin brother, Angelo, and our dear friend, Besi, who runs the best restaurant in all of Italy. Tell my family about yourself, Johann."

I felt totally intimidated but did my best to not bore Angela's lively family. Then, as soon as I could, I turned the conversation and began asking questions.

"How do you like retirement from political life, *Onorevole Farrentino?*" I asked.

"He loves it!" Carla said. "And that's so nice of you to use my husband's title."

"We know *you* love it, Mother," Angelo said.

"Thank you for asking, Johann," Vincenzo said, "I like it, too, almost as much as my wife."

Carla explained, "There is so much pressure lifted from his shoulders. No more drama, crises, and decisions to make."

"Yes, like who to bribe and who to threaten today," Vincenzo said.

"Is it not poetic justice, Father, that one of your sons is tracking down the bribes and the other son is tracking down the threats?" Angela said.

"That is rather humorous," Carla said. "If your sons were in these professions when you were in the Senate, one son would be arresting half your Senate friends and the other son would be prosecuting the other half."

"Yes, both my friends and enemies now laugh when they hear about the exploits of our sons."

"I love hearing all your laughter," I said. "It has been a great privilege to befriend Angela."

"And how is my beautiful daughter Angela?" Vincenzo asked as we all turned our attention to her.

"I have been changing a lot for the good, Father. I'm listening to all the wisdom Mom tried to give me when I was a teenager and did not use. Johann has helped me, too."

I could sense the change and knew it was not time for jokes. I figured everyone at the table knew Angela had lived a pretty wild and risky lifestyle. This was the bad past road that Angela had told me about during our flight.

"I love you all so much," Angela said. Her voice broke up. "Thank you all for loving me and believing in me even when I was not loving myself the way I should. I'm so sorry I made you all worry about me."

I then heard Carla embrace Angela, followed by her father and two brothers. I could not understand Italian I was hearing, but I clearly understood they were words of affirmation and love.

Stefan, who I assumed had picked up his wine glass, said, "Salute, to my sister who has made me and my brother and my father and mother cry tears of joy."

Everyone else in the restaurant overhearing them assumed that Angela had just announced her engagement, but this was better than engagement; she was off the road of self-destruction and on a new road of self-fulfillment.

"I have just two questions for you, Johann," Vincenzo said. "First, have you chased off all of Angela's suitors?"

I was not expecting that and had to say something clever. Angela held her breath.

"I think Angela needs no help in that department," I said. "She is very direct in communicating her interests and disinterests."

"Good answer," Vincenzo said, "I like you, Johann. My next question is how did you and your *Eleutheria Club* friends get mixed up in trying to take down a dangerous criminal like Atlas Churgrill?"

"That is a long story," I said, "and perhaps too long for this joyous family reunion. May I answer that question on another phone call at a better time?"

"Of course, Johann, talk of Churgrill will most certainly spoil our dinner."

We ended the call with plans to talk again.

I wondered how I did and asked Angela about it on a private call later in the evening.

"My family loves you, Johann," Angela said. "I was not surprised by my father's questions, as he asked me the same things."

"What did you say?" I asked.

"I told him I had chased off all my suitors and had one close male friend who is one of my classmates at the University of Chicago. I told him you are a true friend and that you are unlike any of the men I have dated. I told him you are humble and deeply caring at heart, and also gentle and kind and very bright. I said you are still young, but I believe we will be close friends for a long time."

"I hope I can live up to that description, Angela. You are very generous. And what did you say about the *Eleutheria Club*?"

"I told my family the truth. My father always kidded me about being related to da Vinci because of my intellectual proclivities and pursuits. I told him you are an American da Vinci."

"You are too kind, Angela," I said.

"Anything else I should know?"

"Yes, just as they were finishing out last course and thinking about dessert, I received a text message from Chief Ryan. The message was disquieting."

"What did he say?"

"Let me read it to you."

> Atlas Churgrill just landed in Rome. We cannot arrest him yet as we are still compiling evidence. Let Angelo know immediately. There will be two INTERPOL agents following him closely. Also, FBI agent Emily Kelly is accompanying Margarita Bershenko to Florence from Bern to meet her mother Silvia and New York FBI agent Michael Calabrese's wife Natasha, who are arriving tomorrow from New York. They will text you their flight information. They are officially on vacation. Please put them in a safe place. I'm back in Chicago. More later.

"My family is still here at the Brandolino. Can we talk now and you can tell them everything you know?" she asked.

"Yes."

In a few moments she said, "You're on speaker, Johann. Besi moved us all to the back room and no one has any cell phones in the room. It is secure and private. Go ahead."

I shared for two hours, answering questions as I went while they drank wine and took notes. By 2:00 a.m. we were all exhausted. The Farrentino family realized they were in a fight for their lives.

CHAPTER 31

HUΔПG TΔI ΔПD I DECIDED to order Chinese food as Colin and Sarah, who were heading toward a formal engagement, went out on a private dinner date with Commander Fields and his fiancée. We decided to see if we could contact Darrell, Melissa, and Jin to see how things were going in China and whether they had met Huang Tai's uncle yet.

We first sent Darrell a short-encrypted text message, and after about ten minutes we received an encrypted audio file back. We opened the file and huddled around my phone, listening closely.

During a Kung Fu show we attended, Jin had this strong sense that we were being watched. Melissa and I were completely captivated by the performance, so Jin conducted his own surveillance and suspected that we were being followed not by one person, but by a man and a woman. The two suspects were a good distance from each other but seemed to be working together. Jin was trained to recognize this type of surveillance, although he told us that he did not know definitively.

As we walked toward the ShiErLou restaurant, Jin realized that both the man and the woman following them were carrying small backpacks that could contain weapons. There was no easy way to escape a confrontation. He quietly notified me and Melissa. We agreed to split up but to meet in the ShiErLou restaurant in twenty minutes. I wanted to arrive first so I could meet and greet General Hu in private, so I walked straight to the restaurant. Jin paired with Melissa, who took a more circular route so that they would arrive later. Both the man and woman followed me, but I speculated that their real target was the general.

When Melissa and Jin arrived, General Hu and I were deep in conversation. We stopped and General Hu gave Melissa a warm greeting and asked about the welfare of her family back in Hong Kong. The general also greeted Jin, whom he had met two years ago.

Fortunately, the two pursuers did not enter the restaurant, but waited patiently outside for their opportunity. General Hu made some strategic calls during dinner and was able to learn that a rival general had hired professional agents to either injure or assassinate him. The general then contacted a trusted friend in the office of the Chinese president to seek guidance on how he might defend himself, and if necessary, if he was authorized to use deadly force.

After ten minutes, he let us know that he received the text message he was waiting for. "You have permission."

"Excuse me for these interruptions," the general said. "Let's enjoy dinner and conversation. I want you to tell me all about how my favorite nephew Huang Tai is doing. I think you all know Huang Tai is like a son to me."

"And he has become my friend, General, and you already know that he is one of Johann's most trusted friends. He is like a brother to Johann. They have become very close working so hard together," I said.

"Yes, I realized that when I met Johann. I would very much like to meet Johann again. I do believe that he is a true friend to Huang Tai."

When I heard those words, I felt some kind of unity of spirit with Huang Tai. My feeling was difficult to explain, but it was a deeper kind of connection.

After dinner, Jin suggested to General Hu that since the two attackers were outside the restaurant, the attack would probably come in the form of poison darts and that his neck would be likely targeted. General Hu, who told us he was quite familiar with the use of ninja weapons like the blowgun, agreed that it was the perfect weapon for the occasion given the large crowds present.

Also, bamboo blowguns are easily camouflaged; some are even designed to play as a musical instrument. They can be quickly removed from and concealed in a pocket or knapsack. The arrows used, shaped like tiny triangular needles, can be tipped with poison and used with deadly accuracy within ten meters. The neck and eyes are the most vulnerable parts of the body to this type of attack, and the neck is difficult to protect. Jin, however, had prepared for this contingency. In his carry bag was a hard, impenetrable protective neck brace to protect against poison darts and a thin bullet-proof vest. He also carried several pairs of REKS Solux Wrap-Around unbreakable sunglasses with photochromic lenses that adjust to available light.

"I suggest you remain in here, General, and let me, Darrell, and Melissa take care of these attackers," Jin recommended. "We will just need to exchange clothes in a changing room."

The general would have none of that.

"I'm honored that one of you would be willing to dress in my clothes and absorb the attack, but I have always led up front and I don't intend to stop now. Darrell, you can come out beside me. Jin and Melissa, I think you should leave the back of the restaurant and circle back around behind the attackers. Do you have what you need to neutralize them?"

"Yes, we do," I said.

"And you also have a syringe, Jin?"

"Yes, General."

"Good. I will put on the protective gear that you brought Jin, and you can cover me from the front, Darrell, when we leave the restaurant while Jin and Melissa close in from the back."

The restaurant owner provided a small changing room for General Hu. After five minutes, General Hu returned to his chair wearing the protective vest and neck brace under his casual clothing. At 7:30 p.m., the general walked out of the front of the restaurant in plain view, donning his Boston Red Sox cap. I was close behind. At six feet two inches tall, General Hu was easy to spot. He was immediately shot with two darts. One stuck into his neck brace less than an eighth of an inch and then fell onto the ground. The second dart penetrated his outer clothing a couple inches below his larynx but was stopped by his protective vest. He pulled it out carefully and threw it on the ground, grinding both darts into the dirt with the heel of his shoe.

The crowd could not hear anything, and the attack was so quick that no one knew what had taken place. The two attackers, who were about twenty yards apart, looked for immediate cover as Jin begin coming toward them. Melissa, who was standing on an empty crate in the back of the crowd, spotted the female attacker moving quickly through the crowd. As soon as Melissa was able to intercept her, the woman turned on her and with two powerfully placed kicks, knocked Melissa to the ground. Melissa quickly jumped up and then crippled the woman with her own quick kicks to the legs and knees and with a fist to the throat. As the woman crumbled to the ground in pain, Melissa then took out a syringe from her purse and injected the would-be attacker into the left arm with a powerful tranquilizer laced with a virus that would put her in the hospital for two weeks.

While Melissa was efficiently taking care of the woman attacker, she could see the fighting between Jin and the male attacker about thirty yards away. The male attacker was an excellent martial arts fighter, but Jin gained the upper hand, knocking him to the ground just as Melissa arrived to help hold him down. Jin quickly injected a syringe into the man's arm, immobilizing him and also making him sick for a couple weeks. Although we did not know what kind of poison was laced on the darts, we know it would likely have made General Hu very sick or perhaps would even kill him.

With two people now on the ground, the local police would converge quickly, so we slipped back into the crowd and headed toward the Shaolin Zen Music Ritual near the Shaolin Temple, which was to begin at 8:00 p.m. We went our separate ways—the general walking to his hotel and us walking toward the music ritual.

When Darrell and I talked later, I learned this attack was the only disruption to the detailed plans Jin, Melissa, and Darrell had laid out for the three-day tour and rendezvous with the general. During the visit to Zhongyue Temple on the second tour day, General Hu gave Darrell an encrypted thumb drive and the codes to unlock it containing all the coordinates and flight path information of the Chinese weather satellite that had been loaded with a biological weapon.

When Darrell arrived in Taipei, he sent me an encrypted text message:

Good news. Get others together. Will call tonight at 8:00 p.m. California time.

CHAPTER 32

AT 7:45 P.M., DARRELL SENT another text message. He and his friends at the *Jùlèbù Fāxiàn* in Taipei were ready to talk. I was outside our building with Huang Tai, Colin, and Sarah, checking to see how much the San Francisco Bay had retreated. The water was slowly withdrawing from the sandbags around our building. We had seen television news reports indicating that most of the fires were ignited by the earthquake, including several large wildfires, were extinguished. From outside our building, we could still hear a lot of sirens from police, ambulances, and other emergency vehicles. After returning inside, we gathered our notes together and got our phones ready to record our session, and then I responded to the text from Darrell letting him know we were ready.

I had initially recommended that we use Skype for our call, but Huang Tai was not sure if that was best, having heard that Skype could be hacked.

"In the past that was true," Colin explained. "But Microsoft fixed the problem. They now offer end-to-end encryption for audio calls, text, and multimedia messages through a feature called Private Conversations."

"I read about that, too, in *Wired Magazine*," I said. "Skype is now using a robust, open-source signal protocol to implement its encryption services, so that only the devices sending and receiving communications in a conversation can hear or view them. The security is so tight that not even the servers they pass through can see the contents of end-to-end encrypted messages."

"As long as both parties are using the same system," Colin said.

Darrell confirmed that they were using the encrypted Skype system.

They called my Skype number and I was delighted to see and hear that we had a clear connection. It was important for us to see them so we could read their nonverbal behavior while they talked. On the call from Taiwan were Darrell, Chih-wei, Wang Shu, and Cheng-han. After brief introductions, Darrell shared the important highlights of his trip into China with Melissa and Jin to meet Huang Tai's uncle, General Hu. Because Huang-Tai was on the call, Colin, Sarah, and I could not ask the same kinds of questions that Darrell's friends had asked in Taipei. I felt concern for Huang Tai and asked very open questions, listening and watching for any subtle messages that Darrell and the others might try to relay.

"How is General Hu?" I asked.

"He is doing very well. He put himself in harm's way to protect our lives."

"That sounds very much like my uncle," Huang Tai said. "He is a man of great courage. I hope you also experienced his great sense of humor."

"We did," Darrell said, "He made us laugh on many occasions."

We then engaged in a discussion about the quality of the information Darrell had received, not knowing the source from which General Hu received his information. Huang Tai helped us to understand the protocols that would have been enacted to verify the accuracy of the information his uncle had received. We explored questions like, *"Could someone have deceived General Hu? Could someone knowingly give him false information? Could someone be extorting him? Could he be deceiving and misdirecting us for a higher purpose that we had not considered?"*

When we were finished, nearly two hours had gone by and we had not been disconnected a single time. That was almost a miracle in itself. Everyone felt very good and in agreement about moving forward with the information about how to intercept the Chinese weather satellite that Huang Tai's uncle had provided.

Darrell ended the Skype call by saying, "When this is all over, Huang Tai, we need to have a big celebration with your uncle, a big Chinese noodles celebration."

"Let's do it!" Huang Tai said.

We had just gained another big piece of the puzzle, inching closer toward neutralizing the plot seducing two great nations into a biological war.

The aftershocks had ended, but I was still anxious to finish our work and leave the San Francisco Bay area and return to Downers Grove. We now needed the coordinates and flight path information of the Russian satellite. It had been a long time since I had seen my parents and since I had met with my close friends of the *Eleutheria Club*.

I tried hard to put these thoughts out of my mind, knowing we still had critical work to do. The Ames Research Center had become more like a work prison because of the security issues, but I was thankful attacks on my life had stopped. I had not had a nightmare in a long time. Our primary focus was on recalibrating our lasers targeting the Russian satellite to increase the success ratio to above 99.0 percent. We needed to keep our options open so we could both incapacitate the satellite if needed and destroy any WMDs it might launch into space. Huang Tai and I decided to devote a whole day to new simulations after we talked through the issue with Colin and Sarah.

Huang Tai submitted his idea about the Russian satellites for the three of us to consider.

"You all know about Mayak, the Russian pyramid-shaped satellite?"

"Is that the one that students at Moscow State University raised the funds to pay for through crowd-sourcing?" Sarah asked.

"Yes, that's the one."

"I remember the controversy," Colin said. "There was speculation that Mayak could be the third brightest object in the sky, after the sun and the moon. Astronomers don't like lighting up dark skies."

"This is true, I have been thinking about the use of reflective materials."

A rush of excitement invaded my mind.

"How so, Huang Tai?"

"I think Russian satellites use more metallic reflectors than the Chinese satellites."

"So, why is that important?" Sarah asked.

"Brilliant, Huang Tai," I shouted ecstatically as I jumped out of my chair.

Colin then understood, too.

"The light?"

"Yes, Colin, the more reflective light coming from Russian satellites could slightly alter our measurement of its exact location at any point in time. But we can compensate for that small degree of distortion," Huang Tai said.

"Like I've told you before, Huang Tai, you are brilliant. Now we have a strategy to raise our hit accuracy as Chief Ryan asked us to do."

"You both are brilliant," Colin said, elated when he realized we could incapacitate this Russian space weapon.

During the following day Huang Tai and I recalibrated our laser weapon and ran two more simulations on a Russian satellite. Our results were exhilarating. The average success rate rose to 99.92, meaning if we could run 10,000 simulations, eight would result in partial hits, but they would still incapacitate the satellite. There would be no possibility that it would remain operational.

"Now we just need to get the coordinates of the location and flight path of the Russian satellite," I said to Huang Tai.

"Yes, the last piece of the puzzle, Johann. I can hardly believe it."

"I need to call Chief Ryan to let him know our progress," I said.

When I reached Chief Ryan with the good news, he was nearly speechless.

"I have some news, too, are you alone?"

"Yes," I confirmed. I feared something bad had happened to one of my friends. A sickening feeling overtook me. *Is Angela in danger or worse, in peril, or Darrell, or Anna, or Nicole, or Captain Jarvis and his family, or General Hu? Who was it? Did someone die?*

"Just don't tell me one of my friends or family members has been harmed."

"As far as I know, Johann, your friends are all fine. Your family is safe. My wife and I had breakfast with your parents this morning. They are so proud of you."

Chief Ryan could perceive from my inability to respond that he struck an emotional chord deep within me. He just continued to talk.

"Things are getting intense in Florence."

"What's going on?"

"Churgrill is now in Italy."

"What?" I asked with great alarm in my voice.

"We can't arrest him, Johann, without more evidence."

"What do you need?"

"Angela and her two brothers are working feverishly to gather evidence so he can be placed under arrest and interrogated. Churgrill may know the details about the Russian satellite. Angela's father, Vincenzo, is alarmed by the seriousness of the battle his children are engaged in, so much so that he called me to talk about it. He and his wife had been contemplating the international consequences of the work of their children and that potentially millions of lives were at risk. He had difficulty wrapping his mind around how his daughter could go to the U.S. as a student to the University of Chicago and return to Italy working closely with a law enforcement leader of the U.S.'s Joint Terrorism Task Force, all through her involvement in a social club. This did not make any logical sense, despite Angela's best attempt and Johann's attempt to explain it."

"Is Angela safe?" I asked. "I talked with her and her family and they were okay. I tried to explain as much as I could to them."

"Yes, as soon as Vincenzo heard Churgrill was in the country and a few hours away from Florence, he drew from his own extensive resources and relationships to protect his family. He told me they could protect themselves from Churgrill."

I felt much better but still wanted to talk to Angela as soon as possible.

"But that's not the main reason I called you, Johann. You need to know I have been called to Washington, D.C. to personally give our president an update on the *Eleutheria Project.*"

"The what? What is he talking about?"

"The president likes to name things, and once he found out about your club and all that you are doing, he named the U.S.'s counterterrorism plan to stop the plot to push the U.S. and China into a war as the *Eleutheria Project*. However, he has kept your group a secret, just as he said he would. He has referred to you and your friends and associates working here and in Taiwan and China as a secretive group of young scientists whose identities must be protected for national security. The president got these ideas from a book he read on the Manhattan Project during World War II. No one in our government knows about the *Eleutheria Club* or the *Jùlèbù Fāxiàn* other than me, the director of national intelligence, the president, and three of his most trusted advisors in the office of the president. Both the president and the director of national intelligence have assured me that your identities are being protected by a very small circle of trusted people.

"I just want you and everyone you are working with to know what is going on, Johann. You are always at the center of communication with all the *Eleutheria Club* members working together on this project, so let them know. When we finish this call, I'm sending you an encrypted text with a new number where you can reach Angela. It is not a mobile phone number but a secure hard-wired line into the Brandolino restaurant. She is there now with her family."

As soon as I received the number, I called Angela.

"Ciao questo è, Besi."

"Posso parlare con, Angela?"

"Yes, I will go find her," Besi said in English. I didn't think my accent was that bad, but Besi had known I spoke English. "May I ask who's calling?"

"Tell her it's Johann."

"Johann, I am so happy you called," Angela said as soon as she picked up the phone.

"I miss you, Angela, I miss seeing you."

Angela was quiet for a moment. I wasn't quite sure how she was going to react.

"I feel the same way. We are in a battle here, an intense battle to arrest Churgrill before he can do anything against us."

"I heard from Chief Ryan."

"You probably heard that my father has called in the reinforcements. He has many extensive contacts with, shall we say, highly capable men and women."

"He must have a lot of friends."

"You can't survive as a senator in Italy for two decades without making many friends."

"And tomorrow life will get interesting. Natasha Calabrese and Silvia Bershenko arrive in the morning, as are Agent Kelly and Margarita Bershenko, who are flying in from Switzerland. They are all here on vacation and I am making them all feel at home."

"I wish I was coming so you could make me feel at home."

"Me, too. Let's talk again tomorrow. I'll call you, Johann, tomorrow is a big day."

CHAPTER 33

ANGELA CALLED ME VERY EARLY in the morning, though it was nearly lunchtime in Italy. She told me Stefan and Angelo went to the airport in Florence to pick up Agent Kelly and Margarita Bershenko traveling from Bern, and then to pick up Silvia Bershenko and Natasha Calabrese, who were arriving from New York about a half hour later. The New York flight was early, so the two planeloads of passengers came through immigration at nearly the same time.

When the passengers came out of security and into the arrival area, her brothers said Margarita was walking arm and arm with her mother, chattering away in Russian. They had last been together at dinner following the private memorial service for Andrei.

"That sounds great Angela," I said. "How was their trip from the airport?"

"Angelo and Stefan decided how to handle security for the ride from the airport to their apartment building in Florence," Angela said. "Angelo went first with the Bershenkos and Stefan followed with Natasha and Agent Kelly. My father also sent two men to watch over them and make sure they were picked up and safely driven to the Duomo area of Florence."

I was so happy to hear their ride from the airport was peaceful.

Angela said that after settling into their apartments and sleeping for an hour, Natasha, Agent Kelly, and the Bershenkos went out with them for a late lunch to the Mercato Centrale market. The popular market featured a wide variety of Italian food services, including some of the largest and finest steaks found anywhere. Large-screen TVs throughout the marketplace broadcast live sports events, especially European soccer games. The marketplace had security and cameras and was filled with hundreds of people, making it a secure location. Angela told me that she met everyone at the marketplace, ready to be the tour guide.

"You need to take me there in person," I told Angela.

"I don't think you wanted to be here today, Johann, Churgrill showed up at the market."

I was dumbfounded when she told me what happened.

"What do you mean he showed up?"

"While we were strolling peacefully through the marketplace deciding what to have for lunch, outside the marketplace, an attack was being organized as police were closing in on the attackers."

"What happened?"

"My father had sent two men to the marketplace to watch over us. One of the men spotted two foreigners near the entrance of the marketplace who looked suspicious. He took their picture and texted it to Angelo's police surveillance headquarters in Florence to run them through a database. Angelo's staff identified both men as suspected Libyan terrorists and contacted Angelo immediately and sent an experienced trained counterterrorism team to the marketplace to capture the suspected terrorists."

"Did they capture them?"

"Not yet. When my father learned what was going on, he sent text messages to me, Angelo, and Stefan, warning us of an impending attack outside the marketplace and let us know he had dispatched four additional well-trained security agents, two who were already outside and two who were en route. The agents are former mafia who had been rehabilitated after serving reduced sentences on a special rehabilitation program my father had created as a senator. They are in contact with the Florence police and with Angelo's counterterrorism team of six agents. That puts in the field ten well-trained agents who are backed up by an additional dozen Florence police officers."

"Is that enough?" I asked.

"Yes, but we will need every one of those officers, as Churgrill has deployed six experienced Libyan terrorists trained by an Al Qaeda group with heavy firepower. Angelo does not believe they are suicide attackers. His counterterrorism team discovered that they had arrived by a fishing vessel in the port town of Brindisi with falsified Greek passports and planned to repair their ship at the Navalbalsamo Shipyard. While their boat was docked and waiting in line for repair, they removed their hidden weapons and tactical gear and made their way to Florence in a rented car. Angelo does not know what they had brought with them, but expects them to have automatic weapons, probably Kalashnikovs, an assortment of tactical grenades, and perhaps even rocket-propelled grenades. Other Libyan terrorists they had captured in the past wore bulletproof vests and 5.11 tactical gear, including eye and ear protection gear. Angelo also expects them to have an excellent communication system and to be in direct contact with Churgrill."

"I just cannot believe he would show up in Florence," I said, astonished. "What did you do when you saw him in the market? Are you still in the market?"

"Angelo was the first to spot him at the wine bar," she said. "He was wearing a wire and recorded his entire conversation with Churgrill.

I'm sending it to you now, Johann, as an audio file. He is coming over to our table now. I have to go. Listen to it and then call me back."

I accessed the audio file and listened to the following conversation:

"May I buy you a glass of wine, Mr. Churgrill?"

"Yes, I would love a glass of wine."

I heard Angelo ordering two glasses of Brunello di Montalcino.

"Salute," Angelo said. "How does it compare to some of the wines from your vineyards in South Africa?"

"If we could produce wines this good, I'd be a much richer man."

"It seems like you are doing very well, especially now that you are transitioning out of drug smuggling and human trafficking, and into more respectable business ventures like purchasing oil and gas companies in Russia and Eastern Europe and pharmaceutical companies in Canada."

"I see you have done your homework, Agent Farrentino, I'm impressed."

"Despite that you are threatening my family with Libyan terrorists, I'm willing to let you walk out of here, Mr. Churgrill, in exchange for the coordinates of a certain Russian weather satellite that recently accepted a delivery of biological weapons."

"You know I can't do that, Mr. Farrentino, and even if I could, I do not have that information."

"Yes, but I am sure you can get it from your partner, General Nicoli Sarkovsky. Your stock has already increased substantially by just the mere threat of a biological war. Wouldn't it be wise to be content with your gains while you are still alive?"

"You know my profile, Mr. Farrentino, I'm an extreme risk-taker."

"More than risk-taking, you are passionate about proving your father wrong."

There was a long pause. I heard Churgrill ask the bartender for two more glasses.

"This one is on me," he said. "I'm old enough now that it shouldn't bother me, but it still does. My father didn't understand. I could've done a lot of good for South Africa and for the whole continent. I still have another chance at the presidency."

"Mr. Churgrill, I cannot help but strongly agree with you. Why would you risk throwing away that chance now? I have followed you closely for almost a year. You are an extraordinarily gifted man. I have never been able to understand why you have risked giving such a great future away to pursue a life of malfeasance. I cannot understand why you would now risk millions of lives for financial gain or to prove your point that the international community should have banned placing any military satellites in space that could be used to carry weapons. I watched your speech on YouTube on the global need to ban military satellites when you were the South African ambassador to the United Nations. You are very forward-thinking."

"Unfortunately, no one listened and took it to heart. Even after the COVID-19 pandemic has devastated so many countries, no one is listening."

"Mr. Churgrill, at least one person is listening and is taking it to heart."

"Angelo Farrentino, I'm beginning to like you; I don't want to have to kill you."

"That's mutual. Maybe we can come to an agreement. If you will give me the location of Sarkovsky and his command

and control center where I could retrieve those satellite co-ordinates, I will not arrest you."

"I'm afraid the wine is already out of the bottle," Churgrill said.

I called Angela, but she was not free to talk. I waited and called again. Nothing. After ten long minutes I called a third time. She took my call.

"What happened Angela?"

"My older brother Stefan came up behind Churgrill, thrust a gun into his back, and helped Angelo to escort him out toward a back exit of the building. That's when he told my brothers, 'There's a bomb hidden here. If anything happens to me, it will detonate, and your family members and friends will be killed.' My brothers decided the safest thing to do was to bring him to our table, because he would never detonate the bomb while he was with us in the market."

"So, you saw him face-to-face, Angela?"

"Yes," Angela said. "It was surreal. My brothers escorted Churgrill to our table, and Angelo said, 'I want to introduce you all to a greatly accomplished man that I have been following for almost a year now, Mr. Atlas Churgrill.'

"Everyone around the table was so shocked that we assumed Angelo must be joking or that we must not have heard him correctly. But it was no joke. My brothers explained there was an explosive planted in the building and that the safest place to be was close to Churgrill."

"What did you do Angela?"

"We grasped the situation and decided to try and get into the mind of Churgrill. I turned to him and said, 'It is good to meet you in person.'

"Churgrill said, 'And you, Angela. Your beauty has not been exaggerated.' I told him neither had his treachery.

"Churgrill then turned to Silvia and said, 'Mrs. Bershenko, I have met few men who have loved their wives more than I know your husband loved you. I almost did not recognize you because every picture I have seen of you, you had a necklace on with a beautiful locket.'

"She was shocked. She said, 'You know about that?'

"Churgrill replied, 'Oh yes, I was with your husband Andrei when he bought it in Zurich. I hope you still have it.'

"She said she would have been wearing it, but it was being repaired. I observed Churgrill's mouth twitched in response to what Silvia said. He locked eyes on Natasha and said, 'You are wondering, Natasha, how I could possibly be the personification of evil you heard I am. Am I correct?'

"Churgrill sighed and said, 'Everything is not as it seems. You might call it the social application of the Heisenberg uncertainty principle, which states that you cannot measure exactly the position and the velocity of an object at the same time. I believe you cannot know the motivation of a person and his or her intended actions at the same time.'

"While we were all trying to process that statement, he continued, 'Psychologists would diagnose me as extreme bipolar; but that is often a misdiagnosis because our psyche is not always about moods.'"

"Wow," I said.

"I know. He then began quoting the Book of Ecclesiastes, stating, 'There is a time and place for compassion, and a time and place for mercilessness. There is a time for everything . . . a time to kill and a time to heal, a time to tear down and a time to build . . .'

"My brother Stefan said, 'Your FBI profile identifies you as schizophrenic, not bipolar, but I think this is also inaccurate. You are much too intelligent and logical to be schizophrenic. But you do seem disconnected from any moral reality.'

"Churgrill then posed a question, 'But what is morality, Mr. Farrentino? Many scientists say morality is a set of neurons that condition our brains to react in prescribed ways.'

"Angelo then shocked me and put the barrel of his gun on Churgrill's forehead and asked, 'But what do you say, Mr. Churgrill? Would killing you now be simply a matter of neurons that condition my actions?'

"Churgrill showed no fear. I think he knew Angelo would never execute him. He said, 'Conditioning has a definite influence. You have had to kill before, but I doubt that you had adequate time to carefully think through what we call the moral issues of killing another person. Instead, you likely had to instinctively make a split-second decision based on your training and conditioning. But you, Mr. Farrentino, are not conditioned to kill without moral consideration. You are painfully debating whether it is morally right to kill me, and I believe you will conclude it is not moral.'"

"He's also brilliant the way he engaged all of you," I said.

"He is so intelligent. Abruptly, he ended the conversation, looked at his watch and said, 'I must leave now.' He then stood up to walk out of the market. Stefan shouted from across the table, 'He is communicating through his watch! Take his watch!'

"Angelo grabbed Churgrill's arm and attempted to remove his watch, but Churgrill released a toxic gas from the ring on his right index finger and Angelo moved away from Churgrill, who broke free and ran through the crowd toward the back exit.

"Then Agent Kelly, who had left our table to use the bathroom, shouted, 'Let him go! I have disarmed the bomb in this building. There is no danger to us.'

"We froze, stunned by Agent Kelly's shocking pronouncement. She told us, 'You are all safe, I have disabled the electronic signal that Churgrill intended to use to detonate the bomb, which was programmed into his watch.'"

"Did Churgrill get away?" I asked.

"He won't. My brother and his commando unit and the police are now after him. My brother's lead agent, Antonio, is wearing a GoPro and is video recording the action which my phone is receiving. I'm going to describe to you what I am seeing. Hold on."

I waited as she pulled up the live feed, nervous for what she would describe.

"Okay, I've got the feed. Churgrill already exited the back door and is outside Mercato Centrale. I see smoke, probably from a smoke grenade thrown near the exit adjacent to Annibali Chiti. Antonio is out there directing the others. I see two of Antonio's men near the exit closing in on Churgrill. I hear automatic gunfire directed toward them. They just went down on the ground. I hope they're not hit. They are returning gunfire, Churgrill is using the smoke screen to run down Via dell'Ariento toward Biscottini. He's approaching a leather goods store. One of the terrorists is helping him. He just threw a concussion grenade toward Antonio's two agents who were attempting to follow. They are down again. Churgrill took a sharp right and is now running through the crowded outdoor shopping area down Via Panicale. I can hear lots of gunfire. He just reached Banko, a shop on the left. Antonio is on his tail. Two men just emerged from the right side and tackled Churgrill. I think I recognize them—they work for my father. I just spotted two of the Libyan terrorists. They came from the other end of the Via Panicale and are shooting at the two men holding Churgrill on the ground. One of them is wounded; the second one is returning fire. Churgrill was able to get away from them. The terrorist is helping him to the Asian grocery store across the street, but it looks like Churgrill has been shot in the leg.

"Two police cars are converging near the ticket office for the Central Market. The officers are getting out and giving chase on foot. A rocket-propelled grenade launched from the second floor of an apartment building just destroyed the police car, setting it on fire. The two officers are okay—they are continuing their pursuit on foot toward an auto repair shop where the Libyan terrorist took Churgrill. A car is pulling in front of the shop. A Ferrari Portofino is flying down Via Pascala. It looks like it's heading for the auto repair shop. The Libyan terrorist and Churgrill are coming out of the shop and getting into the car! One of the women on Antonio's team is shooting at the car. A terrorist in the car is returning fire. Oh no, she's down. She just dived out of the way of the car.

"Churgrill is in the car and Antonio is now in a police car following. They just turned right on Via Pascala and are racing toward Bar Colazione Italiana. A man is shooting at the terrorists from inside the bar, putting several bullets into the left side. The car turned right on Via Guelfa and is heading toward the direction of SS67 Highway. Antonio is still in hot pursuit.

"I can hear Antonio commanding his team to set up one more containment team in front of McDonald's Firenze Cavour at the crossroad of Via Camillo Cavour. He told his team to block the road at the intersection and to set out two spike strips across the road. Okay, Churgrill's car is out of sight.

"One of Antonio's men said the Ferrari just crossed the spikes and all four tires were shredded. Antonio is at the scene. Now an Alfa Romeo SUV converged on the intersection Via Camillo Cavour and laid down heavy automatic gunfire toward the agents and police officers who had set up the roadblock. I think I see Churgrill exiting the back seat of the Ferrari and jumping into the back seat of the SUV! The terrorist who was driving the Ferrari attempted to get into the SUV but was gunned down before he reached it.

"Antonio is saying Churgrill and the two remaining terrorists in the SUV are driving down Via Degli Alfani. They are going toward SS67 Highway south toward the Arno River. They are racing toward Chiesa Di Sant Ambrogi Catholic Church. Antonio is chasing. Oh my, they are cutting through the parking area and speeding down Borgo la Croce toward the junction for SS67. Antonio has set up another barricade at this junction.

"Okay, hold on, Johann. The car just reached the blockade. Antonio has them boxed in. There is no escape for Churgrill. The two Libyan terrorists just let Churgrill out of the car and then plowed through two police cars and onto SS67. Several spike strips across the road blew their tires. They just got out of the car. They came out fighting with automatic weapons and grenades. It's a big firefight, Johann. Antonio is now out of his car firing at the terrorists. The Libyans are both down. They aren't moving. Churgrill is surrendering! They got him, Johann!"

"Tell your brothers we need the Russian satellite coordinates from Churgrill," I said.

Angela replied, "I will. Antonio told his team to secure Churgrill's watch. I have to go, Johann. I'm cutting the live feed. I'll call again as soon as I am able."

CHAPTER 34

ANGELA CALLED ME JUST AS I was celebrating the near completion of our work at Ames with Huang Tai, Colin, and Sarah. We also had a second reason to celebrate: through working so closely together, Colin and Sarah developed a vibrant romantic relationship. They had just announced their engagement. Commander Fields gave us a bottle of champagne to celebrate the occasion. It was great that our project, which now had a name, was bringing people together. I was anxious to talk to Angela, excused myself, and found a private place to talk.

"Hi Johann, I just want you to know that my family and I are all okay here and that Churgrill is now in jail awaiting his fate. However, we are not happy."

"Why?"

"He is going to be transported to the Hague for violating EU laws."

"And that's not good?"

"No, because the Hague courts are unpredictable. Both my brothers wanted him tried here in Italy, but they were overruled."

"How are Agent Kelly, Natasha, and the Bershenkos?"

"The Florence police just drove them back to their apartment. They are fine considering all the drama and bomb threats. Agent Kelly noticed that Churgrill was keenly interested in a locket that her mother always wore but is not wearing now. She asked Silvia about the locket, and Silvia said it was being repaired at Argyle Jewelers in Melville, New York, not far from her home. Agent Kelly thinks it may hold some important information because Churgrill asked her if she still had it and then had an obvious nonverbal reaction when she said it was being repaired."

"I still can't believe you ate lunch with Churgrill in Florence," I said. "That was wild."

"I can't either. The reason I'm telling you about the locket is because Andrei picked that locket out for his wife as an anniversary present when he was with Churgrill in Zurich, and there may be important information inside the locket. I have tried unsuccessfully to reach Chief Ryan during the past hour, and Natasha has tried to reach her husband, Michael, now for an hour. We cannot get through to either one."

"Do you want me to tell Chief Ryan?"

"Yes, he will read a text from you. Agent Kelly is calling the FBI office in Melville now to dispatch an agent to pick up the locket."

"Chief Ryan was scheduled to meet with the president, which might explain why he is not answering. I'll try to make contact with him now," I said.

Chief Ryan called me ten minutes after I sent him an urgent text.

"I'm in the White House, Johann, I haven't been able to receive calls. Do we have to talk now?"

"Very briefly. Silvia Bershenko has a locket being repaired at a jewelry store in Melville, New York. Churgrill asked her about it in Florence before he was arrested."

"Wait, Johann. Silvia talked to Churgrill in Florence and he is in police custody?"

"Yes. It's a long story. I can fill you in later. Agent Kelly believes the locket may contain important information we need. She tried to contact the FBI Office in Melville to have an agent go to the jewelry store and pick up the locket before Churgrill sends someone after it but could only leave a message."

"Okay, make sure Silvia tells her jeweler an FBI agent is coming and keep me informed by text. I'll contact the Melville office now."

I immediately called Angela back and told her what Chief Ryan requested of Silvia.

Silvia told Angela, "I can call the store now. The store manager, Janie Smith, is a friend."

"Keep me on the line with you Angela so I can hear the call," I said.

"Can you put your phone on speaker, Silvia, so Agent Kelly, Johann and I can hear the conservation with Janie?" Angela asked.

"Yes, I can," Silvia said.

When Silvia called Janie, Janie said a police officer already came by to pick up the locket saying they needed it for an investigation of a burglary in your home.

"My home was burglarized? How can that be, the police were guarding it!"

"I don't know. That's what the officer said."

"Did you give the locket to this officer?"

"No, because George took it home to repair it. I told the officer to come back the next morning but that I also needed to contact you."

Agent Kelly, who also was listening to the conversation, asked Silvia if she could speak to the store manager.

"Janie, I'm going to let you talk with Agent Emily Kelly, an FBI agent who is assisting me in Italy." Silvia then handed her phone to Emily.

"Hi Janie, this is Agent Kelly. There is an FBI office not far from your shop in Melville. I called them and asked them to send an agent to your home to pick up the locket. Is your husband home?"

"Yes, George helps me repair jewelry at his workshop at home."

"Then call your husband to let him know that an agent is coming. I will send the agent directly to your house. I am also going to give you the number to the FBI office, so write this number down."

"Am I in danger?"

"I don't know. But just to be safe, instead of driving home right now, drive directly to the FBI office. If someone follows you, just keep your cool and drive directly there. I will call the office again and let them know you are coming, and they will send an agent to your house to pick up your husband and the locket."

Agent Kelly then called the FBI office and explained to Agent Moyer what was going on. Chief Ryan had already spoken to Moyer, who called George to let him know two agents were coming to his home. George, who had retrieved his shotgun after Janie had called him, was waiting for the agents, hoping no one else came before them. He wondered what might be in the locket but would not dare open it.

When Janie drove from her jewelry store to the FBI office, she noticed that she was being followed. Someone wanted to know where she lived, probably the man who had come into the shop dressed as a police officer. When she pulled into the parking lot of the FBI building, Agent Kathy McClintock was waiting for her just outside the door and the car following Janie quickly drove past her. McClintock saw the license number and recorded it. Janie was visibly shaking when McClintock escorted her into the office. George arrived about five minutes later with the two agents sent to pick him up, holding Silvia's necklace and locket in a metal jewelry box.

Chief Ryan told me on his way from Washington, D.C. to New York that Agent Moyer and his team spent nearly a week evaluating all the evidence from Andrei's two computers, tablet, and phone. Much of the information they retrieved was encrypted. Despite their efforts, they did not find any information about the exact location and flight path of the Russian weather satellite.

Chief Ryan arrived at the FBI office just as Agent Moyer and his team was entering the evidence room to inspect the locket. The FBI forensic expert asked George to carefully open it. Inside, there was a beautiful picture of Andrei and Silvia taken in Italy. They were in the ancient walled village of Anghiari. Opposite the picture on the other half of the locket were the words, "I will always love you Silvia." The thickness of the locket left room for a second compartment. George found it hidden behind the picture. A tiny button just to the right of the picture enabled him to open the second compartment. In it was a piece of paper with tiny writing. It said, "FNB lock box 124. shoekey pwcatheaven." They needed to call Silvia to help them decipher the message.

When FBI Agent Moyer called Silvia, she was relieved to hear from George that Janie was safe and that they were both with the FBI in Melville.

"I am so sorry to disturb you, Mrs. Bershenko, on your vacation in Italy," Agent Moyer said. "We found some coded language in a secret compartment of your locket and we are trying to discover its meaning."

"I never saw any markings in it," Silvia said, "Only my husband's words to me. There is a secret message?"

"Yes, we found a piece of paper hidden behind your picture. On the paper is written *FNB lock box 124. shoekey pwcatheaven.*"

"FNB would be First National Bank. We have accounts there," said Silvia.

"Which branch?"

"The branch on West Main Street in East Islip, but I didn't know we had a lock box there. Andrei must have gotten one."

"Do you know what *shoekey pwcatheaven* means?" Agent Moyer asked.

"Oh yes, the word *shoekey* is where Andrei kept all his keys hidden inside the tips of his shoes on the top shelf of his closet. Andrei abbreviated passwords with the initials *pw*, so I believe the password must be when our favorite cat, *Smokey*, went to cat heaven, December 25, 2018. It was our private shared humor that Smokey died that day as a gift to Jesus. Was our home burglarized?"

"No, we have been guarding your home ever since you left on vacation. Why did you think that?"

"Because the police officer who went to the jewelry shop to pick up my locket told the shop owner, my friend Janie, that my home had been burglarized."

"That was a lie, Silvia, and that was not a real police officer, but an imposter. He wanted your locket."

"Do you still have my house keys?"

"Yes, we have your keys and should now be able to search for the key to the lock box in your home."

Agent Moyer thought about how his agents had thoroughly searched their home for any evidence that might help them, but they did not even consider checking the tips of Andrei's shoes on the top shelf of his closet. It was a clever place to hide keys.

When they returned to the Bershenkos' home, they found car keys, house keys, office keys, and one safe deposit box key in Andrei's shoes. Agent McClintock excitedly drove to the bank and, with her FBI credentials and confirmation from Silvia Bershenko by phone, was given permission to open safe deposit box 124. Inside was an encrypted thumb drive with a note from Andrei Bershenko that simply said, "Documentation for satellite project."

Using the password *Smokey122518*, Agent Jason Turpan, the forensic specialist in the office, was able to open the bank deposit box and retrieve a thumb drive that Andrei had placed there. It was not encrypted and contained the complete documentation for the Russian satellite project, including the exact location of the satellite and the flight path. The thumb drive also provided the exact location of the team that was controlling the satellite from Malta.

Chief Ryan was relaying to me everything that was happening through text. He then called me.

"We've got it, Johann. I have the coordinates of the Russian satellite and flight information on a thumb drive. I'm getting on the next plane to San Jose from New York and will bring the thumb drive with me. I'll text you my flight information."

I received a text from Chief Ryan at 6:00 a.m. California time.

Arrive San Jose 10:30 a.m. See you at Ames soon.

Then a second text.

Sorry, Johann. Couldn't let you sleep in today—too much to do.

I tried to get another hour of sleep but failed.

Huang Tai, Colin, and Sarah were all up by 7:00 a.m., excited that Chief Ryan was bringing with him the Russian satellite information. We all felt that we could finish our work today.

Chief Ryan arrived late that morning with police escort. After very brief and perfunctory greetings, as we had no time to socialize, we went to work. Our programming did not take long. We ran several simulations and were confident we could destroy any WMD launched from the Russian weather satellite.

We finished our last testing protocol that evening. Colin, Sarah, Huang Tai, and I were working together like a well-oiled machine. We now had all the location information and flight paths for both the Chinese and Russian satellites programmed into our laser weapons' system. We were all elated that our initial predictions were confirmed that the orbits of the Chinese and Russian satellites would put them in close proximity to one another. It would not be difficult to maneuver our satellite into position to incapacitate both of them as soon as we received surveillance of a WMD launch.

"I believe that's a wrap," Colin declared with a smile.

"Yes," I agreed. "It is time to get this laser system loaded on a rocket at Vandenberg."

———————————

Chief Ryan gathered us together for the last time.

"I know this is difficult. You have worked together in an extraordinary way, through life-threatening situations. Now that you're done, you will need to go separate ways. Johann, you need to go to Vandenberg with the module you made. You may be needed during the launch. But first you do have one last time to celebrate."

"What about Huang Tai?"

"Huang Tai, your work is now finished with us. You need to go to a safe place until the biological warfare threat is over. I suggest that you work out with your uncle where that is."

Huang Tai smiled but looked sad.

"Colin and Sarah. You two need to go plan your wedding. You deserve the break."

"What about you, Chief Ryan?" I asked.

"I'm going to return home. As much as I want to witness the launch at the Joint Space Operations Center with you, I'm confident the command and control for the satellite and the laser weapon on board will be at Vandenberg and will be launched successfully and fully operational."

Our long work together in the trenches was over. Most importantly, we had successfully built a satellite-based laser system capable of defending the United States against a biological attack. We also had designed a defense that would prevent China and Russia from launching biological weapons from satellites.

"Are you ready to celebrate?" I asked Huang Tai, Colin, and Sarah.

They all indicated they were.

"But first, I need to talk with my uncle about my next step," Huang Tai said.

For our celebration, Commander Fields arranged for us to have a special dinner together, sending two security officers with us. We hid ourselves in the back of the military vehicle, just in case anyone was still conducting surveillance on us. Since we all loved Japanese cuisine, we decided to go to the Sushi Tomi in Mountain View.

After enjoying a Mix Don and White Tuna Tataki, we talked about our experiences in Hawaii, Chicago, and the Bay Area of California.

It would be hard saying our good-byes, so I decided to jump right in as we ate sushi together.

"I'm going to miss you, Huang Tai."

Chief Ryan said, "I imagine you two have grown very close."

"Like brothers," I said. "We have a lot in common. I feel like we've been in a foxhole together fighting a war."

Huang Tai then spoke.

"Our friendship will endure, Johann. We will be lifelong friends."

"I am going to miss you both, too, Colin and Sarah, especially your back-and-forth bantering."

"Me, too," said Huang Tai. "You both made me laugh so much."

"We look forward to your wedding," I said.

"It's been such a great experience," Colin and Sarah said. "We hope you can all come to our wedding."

"We will come," I said.

"I know you talked with your uncle for a while Huang Tai," I said. "What are you going to do?"

"You will not be shocked, Johann, but he wants me to go to Switzerland for a year and study at the University of Bern. Did you hear what happened in Italy?"

"Yes, most of the story," I said.

"Well, Chief Ryan told me the full story this morning."

"You got an inside scoop from Chief Ryan?"

"Yes. I needed his advice. He connected me with another Chinese student who is studying at the university. Switzerland is a very safe place, and my uncle wants to come see me there."

"I will also come see you there," I said.

"You would come?"

"Absolutely! You are now my good friend. I would love to hang out with you in Switzerland."

Sarah spoke up. "We would come visit you, too."

Our ride back to Moffett Field was a quiet one. We were all thinking about saying good-bye and perhaps how well our laser defense system would work. We never talked about it openly, but we knew millions of lives could be saved or lost.

The next morning, Huang Tai's ride to the San Francisco airport arrived. I helped him put his bags in the trunk. Colin and Sarah were there, too. We all did our best to hold back our emotions, so none of us could say very much. We gave each other long bear hugs.

"You are a good man, Huang Tai, and you will always be my friend."

"Likewise, you will always be my friend, too, Johann. I want you to be safe. Also, when you return to Chicago, please give my greetings to my new friends in the *Eleutheria Club*. Be sure to tell them all that we have done together."

"I will, and please greet your uncle warmly for me when you see him, hopefully soon."

As Huang Tai rode out of sight, I hoped we would meet again. I hoped we would both survive the dangers we faced. I hoped our countries would survive.

CHAPTER 35

I AWOKE EARLY TO A short text from Angela.

Churgrill has been released. Call me.

"Released?" I asked Angela as soon as she picked up my call. "What do you mean he was released? How can your government release one of the most dangerous criminals in the world, one who is about to orchestrate a biological nightmare on two nations? What is going on?"

"It wasn't our government that released him. It was the EU."

"How could they do that?"

"When I talked to Stefan," Angela said, "he was so angry he nearly threw his phone on the ground after shouting expletives several times. The EU authorities told him there was not enough evidence to hold him."

"What do you mean not enough evidence? Didn't Churgrill just initiate one of the largest street battles in Florence history? The whole thing was video-recorded!"

"I know. It took the lives of four people and wounded seventy-three people."

"What more evidence do they need?"

"Stefan said they were paid off. He said the EU authorities are corrupt politicians and cowards, as well as a few other choice words."

"Is there any recourse?"

"Anthony Barone, the chief of police and director general of public security for the nation of Italy, is a close friend of Stefan. He tried to hold him for the FBI office in Rome so he could be extradited to the U.S., but because Churgrill is a South African citizen, Angelo's counterterrorism unit was ordered to give custody of Churgrill to the South African embassy in Rome. Our government denied the U.S. request and put him on a flight to Pretoria. The former ambassador will probably be walking free tomorrow."

"How is Angelo?"

"He told me it is times like these that he wishes for our old justice system in Italy. Stefan is still exploring options with Tony Barone to see how they can get Churgrill. Tony has friends who are agents in the National Intelligence Agency of South Africa, working out of the Pretoria office. He wants to connect his friends with FBI agents Michael Calabrese and Emily Kelly, who are working on Churgrill's case. Tony wants to see if Calabrese and Kelly could go to South Africa to assist in tracking Churgrill's activities. Did you finish your work at Ames?"

"Yes, we're all finished here. I'm getting ready to board a plane to Vandenberg Air Force Base to witness the launch our defensive laser system into space."

"Will you come to Italy when this is over?"

"I promise I will come. My parents would want to come, too."

"I would love that."

———————

I boarded the MC-130W Combat Spear, unofficially and facetiously nicknamed the "Combat Wombat" at Moffett Field en route to the Vandenberg Air Force base just north of Lompoc, California. It was my first time flying in a military aircraft and the trip was stunningly beautiful. It was a sunny day and we flew along the western California coast, over Santa Cruz, Monterey Bay, and the Monterey-Carmel area. We then flew over Big Sur and followed the coast south to Morro Bay, home of one of my favorite Alfred Hitchcock films, *The Birds*. We then flew over Pismo Beach and the outskirts of Santa Maria and into Vandenberg. Peering out the window at the beautiful rugged coastline, I put out of my mind the monumental crisis at hand and dreamed of taking a sailboat trip down the California coast from Half Moon Bay to San Diego, with a visit to Catalina Island.

I had initially feared this trip to Vandenberg when I thought we had to go by land. My imagination ran wild with thoughts of assassins bankrolled by Churgrill planting IEDs along the roadside. Then I heard the military was quite capable of transporting our satellite laser weapons' system safely by air.

We still were uncertain how Churgrill learned about the people working with us, but the tentacles of an eccentric billionaire can go quite far, especially one as ambitious as Churgrill. I wondered if he had convinced himself that we were very unlikely to have developed a space defense weapons system in such a short period of time. It must have been expensive to have to continually hire well-trained assassins to follow us and attack us.

We landed safely just after sunset and immediately moved our precious cargo into the building where it would be prepared for the rocket launch. The following day we encountered no difficulties loading the satellite into the cargo bay of the rocket that would carry it into space. The weather was holding to the forecast of clear skies for the scheduled launch at 7:05 p.m.

Shortly after I arrived at Vandenberg, Chief Ryan sent me a long message.

Atlas Churgrill just boarded his private jet with his doctor and six paramilitary commandos. Michael Calabrese and Emily Kelly obtained a copy of his flight plans. His Citation Ultra was flying a 4,930-mile trip with two refueling stops at private airports in Kampala and Cairo and one overnight stay in Cairo. Churgrill has a bullet wound in his left calf from the shootout in Florence. His final destination is Malta. He's joining Sarkovsky at the command and control center for the Russian satellite. You must deploy your defense system without delay. I've already told the team at Vandenberg.

Fortunately, or more likely, providentially, the weather was good and the rocket launch at Vandenberg was flawless. Shortly after liftoff, I followed the live video feed of the rocket, until it was shut down at the request of the U.S. Air Force. This was a routine procedure for military satellite launches. About six hours after liftoff, the satellite began to separate from the carrier rocket, according to schedule. The satellite was then propelled into the geosynchronous orbit above Earth's equator.

The satellite, with its mobile mirrors to be subsequently deployed, was labeled LDS-V1. It was designed to operate our laser defense weapon and to expand existing military satellite communications by relaying messages between senior military officers engaged in an armed conflict emanating from space.

The control mechanism for the rocket and the initial guidance system made calculations that guided the nozzle of the rocket on its specified flight plan, guiding it toward the direction of the Earth's rotation. We followed its path on our monitors. When it reached a height of 120 miles above the Earth, small rockets were fired in order to shift the vehicle in a horizontal position. Additional rockets were then fired to separate the satellite from its launch vehicle and set it on its course.

Once in orbit, the mission control center (MCC) at Vandenberg was able to send commands to and receive data from the satellite and to launch its reflective mirrors. I was excited to watch twenty-four hours later as they began to control the movement of the satellite and its specially designed mirrors that would be used to reflect the lasers. The system was working as designed. The MCC directed it toward the locations of the Chinese and Russian satellites.

Chief Ryan asked if I could call him the following morning when they launched the mirrors. He said he had news for me.

I fell asleep exhausted and awoke at sunrise. Chief Ryan had already sent me a text that he needed me to call him right away.

"Hi, Chief Ryan," I said elated, "It was beautiful to watch."

"I know," he said. "We just learned through intelligence agents in Malta that Churgrill and his security team landed at the Luqa Airport, where General Sarkovsky and two of his security agents met them. Sarkovsky took them to his home in the Dingli Cliffs, a village on the west coast of Malta at the highest elevation on the island. The home is easy to protect with no other structures around it and much of it was underground. It also features a large satellite dish that could be used to directly communicate with satellites in space. Sarkovsky has his space command and control team in place, including two former employees of Roscosmos, the Russian space program, who worked at Russia's Mission Control space center in Korolev."

"We suspected Malta," I said. "It was one of the countries mentioned by Andrei Bershenko and Churgrill said something about coming to Malta.

"We also confirmed that everything is in place for the catastrophic chain of events planned. At the Beijing Aerospace Command and Control Center, General Bingwen Tso has two aerospace engineers and confidants prepared to launch the biological weapon placed aboard the Chinese weather satellite. The two engineers on his team had helped to launch the Fengyun 2H weather observatory from the Xichang Space Center in southwestern China's Sichuan province. The weather monitoring payload was carried into space by a 172-foot-tall Long March 3A rocket, which released the Fengyun 2H spacecraft in orbit. The Chinese weather satellite carrying the WMD is currently in an elliptical transfer orbit ranging in altitude between 144 miles and 22,305 miles with an inclination of 24.6 degrees to the equator."

"So, the group here is the third command and control team in place," I said.

"Yes, and the team there at Vandenberg is outstanding," Chief Ryan said. "You will be able to see them in action today when they launch the reflective mirrors for the laser defense system. They will closely monitor both the Russian and Chinese weather satellites with attached biological weapons. I am confident the laser weapon you designed will destroy any weapons that might be launched from those satellites."

The following day I took an early flight back to Chicago. Chief Ryan was coming to the airport to pick me up. He called me as I was being driven by a military officer to LAX.

"A lot is happening, Johann. A surveillance drone from General Suberov just relayed real time information to us from Malta. After dinner in Sarkovsky's home, Churgrill gathered the mission control team to once more review their procedures and plan of action. A half an hour later, he gave the command that intelligence professionals and law enforcement officers in many countries have worked so hard to prepare for and possibly prevent.

"It's time to launch."

CHAPTER 36

WHILE I WAITED AT THE boarding gate at LAX, there was one more critical task that Chief Ryan had asked me to do. I needed to talk to Nicole about weapons deployment. She had been working on simulations and told me to call her after the rocket launch at Vandenberg. I now had time to make that call.

"Hi, Nicole, how are you?"

"Freaked out, Johann, to tell you the truth. I have the information you wanted on the likely deployment systems of the biological weapons on board the two satellites. Do you have enough time now to talk?"

"Yes, I have about thirty minutes before I board my plane to Chicago."

"My colleagues and I think both satellite weapon systems will use jet-propelled cluster munition bombs. The cluster bombs will be preprogrammed to travel directly to their target areas and be exploded at about 90,000 feet above the Earth. This is much higher than the traditional cluster bombs that have been used in the past, which usually explode at two to three thousand feet above the Earth. This is why they would not simply use planes to drop these weapons. At 90,000 feet, it would be difficult to defend against these weapons and the thousands of cluster munitions would spread out over a wide area."

"How wide?"

"One cluster bomb could blanket many hundreds of square miles with a biological agent in a two-stage process. First, the cluster bomblets would be dispersed at 90,000 feet. Each submunition is about the size of a soda can. They each deploy a little parachute that stabilizes them and ensures that they descend with their nose down. Second, each submunition would then be timed to explode at about 300 feet, dispersing a cloud of biological agent over about 10,000 square yards. If each weapon had 2,000 munitions, then one bomb could cover 6.5 square miles."

"That's devastating. One bomblet could kill tens of thousands of people."

"The hopeful news is that the aerospace engineers from MIT, that we are working with, agree that the feasibility of delivering devices from a satellite to the Earth's surface is very difficult to achieve. The extent of the propulsion installation required on the satellite to eject the warhead is substantial, depending upon the distance to be covered by the bomb during its descent phase. If the descent can be engineered to take place over several thousand miles, then less propulsion is needed. We think the engineers will slow the descent to about 1,000 feet per second.

"Our aerospace engineers also identified another formidable challenge. Additional propulsion capacity is needed to deflect the warhead to the right or left, since a prospective target will rarely lie directly under the orbit path of the satellite that is used to launch such a weapon, making the targeting difficult. Therefore, the engineers will likely control the satellite from a ground radar station to guide its descent."

"This is exactly how we designed our laser defense satellite, Nicole. It can be completely controlled by the command center on the ground."

"It might be the battle of command stations on the ground that will determine the outcomes. Once the Botulinum toxin is released, it can kill in a very short period of time and it will be difficult to distribute the antitoxin fast enough to the areas that have been attacked. If the bombs survive the laser defenses, there is no easy way to prevent their detonation ninety miles above Earth."

"We plan to destroy them as soon as they are launched."

"Remember, Johann, a single gram of dispersed Botulinum toxin can kill a million people, and one cluster bomb can disperse up to half a gram of toxin in each submunition. It is conceivable that one bomb could kill much of the population of a large city."

"Chief Ryan was almost killed by the Botulinum attack in Chicago years ago."

"He was fortunate he had secondary exposure. Surviving depends on how much exposure a person has had. Lethal exposure will usually kill people within twenty-four hours."

"So, you have to get the antitoxin to victims exposed in less than twenty-four hours?"

"Within much less time. Administration of antitoxin minimizes the deadly effects soon after exposure, so it is critical to prevent extensive nerve damage by the toxin. However, the antitoxin cannot reverse paralysis that has already occurred. Also, antibiotics are of no use in treating Botulinum poisoning."

"So, what is the critical treatment time to save people?"

"If we can get antitoxin to everyone within six to twelve hours after exposure, we can save lives. It is possible to do that in some regions, but it could be difficult, depending upon where an attack may occur. Thanks to the swift action by Congress, we have already distributed antitoxins to 390 of the 427 distribution centers around the U.S. The remaining thirty-seven centers will be receiving shipments of HBAT by the end of this week. The ultimate death count will depend on the distance between these distribution centers and the places that have been attacked. Rural areas are obviously more vulnerable if they are attacked, although we expect attacks to be concentrated in large urban areas. Fortunately, Botulinum sickness is not communicable—you cannot be infected by others who have been exposed. So, health workers and emergency medical professionals will have no problem going into areas that have been attacked as long as they wear protective breathing apparatus."

"Will masks help? There are many available because of COVID-19."

"Not much; people in an aerosol attack would need a full-face respirator to protect from exposure to residual aerosol. In an attack, it is difficult to determine the persistence of the aerosol after the initial release."

"We will now begin boarding for United Flight 2039 for Chicago," the agent said.

"I guess you heard that, Nicole. I have to go soon."

"We can't predict how long the dispersed toxin will be dangerous because the temperature, humidity, and the size of the aerosol particles all determine the rate of dissipation into the atmosphere. Even people downwind from the site of the attack could be infected and killed."

"So, what you are saying is that even in the best scenario, if any Botulinum munitions are exploded, the results will be disastrous. That we need to succeed and destroy any cluster bomb that is launched before it reaches Earth's atmosphere and is detonated, or millions of people will die."

"Yes, that's the bottom line."

"One last question, Nicole. What about the planned attack on China?"

"There are six cities in China with more than ten million people: Shanghai, Beijing, Chongqing, Guangzhou, Tianjin, and Shenzhen. In addition, there are 160 cities in China with more than one million people. The total number of dead from an attack would be much greater than in the U.S. Could you imagine if two or three cluster bombs were dropped on the city of Shanghai and its thirty-six million people?"

"I don't want to imagine."

"They have enough antitoxin, for about 100 million people, stockpiled in the most populated areas. Shipments of HBAT from Canada would take two days. A biological attack on China would be catastrophic."

"Final call for passengers on United Flight 2039 for Chicago," the agent said over the airport speaker system.

"I have to board, Nicole. Let's talk again after I return home."

"Safe travels, Johann. I look forward to talking to you when this crisis is over, and especially look forward to spending time with you at our upcoming conference."

"Me, too, Nicole." I felt bad because I knew I'd be disappointing her once I shared with her my developing relationship with Angela.

"Thank you again, Johann, for saving my life and the lives of all my colleagues. We will never forget what you did for us."

I boarded my flight with a strange premonition that it would be the last time I would ever again hear Nicole's kind voice.

I hadn't had much time to play video games throughout my life, but when Chief Ryan described to me what happened in Malta through a long phone message shortly after I departed for Chicago, it sounded a lot like a popular video game. Two Mi-35M Russian attack helicopters departed the French-made amphibious assault Mistral ship cruising the Mediterranean and turned north toward Malta. The helicopters featured a modern "glass" cockpit with night vision goggle compatibility. This special feature, along with upgraded sensors, made the Mi-35M especially well-suited for nighttime operations. Both choppers were armed with four 9M120 Ataka-V SACLOS radio guided anti-tank missiles and ten 80mm 'S-8' unguided rockets. The attack plan called for one of the choppers to approach the target from the south, staying close to the water, hidden by the Dingli Cliffs.

As the attackers approached General Sarkovsky's home, the satellite command and control team were inputting the launch codes to the Russian weather satellite, which they had maneuvered into close proximity to a U.S. military satellite, to release the four biological weapons attached to it.

The Mi-35H Russian helicopter approaching from the north came into view on their radar screens. Sarkovsky immediately gave the command to fire their Type 91 surface-to-air missile, located on a flat part of their roof structure. The Japanese-made portable air-defense system had an advanced infrared seeker. The system employed a third generation-made infrared and ultraviolet guidance system that was able to ignore defensive countermeasures such as flares.

The versatile Mi-35H detected the incoming missile and took immediate evasive action, but it was too late. The missile penetrated the fuselage, exploding the gas tank into a large fireball and killing everyone on board.

Chief Ryan then told me two experienced former Roscosmos engineers at the command center learned for the first time that the payload on the satellite was a WMD. It was too late to think about aborting the mission as they knew they would risk their lives and the lives of their families. They successfully launched their weapon into space.

"That's devastating," I said.

"That weapon will deploy four cluster bombs with jet propulsion systems that will set them on their gradual flight paths toward four cities in China: Beijing, Shanghai, Guangzhou, and Chongqing," Chief Ryan said.

"Fortunately, the second Mi-35H hiding below the cliff out of radar detection, elevated and immediately fired its four radio guided anti-tank missiles, penetrating the reinforced concrete underground floor where the command and control center was, and then quickly dived below the cliff again for protection as two Type 91 surface-to-air missiles were fired at it. We captured this all from our surveillance drone."

"What happened?" I asked.

"The missiles passed above the helicopter. It then rose again above the cliff and fired all ten 80mm 'S-8' rockets, hitting the home from different directions and destroying the Type 91 surface-to-air missile system on the roof of the house. The home was completely engulfed in flames and there was no chance anyone could survive the attack.

"We then traced a call by the ship commander to a private phone number at a Black Sea resort. I should get a copy of that conversation shortly," Chief Ryan said. "I'll call you or text you again soon, Johann."

About an hour later, Chief Ryan sent me the English translation of the conversation between the ship captain and the president.

"It's done, sir."

"Was the launch successful?"

"We don't know yet, Mr. President."

───────────

Chief Ryan was right about what the Russian president and his advisors knew. He told me U.S. intelligence was able to capture the conversation with high-tech surveillance equipment and sent me the conversation electronically. I read the transcript with grave concern.

"If you tell the president of China that a biological attack has been launched on them from a Russian satellite, but that we had nothing to do with it, would they believe you, Mr. President?" asked Russia's minister of defense. "We have obliterated all the evidence in Malta."

"I agree," said Russia's foreign minister. "We cannot prove that it was not us."

"But if we don't tell them," the president argued, "they will have no warning and many more people will needlessly die. They will blame us for not warning them. Just like we blame them for not warning us about COVID-19."

"Not necessarily," rebutted the defense minister. "We do not know where those bombs are heading. There would be no way to prepare for such an attack without that knowledge. China already has its biological attack response capabilities strategically placed in the most populated areas of the country."

"We need to find out if the United States knows about this," the defense minister said. "Maybe they have more intelligence on this planned attack by Churgrill and Sarkovsky."

"What about our initial source of this information?" the president asked, pretending he knew nothing about the plot. "Does General Suberov know anything else about the nature of this attack and the biological weapons being used?"

"I'm not sure. If he doesn't, he may know who does," the prime minister said. "I have known Suberov for many years and he will assist us any way he can."

"I agree," the president said. "Interestingly, Suberov's wife and my ex-wife are still very close friends. Suberov has been loyal to Russia. It was General Sarkovsky who spoke against him and pushed him out as a rival, feeding me what was likely false information about him."

"So do we agree, Mr. President, that contacting the president of China and telling him a renegade Russian general launched a biological attack on them from a Russian satellite in space, is not the best course of action?" the defense minister asked.

"That's how I see it."

All eight leaders in the room nodded in agreement.

"I think, Mr. President, that we should contact Americans that we trust and try to find out what they know," the finance minister said.

The president then posed the question: "Does anyone think I need to warn the American president? If the Chinese believe it is a U.S. attack on them, the Chinese will retaliate."

"I would be cautious about that," the defense minister said. "There are people in the State Department still not loyal to their president that might use this information as a political weapon. We still don't know who we can trust."

"I concur, Mr. President," stated the trade minister, speaking for the first time. "There are still people in the government planted by previous administrations who are disloyal to the American president. They want him to look bad at any cost."

"I think this is wise counsel. I will not call either president."

The Russian president then turned to his director of foreign intelligence and said, "Shogu, I need you to find out what the Americans know as soon as possible. Talk first to General Suberov and then follow the leads. The rest of you do the same, but it is essential not to reveal that we know anything about a biological weapon launched from a Russian weather satellite. Is that clear?" Everyone nodded in agreement.

"I want that weather satellite from which the attack was launched immediately destroyed."

"Understood, Mr. President," replied Russia's defense minister.

CHAPTER 37

I LANDED SAFELY IN CHICAGO. and Chief Ryan and a police escort picked me up from the airport and drove me to my parents' home in Downers Grove. On the way, he told me all that he had learned in the last several hours.

"I know you are emotionally exhausted, Johann, but this is what is happening right now. General Suberov notified the president of Russia that Churgrill and Sarkovsky were launching an attack on China, using a biological weapon deployed from a Russian weather satellite. He was sure that the Russian president probably already knew. He then told the president the exact location of the command and control center in Sarkovsky's Malta home, which the president said he did not know about."

"But wasn't the Russian president pretending not to know?"

"Yes, but General Suberov explained how the Americans would surely be able to prove that the WMD was deployed from a Russian satellite."

"The president of Russia immediately ordered the destruction of Sarkovsky's home in Malta after the WMD was already launched."

"Did China respond?" I feared I already knew the answer.

"Yes, the Chinese had been surveilling the Russian and American satellites and had detected the launch of the WMD. China's military leaders met and General Bingwen Tso shared how he had prepared for this contingency by placing a WMD on a Chinese satellite. The president of China felt he had no choice but to authorize a retaliatory strike against the U.S. Our intelligence agencies believe that based on the film that you, Darrell, John, and Michael had taken in the Diaoyu Islands, that the payload of Botulinum in the WMD launched could make eight to ten cluster bombs.

"Is our laser system now operational?"

"Yes. And we have already tested its mobility. It will be able to destroy all the cluster bombs from both satellites before they are exploded."

"In the slight chance that our laser defense system fails to destroy the cluster bombs, what would be the projected death toll?"

"The initial estimate by the CDC is that sixty to seventy million people in China would die from Botulinum poisoning and another forty to fifty million would be seriously ill but likely saved by the administration of botulism antitoxin heptavalent."

"And in the U.S.?"

"If they targeted our top ten most populated cities: New York, Los Angeles, Chicago, Houston, Philadelphia, Phoenix, San Antonio, and San Diego, that could potentially expose 23.5 million people to Botulinum toxin. However, our distribution of HBAT is much more extensive than that in China and we could get to more than half of those exposed within six hours of exposure."

"I talked with Nicole, and she felt the total casualties greatly depended upon where the attacks were."

"The CDC estimates eight to ten cluster bombs of Botulinum would kill five to ten million Americans and another ten to fifteen million Americans would be sickened but saved in time by the administration of the Botulinum antitoxin."

"This sickens me, Chief Ryan, but I believe our laser system will work. The way it all came together was miraculous. There was something supernatural going on. I believe these weapons will all be destroyed."

"I would expect nothing less from you, Johann. God put you on Earth for a reason. Could you imagine a better reason than to create a laser system that will save millions of people?"

———————

I was so physically and emotionally spent I must have fallen asleep on the way home from the airport. I remember talking to Chief Ryan and then I was asleep and thrust into my reoccurring nightmare. It had been many months since I had experienced it. This one was so real and vivid; more frightening than any of the others. I knew someone was trying to kill me. I saw an evil man with a grotesque and sinister face who was wearing some type of white gown, which was splattered with blood.

Then somehow, I knew where I was in my dream. My mother was about to give birth to me, but I was not in the Hutzel Women's Hospital in the Detroit Medical Center on John R Street. I had always believed that was where I was born; but my mom, in her distress, initially decided to end her pregnancy when she went into premature labor at twenty-six weeks. She was first taken by taxi to the Planned Parenthood Detroit Health Center on Cass Avenue in Detroit, less than half a mile from the Hutzel Women's Hospital. Then I understood the horror of the nightmare that engulfed me.

I heard the man in the white gown speak, then I realized who he was. He explained to my mom what he was going to do. I heard my mom tell the man that she had changed her mind and wanted to be taken to Hutzel Women's Hospital. I heard this clearly but his reply was muffled. I could hear my mom crying. I could feel her anguish. I knew she did not want to do this.

I experienced the emotion of great loss. Again, it was so intense that I cannot describe it adequately in words. It was the feeling of having lost all my dreams in a moment. I was sorry that I would never play baseball, the game I loved. I was sorry that I would never hike to the top of Half Dome in Yosemite National Park with my parents. I was sorry that I would never have my own lab to pursue my love of astronomy and explore space. I was sorry I would never get to look into the amazing telescopes again at the Keck Observatory on top of Mauna Kea in Hawaii. I was sorry I would not be able to go to Taiwan with Darrell and eat the best handmade beef noodles in the world. I was sorry that I would never get to take a sailboat trip down the coast of California. I was sorry that I would never be able to explore Switzerland with my friend Huang Tai. I was sorry I would miss Colin and Sarah's wedding. Most of all, I was so deeply sorry that I would never be able to take a ride in a gondola on the Grand Canal in Venice with Angela on our honeymoon.

Then, just before I thought I was going to die, I thought of all the people who did not need to die, not just because of me not being born, but because of millions of others whose lives had ended early. Would one have created a vaccine that would eradicate AIDS, or discover a radical new treatment to heal breast cancer or lung cancer or cure all cancers in the world, or create a new solar energy system that would eliminate the need for carbon fuels, or lift a poor country out of poverty and despair, or bring peace to the Middle East, or save the world from a deadly virus?

I also thought of others who may not have accomplished great things in the eyes of the world because they were deformed or handicapped or limited by disease and sickness. These children would still have had the opportunity to love and to be loved. It was clear to me that their lives should be equally valued, because the significance of all our lives depends on the significance of each individual life.

Then I awoke from my nightmare. I wasn't sure where I was, but I knew that the recurring nightmare had ended forever. The overwhelming sense of great loss I had felt was gone. I heard Chief Ryan say, "The satellite defense system is working. You've just saved millions of lives, Johann."

When I heard those words, a great sense of hope filled me. My heart then experienced a profound joy as if I had just recaptured all my future dreams. Whatever my life in this world had been and would be, I knew at that moment my life was significant. I knew that every human life is, and was, significant.

THE END

ABOUT THE AUTHOR

W. J. Brown is a professor and Research Fellow in the School of Communication and the Arts at Regent University in Virginia Beach, Virginia. He received a Bachelor of Science Degree in Environmental Science from Purdue University, a Master's Degree in Communication Management from the Annenberg School for Communication at the University of Southern California in Los Angeles, and M.A. and Ph.D. degrees in Communication, also from the University of Southern California. His academic research interests include international media, development, and the use of entertainment for social change. Dr. Brown has published extensively in academic journals and books in the field of communication during the past thirty years and has served as a Fulbright Senior Specialist in the Netherlands and Norway. Dr. Brown serves on the Board of Directors of Friends for Africa Development, a nonprofit organization that has funded and completed numerous development and sustainability projects in East Africa during the past twenty years. He also is a partner of Brown, Fraser & Associates, an international media research and consulting company that has conducted more than 250 media studies in North America, Central and South America, the Caribbean, Europe, Asia, Africa, and the Middle East.

Dr. Brown's first novel, *Into the Winds of Fear,* is a sailing adventure with a young woman who prevents a terrorist attack at one of the U.S.'s most vulnerable places for terrorism in the city of Chicago. During the past sixteen years, Dr. Brown has been teaching a class at Oxford University on C.S. Lewis and his friends, focusing on the power of fictional narratives to change attitudes, beliefs, and behavior and to help readers learn about critical social issues. Dr. Brown especially enjoys giving workshops and seminars to young people on using entertainment media for social change, drawing on more than thirty years of international research and teaching experience.

ENDNOTES

1 Tutu, Desmond and Mpho Tutu. *Made for Goodness: And Why This Makes All the Difference.* New York, HarperOne, 2011.

2 Rowling, J.K. *Harry Potter and the Deathly Hallows.* New York, Scholastic Inc., 2007.

For more information about

W. J. Brown
and
Significant
please contact:

willbro@regent.edu

For more information about
AMBASSADOR INTERNATIONAL
please visit:

www.ambassador-international.com
@AmbassadorIntl
www.facebook.com/AmbassadorIntl

If you enjoyed this book, please consider leaving us a review on
Amazon, Goodreads, or our website.

Made in the USA
Middletown, DE
10 February 2022

60209266R00235